THE **WEREWOLVES** OF **WASHINGTON SQUARE**

NYPD WIZARD DETECTIVE BOOK 3

ARJAY LEWIS

MIND
BENDER
PRESS

Copyright ©2022

Cover Design: Book Cover Designer; www.thebookcoverdesigner.com
Editing: Libby Broadbent

ISBN: 978-1737838104
ISBN-10: 1737838109

Published by:
Mindbender Press
474 South Main Street
Phillipsburg NJ 08865
www.mindbenderpress.com

Prologue 1

One 7

Two 21

Three 39

Four 53

Five 63

Six 79

Seven 95

Eight 111

Nine 131

Ten 151

Eleven 169

Twelve 183

Thirteen 197

Fourteen 211

Fifteen 223

Sixteen 239

Seventeen 253

Eighteen 271

Nineteen 291

Twenty 301

Twenty-One 311

Twenty-Two 323

Twenty-Three 339

Twenty-Four 355

Twenty-Five 371

Epilogue 381

About The Author 390

Also by Arjay Lewis 391

DEDICATION

To composer Ralph Carbone,
my friend and collaborator.
Heaven needed your music
and I am sure you play every day.

"The story goes that he who tastes of the one bit of human entrails minced up with those of other victims is inevitably transformed into a wolf."

-Plato

"A lonely journey in a snowstorm on All Souls' Night, when the dead travel fast. The traveler takes refuge in a marble sepulcher, the tomb of a mysterious Austrian countess, and is attacked by a werewolf."

-Bram Stoker

PROLOGUE

The full moon crested over Greenwich Village, far outshining the glow from the huge marble arch that was the centerpiece of Washington Square Park. Bright lights illuminated the large open plaza as the glow of windows seemed to float in the air from the many high-rise buildings encircling the monument.

The nearby benches and permanent cement chessboards abounded with shadows, lending those usually joyful areas a sinister air.

It was a chilly spring night, and the few New Yorkers walking through the park seemed to sense the strangeness of the hour. They stayed in the well-lit central area, avoiding the murky walkways snaking through the trees.

A tall man with shoulder-length dark hair and a pointed nose stepped out of a grove, holding a pocket watch. He was followed by a shorter man with a white beard and an ebony walking stick in his hand. Finally, a black-haired, tall woman with a tawny cast to her features appeared. The moon glinted off the large stone in the ring on her right hand.

"Marlowe, are you certain this is where Willowdell said we would find the lycanthrope?"

Marlowe nodded his head wearily. "The prophetess was quite sure."

Drusilicus shoved the watch in the pocket of his expensive three-piece suit. "We have had little success pursuing the creature."

"Are you sure it is the beast that killed that man?" the woman asked. "We've only known it was a werewolf since yesterday."

"It killed in Central Park the first night of the full moon. This is the third and final night," Drusilicus replied, an eyebrow raised. "It is unfortunate we didn't realize the danger sooner."

"Oh, don't nag, Drusilicus," Marlowe grumbled.

The woman smiled. "He is right. It does not become you." She looked over at Marlowe with concern. "Are you sure you are up to this? You appear tired."

Marlowe sighed. "Vasant, let us find the beast and be done."

A scream ripped through the night air.

With hardly a thought, the trio ran toward the disturbance, the taller man's stride much longer and faster than the other two. As they ran, their clothes underwent a surprising transformation. Their formal clothing shimmered and became tunics, leggings, and tall boots—Drusilicus in blue, Vasant in golden yellow, and Marlowe in white. All three of them suddenly held tall wooden staffs and raw power seemed to crackle around them.

Drusilicus arrived in a clearing where a woman crouched in fear behind a park bench, breathing hard, her eyes wide with terror.

Before her was an animal. It was a wolf with thick reddish fur, gray around its eyes and ears, and a white belly. Its fur bristled as it growled at the woman. Drool oozed from its muzzle and its eyes were a fiery red.

The monster turned to Drusilicus, staring at the tall man. The air reeked of the animal's strong musk, and Drusilicus saw malice in its eyes. He paused for a moment, then a blue light appeared at the top of his wooden staff. With a gesture, a beam of blue light lashed out at the creature, striking empty pavement, cracking the sidewalk on impact.

The monster leapt into the air, sailing over the stunned wizard.

With heightened reflexes and a century of training, he enveloped himself in a protective dome of magickal light.

The flying wolf landed upon the dome with such force, it knocked Drusilicus to the ground. The dome held, and the creature leapt only to fly straight at Vasant, mouth open and fangs gleaming. A dome of yellow light appeared over her as she dropped to one knee, enveloped under the protective sphere.

The wolf merely bounded off the top of her shield, lunging at Marlowe as he stumbled into the clearing and directly into its path.

"Marlowe!" Drusilicus tried to warn him, but it was all happening too fast as the canine fell upon the older wizard and knocked him to the ground.

Drusilicus and Vasant both jumped to their feet to see a second wolf— this one with a thick gray pelt—leap upon the attacker and shove it off the older man.

The two canines fought, biting and wrestling as they growled and tumbled over the open ground. They were about the same size, but the reddish wolf seemed to have the upper hand. Eventually the gray wolf pushed it off and faced it.

With a glance at the wizards, the red wolf vanished down another pathway, the gray wolf in pursuit.

Vasant moved toward Marlowe, but he was already getting up and gesturing to Drusilicus. "The woman, see to the woman."

Drusilicus approached the terrified woman still cowering behind the bench, her face white with fear.

"What was that?" she stammered. "Who are you?"

"Madam, were you bitten?"

"I don't see how a dog could be that big—"

"Madam," Drusilicus interrupted. "Were you bitten? Tell me."

"No, no," she gulped. "What was that… that… thing?"

"Where were you going?" he asked quietly.

"To my apartment," the woman said. "I was just out for a run, and that creature…"

Drusilicus made a small circle with his staff. "It was nothing. You saw a big dog that scared you, but you ran past it and headed home."

The woman's eyes glazed over. "Yes, I got scared and ran home."

"You saw two men from animal control and they pursued the dog," he told her.

Still spellbound, the woman replied. "Yes, animal control. I recognized the uniforms."

"You are going right home and to bed," Drusilicus told her.

She rose and without another word, she ran off without a look back.

Drusilicus let his shoulders relax and walked back to his companions. "Now we see the problem. There are two of the creatures. Let us pursue them at once."

Vasant looked up at Drusilicus, her eyes hard. "We cannot."

"What? But the night is still—"

"I am bitten," Marlowe confessed.

Drusilicus' eyes grew wide in alarm as Marlowe held out his hand, where a drop of blood dripped from a single wound.

"Which one?"

"The gray one," Marlowe said.

"But it looked like it was trying to save you," Vasant said.

"In the werewolf's defense, it might not have meant to bite me," Marlowe agreed. "But during the full moon, it cannot control itself."

"Marlowe, you know what this means." Drusilicus looked worried. "If it infected you, at the full moon next month you will —"

Marlowe sighed. "I am no good for you. I cannot fight the one that bit me—I am now part of its pack."

Vasant nodded. "Return to the townhouse quickly. Perhaps your vampire friend Daniel can remove the infection from your blood."

"Yes, that's good thinking," Marlowe said.

"I dislike the idea of you going there alone," Drusilicus said.

"I will be fine," Marlowe said. "We can worry about me on the morrow. You two pursue the werewolves. Do not let them strike again."

Marlowe headed into a grove of trees and disappeared.

"This does not bode well," Vasant said, watching Marlowe as he disappeared.

Drusilicus could only nod, his mouth a tight line.

ONE

Lieutenant Eddie Berman walked into the bullpen of the twenty-second precinct in a fine mood, two cups of coffee in his hand. He was a thin African-American man, about six feet tall. With his short hair and neat suit, he looked every bit the NYPD detective.

His one-year-old daughter was finally sleeping through the night, and he was moving past the sleep deprivation since Ellie's birth.

The lack of sleep didn't bother him as much as it had with his two sons, as his body now required less sleep. It had been harder on Cerise, his wife. Having a baby at forty was a delight, but it was a lot of work, especially with her career as a surgical nurse.

Eddie was grateful his mother, Eleanor, lived with them and helped so much, or it would have been a much tougher time.

He reached his desk and placed one of the styrofoam cups on his partner's.

Sergeant Luis Vasquez looked up from his computer. He was a large man, tall and big, but all of it muscle, with light brown skin and a small mustache.

"Gracias."

"Da nada," Eddie replied as he took off his suit jacket and hung it over his chair. He sat at the computer to go over reports from the previous night.

"Any animal attacks last night?" Eddie asked.

"None reported," Luis said with his slight Spanish accent, as he sipped his coffee. "You've asked me that every day since that guy got killed near the Metropolitan Museum of Art."

"If people don't feel safe, they don't come into Central Park—and that makes us look bad," Eddie said and grabbed a paper from his desk.

"We both saw the DB," Luis said, typing out 'dead body' on his computer with two fingers. "Whatever got him, it tore him to pieces. What are we now, friggin' animal control? Robbery, murder, and drug dealers ain't enough for you?"

"More than enough. I don't know why, but that one case just bugs me."

"They checked the big cats and the bears at the Central Park Zoo," Luis said, and shrugged. "It ain't them."

"I know, I know. But a killer animal in Central Park? How did it get there? Worse, where did it go?"

"Admit it, Eddie—you want it to be a homicide. You love a good homicide."

Eddie shook his head. "It's just that there are more questions than answers. We've had a lot of strange animal sightings in the park, but now someone got killed."

"Did you notice it was during the full moon?" Luis said with a stony stare.

"Crime is always up during the full moon," Eddie said, sitting back in his chair and sipping his coffee.

Luis leaned forward on his desk. "Yeah, but I mean—maybe it has something to do with those guys you used to hang with." He lowered his voice. "Something supernatural?"

Eddie leaned forward as well, glancing about the bullpen to make sure no one could overhear them. "Luis, I haven't seen those guys in a year…"

"Yeah, but one of them, that Drew guy? Didn't he have someone who worked for him that was—you know—a werewolf?"

Eddie rubbed his forehead. This was giving him a headache.

Eddie had worked with a group of wizards a year earlier, after being summoned by a decapitated head at a crime scene almost two years ago. Even thinking about the strange group and their odd abilities made his head hurt.

"Now an animal attack is a werewolf?" Eddie hissed.

"Hey, you fought those vampires a year ago and kicked their ass. Maybe this is like that."

Eddie picked up his coffee and shook his head. "My life has been a lot simpler since I stopped dealing with any of that."

A uniformed officer stepped into the bullpen. "LT, there's a man in the lobby who wants to speak to you. Says his name is Drew Gray-something."

Eddie sat up straight in the chair. "I'll be right there."

Luis spoke quietly, "Isn't that the wizard guy with the stick up his ass?"

"Drusilicus Greywacke. I should find out what he wants."

Luis sat up. "I'm coming with you."

"I can handle him," Eddie said, putting on his coat.

"No way," Luis told him as he got to his feet. "If they're gonna pull you in again, I gotta make sure it's on the up and up."

Eddie couldn't help but smile. This was Luis—his partner, his friend, the man who always had his back. Eddie was grateful to have him.

The two detectives strode out into the lobby, where the tall man waited, wearing a black suit and a somber tie.

"Mr. Greywacke," Eddie announced, not offering his hand to shake. "How can I help you?"

Luis stood behind him and folded his arms, a stern expression on his face.

"Lieutenant," Drusilicus acknowledged him and nodded to Luis. "The sergeant is with you, of course." He turned his back to Luis and spoke quietly to Eddie. "Do you have a moment? I need to speak to you about a most urgent matter."

Luis stepped in close behind them.

Drusilicus sighed. "I cannot speak to you about it here."

"If you wanna speak to me, Luis comes with us," Eddie said.

Drusilicus rolled his eyes. "Come now, lieutenant. Are you continuing the charade that the good sergeant is your apprentice? Since you have not practiced the arts in a year, you can hardly suggest you are teaching him anything."

"I'll show you what I do know," Luis growled. "If you try anything."

Drusilicus glared at the large man, who looked eager to knock Drusilicus across the room if he even lifted a finger in a way Luis didn't like.

"My partner and I are on duty. What's this about?" Eddie insisted.

"Marlowe is injured."

The three men made their way to a stunning townhouse on 85th Street and Central Park West. Although it appeared to be a simple three-story brick building, it had a most unusual feature— a tower that jutted out from one side, giving the entire structure a fairy tale aura.

Drusilicus knocked.

A semi-transparent man opened the door. He wore a black cutaway coat, striped pants, and a gray vest. He bowed his head to the newcomers.

"Wraith, my man," Luis said joyfully. "Been a long time since I've seen you!"

The spirit attempted a smile that looked more like a grimace. "Thank you, sergeant."

"How's the afterlife going?" Luis asked.

"Very much the same, I'm afraid," he answered mournfully. "I hope you and Wizard Berman can help Marlowe."

Without another word, the ghost lowered his head, and his entire body sank down into the floor and was gone.

"He sure knows how to make an exit," Luis said.

They walked into the vast living room, with the ceiling several stories high. Although the townhouse looked a normal size on the outside, the inside was much larger than what was possible through construction. There was an enormous spiral staircase that went to a high second floor with a tube-shaped elevator car in the middle, surrounded by ornate metalwork that looked both artistic and frightening.

Vasant came rapidly into the room, wearing a traditional sari and a smile on her face. "Eddie! Oh thank the Divine, you came."

"Vasant!" Eddie beamed. "You look amazing!"

She smiled shyly. "Thank you. And Luis, still there when duty calls, are you not?"

Luis smiled at the Indian woman and took her hand. "You know it, Vasant. And Eddie's right, you look great."

She stepped next to Drusilicus and took his hand. "Being in love makes a tremendous difference."

Drusilicus glanced at her with adoration, and Eddie was glad to see it.

Vasant pulled away, becoming serious. "Come, let us talk in the breakfast room. We have a most serious situation."

They went into a room which held a table that could easily seat ten. Standing near the table was a young Caucasian woman who appeared to be in her mid-twenties with a pretty face, blonde hair, and hazel eyes. She possessed a waif-like appearance that reminded Eddie of a young fashion model.

"Allow me to make introductions," Vasant said. "This is the Wizard Berman, and his apprentice Luis Vasquez."

The young woman didn't make eye contact but bowed her head and said, "I live to serve and learn at your feet."

Eddie glanced at Vasant and Drusilicus. "What's all this?"

"She is our new apprentice," Drusilicus said. "Right now, she mostly speaks when spoken to."

"It's part of learning discipline," Vasant said. "It's a starting place for understanding that one's every word contains great power."

Drusilicus' smile was mocking. "Imagine how much you could have learned, lieutenant, if Marlowe had insisted you keep your mouth shut?"

Luis suddenly stood up straighter. "How about you shut yours, Drew?"

Drusilicus glared arrows at Luis, but Eddie approached the girl. "I'm Eddie. How about you tell me your name?"

"I'm Lovetta. Lovetta Wynter," she responded with a dazzling smile.

"Lovetta," Eddie repeated. "You like studying with these two?"

"Actually, I've waited for an opportunity like this for years, sir," she answered sincerely.

"Sir?" Eddie said, surprised. "I like young people with manners."

Vasant spoke up. "We are training her in the path of the wise."

Eddie frowned, knowing that this entailed situations that could turn a life upside-down. "Have you told her everything that's involved?"

"Lieutenant, I assure you—" Drusilicus started.

Eddie held up his hand to cut Drusilicus off. "I want to hear from her." He turned to Lovetta. "Did they tell you what this is all about?"

"My instructors have told me what I need to know as I learn. They are teaching me to use my mind in new ways."

Eddie nodded. "Instructors? Well, that sounds better than 'masters', I guess."

Lovetta smiled. "One thing they're teaching me is meditation. I've already improved my grade point average, and I need less sleep."

"You're in college?"

"Yes, sir. NYU. That's where I heard about Vasant and Greywacke."

"Really?"

Drusilicus spoke up. "Believe it or not, lieutenant, the young lady approached Vasant and I about becoming our apprentice."

Vasant smiled. "I did the interview with her. She is from a family of Wicca practitioners, which is—"

"Her family practices witchcraft?" Luis said, startled.

Lovetta gritted her teeth and looked at the floor, obviously upset by his reaction and fighting to remain silent.

"Wicca. It's entirely different, a practice of ancient pagan rituals designed to open the mind," Drusilicus claimed. "Having grown up with it, it made her suitable to the ideas of will and intent and the path of the wise. She was an ideal candidate."

"There are also benefits," Vasant noted. "The young lady lives in our townhouse and saves on rent and expenses—"

Drusilicus stepped forward. "That's enough for now." He turned to Lovetta. "We wanted you to be here so Wizard Berman could meet you. Please, return downtown and practice those exercises Vasant gave you."

The young woman bowed and headed for the door.

Eddie grabbed Drusilicus' arm. "She lives in your townhouse?"

Drusilicus pulled free. "Yes, what of it? You've seen my townhouse. She lives in a separate wing."

Vasant stepped in. "Wizard Berman, I assure you, all we are doing is training her. We must expose her to the strangeness of a wizard's life slowly, prepare her for it, and teach her mental discipline."

"Seems like your standards differ from when you were teaching Caleb," Luis snorted.

"Caleb was an idiot," Drusilicus said bitterly. "Also, I am following Vasant's training techniques. I found my own were… inefficient."

"What do you need an apprentice for, anyway?" Eddie demanded.

Drusilicus watched Eddie carefully. "After you left us, I had to make a plan in case you did not wish to continue to walk the path."

"You gotta lotta nerve, Drew," Luis snorted. "Eddie saved your ass twice, saved all of freakin' New York—"

"I have the greatest respect for what the lieutenant did," Drusilicus said, speaking louder than Luis. "But possessing a wizard's staff isn't a toy. It is meant for someone who becomes a member of our coven and will join our battle of good against evil. Eddie never became part of the coven, and walked away after our victory last year, leaving us short-handed on the important work we do."

Drusilicus moved to the table as he went on. "Vasant and I have been working with this apprentice for nine months. It was a logical decision. I still have the staff the vampires used against us, and I also needed to be prepared in case Eddie surrendered his."

Vasant smiled. "Since only an experienced wizard should hold your staff, I thought I could take on yours, Wizard Berman, if you were willing. Our apprentice could then take mine once she is ready."

"And Eddie gets nothing," Luis fumed.

"It is the lieutenant who turned away from us," Drusilicus said. "We did not reject him."

"And that made you mad, Drew?" Eddie said.

"Indeed, it did, lieutenant," Drusilicus snapped. "You have a unique talent for the arts, a quick, flexible mind, and natural skill. You squander a substantial gift, and such waste makes me angry. Now, shall we discuss our current situation?"

Luis and Eddie chose seats that were near the tea trolley. It was an enchanted set, and the two men ordered coffee. In response to their voices, the cups flew to saucers where a silver pot filled them with steaming coffee and added milk and sugar to their liking.

"I gotta say, I missed the coffee," Luis mused as he took a big sip.

"What's wrong with Marlowe?" Eddie demanded.

"A werewolf bit him," Drusilicus said.

Eddie sucked in a breath. "When did this happen?"

"In Washington Square Park, last night."

Eddie shrugged. "So what? A vampire bit me and one bit my wife. We're fine now."

Drusilicus pinched his lips as if he had tasted something unpleasant. "Once again, I find your lack of basic knowledge frustrating."

Vasant patted his hand. "Calm down, dearest. Chiding Wizard Berman will not help our cause."

"Our cause would have been much further ahead if he had not chosen to cut and run," Drusilicus complained.

Eddie got to his feet. "I can walk out the door right now, Drew."

Drusilicus also leapt to his feet. "Give me your staff and don't let the door hit you in the ass on the way out."

Vasant slapped the table, making a sound like a gunshot. "Gentlemen!"

Eddie and Drusilicus stared at Vasant in surprise.

"You will both sit down and be quiet, and I will explain the situation."

The two men exchanged glances and sat.

Vasant sighed and regained her composure. "There was an animal attack in Central Park on the first day of the full moon."

"We know about that. We're the detectives on the case," Luis said. "The victim got torn apart."

"In that case, we were lucky," Drusilicus murmured.

"Why?" Eddie wondered.

Vasant continued the tale. "Because it was a werewolf attack. It is preferable that the victim died, because if he had survived, on the next full moon, he too would become a werewolf."

"Our case in the park was a werewolf?" Eddie asked.

"See, I tol' you," Luis hissed.

Eddie glared at his partner.

"Yes, with the help of the prophetess Willowdell, she tracked the beast to Washington Square Park last night," Vasant said. "We were planning to capture it."

"Why not just kill it?" Eddie said.

Drusilicus shook his head. "Unlike a vampire, a werewolf is a living creature. Our plan was to capture it, bind it, and see if we could contact Matchitehew."

"Who's that?" Eddie asked.

"He is a prominent leader in the werewolf community, though we have not met him. It would be up to him to pass sentence," Drusilicus explained.

Vasant took up the story. "We discovered that there is not merely one werewolf, but at least two. One of them bit Marlowe."

This roused Drusilicus again. "If you had not shirked your duty, you would have been the one out hunting with us instead of Marlowe."

"You can't make this his fault," Luis snapped.

Eddie said. "Doesn't sunlight or a spell fix it?"

"Shall I explain the differences, lieutenant?" Drusilicus said.

"Best to let me, dear," Vasant suggested. "Werewolves differ from vampires. First, a vampire bite cannot convert you, only a large exchange of blood with the vampire can do that. It is an invasive process that transforms one into the undead, killing the body and changing it. Werewolves are shape changers. They are living creatures, not the undead."

"What does the bite do?" Eddie asked.

"The bite of the werewolf contains a virus that causes the human body to evolve, adapting itself to werewolf transformations."

"In modern parlance," Drusilicus added, "it rewrites the genetic code of the victim."

"How could a virus do that?" Luis wondered.

"It is magickal in origin," Vasant said.

"So, every werewolf has been bitten by another werewolf?" Eddie asked with a frown.

"No, some are born with the ability," Drusilicus explained. "My majordomo, Howell, comes from a long line of werewolves. He can constrain his abilities, except on the full moon, when the beast takes control."

"The wolf that killed the man in Central Park also attacked Marlowe last night?"

"Yes, but another wolf saved him," Vasant explained. "It is the second one that bit him, but it might have been by mistake during the skirmish."

"How could this happen?" Eddie asked. "Marlowe is an expert, the coven master. He's the best wizard I know."

"The werewolves are fast," Drusilicus said. "Amazingly so. I could barely defend myself from the attack."

Vasant glanced at Drusilicus and took a deep breath. "The thing Drusilicus does not want to say is that Marlowe... has been slowing down of late."

"What?" Eddie said, rising to his feet. "Why didn't anyone tell me?"

Drusilicus glared at him and said through gritted teeth, "You walked out on him, remember?" Vasant put a hand on his arm, but Drusilicus pulled himself free and stood. "Your leaving took the heart out of the old man, made him feel he was a failure."

This shocked Eddie, and he lowered himself back into his seat. "I... I didn't know."

"Or didn't care," Drusilicus grumbled.

"Ease off, man," Luis warned, and pointed a finger at Drusilicus. "Eddie has a new kid. He has a job and a family. He didn't walk out on anyone."

"There are ways—"

"Says the man who never had a kid," Luis snorted.

"Gentlemen," Vasant said quietly and calmly. "Making accusations or questioning who has a more complicated life does nothing to help. We have a dire situation on our hands."

The three men stared at each other and then turned their attention to Vasant.

"This bite. What will it do to Marlowe?" Eddie asked.

Drusilicus rubbed one hand down his face before he spoke. "The virus strain is duplicating itself in Marlowe's bloodstream, changing his genetics. This will take roughly two to three weeks until fully integrated. He will experience insomnia, headaches, and flu-like symptoms, and perhaps a few external signs."

Vasant nodded. "Then upon the next full moon—he will change."

Eddie tried to get his head around this. "What happens when someone with Marlowe's powers becomes a wolf?"

Vasant and Drusilicus exchanged a glance.

"Bad things," murmured Vasant.

"If we cannot stave off the infection," Drusilicus added. "Terrible things, indeed."

TWO

"We have to do something!"

"Which is exactly why we sought you out, Wizard Berman," Vasant agreed.

"We asked Daniel Kraft to purge the poison from Marlowe, but he could not," Drusilicus said. "The virus in the werewolf's blood is fatal to vampires, which explains why the two creatures avoid each other."

"What's your plan?" Eddie had no idea how he could help, but Marlowe was a friend—even if he might become a werewolf.

"We desperately need information," Drusilicus explained. "Information that we are unable to gather."

Vasant nodded. "We hoped you could tell us everything about the man killed in Central Park."

"I can do that," Eddie said.

"But how you gonna catch either of these werewolves?" Luis asked. "I mean, the full moon is over and those guys won't change again until next month."

"We are already making plans to locate the specific wolf," Drusilicus explained. "This morning I contacted Bankrock and asked him to establish negotiations with Matchitehew."

"The king of the werewolves or something, right?" Eddie said.

"Yes, secondly I have contacted the Wizard Glade. Although she is solitary by nature, she is an expert on werewolves and can give us information about the beasts. I expect her this evening."

"That's good," Eddie said. "What else?"

Drusilicus set his jaw. "We must assemble the Five."

The Five were the leaders of the wizards, each bearing a staff representing the elements of the ancient world. Eddie carried the staff of fire, Drusilicus, the staff of water, and Marlowe, the staff of spirit.

"Have you been able to reach Ahbay and Eugenia?" Eddie asked.

"The bearers of the staffs of earth and air will arrive in New York this evening," Vasant assured him.

"You can see why I had to speak to you," Drusilicus said. "It is possible that with the power of the Five united, we can purge the virus from Marlowe's blood." Drusilicus glanced at Vasant, and went on. "I also believe that it is time for you to consider the facts, lieutenant. If you have no wish to continue the path of the Wise, you should return your staff."

Eddie hesitated. "I don't know…"

Vasant touched Drusilicus' arm. "Let us not talk of this now." She turned to Eddie. "If you could come at six tonight, the others will be here—with the help of the Divine, we can make Marlowe whole again."

"I'll be here to help Marlowe," Eddie said and faced Drusilicus. "I'll go through my files and call the medical examiner to get as much information as I can about the man killed in Central Park. C'mon Luis."

The two men were soon out in the warm spring air, walking down the transverse road back to the precinct.

"Man, I'd like to tell that Drusilicus off," Luis said as they walked. "He thinks he's so high and mighty and—"

"He's right, Luis."

Luis stared at his partner. "You saved New York."

"By killing hundreds of vampires."

"You didn't have a choice! They were going to kill people, destroy the city."

"Yes, and now there are werewolves attacking people. These weird things never stop. Drusilicus is right, he needs someone dedicated to fight these things. If I had been working with Drew, maybe Marlowe wouldn't have gotten hurt. I didn't even know that my leaving had depressed him. Marlowe is a good man. I don't want him to feel responsible for my choices."

"You focused on your family, being home every night for your boys and Ellie. Between being a cop and taking care of a family, who's got time to play with wizards?"

"If I don't, people get hurt."

"You're not responsible for everything, man."

Eddie sighed. "It just sometimes feels like I am."

Eddie returned to the precinct to find a message at the front desk asking him to speak with Captain Jacobs as soon as possible.

Jacobs ran the 'twenty-two' in his own way. Most of the brass of NYPD considered the Central Park Precinct a place for misfits and underperforming officers but it turned out that once there, many of them excelled at their jobs. It was because Jacobs, who held a spotless record, expected the best from his officers and they all rose to the challenge.

Eddie went to his commander's office on the second floor of the facility, which was once the park's stables. The original brick and stone outbuildings were constructed in 1871 and included offices, sheds, and dwelling spaces for park keepers—the first police force that patrolled the park.

The recent renovation combined the older buildings under an enclosed courtyard with a structural bullet-resistant glass wall and windows. This protected the occupants while creating a welcoming appearance for the public.

In the commander's office, Captain Jacobs rose as Eddie entered and asked him to sit.

"How's the little girl, lieutenant? Ellie, is it?" he asked.

Eddie beamed. "Amazing, sir. She's gotten big so fast."

Jacobs smiled as well. "That's good. Now, down to business. There has been a request for your help at the sixth precinct. You know they've had animal attacks in Washington Square?"

"Yes, sir. It's possible that it's related to the animal that killed the man here in Central Park."

Eddie knew it was, but felt no need to mention how he got that knowledge.

Jacobs frowned. "You think it's the same animal?"

"It might be a good idea to find out, sir."

"After your success down there with the strange situation last year, Captain Santaro specifically asked for you and Sergeant Vasquez to help. Do you think this is something that might interest you, LT?"

"I would want to make sure it isn't just someone with a trained killer dog, sir."

This made Jacobs smile. "Always looking for a murderer, aren't you?"

Eddie grinned. "Old habit, sir."

"The situation is this—they're bringing in animal control, but they won't look for this animal unless they're escorted by police."

"Why's that, sir?"

"Animal control agents don't carry sidearms, and to be honest, they're scared."

"So Luis and I would accompany animal control, sir?"

"That's right," Jacobs said. "Look, you can refuse, I know it's not—"

"No, sir, we'll take the assignment. Maybe we can get this taken care of and stop this threat."

Jacobs nodded. "It's the last thing New York needs right now."

"I understand, sir. The NYPD has done work for the ASPCA and Animal Control before. When do you want us to start?"

"Tomorrow if you can. The four to midnight shift, reporting to Detective Brad Thomas at the sixth precinct. He's currently the detective coordinating their efforts."

"We'll be there, sir."

"Why don't you and Vasquez head home early today?" Jacobs said, with a glance at his watch.

"Yes, sir," Eddie said and rose to his feet, heading out the door and back down into the bullpen.

As usual, his partner was typing away with two fingers.

"What's up?" Luis asked.

"The captain asked us to patrol the four to midnight tomorrow, down in Washington Square."

"How did you arrange that?"

"I didn't. Captain Santaro asked for us. They're bringing in animal control and the agents are scared."

Luis looked over his shoulder at Eddie. "Really? Those guys are usually *muy bueno* when dealing with dangerous animals."

"They want armed cops to go with them or they won't do the job."

"I guess that makes sense," Luis grunted. "No one who joins animal control expects to face deadly force."

"I have to call the detective running the case, get what info I can. In the meantime, Jacobs gave us the rest of the day off."

"Really?" A smile grew on Luis' face. "You mean I can leave now and avoid the rush hour traffic?"

"Yeah. Finish up, I'll walk you to your car."

"Aren't you going home?"

"I have to meet the others and try to help Marlowe."

"Do you want me to stay?"

"No, you go home. I'll visit Marlowe and let you know how he's doing."

As Luis typed, Eddie called his contact at the Medical Examiner's office, Doctor Beverly Warren. She picked up on the second ring.

"Doctor Warren."

"Beverly, it's Eddie Berman."

"Did someone else die in Central Park and I didn't hear about it?"

"Nothing of the kind. They've assigned me to Washington Square because of a wild animal spotted there. I haven't spoken to you about our Central Park victim who got torn apart—do you know who did the autopsy?"

"I should," she chuckled. "It was me."

"Great," Eddie said, and grabbed a piece of paper on his desk to take notes. "What can you tell me?"

"I'll email you the report, but I take it you want the highlights."

"If you don't mind."

Eddie heard her rustling pages as she spoke. "Definitely an animal attack. From the wounds, I would say it was a large canine. Elongated bites from a creature with a muzzle, as opposed to a big cat which uses wide, tearing motions in its attack."

"Mad dog, maybe?"

"We tested for rabies in the wounds, and it didn't show up in the test results. If it is a canine, it's a big one, bigger than a German Shepherd."

"Thanks, Beverly, I'll review the report."

"You want the weird stuff?"

"Do I have a choice?" Eddie asked.

"You know it ripped open the chest cavity, right?"

"Luis and I saw the body, yes."

"Difficult to break open the sternum, and not an attack most animals would do. What's weird is—the heart was missing."

"Missing?" Eddie gulped.

"Yes. Also strange, he had a flower in his lapel."

"That's not as strange as a missing heart. He liked flowers, so what?"

"That's just it. The flower was Monkshood, and it's highly poisonous. You can't even touch it with your bare hands."

"Why would he have it in his lapel? Anything special about this flower, other than it being deadly?"

"Not really. It's common enough, and goes by several names: Queen of Poisons, Devil's Helmet, and Wolfsbane."

Eddie paused. "Did you say Wolfsbane?"

"Yes, does that mean anything?"

"It might. What was the victim's name?"

"Stubbe. Harold Stubbe."

"Any other personal items of note?"

"Wallet, keys, no phone, and a flyer for a show at MOMA—"

"That makes sense, his body was found near the Metropolitan Museum of Art. Anyone get in touch with the next of kin?"

"No. We found a name and number on a piece of paper in his wallet. Sophia Stubbe. We don't know if it was a wife or relative or what."

"Give me the number," Eddie requested and wrote it on a pad as Beverly rattled off the digits. "That's a long number."

"It's international. I looked up the country code, and it's in Austria. Let us know if you have any luck with next of kin. We can release the body—well, what's left—any time."

"Thanks, Beverly," Eddie said and hung up.

Luis was still working on the report, so Eddie put the number in his smart phone, and waited as it rang.

"Ja?" a deep, sultry woman's voice answered.

"Mrs. Stubbe? This is Lieutenant Berman with the New York Police Department."

She immediately switched to English with a German accent. "It's not Missus, it's just Ms."

"We found your number in the belongings of Harold Stubbe —"

"*Mein Gott!* Vhat has happened?"

"I regret to inform you that Harold Stubbe is dead. Are you related to the deceased?"

"He is—vas—my cousin," she answered. "Ve vere not terribly close. In fact, I am surprised he had my number—vhere did you find it?"

"In his wallet on a folded piece of paper."

She was silent for a moment, then asked, "How did he, I mean, vhat did he die of—"

"He was the victim of an animal attack."

"Are you the investigator?"

"Yes, I'm assigned to the case. We're working with animal control to hunt down the animal."

"And you are in New York? The City?"

"Yes, NYPD. Can you tell me any reason he might have been wandering around at night in Central Park?"

"I cannot think of one," she replied.

"We found his body at a children's playground, off Fifth Avenue and 80th Street, near the Metropolitan Museum Of Art. Does that mean anything?"

"I am afraid not."

Eddie sighed, knowing he could get nothing new from the woman. "We need the next of kin to make arrangements for the body—"

"I can do that," she responded. "I am really the only family he had."

Eddie gave her the information about contacting the medical examiner, the case number, his own number, and made a few suggestions as to funeral homes that could take care of things for her.

"Will you be able to come over from Austria?" Eddie asked as he finished with the information.

"I am already in America. I have been staying in upstate New York. This is probably vhy my cousin had my number in his vallet. Ve vere planning to meet later in the month."

"Contact me if I can be of any help," Eddie said.

"I vill."

After Eddie ended the call, he transferred the information about the victim into the notes app on his phone.

Luis was done with his report, and the two men walked out of the building and across the transverse road to the parking lot for the precinct.

"I feel guilty," Luis said. "I mean, if you're going to work with that Drew guy, shouldn't I be there to help?"

"Relax, Luis, it's all wizard stuff tonight. There isn't much you could do. Hell, I'm not sure what I'm supposed to do—"

They stopped at the back of Luis' car and Eddie's mouth fell open.

"Oh, yeah—I guess you haven't seen what I've done," Luis boasted.

It was still Luis' car, an older vehicle from the late 1990s, but the formerly beat-up automobile looked like new. Better than new, it looked like a classic car painstakingly restored. The rust spots that had pockmarked the lower edge of the car were gone and it was without blemish. There was a fresh coat of paint, and when Eddie peeked in, instead of the worn cloth seats and heaps of fast-food bags in the back, the car had leather seats and new floor mats. It was definitely the same car, but completely restored to its showroom luster.

"This is amazing," Eddie said. "When did you do this?"

Luis shrugged, a bit embarrassed. "I did it slowly, over the last few months. A friend helped me."

"He's good," Eddie said, his attention on the car.

"Yeah, he's… um… a wiz at this kind of thing." Luis said and flushed. "I gotta go."

The car turned over with no trouble and didn't belch a fog of gray smoke, as it had the last time Eddie rode in it. With a wave, Luis pulled out of his parking space and headed down the transverse road.

Eddie shook his head, and walked toward Central Park West and Marlowe's townhouse, retrieving his smart phone as he walked. He hit the button to call his wife.

"Hello, husband." Cerise answered with a sultry tone. He pictured her in his mind, her dark, firm body, probably dressed in scrubs as she spoke. Her voice carried the lilt of her accent, having grown up in a house where her parents, emigrants from the African country of Botswana, spoke Setswana.

"Hello to you. You at work?"

"Yes, for a couple more hours. It's a light day, no surgeries this afternoon, so I'm catching up on the paperwork."

"You've been busy the last few weeks."

"Don't I know it! I'm so grateful *your* daughter is finally letting us sleep."

"*My* daughter? I thought she was *our* daughter."

"She's a daddy's girl. I can tell by how she looks at you."

"Cerise," Eddie said, getting serious. "I have to stay in New York late."

"Something wrong?"

"Do you remember Marlowe?"

There was a pause. "How could I forget?"

"He's been injured, and they need me to help him." There was no sound on the other end of the phone and finally Eddie said, "Hello, did I lose you?"

"No, I'm here. It's just that—I thought you were done with that."

"It appears not. I still bear the staff of Fire. Though Drusilicus may have someone I can give it to."

"Is that what you want?"

"I want what's best for our family."

"Eddie, those wizards and what they do—it scares me."

"Scares me too," Eddie replied.

"I'm the wife of a cop. Any day you might not make it home. I just don't want it to be fighting some monster you could have avoided."

"That's a good point," Eddie agreed.

"I know how important duty and honor are to you, sugar. I support what you feel you need to do."

"Thanks, that helps."

"Get home as soon as you can. Take care of my big, black man."

This made Eddie smile as he ended the call. It was a running joke between them, going back to when they were dating. He was so much lighter than his wife, and thin, so Eddie laughed the first time she said it, and she had used it ever since.

He stopped at Marlowe's townhouse to stare up at the brick structure. It only took a moment for Wraith to respond to his knock.

Eddie stepped in. "Hey Wraith, can I visit Marlowe, see how he's doing?"

The transparent man looked solemnly at Eddie—he couldn't help looking solemn most of the time. "I will have to say no, sir. Marlowe is resting right now."

"Drusilicus and Vasant still here?"

"I am afraid they have left, sir. They shall return this evening."

"They left Marlowe alone?" Eddie said, suddenly angry.

"No, sir. Mister Kraft is sitting with Marlowe. He insisted, sir."

"Oh, that's all right then," Eddie said, calming down. He glanced over at the door that led to the basement, where Marlowe trained him in the weeks and months after gaining the power of his staff. "Anyone in the basement?"

Wraith turned his spectral head and looked. "No, sir. Marlowe prepared nothing down there. The space is quite empty."

"Could I go down and… um… practice?" Eddie said, feeling embarrassed to admit, even casually, that he had not kept honing his skills in the months since he stopped working with his mentor.

The ghost returned his gaze to Eddie. "If you wish, sir. Would you like me to inform you when the others arrive?"

"Yeah, thanks."

The spirit bowed his head, rose into the air and disappeared into the wall.

Eddie walked to the basement door and hesitated. He vividly recalled the crash course Marlowe had worked him through in that basement almost two years ago, teaching him how to take down dragons, monsters, and the creatures of legend.

He hit a wall switch for lights and descended the long stone staircase into the deep recesses of the building.

In the center of the large room was a circular raised platform with an enormous cauldron. Eddie carefully approached and looked in to see a green liquid half-filling the large pot. The liquid just sat there, still and murky.

He held out his right hand.

A six-foot tall wooden staff slapped into his empty palm. Eddie ran his fingers over the surface of the wood, which glowed with layer upon layer of wax that gave it a surface as smooth as silk.

He had not held his staff in twelve long months.

He lifted the staff and with a flash of red light, his clothes melted, shifted, and reformed into robes—a tunic that went half-way down to his knees, leggings, and tall boots on his feet, all a scarlet hue.

He examined himself in his fighting robes, the garment he had worn into battle against demons and vampires, and he felt the power of his magick rising within him. He faced the cauldron, and with the slightest of gestures, it rose into the air and hovered unbound from the laws of gravity.

Eddie couldn't help but smile. Twelve long months and he still possessed the power of a wizard.

The liquid in the cauldron glowed with a greenish-yellow light, and smoke poured out of the open top, filling the room with the stench of brimstone.

Being careful not to let this throw him, Eddie carefully lowered the large container to its pedestal and stepped back, in case something unpleasant materialized out of the smoking vessel.

The glow in the pot increased, and the smoke coalesced as a shape rose in the center. A demonic face peered out with an enormous mouth, oversized pointed ears, and small horns on the skull-like head. It pulled itself up to expose its red skin and a naked chest.

"I seek the wizard Marlowe," the desiccated demon testified, with an air that suggested he wouldn't actually care if he got to Marlowe or not.

Eddie stepped forward. "I speak for Marlowe."

The demon lowered his tired eyes to Eddie. "You?"

"I am the Wizard Berman, and I will hear your message."

The weary demon put an elbow on the edge of the cauldron and rested his chin on his forearm as he scrutinized Eddie. "The Wizard Berman? Never heard of you."

Eddie thought about the name of the wizard whose staff he had received. "I am also known as Riftstone."

The monster shrugged. "Thought he was dead."

Eddie felt anger course through him. "Did you hear of the wizard who stopped the Great Evil? Or the wizard who brought vengeance down upon the vampires?"

This made the fiend look up questioningly. "Yeah, sure," he said with suspicion.

Eddie released a blast of light from his staff that smashed a chunk out of the stone pedestal where the cauldron stood. "I am that wizard. Now give me the message for Marlowe, before I lose my patience."

He held his staff aloft, ready to make his next attack directly against the demon.

The Hellish entity held up his hands defensively. "Hey, calm down, I'll tell you."

The creature cleared his throat. "The great and powerful Matchitehew sends greetings to the coven master Marlowe. Matchitehew agrees to an audience to discuss their mutual concerns of werewolves and the unintended slaughter of innocents upon the morrow."

The creature looked down at Eddie, his speech finished.

"That's it?"

The demon shrugged. "I'm just the messenger. It's not my job to explain the messages."

They stared at each other.

Finally, the demon broke the silence. "It is tradition to offer a messenger a gratuity upon delivery."

Eddie sighed. He was ready to tell the demon to go pound sand. Even though it was a year since he had taken on any wizardly duties or even conjured his staff of power, he recalled how often Marlowe reminded Eddie to treat magickal beings with great courtesy. The last thing he wanted to do was unleash an annoyed demon to bother Marlowe, just because he'd been a poor tipper.

"I... um... have a few dollars I could give you," Eddie attempted.

"I cannot touch your money," he scoffed. "It has 'In God We Trust' written upon it."

Eddie paused. "Yeah, I can see that it might be a problem for you."

The demon stared at Eddie.

"I guess I owe you one." Eddie shrugged.

A wide smile appeared on the demon's face. "As you wish, wizard."

Smoke enveloped the figure, and it sank down into the greenish slime in the cauldron and was gone.

"That was easier than I thought," Eddie said.

"Wizard Berman," a voice said next to him.

Eddie shrieked and spun around, his staff held high as power crackled around him.

Wraith stood, hands clasped in front of him, his shadowy eyes looking at the staff.

"Sorry, sir. The Wizard Obaru and the Wizard Philalethes have arrived and await you upstairs."

Eddie was breathing hard. "Yeah, sure. Don't sneak up on a guy, okay?"

"Sorry, sir. Please, you must help Marlowe. He is one of the few reasons I remain on this plane of existence."

"I'll do my best, Wraith."

The ghost looked downcast and passed through the wall as Eddie started up the long staircase.

Eddie hoped that his best would be enough.

THREE

E ugenia and Ahbay were sitting in large overstuffed chairs when Eddie entered the living room.

The Asian man rose and bowed. His hair was white and the lines in his face were deep. He wore a very nice burgundy suit that enhanced his straight back and sturdy shoulders.

Eddie bowed in return. "It is a pleasure to see you once again, Ahbay-san."

"You have learned some customs from my homeland since we last met, Wizard Berman," Ahbay Obaru replied with his slight accent.

Eugenia Philalethes rose from her chair and moved to the two men. She was a tall, thin woman with dark hair and striking features, including marvelous cheekbones. She smiled and hugged Eddie.

"Such a pleasure to see you again, Edward," Eugenia said with her high-class British accent. "It is a pity that we only meet when there are dire situations."

"We heard about the vampires," Ahbay said, his voice warm with praise. "There has been much less trouble with them over the last twelve months, now that they are not so emboldened."

"Is there a new Drakula?" Eddie asked, referring to the name not for a specific individual, but as an honorary title given to the ruler of the vampires.

"Not that I am aware of," Ahbay said.

"We've heard so little about you, Edward," Eugenia said. "Marlowe can be as tight-lipped as a clam."

"I have a one-year-old little girl, along with my sons," Eddie boasted as both Ahbay and Eugenia smiled. "But to be honest, I haven't been involved for the last year."

The two exchanged glances, and finally Eugenia said, "Not involved—what does that mean?"

Eddie rubbed the back of his neck. "I... took a break, decided to not do magick." He lifted his arms to display his scarlet robes. "This is the first time I've worn this, or even held my staff in the last year."

The two older wizards stared at him.

Eddie went on. "After the vampires—I needed some time away to figure out how I felt about all this."

"Edward," Eugenia gasped. "I am surprised. You do not seem like a man who walks away from things."

"Hey, that's not—"

"A wizard of your gifts, and you did not practice?" Ahbay said, obviously upset.

"I killed them," Eddie said, louder than he wanted to. "Hundreds of vampires. I destroyed them all in moments, like it was nothing."

Eugenia and Ahbay watched him with knowing eyes.

"You had no choice," Eugenia said softly. "From what we heard, they were raising the dead, planning to destroy the city. Thousands of innocents would have died if you had not acted."

"I didn't see that I was any better than they were," Eddie said, shaking his head. "I killed so many vampires that night, as if their existence was meaningless."

"I can see you are in pain, confused," Ahbay said. "You became a police officer to save lives, and a wizard to save the world. You do not feel right, killing."

"And I did it so easily…" Eddie said.

There was a knock at the door. Drusilicus entered in a fine blue suit complete with matching tie, followed by Vasant wearing pants and a long-sleeve full top with a belt at the waist.

Eugenia stepped forward with a cry of "Vasantbainkon!" as she took the other woman into a hug. Drusilicus greeted Ahbay with a bow, which the shorter man returned.

Drusilicus moved to Eddie. "Nice to see you in robes and with your staff."

"I was planning to work out a little, but a message came through for Marlowe."

"A message? What kind of message?"

"A demon said that this *Match-at-you* guy is ready to meet with Marlowe to discuss the werewolf problem—on the morrow."

Drusilicus stared at Eddie. "Apparently, Bankrock has been successful in making contact. I am surprised he responded so quickly."

"Why?"

"He is immortal and prefers being with his own kind," Drusilicus acknowledged. "He usually has no desire to work with wizards."

Eugenia had been talking to Vasant, but now she stepped forward. "The Five are now all present. Drusilicus, you passed word that a werewolf bit Marlowe, is that correct?"

"Quite," Drusilicus responded.

Ahbay also stepped closer. "You wish for us to purge the toxin from his blood?"

"Also correct. If we cannot—by next month, Marlowe will carry the werewolf curse."

"We cannot allow someone with Marlowe's powers to become a werewolf," Ahbay stated sternly. "No prison could contain him nor barrier stop him."

"Wait, wait," Eddie said. "You cannot allow? What would you do to him?"

"It is unwise to get ahead of ourselves, is it not?" Eugenia said. "Tonight, we must focus on healing Marlowe. Perhaps we will be victorious."

"We shall have to make two trips with the elevator," Drusilicus stated. "Eugenia, Vasant, and Ahbay, if you could go up first?"

Vasant led the other two to the elevator, leaving Drusilicus and Eddie to watch them as they ascended.

"I'm surprised that Bankrock didn't show up and tell us we were doing everything wrong," Eddie said.

Drusilicus grimaced. "Bankrock went upstate, where Matchitehew has a compound."

"Werewolves need a compound?"

Drusilicus shrugged. "I've been told he has hundreds of untouched acres on which his pack can hunt and roam. Wizard Claremont drove Bankrock up there."

Wizard Claremont—Rusty—drove a perfectly preserved Checker Cab with a huge passenger section and an enormous trunk. He claimed he enjoyed being a cabbie. Eddie always liked him, because unlike most of the wizards, he was down-to-earth and didn't put on airs.

"How is Rusty?"

"Same as always. It's been convenient for Marlowe that there has been someone to drive him places."

"Look, I didn't know my sabbatical depressed Marlowe."

"Is that what you're calling it?" Drusilicus inquired with a lifted eyebrow. "A sabbatical?"

"It sounds better than a re-evaluation. I haven't sorted out how I feel."

"Very well, lieutenant. How do you feel?" Drusilicus sneered as they got into the elevator.

The cage began its ascent. "Confused. I want to help people. I enjoy needing less sleep and having more energy that I get from bearing a staff—but Marlowe's been alive for over a thousand years. That means I will outlive my wife and my kids. I don't care for that idea at all."

"I am over one-hundred-forty, and still in the prime of life. I find it beneficial indeed."

"You and I are very different, Drew. I'm glad to see you're involved with Vasant, but she's as immortal as you are. The idea of losing my wife is crushing to me."

The pair stared forward as the elevator stopped at its destination.

The other three waited for Drusilicus and Eddie to join them and then walked down the long hallway to Marlowe's room. The upper hall was a large balcony that wrapped around the open living room with doors to the many bedrooms. Eddie often wondered how this was architecturally possible but had given up trying to understand.

The hall was always dark, and sconces on the wall held lit candles that burned but never melted. Vasant, in the lead, opened Marlowe's door.

They all easily fit in the enormous room, and Marlowe sat up in bed.

At Marlowe's command, several candelabrums burst into flame around the room, filling it with a yellow light. Marlowe blinked, looking at the group.

It shocked Eddie to see how thin and frail the old man appeared. He had lost weight since Eddie last saw him and was very pale.

He was in a large four-poster bed, and with a gesture, the pillows moved behind him to allow him to sit up easily. He lay back against them as he surveyed the assembly.

Marlowe spoke weakly. "Look upon your sorry coven master."

"You are sick, nothing more," Vasant said. "We are here to cleanse you of the infection."

Marlowe pursed his lips in thought. "And what is your function in this, my dear?"

Drusilicus stepped forward. "After the incident with Trefoil years ago, I thought it best to have an extra wizard to supervise, in case anything should go wrong."

Eddie nodded. He was there when the Five had attempted to heal a wizard named Trefoil, and it went horribly wrong. There was a talisman the unconscious wizard was wearing designed to steal their powers. If it hadn't been for his own fast thinking, the wizards might have lost their powers completely.

Marlowe nodded slightly. "Wise indeed. Who says we cannot learn from our mistakes?"

Vasant took charge. "Wizards, if you would please go to the four corners of the bed, we may begin."

Each member of the group moved to one of the four posts. Eddie stood at the head of the bed and gently touched his mentor's shoulder.

Marlowe patted his hand and looked up at Eddie. "I am most grateful to see you here."

"I wish it were under better circumstances," Eddie said, still in shock over Marlowe's appearance.

"The part that troubles me is that it was barely a bite, really nothing more than a nip, as if the werewolf did not intend to hurt me seriously."

Vasant spoke up. "Please, I need your full attention. Wizard Philalethes, if you will begin."

Eugenia touched the wooden comb in her hair, and her clothing swirled into buttercup-yellow robes as a staff appeared in her hand. A slight breeze passed through the room and her staff glowed with a lemony light. "Isa ya!" she offered. "The power of air, the breath of life, is with thee."

Ahbay held up his wooden cane, and he was instantly in long green robes and holding a staff with a green light on top. "Isa ya! The power of earth, the mother of us all, is with thee."

Drusilicus' suit melted into blue robes as his staff leapt into his hand, and he spoke clearly and powerfully. "Isa ya! The power of water, the mighty ocean, is with thee."

It was Eddie's turn, and as a red light appeared at the top of his staff, he announced, "Isa ya! The power of fire, the heat of the sun, is with thee."

Vasant spoke. "Marlowe, are you strong enough for this?"

Marlowe held up his walking stick, which grew into a staff that he held to his chest. "Isa ya!" Marlowe intoned. "The power of spirit that binds the elements is with thee."

"So mote it be!" Eugenia declared as her yellow light shot forth from her staff to touch Marlowe and became a pale yellow.

"So mote it be!" Ahbay agreed, and his emerald light joined the other two to become a pale light green.

"So mote it be!" Drusilicus uttered, and his blue light joined the rest, making the aura surrounding Marlowe a bright aquamarine.

"So mote it be!" Eddie focused his attention on Marlowe and the aura shifted to a bright violet.

"So mote it be!" Marlowe vowed with closed eyes. His body rose from the bed, suspended on beams of light.

"Focus, all of you," Vasant said. "Remove the poison from his blood, cleanse him of all that ails him, and restore his strength."

Eddie concentrated. He felt as if he could see into Marlowe's body, see his skeletal structure and the arteries and veins as the heart pumped and moved the blood. He sensed the lungs pulling in air and all the organs as they performed their necessary functions.

He also sensed something dark that moved through the blood, snaking its way throughout the body and evading his grasp.

They held Marlowe aloft for at least five minutes and then he slowly lowered back to the bed, as Vasant called out, "It is done. So mote it be!"

"So mote it be," the others repeated. The wizards called back their powers, and the beams of light faded and disappeared.

"How do you feel, old friend?" Ahbay asked, as Marlowe sat up.

"Better," Marlowe replied with a nod. "Stronger."

"Are you cleansed of the infection?" Eugenia asked.

"I am not sure," Marlowe said, but he appeared more alert. "Let me meet you all downstairs, and we can discuss it over a meal."

With a glance at each other, the group left the room, heading back to the waiting elevator.

Eddie and Drusilicus took the elevator first and discovered a figure sitting in one of the living room chairs.

The woman rose, pushing herself to her feet with her staff which seemed much taller than her petite frame. She wore battle robes the same as Eddie's, yet the color was a light green-blue hue. She had brown shoulder length hair, a small nose and full lips. Her violet eyes observed the wizards as they approached.

She only glanced at Eddie before turning to Drusilicus. "I be the Wizard Glade. The ghost at the door told me to wait here. Didst thou summon me?"

Her voice was light but held a hard edge, with the lilt of an Irish accent.

Drusilicus' face rose in a patient smile. "Yes, thank you for coming, and no need to be so formal. Please join us?"

He gestured toward the breakfast room, and the unsmiling woman turned and headed toward it.

"She's your expert on werewolves?" Eddie whispered.

"Yes, quite an authority from what we are told," Drusilicus mumbled back.

In the breakfast room, chafing dishes of food awaited, with plates and flatware nearby.

"Aye, this be quite fancy, don't it?" Glade said, again not looking pleased.

"Help yourself," Drusilicus offered, but she merely stared at the chafing dishes.

Eddie inquired, "Who puts out the food?"

"Hm?" Drusilicus replied, a bit distracted. "I imagine Wraith does."

"He's a ghost. How does he carry these things out here?"

"With practice, a spirit can lift and move objects. Have you never heard of a poltergeist?"

"Is that what Wraith is? A poltergeist?"

"Wraith is a rather unique being. He's been with Marlowe for centuries. As I recall, he was engaged as a servant by Marlowe in the 1800s when, after years of loyal service, he died. Even so, he was so attached to Marlowe that he didn't want to leave, so he's been with him ever since."

"Why is he always so glum?"

Drusilicus shrugged. "That's just his personality."

The others arrived and they made introductions, though Glade didn't appear pleased to meet the rest of the wizards.

Eugenia and Ahbay helped themselves to food as Vasant tried to welcome the newcomer.

"So glad you could join us," Vasant said.

"I dislike cities," Glade complained. "I prefer livin' at one with nature without the stink of humanity."

Drusilicus and Eddie exchanged a worried glance.

Marlowe entered, leaning heavily on his walking stick. Daniel Kraft stood with him in a black velvet suit, helping him along. His pale skin made him look as if he was carved from marble.

The wizards all stepped back from Daniel, giving both him and Marlowe a wide berth.

Eddie took Daniel's hand in a warm handshake. "Good to see you, Daniel."

Kraft merely smiled tightly. "Let me get Marlowe settled." He helped Marlowe into a chair and got a plate for him.

Eddie looked at his fellow wizards, surprised that they moved away and avoided looking at Daniel. In the past, they always seemed to accept the vampire and his unique presence in Marlowe's townhouse. Had Eddie's battle with the vampires a year ago made the wizard suspicious, even paranoid?

Daniel set the plate in front of the old man and stepped through the archway toward the living room. With a glance at the others, Eddie followed, catching up with Daniel at the bottom of the circular staircase.

"Daniel," Eddie called out, and the tall vampire stopped. "What's going on? Why was everyone looking at you that way?"

"I am sure I don't know what you mean, Wizard Berman," Daniel replied.

Eddie frowned. "Wizard Berman? Daniel, it's me, Eddie. You were never formal with me in the past."

"Things have changed, haven't they?" Daniel answered curtly.

Eddie met Daniel's eyes. "Tell me what has changed… I've been away."

"Yes, and you broke Marlowe's heart."

"Daniel, you know me. I would never hurt Marlowe for any reason—I have a new daughter, a family. I have responsibilities."

"And we both know Marlowe is low on your list," Daniel stated coldly. "If you don't mind, I best leave before you extinguish my existence as you did so many others."

Daniel headed to the front door, and out into the night.

Eddie's face burned with shame. The terrible events of a year earlier seemed like a weight about to crush him. He headed back to the others. By now, they had all filled their plates with food and sat around the large table.

Eddie sat heavily next to Marlowe, his appetite gone.

Vasant positioned silver goblets at each place setting. She brought out a jug of wine and filled the goblet in front of Marlowe, then her own.

Marlowe was eating, and Eddie was glad for it.

"How do you feel?" Eddie asked.

"Much better, thank you," Marlowe said. "It quite surprised me to open my eyes and see you standing nearby."

"You needed the Five. I wouldn't stay away from a situation like that."

"I feel better than I have for several days," Marlowe said and looked around the table. "And it's good to see you all."

Ahbay spoke up. "It was our duty to help."

"Do you think we purged you of the werewolf curse?" Eugenia asked.

Glade made a snort of derision but said nothing.

"I am not sure," Marlowe said. "But I am grateful you could all come together. Ahbay, Eugenia, I invite you to stay here in my townhouse until we can be sure."

The two wizards nodded in agreement.

Eddie turned to Marlowe. "I have to head home soon. I'm on the four to midnight in Washington Square tomorrow. Luis and I will help animal control hunt for the werewolves and get any information you might need."

"The full moon is over, I am afraid," Marlowe said.

Glade spoke up. "A werewolf can transform even on nights past the full moon. It is only during the full moon that there be no choice. There be ways to make a werewolf show itself."

The others stared at her.

Ahbay shook his head. "If this werewolf is hunting beyond the full moon—this suggests that it wishes to kill the innocent."

"There be cases of werewolves driven mad by their own needs," Glade intoned. "I've hunted down several."

"I hope this will be the last I have to worry about such things," Marlowe said, and stood. Eddie hopped up to help, but the old man waved him away.

"A toast to the Five, and my good friends," Marlowe said, and picked up the silver goblet.

He grimaced, and the chalice fell from his hand, clunking to the table, the red wine spilling over the surface of the wood.

Marlowe gaped at his hand, as several angry marks appeared on it.

Eddie took Marlowe's hand in his own. "Those look like burns."

"Silver burns a werewolf," Glade stated with no emotion.

Marlowe frowned, his face twisted in pain. "It would appear I am not cured after all."

Eddie watched the red wine as it dripped off the table in droplets as dark red as blood.

FOUR

After they'd eaten, Vasant helped Marlowe back up to his room as the other wizards sat around in a circle in the living room.

It wasn't until the door to Marlowe's room shut that Glade finally spoke. "A werewolf bit the old man, then?"

"Your grasp of the situation is astounding," Drusilicus snapped.

"Drew, there's no need for sarcasm," Eddie said. "Can you help us?"

"I be not sure," Glade said. "What did ye do for him?"

"We used the power of the Five united," Eugenia explained, "to cleanse him of the curse."

Glade made a derogatory sound. "You see how well that worked."

"Since you are the expert, perhaps you can tell us what would succeed," Drusilicus demanded.

"I'll not be talked to in such a way," Glade said, getting to her feet.

Eddie held up his hands. "Everyone calm down." He looked at the group, who grew silent as he turned to their newest member.

"Glade, if you can offer anything to help Marlowe, we would appreciate it."

She gazed from wizard to wizard. "What did the wolf look like?"

Vasant spoke up. "There were two. The first had reddish fur with gray around the face and ears, and the belly was white."

"Ah, an Eurasian wolf from the description. You say there be two? How did the other appear?"

Vasant closed her eyes, searching her memory. "The other one was more gray and white, and the ears and muzzle were smaller."

Glade nodded. "A timber wolf, to be sure."

"Do you know of a cure?" Eddie asked.

"There be few cures, but several remedies. Tell me, what other steps have ye taken?"

"We are in contact with Matchitehew, seeking his help," Drusilicus said.

This made Glade sit up. "Really? And he wouldst meet with ye?"

"We reached out to him," Drusilicus said, obviously suspicious of her reaction. "We were told he holds sway in the community."

"And he offered to help," Eddie added.

Glade considered it. "I be most surprised at this."

"You're familiar with this Match guy," Eddie said.

Glade opened her mouth to speak, just as the elevator opened and Vasant stepped out. Glade waited for her to sit before she went on. "Our paths have crossed."

"What can you tell us about him?" Eddie asked.

"He be a man and wolf that others look up to, and well deserved. Y'see, like we wizards, he is old—centuries old."

"How did he become a werewolf?" Eddie asked. "Was he bitten?"

"Nay. Long ago, before the Europeans came to this land, there be a spirit-god named Wisakachek who lived in the woods. One day he saw two brothers, Keme and Matchitehew, who killed a deer with bow and arrow. Wisakachek claimed he be a lost and hungry wanderer and the brothers offered him some of the deer meat."

"Following the tradition of treating magickal beings with respect?" Eddie suggested.

Glade nodded. "Aye. Wisakachek, in gratitude, shared his ability to shape-shift into a wolf so that they could catch deer more easily. The only condition he set was that they could not use their wolf-forms to hurt humans, only to hunt."

"I take it things did not go well?" Vasant asked.

"One day, Matchitehew tried to help a boy in the village hunt for game, and he became the wolf. The lad was so shocked, he turned to flee, fell off a mountainside, and killed hisself. Wisakachek was furious, blaming Matchitehew, though it t'weren't his fault. He cast a spell on Matchitehew, so from that day onward, he would take on human form and 'ere the full moon he would transform into a mindless wolf."

"Was that the beginning of the werewolf curse?" Eddie asked.

"Perhaps here in America, it was. Matchitehew be known as the Father of Werewolves. Through his bite, he created many others."

Vasant cleared her throat. "Which begs the question, why is he willing to help?"

Glade looked over the group. "Tell me, how did the old man get hisself bit?"

"There was a werewolf attack in Central Park," Eddie explained. "It killed a man."

"Who was that?" Glade's violet eyes focused on Eddie.

Eddie pulled his phone to review his notes, speaking as he did. "He was a mess, all torn up, but we got fingerprints and he had identification. The victim's name was Stubbe. Harold Stubbe."

The color left Glade's face.

Drusilicus frowned at her. "Are you all right, Wizard Glade?"

"Aye, just surprised," she said, recovering quickly.

"That name is significant to you?" Eddie asked.

Glade pondered this for a moment. "Understand how I know of this, why I be an expert? I have lived among werewolves."

"How is that even possible?" Eugenia asked.

"'Tis quite possible. I spent many years livin' one with nature, out in the wild, and among werewolves seeking ways to control their gifts. I've learned of many potions and spells, ancient books, and strange rites to relieve some fine people from the burden they carry. I have known for many a year the family name of Stubbe."

"Anything you can tell us might help," Eddie persisted.

Glade took a deep breath. "In 1589, in Germany, in a town near Cologne, a vicious werewolf preyed upon the citizens. It started with the villagers' livestock. Day after day, they found dead cows, ripped open and slaughtered."

"Could it have been actual wolves back then?" Drusilicus asked.

"Not at all. The animals were just the beginning. The creature murdered seventeen women and children. After the killing and disembowelment of a pregnant woman, the men formed hunting parties to kill the beast."

Eddie frowned. "I don't see what this has to do with our case."

"The hounds of the search party pursued the monster and cornered it. Whereupon it took off a belt and transformed from a wolf into a man."

"Wait," Eddie said, amazed. "The *belt* turned him into a wolf?"

"Aye. Made of wolf's fur it was, and enchanted. What we wizards would call a talisman. The captured man claimed the devil hisself taught him to make it." Glade turned her violet eyes to each person. "That man's name was Peter Stubbe."

"A distant relative of our victim?" Eddie asked.

"Perhaps. They convicted the man and put him to death—rather brutally, but ne'er found the magic belt."

"Where do you suppose it went?" Drusilicus asked.

"That be a mystery, but one I have long since uncovered. Stubbe had a brother, Hermann, who came to the town before the trial and left after the verdict."

"You think he found his brother's belt?" Eddie asked.

"That I do. He also gained the knowledge of how to construct it, and the spells necessary to make it work. According to legends, his family has passed down that knowledge for generations."

Eddie stroked his chin as he'd often seen Marlowe do.

"I do not know of werewolf attacks using an enchanted belt," Drusilicus huffed.

Glade's eyebrows went up. "In 1901, there was a serial killer, Ludwig Tessnow, who killed sheep and people, rippin' them apart viciously. Two of his victims were children named Stubbe.

Methinks Ludwig got one of the magic belts and killed the Stubbe children instead of paying for it."

Ahbay shook his head. "I do not see the connection to the wolves we seek."

Glade sighed. "There be rumors in the werewolf community that there still be members of the Stubbe family with the ability to create the magickal belt."

"If this Stubbe person knew how to make these belts, why did he end up dead?" Drusilicus asked.

Eddie spoke. "From a police point of view, there could be only one of three possibilities." He counted off on his fingers. "One, someone killed him to stop him from making the belts. Two, he made someone a belt, and the guy transformed and lost control. Or three, someone purchased a belt and killed Stubbe so he couldn't tell anyone who the buyer was."

"That adds to our problems then," Drusilicus surmised. "The werewolf we are seeking might be someone using a magic belt."

"It couldn't have been such a wolf that bit Wizard Marlowe," Glade said, holding up a hand. "Using the enchanted belt, the wearer does not have the virus and cannot infect a person."

"There were two werewolves," Vasant said. "The second one, the timber wolf, was attempting to protect Marlowe, and it only bit him while fighting off the attacker."

"Aye, then the timber wolf be the true werewolf."

"What can we do?" Drusilicus said. "That werewolf will not change for a month, and by then, it will be too late for Marlowe."

Glade shifted her eyes to Drusilicus. "I have ways to conjure the wolf, force it to return to a place it has been. This spell would compel even a user of the belt to return. Then I have me ways to mesmerize the beast."

"Will you share these techniques with us?" asked Eugenia.

Glade looked at the woman, and her lip curled in derision. "I think to a fine lady as yourself, such a spell wouldst only be a burden."

Vasant said calmly. "Can you help us, then?"

"Aye. I can do a spell and I have ways to contain and control the beastie," Glade announced. "But we must do it at the stroke of midnight, and not this night. I must mix some special potions and prepare meself."

"Is there anything that will cure Marlowe?" Eddie asked.

"There be only one potion I know of. But I can make no promises as to how well it moight work." She reached into her robes and extracted a small rolled up parchment and offered it to Vasant. "I've written it out for ye. It uses ingredients that are quite rare—it also requires several hairs from the wolf who bit Wizard Marlowe."

"An actual case of 'hair of the dog'?" Eddie said.

The other stared at him blankly.

Vasant looked over the scroll. "I believe that if we can attain some of the animal's fur, myself or Ahbay could make it."

"I would be glad to help," Ahbay announced. "I have mixed many potions in my time."

Drusilicus stepped close to look over Vasant's shoulders. "I'll get you anything you need."

Glade reached into her robes and pulled out another small parchment. "Since ye be offerin', I need this for the conjurin'."

Drusilicus took the parchment. "Wolfsbane oil?" He did a double take at the writing. "This is an unusual concentration."

"I need it at the exact mix I ask ye," Glade explained. "It be to bind the animal once I have it in me spell."

"This actually might work out," Eddie said. "I'm patrolling Washington Square Park with an animal control agent tomorrow night, and his shift ends at eleven. We can assemble there, and if you can conjure the wolves at midnight, we can capture them."

"What if they come in human form?" Ahbay wondered.

"When they feel the pull of the spell, they will change," Glade said. "Of that ye can be sure."

"Since you are staying until at least tomorrow, we would like to provide you a room to stay here in the townhouse," Vasant said.

Glade looked around the large living room. "That be not necessary. I have an arch in Central Park where I stay when needs arise. I would not be comfortable here."

Eddie nodded. Wizards had been around during the construction of Central Park and the designers built arches named after many of them. Each one of those arches contained a hidden room which only that wizard or certain people could access.

The strange woman rose with a glance at the other wizards. "I have much to make ready before the morrow. I shall see thee at the witching hour in the park."

Without another word, she headed straight to the door and was gone, leaving the other wizards stunned.

"That was a bit... abrupt," Eugenia said.

"I would use the word rude," Drusilicus said, looking at the parchment in his hand. "I will need to mix up this wolfsbane oil. I do not have any concentrations this high."

"Yeah, about that," Eddie asked. "Wolfsbane is a flower, right?"

"A most poisonous one, yes," Ahbay pointed out.

"Quite," Drusilicus agreed. "It is so toxic you cannot touch it without wearing gloves."

"The Medical Examiner said that Stubbe was wearing wolfsbane in his lapel the night of the murder," Eddie reported.

Ahbay nodded. "It appears he knew a werewolf was pursuing him."

"Why kill a man who could make such an unusual talisman?" Eugenia wondered.

"Perhaps it was a wolf that didn't want competition?" Vasant suggested.

"There is still much we do not know," Drusilicus said.

"Right," Eddie said, taking charge. "We need to become more knowledgeable." He faced the others. "All of you need to find any information that exists about werewolves: potions, spells, anything, no matter how esoteric. We have only this one cure that Glade gave us, but I want several to choose from in case it doesn't work."

Ahbay and Eugenia nodded in agreement.

"I shall contact Bankrock and find out when we can meet with Matchitehew," Vasant said.

"Good!"

"And what will you do, lieutenant?" Drusilicus demanded.

"I'm a cop, so I'll do what a cop does. I'll search Stubbe's apartment and find out anything I can about him and his wolf belt."

"Do you think we will get the hair of the timber wolf tomorrow?" Vasant asked.

"If we do, that's great," Eddie agreed. "But I want a backup plan so we don't depend on Glade if things go wrong."

The wizards looked at him, their jaws firm. They all knew what it meant if they failed.

FIVE

The next morning, Eddie heard a voice near his ear saying "Da! Da!"

He had gotten home well after midnight, when the house was dark and everyone asleep, getting into bed quietly so not to disturb Cerise.

At seven AM he opened his eyes to see his one-year-old daughter holding herself up on the edge of the bed.

With a glance to Cerise, Eddie got out of bed, and lifted the giggling girl.

"How the heck did you get out of your crib?" Eddie whispered as he carried her into the nursery and onto her changing table to replace her diaper. He glanced at the crib— the sides were all up. Usually, Ellie pulled herself to her feet and woke her parents by crying for them. Yet, she not only got out of the crib, but wandered through her parents' closed bedroom door.

Eddie carried her downstairs to start coffee. His wizard abilities allowed him to need less sleep, so he was wide awake and ready to face the day.

He placed Ellie in her high chair and prepared a sippy cup.

"Ba-ba," Ellie stated, not pleased when he placed the cup in front of her.

"No more bottles, Ellie," Eddie said, and reluctantly, the toddler picked up the cup and drank.

As Eddie waited for coffee and heated a pot of cereal for Ellie, he quickly texted Luis:

Heading in early today

to toss Stubbe's apartment.

You in?

"What are you doing up?" a female voice said behind him.

Eddie turned to see his mother, Eleanor, coming down the back stairs. She was an older woman only about five feet five, with silver-white hair, thick glasses, and a trim figure.

"Hey Momma," Eddie said. "Ellie was awake, and in my bedroom."

Eleanor frowned. "How did she get out of her crib?"

Eddie chuckled. "I have no idea, Momma."

"When did you get in las' night?" his mother asked, setting up pots on the stove to make breakfast.

"Pretty late," Eddie said. "It's gonna be that way for at least the next week."

"Hey Dad," William said, coming down the stairs like a herd of elephants.

"Keep the noise down," Eddie said, shushing the young man. "Your mother's off today, and I want to let her sleep late."

Ellie put down her cup, held up her arms excitedly, and said, "Wee, wee."

"Morning, squirt," he said, and gave the girl a hug. She clung to him, but William disentangled himself from the child and handed her the cup again.

"Let Mom know I'm gonna get home late today, okay?" William said.

"What's up?"

"Tryouts for next year's basketball team."

Eddie put cereal in a plastic bowl to feed Ellie. "I know you've been working really hard to get your game up."

"I think I got it this year."

"Let me know when you know. And don't slow down this summer, thinking you have it made."

"No way, Dad."

"Guess I'll have to go one-on-one with you a lot."

"You, I can take. It's the other guys I worry about," William said, smiling.

"I still got a few moves I can use," Eddie said as he sat down next to Ellie with the cereal.

"Why don't you go back to bed?" Eleanor said from the stove. "I can feed the boys and take care of Ellie."

Eddie looked at his momma, his son, and his daughter—this was what he really loved. These people, his family, sharing a life together.

Eddie rose. "I think I'll do that, Momma. If it's not too much on you."

"Go be with your wife," Eleanor chuckled.

As Eddie went up the stairs, Douglas was coming down. Although he'd grown, Doug would never be as tall as his brother, as he took after his mother. "Dad, you're around this weekend, right?"

"Unless something big comes up, why?"

"My first magic show, Dad! For money."

"That's right, I'm your driver. Think you're ready?"

"I sure hope so."

Eddie headed back to the bedroom and lay down next to his wife with a sigh.

"Why are you sighing?" Cerise said, her accent coloring her words.

He took her hand under the sheet. "Just thinking how lucky I am to have this family and to have you."

"Oh, that's an excellent answer," she said and moved her lips to his.

"The boys are so big," Eddie said.

"So is Ellie. It's hard to believe I pushed her out of my body a year ago." She kissed him again. "What do you have in mind, coming back to bed?"

"We need to talk."

"That certainly kills the mood," Cerise said, lying back down.

"I'm serious."

"What's bothering you? Is it about your friend Marlowe getting hurt?"

"Yes. That animal attack in Central Park? I think it's a supernatural creature."

"Supernatural? Like those vampires?"

"Only this time it's werewolves."

Cerise sighed. "Should I expect a mummy to show up any day?"

"It's just—I have to get involved again. They need me. But once it's over, I have to decide about my staff."

"What do you have to decide?"

"I think I should give it up, pass it on to someone else."

Cerise frowned. "That is a big decision."

"I wasn't completely honest with you when I got it—if you have a staff, you age a lot slower."

"What do you mean?"

"Marlowe is like a thousand years old. Drusilicus is over a hundred and forty."

"Really? Why is that a bad thing?"

Eddie faced his wife. "Because everyone I know and love will age at the normal speed, and I won't."

"Ah."

"The other wizards told me they've had numerous families. One of them, Vasant, she's had dozens of husbands and over one hundred children."

"Oof! Three times was enough for me."

"I always saw us growing old together, watching the kids become adults, becoming grandparents. The thought that I could outlive you, and the kids, and their children—it just isn't something I want to face."

Cerise lay in their marriage bed, considering it. "Maybe I would enjoy being an old lady with a young husband."

"Come on, Cerise, I'm serious."

She nodded. "I know. It's hard for me to get my head around it all. Tell you what, let's focus on the small things."

"Okay, what would that be?"

"Your friends will help you catch this animal. You should do that, make Central Park safe again. Then decide if you want to continue working with them."

"The problem is—these werewolves—I've been told they're fast, very fast. I might get hurt."

"But you're planning to stop it, am I correct?"

"I have to. It killed a man and bit Marlowe."

"Then get your friends to help. Don't go in alone. And do what you do best."

"What's that?"

"Think outside the box." She reached over and caressed Eddie's chest. "Now, I have a day off, and I know a perfect way to start my day."

She slid on top of Eddie, pulling her nightgown off over her head.

It was—indeed—a terrific way to start the day.

Eddie was dressed and showered before Luis replied to his text:

When and where? I'll be there.

Eddie made the call to get a warrant. It wasn't legally required to search a dead man's house but Harold Stubbe had lived in a high-rise in Manhattan and the warrant would open doors more easily.

He left his car in New York the previous night, so instead of driving, he walked to a park close to his house and entered the trees. Using the woods to teleport was one of the first abilities that Eddie mastered as a wizard. He transformed the wood-grain credit card he carried in his wallet into its true form, his wizard's staff, and entered the copse of trees. Instantly, he stepped out of the woods in Central Park near his precinct.

Marlowe explained that this was accomplished through an act of sympathetic magick. The idea was that all the forests on earth are really just one giant forest, not aware of borders or different countries. If a wizard focused on where he wanted to be, through will and intent, he could teleport to the forest of his choice immediately.

He met with Luis at the twenty-second precinct, got the warrant and an evidence collection kit, and drove the pair of them in an unmarked police car to the upper East Side. He brought Luis up to speed on what happened the previous night with the wizards and what they were looking for in the apartment.

He pulled over on East 80th Street and parked in front of a twenty-story modern building. Individual metal letters built into the facade announced that this was 'The Wentworth.'

It was a newer construction and towered high over their heads, with large windows and balconies on every floor starting at the third floor. A revolving door led to a lobby and a uniformed doorman came outside.

"You can't park there," the man said as they approached.

Luis pulled out his billfold with his shield. "This says I can. We need to go into one of your apartments."

The man looked flustered. "You'll have to come inside and talk to the manager. We don't want to alarm the guests."

He escorted Eddie, carrying the evidence kit, and Luis, through the revolving door. The interior was all marble—floor, walls, and even the trim. As they entered, a concierge desk was to their left, and a small sitting area to their right with large sturdy chairs and a pair of sofas, one in a green velvet and the other done in leather. Bookcases with tastefully arranged books framed one couch, creating a relaxed atmosphere. The doorman led them through a side door, and into a windowless back office.

Behind a desk sat a matronly woman with gray hair and glasses. She lifted her head as the group came in. The doorman quickly left.

"Good afternoon, Mrs. Caitlan," Eddie said, reading the name plate on her desk. Luis handed her the paper. "We have a warrant for one of your apartments—the residence of Harold Stubbe."

She frowned and looked down at the paper. "This is most unusual. It states you are looking for any evidence regarding the untimely death of Harold Stubbe. I thought a wild animal killed him. Why are the police involved?"

"It's an ongoing investigation and I am not at liberty to say," Eddie replied.

She continued to go over the form. "May I see your identification, please?" She took a careful look at their shields and ID. "The next of kin asked us to seal the apartment. No one in or out until she arrives to take care of Mr. Stubbe's possessions."

"Yeah, well, our warrant takes precedence over her request," Luis said.

"I see. Shall I escort you?" She rose from her desk, and unlocked a box on the wall that was filled with carefully marked keys. "Will this take long?"

"As long as it needs to," Eddie assured her.

They rode up in a service elevator with quilted fabric lining the walls up to the tenth floor. They traveled in silence as Mrs. Caitlan led them to the door for 10E and unlocked it with the two keys on the small key ring.

She stepped in and Eddie put his hand out for the keys. "We'll lock up when we're done."

"I really should stay and make sure everything is on the up and up," she reasoned.

"That won't be necessary. We'll bring the keys back to your office," Eddie said, then as politely as he could, shut the door in her face.

Eddie put the plastic box on top of the nearby kitchen counter, and Luis opened it to pull out nitrile gloves. He offered a pair to Eddie and slid one on his right hand.

The apartment was a one-bedroom with a living room and a separate kitchen, bath, and a stacked washer and dryer in one closet. Floors of fine wood gleamed throughout the rooms. The living room had several straight-backed chairs, a couch, a coffee table, and a large screen TV mounted on the wall.

"How much does a place like this go for?" Luis asked, pulling a glove on his left hand.

"According to their website," Eddie said, "this apartment rents for about six thousand a month."

"Jeez," Luis winced. "How can anyone afford to live in Manhattan?"

"The real question is, how did a guy who makes wolf belts get the money he needed to live here?" Eddie wondered.

"Yeah, and there's something wrong," Luis said. "I mean, the guy had to have tools if he made things like a belt, right?"

Luis opened the closet that contained the washer/dryer combination with a thick PVC pipe going up beside the pair. From the space next to the lower machine, Luis slid out a folding table. "Maybe this would help?"

He brought it into the living room, moved the coffee table aside, and opened it. It was heavy plastic and folded in the middle, so once opened it was about eight feet long and sturdy. Brown stains discolored the white plastic of the surface.

"This could be his workspace," Eddie said.

"So, where are the tools?" Luis wondered.

"More important, where are the talismans and spells?"

"He wouldn't keep the tools he used in plain sight. You got a spell to help you locate hidden stuff?"

"Sorry, fresh out."

Luis glanced into the bedroom. "There's a bookcase in here. I'll look through what's there."

Eddie said, "According to the Glade woman, Harold Stubbe was an enchanter from a long line of enchanters. I think he knew enough to keep us from finding his hidey-hole."

"Great," Luis muttered from the bedroom.

Eddie stopped at the plastic table and peered under it. He put it on its side to expose a pentagram carved into the plastic on the underside.

"I found an inverted pentagram," Eddie said.

"What does that mean?" Luis said from the other room.

"Some say it's the sign of the devil. We're definitely in the right apartment."

"I may have something here," Luis said as he strode back into the room holding a large leather-bound book. It had the head of a wolf carved into the heavy leather cover and, in elaborate print, the words:

Lupus Libre

"What does that mean?" Eddie asked.

"I dunno," Luis said. He handed Eddie the book and pulled out his smart phone. "Let me look it up online."

Eddie opened it. The pages were larger than letter size and a light brown color. Each page was hand-written, filled with an odd script and covered with many diagrams and notes.

Staring at his phone, Luis spoke up. "The Book of the Wolf."

"What?" Eddie said, taken aback.

"That's what it means in Latin," Luis said, pocketing his phone and looking over Eddie's shoulder. "Wow, that looks cool. What language is that?"

"I don't know, Latin, maybe some German," Eddie suggested. "Some of these letters are Greek."

"Put it on the table," Luis said. "That way, we both can look at it."

Eddie laid it down on the table and opened it up.

"What kind of paper is this?" Luis asked.

"I don't think it's paper," Eddie explained. "It looks like parchment."

"What's the difference?"

"They make parchment from the skin of an animal." Eddie turned another page. "Could this be the original instructions written by Peter Stubbe?"

"You mean we got a book from the sixteenth century?" Luis asked, feeling one of the brown pages.

"Could be. Or it could be a copy. But it's handwritten on parchment. Maybe a member of the Stubbe family wrote it up."

"Anything useful?" Luis said, as Eddie continued to turn pages.

"I can't tell. I don't have any idea what the instructions say or what the symbols mean. If I can get it to Marlowe and the other wizards, they might decipher it."

Luis opened it to the back. "Look here, someone cut out pages."

At the back of the book near the binding, someone had cut out several pages, leaving only remaining slivers in the spine. "That's not a good sign."

Luis raised his head to glance around the room again. "How about the tools? You getting any vibe?"

"No, maybe it's time we do this the old-fashioned way," Eddie said, closing the book.

Luis grinned. "I'll check the tank of the toilet and the mattress."

"I'll check the frozen food," Eddie proposed, and headed into the small kitchen.

One of the most popular places people like to hide money or narcotics was to wrap the item in aluminum foil and stick it in a box of food made to look unopened.

Eddie opened the top compartment of the refrigerator and pulled out boxes of frozen items, opening the boxes, but each one contained the named product. Frozen waffles, peas, broccoli, corn, all were in the inner plastic bags.

He emptied the freezer and finally checked the back wall of the empty refrigerator to make sure it was real. Then he put everything back in, just as Luis came into the room. He was carrying a rectangle covered with a thick pelt.

"I found this zipped into the lining of the mattress."

Eddie rubbed the fur. "It's an animal skin."

"What do you think it is?"

"The lady wizard said you needed a wolf pelt to make the belt," Eddie asserted. "That would be my guess."

Luis turned the skin over in his hand, looking at the leather side. "This hide is thick. It would make a pretty sturdy belt."

"Yes, but we still haven't found either leather tools or enchanter's tools."

"What sort of tools would he use?"

"There is someone we could ask," Eddie suggested. "Caleb."

"That creep who used to be Drew's apprentice?" Luis said. "I thought he had that 'Psychic-Reader' scam at a place on Sullivan street."

"It might not be a scam," Eddie said. "I mean with those talismans of his he can actually read minds and stuff."

Luis snorted. "He's trouble! We had problems with him back in the day. Hey, maybe this Stubbe guy had tools he stored elsewhere, y'know, rented a space."

"I doubt it," Eddie said. "From what the others have told me, an enchanter wants to keep his tools close." Eddie pulled open the closet with the washing machine and dryer. He opened the front-loading washer and looked in, then did the same to the dryer. Then he looked at the space above the combo. "The ceiling in this closet is lower than the ceiling in the rest of the apartment."

Luis joined Eddie and looked at it. "To cover heating pipes or vents or something?"

"That's what someone wants us to think."

Luis reached up and pressed the front of the lower wall. "Feels solid."

Eddie smiled. "He was an enchanter. He knew how to make a lock most people could not get past." Eddie held out his hand, called his power to him and whispered, "Patentibus."

The wall in front of him fell open on hinges, revealing a space crammed with items. There was a strange lock mechanism on the top, and solid two-by-fours lined the plywood attached to the walls.

"Your spell that opens any lock comes in handy," Luis admitted.

"It certainly does," Eddie said as he pulled out several plastic toolboxes and an enormous pair of scissors. Luis took the plastic boxes and moved them to the table, opening them up.

"Leather sewing kit," Luis said, looking inside a smaller plastic box. "There are awls, leather needles, thimbles, pliers, and heavy waxed thread. The other one has a bunch of knives and stuff."

"I have a box that has an electric engraver," Eddie said, opening it. "And the last one is a small drill set with a rechargeable battery."

Eddie carried a leather bag with a drawstring to the table. "This was in the back." He poured it out to reveal gold and silver disks, many with engraved symbols on them and a collection of sparkling gemstones with holes drilled into them.

"Why are there holes in the stones?" Luis asked.

"To sew them onto the belt," Eddie explained. "And look, someone already engraved some stones with magickal symbols. Looks like Harold Stubbe had everything he needed to make several wolf belts. The question is, who did he make them for?"

"I think I saw a date book in the bedroom," Luis said.

"Do people still use those?"

"I'll let you know."

Eddie returned to the closet and examined the PVC pipe on the side of the closet. It came out of the wall about chest height, bent at a forty-five degree angle, and went up into the bottom of the hidey-hole. He reached into the open space, felt for the pipe, and found the unconnected top of it poking into the false construction.

Frowning, Eddie grabbed the pipe, gave it a twist, and felt it turn in his hands. He pushed upwards, and it came loose from the fitting. As it did, something furry fell out.

Eddie stepped back, afraid it was alive, but it just lay on the floor. It was about six inches wide and covered with a thick, dark pelt. He saw gold and silver disks and sparkling gems reflecting on it, ending with an overlarge silver buckle.

He slipped the pipe back into place and picked up the elaborate belt from the floor and carried it into the living room. "I hit pay dirt."

Luis walked in, the datebook in his hand. "Is that a belt that can turn people into wolves? That looks big enough to fit me. Are you sure it's safe to touch it?"

"I don't know how it works, but I don't think touching it will do anything," Eddie said.

Luis held up the book in his hand. "I've got the vic's datebook."

Eddie perked up. "Anything for the night of the murder?"

Luis shook his head. "He got a lot of entries, people to meet and all that. But that night, there's nothing except GA, 7:30 and Group of Bears, 8:00."

"The Group of Bears statue is in the playground where they found the body. I wonder who G.A. is?"

There was a click at the door and Eddie and Luis turned to see a tall woman in a brown pants suit open the door. She had lovely brown eyes, a splendid figure, and reddish hair.

Anger contorted her face.

"Vhat is the meaning of this?" she demanded.

SIX

"e're with the police," Eddie explained, then turned to Luis. "Show her your shield."

The woman gazed at the identification and frowned.

"We're investigating the death of Harold Stubbe," Eddie went on. "Are you... Sophia Stubbe? We spoke on the phone. I'm Lieutenant Berman and this is my partner, Sergeant Vasquez."

The woman glared at Eddie. "Vy have you broken in?" she demanded.

"We're trying to find out who killed your cousin," Eddie said.

"You said my cousin's death vas because of a vild animal," she said and gazed at the table with the book, pelt, and medallions spread about. "Vhat are you doing with my cousin's things?"

"We're investigating," Eddie said. "Look, a wild animal killed your cousin, but I have to tell you—I am aware of your family history. I know about Peter Stubbe and the legends of the wolf belt. From what we found, I think your cousin could make these belts. We think he sold a wolf belt, and the buyer killed him."

Her eyes blazed. "And that gives you the right to pry into my family business?"

"Look, lady, we got a search warrant," Luis pointed out, holding out the piece of paper.

"Ms. Stubbe, we're aware of your family trade, and we are looking into a supernatural explanation for his murder."

Sophia stared at the two men, unmoving. "You seem to know much more than police officers normally vould."

Eddie looked at Luis who shrugged and said, "I guess you gotta tell her."

Eddie put out his hand and his wizard's staff flew into it as his clothes swirled around him, moving like mist from a suit jacket and pants to his battle garb.

The woman took a step back from this stunning transformation but did not seem totally surprised. "You are a vizard!"

"Yes," Eddie said. "But also a New York City detective."

She considered this for a moment. "And you, the big fellow, you're a vizard as vell?"

"I just help my partner," Luis clarified.

"Then you are people I can speak to openly," she said and sighed deeply. "I vould be hard-pressed to discuss such things vith ordinary policemen."

"I am aware of werewolves, as well as your family legacy. I am working with a wizard bitten by a wolf. We are trying to find a cure."

She frowned. "He vas bitten by a verevolf vearing a belt? They do not carry the infection."

"No, a... um... genuine werewolf bit him," Eddie advised.

"Ah!" she said and shook her head. "Then you cannot save him."

"We were going through your cousin's things to see if we could find anything that might help."

"I came to Manhattan to organize his things and take his ashes back to Austria." She pointed at the open manuscript on the table. "That book has been passed down in my family for generations. How did you find these things? My cousin must have hidden them."

"The book was on a shelf in his bedroom," Luis admitted with a shrug.

"As far as the other items, it's not the first time we've searched a place," Eddie said and pointed to the things laid out on the table. "We also located a finished belt. As next of kin, these items are yours. However, if I could borrow the manuscript—"

Sophia raised her eyebrows. "That book is priceless as vell as a family heirloom."

"I understand, and I am more than happy to bring it back to you, but there might be something we can use. The wizards I work with can read Latin and German and are good with potions."

She frowned. "Vhy can't you just use your magicks to cure your friend?"

"Our magick appears not to work on this. We need something to cleanse the infection totally. Also, in the manuscript, there appear to be pages missing. Do you have any idea what happened to them?"

She moved to the table and opened the book. "Missing pages?"

She flipped to the back of the book, rubbing her hand up and down the book as if it were a holy relic. She touched the shorn pages and frowned. "Cut out?"

Eddie nodded. "Do you know why anyone would do that?"

She shook her head. "I cannot imagine it. But I must varn you, no one has ever cured a verevolf."

"We're going to try," Eddie said.

"Very vell," Sophia said, and flipped pages, studying them carefully. "Do any of your vizards make enchanted items?"

Eddie and Luis exchanged a glance, and Eddie spoke up, "I know an enchanter. He has a storefront downtown on Sullivan Street."

Sophia raised her eyebrows. "A storefront? I doubt he vould be competent."

"Actually, he does good work with talismans."

"Then here," Sophia said, turning to a specific page. It showed an elaborate sigil that formed an odd design, and there were several lines of instructions above and around it. "This is an old rune design."

"What's a rune?" Eddie asked, looking at the symbol.

"Runes are ancient Norwegian symbols of power," she said and touched the page. "This one might be vhat you need."

"Can I take a photo of that page?"

"Ja, take a photograph and this vill give your enchanter a useful design."

"How do these belts work?" Luis asked, holding up the long wolf-hide belt. "Do you use a special word, or what?"

Sophia looked Luis up and down. "Vhy do you vish to know?"

"I'm a cop that sees a lot of weird stuff and I'm curious," Luis said.

Sophia nodded. "The creator of the belt must cast the spell for the vearer, and then transforming is merely a matter of vill and intent."

"The same way my staff works," Eddie replied.

She shrugged. "It is the vay all magick vorks. However, the vearer must also touch the belt, vhile focusing on the transformation."

Luis shook his head. "That's pretty amazing."

"Ja," Sophia agreed. "However, I must insist, I cannot allow you to take the manuscript."

Eddie finished photographing the page, and it came out clearly on his phone. He turned to the woman. "Ms. Stubbe, this book could help my friend, or more important, find the one who murdered your cousin—"

"Hey Eddie," Luis said, still going through the small date book. "I have a scanner app on my phone. I could take pictures of the pages of the book, and then organize them, keep them in order."

Eddie looked hopefully at Sophia.

She shrugged. "I vould have no objection. I vill allow you to photograph the book, but it must not leave this apartment."

Eddie brightened. "It's the information we need, not the physical book. Luis, can you get started?"

"I'll get on it," Luis said, the small datebook still in his hand, he gently turned Eddie to face away from Sophia and whispered. "I got a series of meetings in this date book that Harold Stubbe went downtown to meet someone named C.H. and, more recently, a C.H. and L.W."

"That's not much help," Eddie whispered back.

"What can I tell you? The guy was pretty secretive."

Eddie glanced at Sophia. "It runs in the family."

While Luis photographed the book, Eddie drove the car down to 10th Street in the West Village at 3:45 and reported to the sixth precinct, an older brick and stucco building between Hudson and Bleecker. At the main desk, he asked for Detective Brad Thomas. A tall, heavyset man with a thick mustache and a receding hairline brought him to a conference room.

Brad pulled out maps of the area around Washington Square Park and reviewed his plan for helping the animal control agents hunt down the wild animal.

"I appreciate having you down here," Dan said as he rubbed his balding head with his free hand. "Where is your partner?"

"He's meeting me in Washington Square. I'll bring him up to speed."

"Fine, fine," Thomas said. "I gotta tell ya, this is the damnedest thing I ever heard. Animal attacks at night and we can't find the thing during the day."

"Wild animals usually only hunt at night," Eddie suggested. "Maybe it found a tunnel or a cave to hide in."

"The witnesses said it was like a dog—only really mean. At first, I figured it was rabies, right?"

Eddie nodded.

"But a rabid animal wouldn't hide. It freaked me out, I gotta tell ya, because this thing started showing up during the full moon."

Eddie frowned. "How does that make it worse, Brad?"

The big man shrugged. "I dunno, those legends of werewolves, I guess. I want you two to shadow the animal control guys, starting at seven, as it gets dark around eight. You guys can split at eleven."

Dan gave Eddie a copy of the file, and Eddie drove to Fifth Avenue and parked on a side street near Washington Square Park.

He walked over to a fashionable townhouse on some of the most expensive real estate in all of Manhattan. It was an elaborate, six-story building constructed in the 1800s with large marble columns out front, several small balconies, and intricate architectural touches from another age.

The building was owned by Drusilicus Greywacke.

Eddie knocked on the door, and a manservant opened it. He was average height with a lithe body and a shock of white hair on his head. He smiled when he saw Eddie.

"Wizard Berman, this is a surprise," the man said.

"Howell, good to see you. Is Drew here?"

"The master is creating an oil for the Wizard Glade and preparing for this night. Shall I get him for you?"

"Please," Eddie said, then hesitated. "Um… Howell, if I need you to… um… consult on this case…"

Howell smiled. "Because I am a werewolf?"

"Um… yeah. Is it all right to ask?"

"Wizard Berman, I will be happy to help in any way I can. I am most distressed by Wizard Marlowe getting bitten, and the master and I are working together to think of anything that might help."

"Good to know, thanks, Howell."

As Eddie came through the door, he noted an old-fashioned broom made from a sturdy, gnarled branch with twigs around the bottom. It was sitting with the bristles up near the front door.

"Wizards really use those things?" Eddie wondered, picking it up.

"That is called a besom broom," Howell said. "The lady of the house wished it for traditional reasons."

"Vasant is now the lady of the house?" Eddie asked.

"Of course, sir," Howell said with a smile. "According to several legends, leaving it near the front door with the bristles up wards off evil. Please follow me."

Howell led him into what Drusilicus called the drawing room. It was an overdone chamber, filled with antique furniture, far too opulent for Eddie's taste. Thick carpeting was on the floor and heavy drapes covered the windows. The space was lit only by a few lamps scattered about.

Drusilicus also had an enchanted tea trolley, similar to Marlowe's, but far more ostentatious. Eddie ordered coffee, and instantly the pot poured dark liquid into a mother-of-pearl cup as a matching saucer flew under it, and the pair flew into his hands.

"Really, lieutenant," Drusilicus said as he stormed into the room. "What is it now?"

"Luis and I searched Stubbe's apartment, and we found a completed wolf belt, talismans, and a book, *Lupus Libre*."

"Really?" Drusilicus replied, impressed. "I thought that book was nothing but a legend."

"Luis is photographing the pages and I will email you all of them once we organize them."

"That would be helpful."

"During a search we found a date book and Harold Stubbe had several meetings with someone with the initials C.H. and L.W."

Drusilicus' face turned to stone. "That means nothing to me."

"I wanted you to know in case anyone comes to mind. Have you been able to make the wolfsbane oil Glade asked for?"

"Indeed I have, as well as locate the ingredients for the potion she recommended."

"Do you think we can capture the werewolf tonight?"

Drusilicus pondered this. "One hopes so, if the Wizard Glade is up to the task."

"What do you know about her, anyway?"

"Very little, I'm afraid," Drusilicus said.

"That's not very helpful," Eddie said, heading for the door. "See you later, and be ready in case anything goes wrong tonight."

"I assure you, lieutenant, I shall be on my guard."

"As will I."

Eddie met up with Luis in Washington Square Park.

"Did you photograph the entire book?" Eddie asked when he saw his large companion.

"Yeah, I'll email the pages to you tomorrow," Luis said, as they headed to the park office, a small squat building.

"How did it go with Sophia Stubbe?"

"By the time I left, we were old friends. Once she really believed we want to catch the guy who offed her cousin and we didn't want to steal her magickal books and stuff, she was a pussycat."

Eddie said. "Good, once you send me the pages, I'll email them to Drusilicus, and he can print them up for the others."

"The other wizards don't have email?" Luis wondered.

"Luis, I only taught Marlowe how to use a computer about a year ago."

Luis shook his head. "Man, I thought I was behind the times."

At the park office, he and Luis met the supervisor from the NYC Department of Animal Control and the supervisor paired up Eddie with an agent named Perry, a high-strung little man who expressed his nervousness by talking all the time. It seemed he had a direct connection between his brain and his mouth—anything, no matter how unimportant or unrelated to the conversation, once it went through his mind, had to be expressed in a never-ending stream of consciousness.

Luis partnered up with a man named Javier. The animal control agents carried hand-held radios and the detectives had their cell phones to communicate.

Eddie and Perry soon were strolling up and down the southern-most walkways of Washington Square Park, Eddie wishing he could be with Luis as Perry went on and on, talking endlessly.

Perry carried a device he called an animal control noose, — a five-foot-long aluminum pole with a loop of braided, plastic-coated aircraft cable at the end. The loop went over the animal's head, then tightened by sliding the handle. It could lock in any position with a twist, which allowed the user to keep the animal from biting and helped to control it.

"Did I tell you I once had to go to a building where a lady was keeping a cougar—a cougar! Let me tell you, it was a pretty hairy experience. Get it? Hairy? So, like I was saying—"

The thin little man went on as he and Eddie walked the darkened pathways of Washington Square. Eddie worried about the spell that Glade would cast tonight, and if he could really trust her. Could she be the one Stubbe met with frequently? She knew a great deal about the man. But if she was meeting him, why didn't she bring it up last night? Was she hiding something?

"I finally got the bat out of the house, but you'd think the lady was sure it was a vampire or something, the way she reacted. I mean, a bat is just a flying mouse, right? Tiny little thing, I felt bad for it—"

"Perry," Eddie interrupted.

"Hm?"

"We need to listen."

"What do you mean?"

"We need to listen for the animal we're tracking. If it hears us, it might run or attack. If we're talking, we won't hear its approach."

Perry peered around nervously. "Really?"

"Really. Let me check with the other team."

Eddie pulled out his cell phone to call Luis. They had set the devices to vibrate so the ring wouldn't distract them—or make them an easy target.

"What's up?" Luis answered.

"Checking in. Seen anything?"

"Nothing so far. You?"

"The same. Stay alert," Eddie said and ended the call.

"I don't think we'll have any luck," Perry said, and held up his animal control noose. "Let me tell you, I was hoping to use this —"

Eddie held up a hand, catching the sound of something moving through the brush. "Shh! Did you hear that?"

"No, I didn't," Perry whispered.

Eddie turned, listening intently to his surroundings.

"I don't think it was anything but the wind," Perry stated in a normal tone.

A four-legged creature with a red pelt appeared out of nowhere ten feet behind Perry. It happened so quickly that it startled Eddie. It was too large to be just a dog and covered in reddish fur with large ears and a long muzzle. Its nostrils flared as it took in the scent of the two men. The eyes stared at Eddie with a menacing anger. Its gums curled to reveal stained teeth as it let out a low rumbling growl.

"What are you—?" Perry began, turning his head to see the wolf, his mouth falling open as Eddie slowly reached into his coat to pull his sidearm.

In a flash, the creature leapt at them, and Eddie braced for an attack. Perry screamed in horror and raised the noose as the monster shot past him like a freight train, knocking him off his feet.

Eddie crouched into a shooter's stance, stunned that the creature moved so fast. Instead of attacking, it ran past him and back toward the brush as Eddie fired two shots directly into its flank.

His ears rang with the percussion, and the smell of hot metal and sulfur filled his nose. The wolf howled in pain and disappeared into the underbrush, still moving fast.

Eddie ran to the spot he had last seen the creature and used the light from his phone to look at the underbrush.

There were two drops of blood, but no more. Eddie frowned. The creature should have bled a lot more than that.

Eddie walked back to Perry, holstering his weapon. Perry was sitting up but hadn't moved from where he fell, and Eddie helped him to his feet.

"That hurt so much," Perry complained, his hand on his chest.

"Lucky he didn't bite you," Eddie said, and picked up the animal control noose on the stick. "Here."

Perry shook his head. "No, I quit."

Eddie stared at him. "What?"

"Look," he said, fighting to pull in a breath. "I've taken on cougars, rabid raccoons, and aggressive squirrels, but I didn't sign up for whatever that thing was. No dog, even a rabid one, can move that fast." He put his hands on his chest and felt around. "I think I broke a rib when I fell."

"Maybe we should get you to the hospital."

"That's a good idea," he whined.

Eddie had Perry put his weight on his shoulder and helped the man toward the well-lit monument at the north end of the park. As they walked, he pulled his cell phone and called Luis.

"You okay? We heard shots," Luis said.

"Fine, did you see it?"

"We din't see nothing. What happened?"

"We have an injured man," he said. "Call an ambulance. I'm heading for the arch."

He helped Perry along until they reached the monument, where Luis and Javier rushed to meet them.

"What happened?" Javier asked. He was a sturdy man with olive features and quick brown eyes.

"We saw the animal. It leapt at us," Eddie said.

"Did it bite you?" Luis demanded of Perry.

"No." Perry leaned against the arch, still holding his chest. "Your partner shot it."

"Did you kill it?" Javier asked Eddie.

"Only wounded it, or I might've missed it completely. It was too dark. I think the noise scared it off more than anything else."

"It was big," Perry groaned. "And so… damned fast."

As they spoke, an ambulance pulled down Fifth Avenue and stopped right in front of the arch, pulling off the street. Two EMTs jumped out of the ambulance and one ran to the group while the other pulled a medical bag.

"You the cops that called in the report of an injured man?" the first man asked as he approached.

"Yeah, a big dog knocked him over, maybe broke a rib," Eddie reported.

"Hurts," Perry added for emphasis.

"We can get you to New York Presbyterian Hospital pretty quick."

Perry nodded with a pained look on his face.

The two EMTs escorted Perry to the ambulance as Javier collected the walkie-talkies and handed them to Luis.

"I'd better go with him and write up an incident report," Javier said. "Do you guys mind if we call it a night a little early?"

"We're done in a half-hour anyway," Luis answered.

"That's fine, Javier." Eddie pulled out one of his business cards and handed it to him. "Please forward a copy of the incident report to me."

"You got it," Javier said, as he got in the back of the ambulance.

In minutes, the ambulance was gone, lights flashing as it went.

Luis turned to his partner. "What really happened?"

Eddie shook his head. "The werewolf shows up, and it matched the description Drusilicus gave. Weird thing, though, it just knocks Perry down, and then runs away. I mean, the speed that thing moved, it could've easily killed both of us."

"Why didn't it?" Luis asked.

"I don't know," Eddie said, shrugging. "It was like it just wanted us to see it."

Luis looked up at the vast arch towering over their head. "Let's hope the stuff with the wizards tonight goes better."

"It can't go any worse," Eddie grumbled.

SEVEN

As they had time before the wizards arrived, Eddie and Luis made plans as they made their way back to the unmarked police car.

"I don't see why you want me on top of the Washington Square Arch," Luis protested. "I should be with you."

"I need someone with a bird's eye view of the entire park," Eddie said, as he opened the trunk. He handed Luis a set of binoculars in their leather case and a flashlight. "With you on top of the arch, and these walkie-talkies Javier gave us, you can keep track of things and radio me and the team." He closed the trunk and locked the car.

"I think you just want me to be where I can't get hurt."

"Or bitten? Look, Luis, you've been inside the arch before. You know the layout."

"Man, that place gives me claustrophobia just thinkin' about it."

"We'll open the door on the street and I'll get you to the top through the hatch up there. You'll have a view of the entire park. This way, you can monitor things and let us know if Glade is successful and the werewolves show up."

As they walked back to the park, Luis wondered aloud, "If they're werewolves, what do they do during the day?"

"No idea," Eddie said. "They can become human, so they could be anywhere. We don't know what they look like in human form."

They passed two young college coeds, each carrying laptop bags and wearing jeans they appeared to have been poured into.

Luis glanced at them. "With New York University campus right here, there are lots of people around."

"One werewolf could even live nearby in a dormitory, for all we know. There are several dorms in this neighborhood."

"*My Roommate Is A Werewolf.* Great name for a horror flick."

"Look, if the wolf could find a place to stash clothes and a safe place to transform, a roommate might not even notice."

"Unless they get fleas."

Eddie and Luis approached the seventy-foot arch, carefully illuminated to be the centerpiece of the park. They strode over to the western side, where a short and squat white wooden door blended into the marble.

Luis shook his head. "I still don't enjoy going in there. There are no lights, right?"

"I'll be there to light the way for you, Luis," Eddie said. "And you have a flashlight."

"Still don' like it," Luis muttered.

Eddie leaned to the hasp and whispered, *"Patentibus,"* and the very impressive deadbolt released. Eddie pushed the door open, ducked low, and stepped in. With a gesture, his staff was in his hand and a light on top of it produced enough brightness that it flashed onto the dark sidewalk through the open door.

With a sigh, Luis ducked as low as he could and guided his enormous frame sideways, carefully going through the short door, and closing it once he was inside.

Luis glanced around the narrow corridor, brick on both walls. "Man, it's worse than I remember."

Eddie was once again reminded that the marble of the arch was only on the outside façade. Inside, brick and steel supported the structure. He moved to the tiled circular staircase. "Come on, Luis, once you're upstairs, you'll have plenty of space."

Luis looked at the staircase. "Man, these tiles are fancy for a place no one ever sees."

"They're Guastavino tiles, same kind as used in Grand Central Station. Pretty common back then."

Luis frowned as he slid his way along the wall to reach the stairs. "How do you know this crap?"

Eddie shrugged. "I know stuff. Let's get moving."

With Eddie in the lead, they walked up the circular stairs, the walls curving around them as they went up the long first flight. They reached a landing and a brick archway opened to a seventeen foot tall room, which stood empty except for an old wooden ladder. The same terra-cotta tiles lined the ceiling, which rose in majestic curves over their heads. Light from spotlights on the roof shone down through several rectangular skylights into the oddly shaped room.

"This is where you had your confrontation with that Drakula guy, right?" Luis said, his voice echoing in the empty space.

"Yes, there were a pair of thrones up here. I wonder what happened to them?"

"Who knows? Maybe your wizard posse took them out."

They continued up the circular stairs, and came to a stop at a pair of glass and metal double doors that opened onto the roof. A sturdy metal bar with a padlock secured the doors. Eddie once again whispered, "Patentibus."

The lock opened and fell off as the bar swung by itself out of the way. Eddie pushed the double doors open and stepped out onto the roof. Luis breathed a sigh of relief once he was out in the open air. He sat on the wooden frame of the open doorway and observed the short wall that surrounded the roof and gazed down upon the park.

"I *can* see everything up here," he said, looking around and down at the fountain. "No, wait, I can't see in the wooded areas so good. There's too much light around the arch."

"I'll take care of that," Eddie said, and lifted his staff. The lights around the arch and the fountain faded until they were no brighter than the street lamps down the walkways. He lowered his staff. "How's that?"

"Bueno," Luis said, as he pulled the walkie talkie from his waistband and turned it on.

Eddie turned on his walkie-talkie and easily heard Luis when he said, "Radio check."

"You're good," Eddie declared. "I'll check it down there. You need to let me know if you see anything."

"I got it," Luis grumbled, still unhappy with his assignment.

Eddie headed back down the stairs and soon stood outside the arch. He closed the door and made it secure. Luis could open it from the inside, but no one except a wizard could get in from the outside.

"Hey Eddie, how ya doing?" a voice with a heavy New York accent said.

Eddie turned to see his fellow wizard, Rusty Claremont, step into the light. He was average height and stocky, with short brown hair and wore a white shirt, tie, and yellow jacket with a matching hat on his head.

"Rusty! How are you?" Eddie approached the wizard cabby to shake his hand.

"Great. What do you think of Luis' car, huh?" Rusty asked, all smiles.

"Wait a minute," Eddie exclaimed. "You're the one who fixed up his car?"

"Sure, why not?" Rusty gushed. "I mean, I got da shop in my arch in Central Park. Luis asked, and I said sure. Had to conjure a few parts for him, but hey, he helped on da restoration."

Eddie shook his head. "You mean, while I wasn't doing any magick, my partner took advantage of you to get his car fixed?"

"No reason we couldn't," Rusty said. "And y'know, he's good people. Nice to hang out with. We're talking about fixing his wife's car."

"Rusty, you're not out here alone, are you?"

"Of course not," another voice said.

Eddie whirled about to find a short, thin man in a tight suit and a bowtie staring up at him.

"Bankrock!" Eddie rolled his eyes. "You shouldn't sneak up on people."

The short wizard folded his arms, a smug smile on his face. "I was here the entire time. I was merely using an invisibility spell."

This made Rusty smile. "We figured the werewolf would be more likely to attack if it thought I was alone."

"I don't know how smart that is," Eddie said.

"Whatever do you mean?" Bankrock demanded haughtily.

"First, the werewolf could smell you, even if it couldn't see you." Eddie ticked off his fingers. "Second, under that invisibility spell, everything looks misty—I know, I've done it. Third, the werewolf is fast—faster than a wizard. You need to be aware of what's around you and be ready to respond a lot quicker than you think."

Bankrock lifted his nose in the air. "Some of us have remarkable reflexes from centuries of practice. I take it from the ambulance and the injured compatriot we saw earlier that you confronted the beast."

"Yes, and I don't understand it. It didn't attack us, it just showed itself and knocked the guy with me over," Eddie said.

"Perhaps to get rid of the non-wizard?" Bankrock said.

Eddie frowned. "Maybe, I hadn't thought of that. Are you two here to help?"

Rusty spoke up. "Yeah, we heard Marlowe got bit and that the Wizard Glade is going to summon the werewolves."

Bankrock adjusted his bowtie. "We decided that the more wizards, the more likely we can capture these errant beasts."

Eddie nodded. "I understand you've been reaching out to this Match guy, the father of the werewolves."

"Matchitehew," Bankrock corrected. "Yes, he has offered to have us turn the werewolves over to him once we capture them. Not that it helps us find a cure for Marlowe—"

"Don't panic—at least not yet," Eddie tried to sound reassuring.

Bankrock shook his head. "Marlowe is the coven master. If he loses his mind to the beast, the ramifications are terrible."

"What do you mean?" Eddie asked.

"He would have to give up his staff, abandon the coven," Bankrock clarified. "According to the Werewolf Protection Act of 1885, any wizard who becomes infected must surrender their staff."

Rusty shook his head. "If we lose Marlowe—"

"Bankrock, you have a lot of arcane knowledge—are you aware of anything to cure the werewolf curse?"

"The common belief is that there is no cure," Bankrock replied. "There is supposed to be an ancient Grecian remedy, but experts believe it is merely a legend."

Drusilicus walked up holding hands with Vasant. He wore a pair of dark pants and a topcoat over a suede suit jacket, while Vasant was in an outfit that made Eddie think, 'Victorian Lady Adventurer.' She was dressed in riding breeches with tall boots, a full blouse with large sleeves that went to tight cuffs, and a brocade vest.

"Nice to see you all on time," Drusilicus said.

"You look professional," Eddie said to Vasant.

"I come prepared," she said and extracted a throwing knife from a hidden spot at her waist. The knife gleamed in the dim light from the street lamps.

"Silver?" Eddie asked.

Vasant nodded. "It was effective against the vampires, and I am sure it can stop a werewolf. When Marlowe, Drusilicus, and I tried to capture the wolf during the full moon, we counted too much upon our wizardly powers to bring the beast to heel. Now, I am going to go old school. I have a half-dozen silver knives upon my person, and I am very accurate at throwing them."

Drusilicus gazed at her with pride. "You're good at everything you do, dear. Now pardon me, I must speak to the lieutenant."

Eddie and Drusilicus stepped away from the others.

"Just so you know, Lieutenant," Drusilicus said quietly, "I have backup if needs arise."

"What kind of backup?" Eddie asked.

"Hopefully one we won't need."

"You're being mysterious, Drew."

"Let's just say, we don't want anyone else getting bitten."

The two men returned to the group and Eddie said, "So you all know, my partner Luis is on top of the arch monitoring things." He keyed his walkie-talkie. "Radio check."

"Radio check," Luis replied, and the others looked up to see Luis' hulking form on top of the arch.

Eugenia and Glade appeared at the south end of the park, walking toward them. Glade had a full leather bag hanging from her shoulder.

"Here are the rest of us," Eddie said, then frowned. "Where's Ahbay?"

"We thought it best that he stay to keep an eye on Marlowe," Vasant explained.

"Nice of Wizard Glade to show up," Drusilicus muttered as he removed his pocket watch to glance at it. "With only fifteen minutes to spare."

Eddie and his group walked south to meet the two newcomers next to the embellished stone ring that surrounded the enormous fountain in the center of the park. It was usually filled with about two feet of water, and it contained multiple water jets that sprayed in changing patterns during the day. This night it was not operating, and the fountain was empty and dry.

Eddie glanced over and frowned. It was odd that they drained the fountain, as the city usually only did that during the winter, when the water might freeze. The rest of the year, the fountain acted as a reflecting pool when the jets were not operating.

Glade pointed at the raised circle that stood in the middle of the overlarge empty fountain. "We have our summoning circle. Let us prepare."

Without another word, the woman stepped over the four-foot-high stone surround and walked down the stone steps towards the center of the fountain.

Eugenia glanced at the others, shrugged, and followed the petite wizard.

Drusilicus shook his head and followed, as did Vasant, Rusty, Bankrock, and finally Eddie.

Glade took out several candle sticks, shoving large white candles into them and placing them at the four cardinal points around the raised stone platform.

"We be using the stone circle to bind the beasts." Glade turned to Drusilicus. "Did ye bring what I asked for?"

Drusilicus reached into his pocket and pulled out a round white stone about the size of his thumb, which he handed to Glade. "One moonstone, untouched by silver, as you requested."

Eddie looked at the stone in Glade's hand, and it seemed to shimmer with a light from within.

Drusilicus offered a small vial containing an amber liquid. "Here is the wolfsbane oil, which I reduced to the percentage mix you specifically requested."

Glade nodded, not smiling. "Aye, we need this to contain the beast."

The small woman raised her hand, and her staff appeared in it. With a gesture the candles all lit at once. Since Eddie's staff was the staff of the element fire, he could control flames of any size and type. He had not seen another wizard do things with fire before.

"Let us form a circle," she ordered, "with our staves and robes, if ye please."

The group instantly transformed as if by an agreed command, and all of them stood in their battle robes of different colors, with their individual staffs. This included Rusty in his yellow robes and Bankrock in his gray.

Eddie leaned toward Bankrock, "I don't see you in battle robes very often."

Bankrock flushed. "I prefer not to be involved in battles."

"Aye, but the robes suit ye," Glade said with a smile, as she positioned Bankrock on the tiled floor.

Bankrock flushed, so obviously Eddie could even tell by the light of the dim street lamps.

Glade positioned each wizard, and one at a time, they each sat cross-legged on the hard stone tiles to create a circle around the center stone. She had each wizard lay their staff across their lap, which effectively spaced them apart from one another perfectly.

Glade placed the moonstone in the center of the raised stone platform, then stood outside this circle of people and handed the small vial of oil to Eugenia. "Once we capture the beast, a drop of this on the four cardinal points will entrap it within the circle. You put a drop where ye are, and then hand it around to the others."

"Excuse me," Drusilicus interrupted. "Wouldn't I be a more appropriate person to supervise this? I created the oil."

"Aye," Glade agreed. "Which is why I canna let ye. Ye still have the stink of it on you. The monster be expectin' ye to do it and be on guard. The fine lady will arouse less suspicion."

Eddie leaned to Bankrock again. "Are you familiar with any of these rituals?"

The little man stared back at Eddie. "No. This is why we called upon her to help."

Glade stood a few feet back from the others, her staff in her hand. "Once I begin, I be the only one to move about. If ye break the circle, we canna contain the beast."

Eddie exchanged glances with the others and Drusilicus took a deep breath but didn't look pleased.

Glade raised her hand, and the moonstone on the center platform glowed almost as bright as the moon overhead.

Glade reached into her robe and pulled out a small metal tube with a notch in it. One end was cylindrical but cast in the other end was a wolf's head, with the mouth open and fangs showing. She raised the tube to her lips and blew into it, her cheeks puffing as she did.

"Ah!" Eddie exclaimed, his hand going to his ear. He felt a high-pitched whine go through his head. "Did you hear that?"

"Afraid not," Bankrock chided. "Please be quiet."

Glade looked out at the open space in the park and blew on the whistle a second time.

Eddie grimaced as the ultrasonic whine pierced his brain again.

In the distance, a single lonely howl responded.

Glade's eyes filled with excitement. "It be comin'."

She pointed at the small moonstone and it rose into the air, where it hovered six feet off the stone disk.

"Come on, beastie," she muttered, turned, and walked into the woods.

Eddie followed her movement as she disappeared among the trees and whispered, "Where is she going?"

"Sh," Bankrock hissed.

Eddie's radio crackled and Luis spoke. "We have a large—I don't know what the Hell it is—coming from the west entrance of the park, and coming fast."

Eddie pulled the radio from his belt, keyed the control and said, "Roger that."

Eddie was facing the west side, and he squinted to see what was on its way. Bushes were moving and he heard labored breathing.

At the edge of the clearing that was the park plaza, a large animal peeked through the bushes and stopped to stare at the wizards. The thing was the size of a large dog, and covered in the reddish fur with a white belly.

It was the same one he'd seen earlier. Eddie glanced to see if there was any blood or wounds on it, but he could see none. He knew at least one bullet hit the animal before, and yet there was no sign of any wound now.

The creature did not come into the clearing, but stood on all fours in the bushes, growling.

A beam of light came out from the moonstone hovering in the air, that projected a six inch wide dot on the ground in front of the creature. The monster stared at the dot, and the dot moved closer to the fountain. The creature stepped forward, its eyes completely focused on the circle of light on the ground.

"It's hypnotized by that light," Eddie murmured, as the wolf slowly walked, following the glowing dot, and the moonstone floated above the fountain.

"Come on, be a good little wolf, now," Eugenia whispered as the huge canine drew closer.

The moonstone pivoted in midair so it brought the dot past the stone surround of the fountain. The werewolf leapt over the small wall easily, still hypnotized by the light, following it.

Soon, the circle of light was on the stone in the center of the wizards.

"Nobody move," Drusilicus advised.

The werewolf leapt over the sitting wizards, which almost made Eddie fall back. The monster stood only a foot or two away from him in the center of the fountain, its eyes still on the dot.

"A little on the four points," Eugenia murmured, putting a drop of oil in front of her as the creature continued to stare at the dot. She handed the bottle to Rusty, who passed it to Bankrock. The little man dripped oil in the correct place.

As Bankrock passed it on to Vasant, another wolf howl rang out, deeper and louder than before. The creature looked up, the spell of the beam of light broken.

Eugenia's eyes grew wide, and she insisted, "Hurry, we must bind the beast."

The werewolf was having none of that. It went from being a docile canine to becoming the creature of nightmares. It bared its teeth and roared right in Eddie's face.

"Oh, shit," Eddie exclaimed, and instantly covered himself with a dome of red light, just in time as the snarling beast pounced upon him.

All the wizards cried out as the monster fell on Eddie, biting and clawing at his protective red light covering.

It then leapt off Eddie and ran into the nearby woods as the wizards rose and raised their staves.

Eddie was panting hard, his adrenaline pumping as Rusty helped him to his feet and they both looked at where the monster had gone.

The wizards were moving out of the empty fountain as Bankrock ordered, "Remain calm. I am sure Wizard Glade has everything under control."

"Where the Hell was she during all of this!" Eddie exclaimed.

"It would be wise to stay here and defend our position," Drusilicus shouted. "We don't want anyone else getting bitten!"

Eddie was at the edge of the fountain and turned to look at the woods, only to see a pair of red eyes staring at him. He barely had time to conjure his red dome of protection before being bowled over by the large, red-furred canine. It apparently had doubled back to attack again.

As he fell, Eddie cursed the fact that he forgot the werewolf had human intelligence and could move so quickly that it could attack from almost any angle.

There were shouts from the other wizards as the monster struck at his protective dome. A shape moved over Eddie and the werewolf fell away. Eddie raised his head to see a second wolf, a gray one, growling and snapping at his attacker.

The red wolf and the gray one rolled, each biting and attacking the other.

Drusilicus raised his hand and yelled, *"Oppressio!"*

A wall of force struck both wolves, and it threw them apart, the red wolf flying in one direction and the gray wolf in the other. Eddie pushed himself to his feet as the red wolf landed—he let loose a blast of fiery light from his staff right at the creature.

Though off-balance from the awkward landing, the beast avoided the blast and leapt straight at Eddie again.

Time seemed to slow, the creature flew toward his face, its mouth open, its teeth bared, and drool flying from its open mouth.

A shape whizzed past him, crashed into the red wolf in mid-air, and knocked it to the ground, mere inches from Eddie's face.

Eddie stepped back, his shielding dome finally in place, to see these two wolves fighting each other. The wolf that had stopped the attacker this time was not the gray wolf—it was a bigger and more powerful white wolf.

The two lunged at each other with growls and cries, jaws snapping and fur flying. The gray wolf was on its feet, watching the other two as they battled.

"How many werewolves do we have?" Eddie yelled in frustration.

The wizards all raised their staves, and bursts of light shot at the embattled canines, but they moved with such blinding speed none of the beams hit home.

After one more brief charge, the red wolf turned and ran off into the underbrush. At the same time, the gray wolf ran off as well.

The remaining wolf watched them go, panting with exertion, its white fur luminous in the moonlight.

"Don't hurt him!" came a shout.

Drusilicus stepped over to the creature, his staff in hand.

Eddie looked from the wolf to the advancing wizard. "You know this wolf?"

"Of course," Drusilicus said. "This is Howell."

The animal lowered its head and moved to Drusilicus. It was limping, and it appeared the red wolf had injured him.

"I must get him home and treat him," Drusilicus said. "A bite from another werewolf does not heal instantly, as do other injuries. Good night, my friends."

Drusilicus walked away with the limping wolf as the other wizards lowered their staffs.

"That didn't go well at all!" Bankrock complained.

Eddie's walkie-talkie crackled.

"Can I come down now?" asked Luis.

EIGHT

"Where did Glade go?" Vasant asked, stepping out of the fountain.

"She went into the woods," Rusty said. "Before either werewolf showed up."

"But she was operating the moonstone," Bankrock said. "She had to be watching."

"Then where the Hell was she when that red wolf attacked me?" Eddie demanded.

"I be here," Glade said, coming out of the shadow of the trees with a tall man by her side.

"Hey, where was ya when the wolf attacked Eddie?" Rusty demanded.

"That was my fault, I'm afraid," the tall man said. The stranger was well-muscled, with long black hair and a reddish hue to his skin. He wore denim pants and an open vest showing off a well-muscled chest. "I distracted her."

"This be Matchitehew, father of the werewolves," Glade said. It was obvious that the two knew each other.

The big man chuckled. "Now let us not put on airs, and make me more important than I deserve." Matchitehew's voice was deep and commanding, his long hair a gleaming black in the subdued lighting of the park.

"That's odd," Eddie said. "We get attacked by a werewolf. It runs off and you show up— any chance you were our attacker?"

"That be nonsense," Glade scolded. "I meself asked him to come this eve. I was hoping the werewolf would be bound, and while it be helpless, he could take it away from the city."

"You know dis guy?" Rusty asked.

"Aye, I tol' the others that our paths have crossed," Glade responded annoyed and gave an admiring glance at the tall man.

"I was pleased to offer help," Matchitehew said. "If a wolf is attacking innocents, I need to be aware of it. I do not approve of lone werewolves."

"Your whistle and the moonstone attracted the red wolf," Vasant stated. "The gray wolf is the one we needed."

"Which showed up as well, did it not?" Glade replied, annoyed. "If ye had used the wolfsbane oil as I instructed, you'd have both beasties bound even now!"

"I'm sorry I couldn't assist," Matchitehew explained. "But everything happened so quickly. Both Glade and I were unprepared for the wolf to attack." He eyed Eddie with suspicion. "I thought you wizards had spells for such things?"

Eddie set his jaw. "Yes, for some reason that werewolf wants to attack me."

Bankrock stepped forward getting between Matchitehew and Eddie. "Nice to see you again, sir. Your help is most appreciated."

"Yeah, big freakin' help he was," Rusty muttered.

"Ah yes, Wizard Bankrock," Matchitehew replied to the little man with a smile. "I traveled down from upstate as you requested, and I brought a vehicle that can transport our misunderstood friend. We must prove to him that he will not come to harm."

"Upstate?" Eddie asked. "You live in upstate New York?"

Eddie noticed Luis walking up.

Matchitehew frowned as Luis arrived. "Perhaps we shouldn't discuss this in front of… strangers."

Eddie pointed a thumb at Luis. "He's my apprentice. We can speak freely."

"Ah!" Matchitehew said, again the benevolent guest. "Yes, I have several hundred acres up north, where I and my friends run free far from civilization."

"I did me best this night, but the creature be distracted, afore we could contain it," Glade said. "Now we canna try again until tomorrow at midnight."

"I believe we need a better plan," Eddie pointed out.

"Nothing against your skills, Wizard Glade," Bankrock quickly added.

"Are you kiddin'? We almost ended up dog chow," Rusty snapped.

Matchitehew smiled broadly. "Don't worry yourselves, good wizards. Tomorrow night I shall be here with help to bring our errant child back to the pack. You can leave it in my hands."

Matchitehew turned and walked away, still chatting amicably with Glade.

"Do you trust that guy?" Luis asked the group.

Eddie glanced back at Glade and Matchitehew. "What's the story with Matchitehew's attitude?"

"He is an ancient being, used to getting his own way," Bankrock insisted.

"He's got a high opinion of himself," Rusty observed.

"And Wizard Glade was not quite correct in the history she gave us about him," Vasant added.

Eddie frowned. "What do you mean?"

"She told us that Matchitehew transformed into a wolf and accidentally scared a boy, which led to his death."

"That ain't what happened?" Luis asked.

Vasant shook her head and spoke in a quiet tone. "According to the legends I have researched, Matchitehew argued with the boy, became angry, transformed into a wolf, and slew him."

"That's a very different story," Eddie remarked.

Vasant nodded. "That is why Wisakachek cursed him with the wolf transformation and condemned him to a long life. It was in punishment for his crime."

"It is not our place to judge an ally," Bankrock objected. "If we are done here, I have other places to be!"

Bankrock walked into the woods, disappearing into the trees.

"I'd better go as well," Rusty said and, with a wave, followed Bankrock.

"I don't trust Matchitehew," Eddie said. "But I know someone who can tell me the truth."

"Yeah, who would that be?" Luis asked.

"That's not important now," Eddie deflected the question. "I wonder— when Glade ran into the woods, and then the werewolves showed up did you see where she went from your vantage point?"

"No, she vanished under the trees and then, like a minute later, that wolf showed up. And then that gray wolf and the white one."

"The white one was Howell," Vasant explained.

"Howell?" Luis repeated. "The guy who works for Drew?"

"The same," Eddie said. "Luis, take the police car back to the precinct and go home. I'll go with Vasant to see if Howell can give us any insight into any of this."

Luis glowered. "I should go with you. We're a team."

"Luis, I appreciate it. But the wizard thing means I only need about three hours of sleep a night, and I can teleport home in seconds. You should get home to Maria, and get a full night's rest —we're doing this again tomorrow."

"Hopefully with better results," Vasant said.

"Please send me those photos of the pages from Lupus Libre," Eddie said, and then paused as an idea struck him. "He said he came from upstate. Didn't Sophia Stubbe say she was staying in upstate New York?"

"Yeah… and a funny thing I saw from the top of the arch."

"What?" Eddie asked.

"Before I came down, I thought I saw Sophia Stubbe walking out of the park."

"Are you sure?" Eddie asked, stunned.

"It's hard to be positive looking from above. But she had red hair and carried herself the same way that the Stubbe lady did."

"What was she doing down here in the park?"

"I dunno."

Eddie set his jaw. "We should do a little more research into her background."

Luis shrugged. "Okay, but it might not have been her."

Eddie escorted Vasant back to the townhouse, and she opened it to find Drusilicus waiting at the door.

"Your timing is excellent, both of you," Drusilicus said. "Perhaps we could all have some refreshments in the sitting room."

"Wizard Berman has questions for Howell," Vasant said. "I am all in. I wish nothing more than to soak in a hot bath."

"Very well, my dear," Drusilicus agreed. "Lieutenant, Howell is getting dressed and will join us shortly."

They sat in the drawing room, and Eddie helped himself to coffee. Drusilicus had a cup of tea, which he carried as he paced the room.

"I want to get Howell's perspective on those two werewolves," Eddie said. "Perhaps he could give us some insights into fighting them. They seem to always have the upper hand."

A floorboard creaked and the men turned to look at the doorway. Instead of Howell, however, it was the young woman Eddie met at Marlowe's. Her hair was damp, and she wore pajamas with a ratty bathrobe.

She inclined her head. "Forgive me, teacher. I didn't know you had guests."

"Quite all right, my dear. I believe you know the lieutenant."

Eddie stood up. "Yes, you're... Lily... Lana..."

"Lovetta," the girl said, glancing up at Eddie. "Most people call me Luv or Luvee."

"You're up late," Drusilicus said curtly. "Don't you have morning meditation?"

"I had a late class, and I was practicing those incantations you assigned me," she said. "They were so exciting, I found I couldn't sleep. I thought a cup of tea would help relax me."

"Help yourself," Drusilicus said and then added gently, "morning comes early, so get some rest."

The young woman stepped to the trolley to pour herself some tea, adding sugar and cream.

Eddie watched her serve herself and said, "It's enchanted. Why don't you just tell it what you want?"

Lovetta faced Eddie, meeting his eyes. "At this stage in my training, I may use nothing that carries an enchantment, except my own that I have constructed. I have to master my use of talismans and simple incantations first."

Drusilicus smiled with approval. "And why is that?"

She grinned. "So that I become adept at using the magick I have and not rely on enchanted items to do things for me."

"Very good," Drusilicus beamed.

She glanced at Eddie one more time, then with a nod left the room.

Eddie paused, thinking he had seen an odd reflection in her eyes.

"She's quite bright, and coming along very well," Drusilicus said. "She made her first talisman last week, a first Pentacle of the Moon, and it worked on the initial attempt."

"What does that do?" Eddie asked.

"Hm? Oh, nothing much," Drusilicus said. "It can unlock any door."

"Comes in handy if she wants to become a thief," Eddie suggested.

"That's not the point," Drusilicus snapped. "It's about learning control, mastering skills, and training the mind. That way, when one receives a staff, one is ready to be of service."

"Didn't succeed so well with your old apprentice," Eddie pointed out.

"Caleb was incredibly gifted with talismans, and I allowed his talent to cloud my judgement of his obvious flaws," Drusilicus said haughtily.

"You wanted to see me, sir," Howell said from the doorway. In his human form, he wore a white shirt, tie, black vest and black pants, his hair neatly combed. He looked every bit the formal servant, even though he was now off duty.

Howell's right hand bore a bandage covering the fresh wound.

Drusilicus turned to the door. "Ah, Howell, do come in, have some tea. The lieutenant wishes to speak to you."

"If it would not be unseemly, sir," Howell said with a bow of his head.

"I think we can all be informal here, Howell," Drusilicus said and sat in one of the overdone chairs.

Howell poured himself tea, and Eddie suddenly realized why the manservant always wore gloves. The tea pot was silver and would burn the hands of a werewolf, even in human form.

Howell moved to a smaller chair and faced the others. Eddie spoke. "Thank you for saving me tonight. If you hadn't tackled that wolf, I don't think I could've put up my protective shield fast enough."

"Thus explaining why training on small things is necessary," Drusilicus murmured.

Eddie glared at his host, but went on. "I wanted to ask you for any thoughts you might have—why are these werewolves out after the full moon? I mean, I know Wizard Glade attracted them with that magick whistle but I ran into the red wolf earlier in the night, as if it wanted me to see it."

Howell nodded. "Really? Most curious. I am not as involved in the community as I once was, but I still hear the occasional rumor. My first deduction is that since the vampires have... left..."

Eddie glanced at Drusilicus who said nothing. They all knew that the vampires had not left. Eddie had exterminated them.

Howell continued. "This has opened feeding grounds that have not been available to the werewolf community in the past. Usually werewolves in town go to Pelham Bay Park to hunt during the full moon. Many of them leave town completely when the time is at hand. Some, like myself, have a place in their homes where they can be... safe."

Eddie nodded. A year ago, when they were fighting the vampires, Drusilicus had taken Eddie and several others to his basement. There, behind a vault door, was a cage with thick steel bars. There were scratch marks in the concrete around the cage created by sharp, strong claws.

"Pelham Bay Park is the preferred area," Howell went on. "It is the city's largest park, and few people are there after dark. There are almost three thousand acres, and plenty of game to hunt, even in winter." He shook his head. "Most of us who carry the werewolf curse have no desire to injure anyone and do our best to be far away or secured when the moon is full."

"But the full moon is over, and you transformed tonight."

Howell nodded. "As did your attacker, Wizard Berman. I can change any time I wish, day or night, and maintain my human intellect. It is only during the full moon that I change whether or not I wish to, and the animal has full sway. Every werewolf becomes an unreasoning beast during those three days each month, which is why we must take care to be far away from anyone we might... injure."

Or kill, Eddie thought.

"I am a genetic werewolf. My family has passed the Wolfen curse down for centuries, skipping some generations," Howell said, shaking his head. "In my case, I experienced a very normal childhood, and the transformations began when I hit puberty. Fortunately, my family was well-versed in dealing with the curse, and kept me under lock and key for my protection during the full moon. I have learned to live with the limitations that being a werewolf has created in my life."

"I can imagine so," Eddie said.

Howell's voice was low and measured. "Losing control during the full moon was terrifying to me, but another part of myself reveled in the power of it. In my twenties, I often changed during other phases of the moon, just to feel the ground under my paws and the thrill of the hunt. In ways, even on those other nights, when I kept my human mind, there was a wildness that felt— right."

"You don't think a werewolf would wish to be cured?" Eddie asked.

"Oh no, quite the opposite. I am sure that almost any werewolf would seek a cure."

Eddie frowned. "But you just said…"

"I have learned to work with that aspect of my life. It can be beneficial, as when I rescued you. But I have also had to be careful whom I associate with. I have had to turn aside the idea of a spouse or family, knowing that in one unguarded moment, I might lose control of the beast and slay them all."

Eddie nodded. This made sense.

"It is much harder for a woman, because she knows that if she has children, it is possible her curse will burden them. She could not be in a long-term relationship, as there would be the constant danger of exposure or loss of control."

"When Howell joined my household," Drusilicus added, "the pair of us made provisions for him to stay here, or I teleport him to Pelham Bay Park to let him roam freely."

"Wizard Greywacke has done much to address my condition, and I am grateful."

Drusilicus smiled. "No less than you deserve, old friend."

Eddie looked at Howell and Drusilicus and saw that it was more than a man and a faithful servant. They both cared about each other.

"I want to ask one thing," Eddie interjected. "Howell, did you ever kill anyone?"

Howell and Drusilicus exchanged a glance, and Drusilicus demanded, "What does that have to do with this situation?"

Eddie met Drusilicus' eyes. "I want to know. Avoiding the question suggests that the answer is yes."

Howell held up a hand to Drusilicus, who appeared ready to protest. "It's all right, sir. Yes, I have killed, but not for any reason you might think. Many years ago, I was living in a city that shall go nameless. I saw a man attack a young woman. He slapped her unconscious and pulled her into the brush to have his way with her, ripping and pulling away at her clothing. It so enraged me I transformed. I planned to only stop the man, scare him away. But I was in wolf form, and so overcome by that predatory nature, I threw the man to the ground and tore out his throat."

Eddie said nothing.

"I wanted to change back, put on my clothes and escape, but the attack covered me in blood. I ran to a fountain and leapt into it, washing myself. A police officer approached me—and I found I wanted to lunge at him and rip his throat out as well. You see, killing the criminal had excited me, pulled at my baser instincts. Fortunately, I still had enough of my human mind to realize I had lost control. I ran back to where I had thrown my clothing, changed back and got dressed, monitoring the fallen woman. When the police officer came by, searching for the wolf, he found the woman and radioed for an ambulance. I crept away, unnoticed, but the experience chilled me. I had lost control on a night without the full moon. It was then that I moved to New York to escape what I had done."

The room was silent as Eddie considered Howell's tale.

Drusilicus spoke first. "I took Howell on, and it was the wisest choice I ever made."

Howell smiled at Drusilicus, then looked over to Eddie. "Is there anything else?"

"Do you know any of the history? I would like to know how long there have been werewolves."

"I believe I can answer that, lieutenant," Drusilicus said. "The earliest recorded legends of someone who would transform go back to the ancient Greek myth of Lycaon, hence the word, Lycanthropy."

"Who was that?" Eddie asked.

"An ancient Greek king. According to the legend, Lycaon attempted to trick Zeus into eating human flesh. The god discovered the deceit and transformed him into a wolf. There is a mountain where a magnificent temple used to stand, Mount Lycaeus. There, they performed a ceremony to honor this creature until the second century."

Eddie nodded. "Howell can you think of any way we could cure Marlowe of the curse?"

Howell stroked his chin. "In medieval times, there were people who offered cures, but some of them were so awful as to kill the patient."

"That's not good," Eddie grunted.

"You must admit, that cured the condition," Drusilicus offered wryly.

"There are several potions made from wolfsbane that can affect a werewolf's abilities, though none are a cure," Howell suggested.

Drusilicus sat back in his chair. "The problem is that no one knows the correct proportions or other ingredients to make it work. Wolfsbane is extremely poisonous, and I would want to be very careful with any potion that contained it."

"But Glade asked you to bring that tonight," Eddie pointed out.

"That was wolfsbane, soaked in oil and highly diluted, and not intended to be ingested. As you saw, it was to be placed around the enchanted circle and would've bound the wolf if we'd been able to place it on all four cardinal points."

Howell spoke up. "Master Greywacke and I have attempted several wolfsbane potions over the years, with varying degrees of success."

"Marlowe has an extensive library," Eddie said. "Now that he isn't bedridden, We should have him wear the Hat of Remembrance and help search his records to see if there is a potion that could help."

Drusilicus nodded. "Not a bad idea, lieutenant."

Eddie turned to Howell. "Is there anything we can use against the werewolf we're fighting? He's too quick for striking down with magick."

"*She's* too quick," Howell said.

"What?"

"Both the red wolf and the gray one are female." Howell smiled and touched his index finger to the side of his nose. "I caught their scents. Definitely both female."

"Okay, that changes nothing," Eddie said. "Is there any substance to use against either of them?"

"Silver bullets," Howell said. "In fact, silver implements of any kind. If a werewolf is stabbed with a silver knife it can force it to change back to human."

"What about ordinary bullets?" asked Eddie. "I shot the red wolf twice. Didn't even slow it down."

Howell nodded. "Lead bullets might knock a werewolf aside because of the impact, but it will expel the bullet and heal in seconds." He lifted his bandaged hand. "A bite from another werewolf is one of the few wounds that doesn't heal rapidly, along with touching silver or a severe burn. My hand will be undamaged by tomorrow."

"You heal quickly, even in human form?"

"Yes, but in wolf form, I can recover from most life-threatening injuries in mere moments."

Eddie walked to the tea trolley and poured himself more coffee. He turned and focused on Howell. "Can a werewolf kill a werewolf?"

"They often do," Howell agreed. "Werewolves traveling in packs fight over food, status, or mates, until they consider one wolf the alpha. The alpha will often kill a challenger."

"Okay, silver, another wolf, and wolfsbane," Eddie said with a glance at his watch. "I'm going to head home. Thanks for opening up, Howell."

"We must stop these werewolves, gentlemen," Howell said. "My community is very careful about hiding their existence from others. If these attacks do not stop, it endangers every one of us."

Eddie headed for the door. He knew Howell was right, but he also knew that these werewolves endangered wizards as well.

Eddie stepped onto Fifth Avenue heading south toward the park. He kept his staff with him, using it as a hiking stick as he went.

He knew what he wanted to do and where he wanted to go. The problem was that he just wasn't sure how to go about it. He closed his eyes, focused on his memory of a ring of large stones around a fire, and stepped into the woods of the park.

Eddie felt the air change, the smell of greenery struck his nose, and he no longer heard traffic. He opened his eyes, stepped out of the grove of trees to see the ring of stones, with a bright fire burning in the middle of it, just as he pictured it.

He walked toward the fire and saw a huge shape lurking on the other side of the campfire. Dark brown fur covered the hulking form, and a very human face lifted to stare at Eddie.

"Wondered when you'd get here," the Sasquatch said.

Eddie approached the fire and warmed his hands. "Stone Face, I'm glad to see you."

He met the mighty Sasquatch the previous year, living in the huge Watchung Reservation in New Jersey. The giant had advised Eddie when the vampires were battling the wizards. He even joined the fight in the end, but Eddie hadn't seen him since the night of that battle.

"How did you know to be here?" Eddie asked.

"You thought about it earlier in the evening, and I knew you would come," Stone Face answered. "Smoke?"

"Please," Eddie said. "May I sit at your fire? I seek your wisdom."

"I know," the beast answered, and pulled a pipe and a small leather pouch from behind the rock next to where he sat. "I accept or I would not have offered to smoke with you."

Stone Face packed tobacco into the pipe, but even his pinky was almost too big for the bowl. He took a burning branch from the fire, touched it to the pipe and puffed, blowing a long plume of smoke from his mouth.

Eddie sat on a nearby rock, and Stone Face handed him the pipe. Eddie took a small drag on it, and then fell into coughing, returning it to his host.

"You are worried about werewolves," Stone Face said, puffing on the pipe.

"I wanted to see if you could advise me about Wisakachek or Matchitehew. I mean, you've been around a long time, and if anyone knows anything, it would be you."

Stone Face nodded sagely. "I have smoked and shared a fire with Wisakachek many times."

"Can I meet with him, tell him of our problem?"

"I have not seen him for many moons. He is an immortal and travels a lot. But he enjoys a good smoke." Stone Face held out the pipe for Eddie.

Eddie took a small drag on the pipe and this time the smoke didn't make him cough. He blew it out and asked. "What about Matchitehew?"

"Matchitehew is another matter."

"I get that."

"No, you don't. In your parlance, he is bat-shit crazy. The extension of his life with centuries of becoming a wolf has affected his brain. No werewolf is more vicious or destructive than Matchitehew."

"He has offered to help us."

"I would take such an offer with care. Matchitehew is not charitable. If he offers to help, it is only to get him something he desires."

"What about his control over other werewolves?" Eddie asked.

"The members of his pack obey his word. They will follow him, even unto their own deaths. You must know this, if you are to face him."

"Unless myself and the wizards are there to intervene."

"Yes. Which brings us to the real question you have come here to ask," Stone Face said, his eyes looking up at the sky full of stars.

"My real question is how to stop the werewolf before anyone else dies."

Stone Face shook his hairy head. "No, it is not. Your real question is whether you should remain a wizard or return to your simple mortal life."

Eddie frowned. "Do you, like, read minds or something?"

"Not really, but I have experience. You feel bound by duty to so many things: your job, your family, your marriage."

"I like my job, my family, and my wife."

"I am aware of this. But you have a strong desire to protect and serve. Being a wizard grants you the ability to do so for many more people than your job as a police detective ever could."

"That's true," Eddie said.

"Yet you fear the loss of your family in the years that lie ahead if you remain a wizard. To continue to exist after your wife and children are dead offends your sense of duty, even if they lead long and happy lives."

Eddie rubbed the back of his head. "That *is* how I feel about it."

"And it also offends your sense of duty that you can change things so dramatically using magick, and yet you carry a strong wish to walk away, make it someone else's problem."

"That sums it up for me. Any suggestions?"

"Your powers work through will and intent. If you are unsure, filled with doubt, your powers, great though they are, cannot save you." Stone Face pointed at Eddie's chest with his overlarge index finger. "Listen to your heart."

"Really," Eddie said, annoyed. "That's it? Some kind of greeting card answer to an overwhelming question?"

Stone Face shrugged again. "Not all of my advice can be gems."

"For my more immediate problem, is there anything you can do to find Wisakachek?"

"I shall see what I can do. What would you ask of him?"

"If he could make Matchitehew a plain human again, that would help."

"I can tell you now—he cannot."

"Why not? He's the one who cast the spell."

"Matchitehew is the progenitor of many American werewolves. He has infected many people, and then they went forth to infect others. If Matchitehew became human again, it would collapse the werewolf bloodlines."

"Sounds like a fine answer to me."

"I doubt Wisakachek would see it the same way. His curse has traveled to people far beyond the original intent. It has become so immense that even Wisakachek's powers cannot alter what has occurred."

"If you can set up a meeting, I would be most grateful."

"I make no promises, Eddie Berman. But I can assure you of one thing."

"What's that?"

"If Matchitehew attacks you, he will happily rip your heart out."

NINE

"Eddie, nothing else is coming to mind," Marlowe complained.

They were in Marlowe's basement. The cauldron and its platform were gone, replaced by bookcases, wooden file cabinets, and tables filling the room, weighed down with old books, scrolls, papyri, and even carved stones and clay tablets.

Marlowe was walking up and down the aisles wearing the Hat of Remembrance, which allowed him to recall any tome he'd ever placed there. He pulled two books and handed them to Eddie, who paged through them only to find one written in Latin and the other in something unrecognizable.

"By any chance, do you have spells or potion books in English?" Eddie complained.

"The Latin will be easy for Eugenia. She is quite fluent in the language."

"That's great, but none of the pages look like they have any recipes for potions."

"Ancient measurements were much less precise," Marlowe said. "Come, we can have Eugenia review the Latin, and I'll take a crack at the Cuneiform."

Eddie looked at the book Marlowe held, and the writing seemed to be nothing more than a series of triangles and rectangles. "Is that what this is?"

"Yes, it's rather simple once you get the hang of it." Marlowe turned to face the cluttered room. Giving his staff the lightest movement, the library disappeared, leaving the room empty again.

They started up the long stairs. "Are you in touch with that guy who sent you the demonic message?"

"Hm? Oh yes, Matchitehew."

"I met him last night."

"Oh? Any insights?"

"He came across as a pompous ass," Eddie declared. "Personally, I wouldn't trust him farther than I could throw him."

"Good to know, since I expect to meet with him this day."

"That should be interesting."

"Tell me, how did you pay the messenger?" Marlowe said, concern coloring his face.

"Oh, that skinny demon? I told him I owed him one."

Marlowe stopped and turned to face Eddie. "You did what?"

"I offered him money, but he said he couldn't take it, so I said I owed him one. What's the big deal?"

Marlowe scowled. "Eddie, you told a demon that you owe him. Do you have any idea what that means?"

"That I should have some gold coins for next time?"

"You have given your oath that you owe a demon a debt." Marlowe paced the step he was on, back and forth. "This is terrible! Who knows what that monster could ask for?"

"I figured we just double the tip the next time."

"No, Eddie—you are now bound to give that demon whatever he should request."

"I didn't know that."

"Sometimes, Eddie, what you do not know might be the death of us all!" Marlowe said and stormed up the stairs.

Eddie followed silently, but inside felt his temper rise. How did he know he had to grant some demon's wish? There were so many rules to being a wizard. Once again, Eddie felt he wasn't a part of the club, just an outsider looking in.

For an old man, Marlowe got to the top of the stairs much sooner than Eddie, and Eddie didn't catch up to him until he reached the breakfast room. There Eugenia was looking through a small book of her own, and Ahbay was writing on a scroll with a quill, a bottle of ink open in front of him.

Eugenia looked up. "Any luck?"

"Little, I'm afraid," muttered Marlowe. "Do you mind looking over the Latin in this book? I'm going to work on the Cuneiform."

"What do you want me to do?" Eddie asked. "I mean, considering that I need to be in Washington Square before dark."

"Drusilicus, Vasant, and Claremont should arrive soon, if you could please escort them here," Marlowe sighed. "And try not to make any agreements with the dark forces today."

Eddie headed out of the breakfast room to wait at the front door. Marlowe was getting impatient far more easily and seemed to have anger boiling underneath his usually calm demeanor. Perhaps Eddie had made a mistake, but usually Marlowe would focus on solutions and not on blame.

The idea of becoming a werewolf no doubt frightened the old man, and they were no closer to a cure than they had been the previous day.

Wraith stepped out of the wall next to Eddie. "Drusilicus, Vasant, and Wizard Claremont are coming up the front steps, sir."

"I'll let in the guests. Thank you, Wraith."

The ghost faded into the wall next to the door without a word.

Eddie pulled the door open and invited in the trio.

"Any luck on your research project?" Drusilicus asked as a way of greeting.

"Marlowe found a pair of books, and needs to translate them," Eddie said. "Did you get the photos of the pages from *Lupus Libre*? I sent them to you this morning."

Drusilicus sighed. "I have only glanced at them. There is useful information on how to create a wolf belt, but little else. The page with that odd rune might be promising. I will give it more thorough study before tonight."

Vasant held up a small leather case. "I travelled to meet with some wizards in India last evening. They gave me several Sanskrit copper plates, which may contain a potion, but I have not yet translated them."

"I'm just here to help," Rusty said with a shrug.

"Glad to have you here, Rusty," Eddie said, and turned to Drusilicus. "Drew, you made that potion that unmasked that vampire, and put it in a ball that exploded in the air and turned the potion into a mist. Is there a way to do the same exploding ball with a werewolf potion, if we find one?"

"A mist ball that might be effective on a werewolf?" Drusilicus pondered, looking doubtful.

"The point is, if you could make something a werewolf wasn't expecting, it would slow it down and give us an advantage."

"That sounds quite clever," Vasant said.

Drusilicus looked up at the ceiling. "I am concerned because a mist would get into the lungs, and wolfsbane is poisonous, even in the smallest quantities. It would take extraordinary skill to balance the amount."

Eddie grinned. "You have extraordinary skill, right?"

Drusilicus lifted an eyebrow. "Yes. But, as usual, lieutenant, you ask for the impossible."

"Only because you can usually deliver," Eddie replied.

Drusilicus attempted to look stern, but grinned. "You have a point." The man frowned and looked thoughtful. "I have a tincture I have been working on for several years as a potion for Howell."

"What does it do?"

"It forces the werewolf back to human form."

"Any success?"

"Howell and I have come very close, but not succeeded—as a potion. But if they inhaled it as a mist…" Drusilicus' eyes lit up and he turned to Vasant. "I must go to my laboratory. Is it all right that I leave you, my dear?"

"Of course," Vasant said.

Drusilicus nodded and headed for the door.

Eddie stepped next to Vasant. "You're doing wonders for him."

"He is a challenge, I admit," Vasant said with a smile as Drusilicus walked out the door. "But then again, so am I."

"You two are good for each other."

"And it only took us a hundred years of separation to realize it," Vasant added. "Come, let us talk with the others."

The three of them headed into the breakfast room. Eugenia was now going through the Latin book, writing on a notepad, apparently translating as she read. Marlowe was deep in the study of Cuneiform, and Ahbay was still writing in Japanese with the scroll and quill.

"I have brought what information I could find," Vasant announced, as she took the leather bag and removed several flat, rectangular plates that gleamed orange in the light.

Marlowe looked over. "Sanskrit on copper? And it looks like you polished it."

"Yes, with a simple spell," Vasant proclaimed. "They were all so tarnished and green I could barely read them."

"Are those about werewolves?" Eddie asked. "I thought werewolves were only in Europe or America."

"Oh, no," Vasant said. "There was a terrible werewolf attack in India in 1878. Over 600 lives lost at a village in Uttar Pradesh."

"That's correct," Eugenia responded. "But as recently as 1985, a group of werewolves called the Wolves of Asta attacked an Indian village. Wizards had to be called in to stop them after they killed several children."

"That was when I was living in a cave studying the mysteries of the Atman," Vasant explained.

"We did miss you, dear," Eugenia said. "But you were quite committed to your hermitage."

"I enjoy the new world I have come into. Though it is very loud."

Eddie spoke up. "While the rest of you do the translating we hope to—"

A loud knock came from the front door.

"Now what?" Marlowe complained. "With all these disturbances, it is amazing we get anything done at all."

Marlowe rose from the table when Bankrock walked into the room.

The small man wore his typical bowtie, which made his neck look too thin. He carried a notebook and then looked about the room at the assembled group. "Marlowe, I hope you are ready to go. This is a sensitive negotiation!"

Marlowe sighed. "That's right, we are meeting with Matchitehew. Do you have a location?"

"Of course, I was the one who negotiated it."

Rusty, who was sitting on a chair sipping a cup of coffee, looked up. "I can work on that Cuneiform for ya, Marlowe."

Eddie turned to the cabbie. "You know Cuneiform?"

Rusty shrugged.

Marlowe glanced at the others. "Please, Bankrock. Let us discuss this in the other room."

Ahbay looked up from his writing. "Can we be of assistance, Marlowe?"

"Bankrock and I have this under control," Marlowe said, putting off the other's concerns as they left the room.

Eddie followed, catching up to the pair. "Marlowe, you're meeting with the head of the werewolves with just Bankrock?"

"What is wrong with me?" Bankrock glared at Eddie.

"Are you sure meeting with him is a good idea?"

Marlowe stopped walking. "It is a necessity if we are to end this. Matchitehew holds sway over werewolves and has a place to take them if we can capture them."

"Yes—but what if he holds sway over you?" Eddie pointed out. "You're infected."

Bankrock's eyes bugged out, and Eddie was afraid they might push his glasses right off his face. "He has a point. Once bitten, the influence of the pack might affect even you."

"The power of the Five has made me much better," Marlowe said to Bankrock.

Eddie stared at Marlowe suspiciously. "How about I get a silver goblet for you to hold?"

Marlowe's face flushed in embarrassment. "What is it you wish, Eddie?"

"I want to go with you to meet this guy and make sure he doesn't control you or your powers."

"This was not part of the negotiations," Bankrock fussed.

"It's me going or Marlowe holding a silver goblet," Eddie said, crossing his arms and staring down at the pair of them.

"Very well," Marlowe said through clenched teeth. "Come with us, check the situation, and once you are sure I am unencumbered, you can be off."

"And for once, don't be yourself," Bankrock added.

Eddie followed them out of the building and they all turned uptown and walked into the park.

A few minutes later, the trio emerged from a grove of trees and on to a different dirt path in Central Park.

Since Eddie was with the Central Park Precinct for over two years and knew the park well, he could tell with just a glance that he was now at the north end of the park near Harlem.

Marlowe turned north. Up on the hilltop, among the bushes and trees, sat Blockhouse Number One.

The old stone structure was built on a rock outcrop in the North Woods. It was part of a fortification to protect New York from the British during the War of 1812. The windowless fort was never utilized and fell into disuse, but because of the remarkable stone construction, it remained solid over the years. Although not an active fort, an American flag was raised daily on a single flagpole inside the blockhouse. To discourage people from going into the old structure, there was a very solid metal gate at the one doorway atop a set of stone steps.

Marlowe climbed the hill as Bankrock and Eddie followed.

"We're meeting him in the Blockhouse?" Eddie asked, breathing hard from the climb.

"We needed neutral ground, and this was acceptable," Bankrock told Eddie.

"We asked to meet in daylight," Marlowe clarified. "Although a werewolf can transform at any time, it is far easier to do so at night."

They reached the eight stones steps that led to the iron gate and the entrance. The building was square and rose two stories off the ground, the cut and squared reddish stones fitting together with only scant amounts of mortar.

Marlowe was the first to ascend the stairs. When he arrived at the top, he tapped the heavy padlock with his cane, and it immediately unlocked and fell to the ground.

As Marlowe pulled the gate aside and stepped through, his clothing vanished beneath the swirl of his white robes, brilliant in contrast to the dark grey of Bankrock's vesture. Eddie felt the reassuring thrust of his staff into his hand as he followed them, his crimson robes rippling like water over his shoulders.

Inside the Blockhouse were two men and a woman, waiting. Eddie recognized the tallest man as Matchitehew, who stood with crossed arms looking as if he lorded over all of creation.

Marlowe bowed his head to the tall man. "Matchitehew, it is good of you to meet with us. I am the coven master, Marlowe."

"I came to witness the truth of your words for myself," Matchitehew said with his commanding voice.

The other two—whom Eddie immediately dubbed Biker Guy and Biker Chick because of a preponderance of leather in their outfits—stood half in the dim light as surly bodyguards.

Matchitehew's eyes went to Bankrock. "It is good to see your negotiator with you, as well as this wizard I met last night." His eyes narrowed as he peered at Eddie.

"He is the Wizard Berman," Marlowe said. "He has a special interest in Central Park."

Matchitehew's eyebrows lifted and he chuckled. "Special interest?"

"I'm a detective, assigned to the Central Park precinct. Your lone werewolf killed a man in my park," Eddie said.

Marlowe and Bankrock exchanged a worried glance.

Matchitehew considered Eddie. "You speak plain. I like that. No careful words, no flowery language, just what you want and why."

Eddie didn't move, his eyes still on Matchitehew. "I see you brought some backup. Does that mean you can stop these wolves?"

A smile played on the big man's lips as he glanced back at his leather clad associates. "Yes. In fact, if my friends had been with me last night, we could have easily captured the two wanderers." He turned to Marlowe and his nostrils flared briefly, and he frowned. "But I believe your situation has changed."

Marlowe sighed, aware that their host knew his secret. "One beast bit me."

Matchitehew's face became like stone. "Have you been able to stop the infection with your magicks?"

Marlowe shook his head, lips tight.

Matchitehew sighed. "If it is any help—we would welcome you to our pack."

Marlowe nodded, his jaw set. "That is most kind. But I have weeks until the next full moon, and my friends are seeing if they can help me. If not, I shall have to put aside my magicks, as I would become a much larger threat than the wolves we seek."

Matchitehew nodded gravely. "Which one bit you?"

"The gray one," Marlowe admitted.

"There's also a red wolf with a white stomach," Eddie insisted. "As far as I can tell, she's the aggressive one. Is she a member of your pack?"

All signs of amusement were gone on Matchitehew's face. He was not used to being questioned in this way.

"I will do what I can to learn the identity of both wolves," Matchitehew replied calmly.

"That doesn't answer my question," Eddie challenged.

Bankrock looked nervously from Eddie to Matchitehew, unhappy with the direction his carefully negotiated meeting was taking.

Matchitehew forced a smile. "I shall look into it. After I remove this gray wolf from my hunting ground."

"Your hunting ground?" Eddie snapped. "What the Hell are you saying? That you have a right to hunt *people* in New York City?"

"I am sure that Matchitehew merely meant the area that the members of his pack watch over," Bankrock stammered.

"Didn't sound like that to me," Eddie said, stepping forward.

Biker Guy and Biker Chick moved in closer to Matchitehew protectively, which made Matchitehew smile.

"I think we all need to calm down," Marlowe advised, stepping between Eddie and the bodyguards. "We are here to find solutions." He faced Matchitehew. "The white wolf is a friend named Howell. The gray wolf's identity is unknown to us but getting some of her fur might allow us to find a cure for me."

"Why would you want a cure?" Matchitehew asked. "Trust me, once you embrace the nature of the predator, it will only set you free."

Eddie frowned. *This guy enjoys being a wolf. He thinks we all should want it.*

Eddie stepped back and glanced at his watch. He had to go meet Luis. "I mean no disrespect—but I must report for my duties."

Confusion clouded Matchitehew's features. "Duties? Are you not a wizard?"

"As I said, I work as a police detective and I have to report for my shift. My partner will be waiting."

Matchitehew frowned. "You really are a police officer, and work in the parks?"

"This week I'm assigned to Washington Square Park downtown, to stop the werewolves," Eddie explained. "And let me assure you—if you don't stop them, I will."

Matchitehew's jaw tightened, but he said nothing. Eddie turned and walked away.

"Now, what we are seeking…" Bankrock began as Eddie went out through the gate, his robes swirling and changing back to his suit jacket, shirt, and pants.

He strode down the hill and into the trees and instantly stepped out onto a path in Washington Square Park. No one noticed him walking from the woods or acknowledged that he appeared from nowhere.

Eddie headed to the north end of the park and the Washington Square Arch, the planned meeting place for his patrol.

Eddie saw his large partner approach, but he was alone.

"What's up?" Eddie asked.

"No animal control agents tonight," Luis said, opening his arms wide and looking around as if they might turn up. "Last night scared the *cobardes* and they refused to help."

"Have you spoken to Detective Thomas?"

Luis nodded. "Yeah, I called, and he asked us to continue the patrol."

"They really don't need us to do it until sundown, right?"

Luis lifted his eyebrows. "You planning to goof off?"

"No, but since we have some time, I thought we could visit Caleb, and show him that weird symbol I took a picture of. Drusilicus said it might be useful."

"You want us to go all the way to his place in Alphabet City? Do we even have that kind of time?"

"Caleb has his fortune-telling place over on Sullivan Street. That's only a few blocks away."

"That *tarado*," Luis spat. "Why do you want him to be involved?"

"He's an expert at making talismans," Eddie said. "Like it or not, he should be able to make it and it might cure Marlowe."

They headed out of the park and strolled down Sullivan Street. As they approached Bleecker Street, they saw a small shop with walls that jutted out onto the sidewalk made of metal and plexiglass. An awning sported a hanging sign reading: Psychic and Tarot Card Readings

A neon sign glowed bright with the word READER on top, an outline of a human hand, and the word ADVISOR on the bottom. The glass door was closed and a little sign stated the hours of operation were four to midnight most days.

Luis peeked at his watch. "It's four, he's open."

Eddie pushed through the door. The two men went in and sat in a pair of rattan wicker chairs in front of a small round table with a red brocade tablecloth. A deck of tarot cards sat on the table right next to a crystal ball on a three-legged metal stand.

"Just a moment," a familiar voice said from behind a curtained space.

"No rush, we got time," Luis said.

There was a rustle behind the curtain and then a finger opened a small space enough to take a peek, then closed. Caleb Heinz parted the curtain. He looked different from the last time the detectives had seen him. His body piercings were gone, and while he was thin, he looked healthy and his color was good. He wore a long shirt of Indian design, going down past his knees, with buttons down the front and gold braiding around the collar.

His hair was long and hung loose, and he sat in a larger wicker chair opposite Eddie and Luis. He smiled and spoke in a soft voice. "Lieutenant Berman, Sergeant Vasquez, I'm surprised to see you both."

Luis gestured at the plexiglass booth around them. "Doesn't that ruin your whole 'psychic' claim?"

Caleb's smile returned, which surprised Eddie. This was very uncharacteristic for the young man. Every time they had spoken to him in the past, he had been sullen and uncooperative.

"I can sense most people who come for a reading, but the lieutenant's unique abilities create an energy around him that my talismans cannot penetrate."

"You're still using those trinkets?" Eddie inquired.

The smile didn't falter. "I'm an enchanter, I make talismans. In fact, I've improved with them."

Luis stared hard at the young man. "You on drugs or something?"

Caleb chuckled. "No. I've been crafting talismans that give knowledge and perspective. I've cleansed my body of everything —alcohol, grass, dope. I'm on a whole different high."

Eddie looked around the tiny room. "How's business?"

"It brings in more than I need, but there are times it is quite slow. I take that time to meditate and center myself," Caleb replied dreamily.

Eddie and Luis exchanged a glance.

"Do you know about the wild animal in Washington Square?"

Caleb met Eddie's eyes, and his face clouded. "Yes. The werewolves."

Luis jumped in. "Werewolves? That's crazy, man."

Caleb peered at Luis. "No, you don't think so, sergeant. The lieutenant has powers to keep me out of his mind, but you're an open book. You have seen the werewolf." Caleb's eyes grew wide. "You have seen three of them."

"All right, cut it out," Eddie snapped. "You've proven your point."

Caleb's attention returned to Eddie. "Sorry, I meant no offense."

"So, you've found enlightenment?" Eddie said.

"Yeah, and you convince people to give you money," Luis grumbled.

Caleb shrugged. "My customers meet my material needs. I have little desire for more."

Luis spoke up. "Aren't you worried, going home at midnight?"

Caleb reached into his collar and pulled on the many chains that rested there. Each chain had a disk the size of a silver dollar, all made from gold, silver, and precious metals. He let the circles of metal rest on the outside of his shirt.

"I have nothing to fear. One of these pentacles keeps wild animals away. You might say, it repels them."

Eddie kept going. "My question is—why are you wearing it?"

Caleb's eyes met Eddie's. "I get glimpses of the future. I knew what was coming." He put the many medallions back under his shirt.

"Can I show you a design that might help us?" Eddie asked.

Caleb seemed surprised by this. "Of course."

Eddie held out his phone and brought up the photo of the page from *Lupus Libre*. He handed the phone to Caleb who studied it carefully.

"We had an… expert who said this might help," Eddie explained.

"It is a unique bind rune. I've seen nothing like it," Caleb replied.

"A bind rune? What is that?" Luis asked.

Caleb spoke, his eyes focused on the image. "A bind rune or binderune is a combination of nordic symbols put together to form a new design that also contains the original power of each individual rune symbol. Ancient Germanic people used runes commonly."

"What other runes is this one made from?" Eddie asked. "To me it's just a circle with a series of lines that looked like two letter R's back to back."

"I'd have to do a little more study, but I think this combines the Nordic symbols for wolf. The original runes suggest a battle with a giant and one's animal nature."

"Do you think this, made into a talisman, could cure someone bitten by a werewolf?" Eddie asked.

Caleb typed on the small screen. "I am sending the image to my phone. I need to study it more."

"But do you think it can cure—"

"It's possible," Caleb interrupted. "It is a transformative talisman. Maybe if I cast it in gold, it will have a high enough energy."

"What is the writing all around it on that page?" Eddie asked.

"I think they are the instructions for making the talisman," Caleb said. "I will have to translate that part before I begin."

Luis gave him a dirty look. "How much this gonna cost?"

"Let me see if I can even create a working charm. If I fail, I can melt it and reuse the gold for something else."

Eddie nodded as Caleb handed back his phone. "Is there any other advice you can give us?"

Caleb lowered his head and looked at the crystal ball in front of him. The ball appeared to glow a bit as he stared, and Luis rolled his eyes.

"There are things you don't see, hidden from you," Caleb intoned. "You must be careful with whom you place your trust. There are those who wish to direct you away from the answers."

"Why should today be different?" Luis muttered.

"There is a dark purpose behind the attacks, but how it ends I can't foresee," Caleb said, as he leaned back and closed his eyes. The glass ball ceased glowing.

"That's all you have for us?" Luis demanded. "A bunch of riddles?"

Caleb shrugged apologetically. "Sorry, but the lieutenant's abilities make it impossible for me to gaze into his future."

He pulled up his sleeve and looked at a watch halfway up his arm. "Now, gentlemen, you must excuse me. I have a client coming in ten minutes and I must prepare."

"How do you go home after midnight?" Luis teased. "Through the park?"

"No, over to Sixth to catch the bus, uptown, then across on 14th. I avoid the park, Fifth Avenue, and *his* house."

Eddie knew Caleb meant the home of his former teacher, Drusilicus.

"He might surprise you. Drew has mellowed," Eddie said.

Caleb appeared perplexed. "Mellowed?"

"Got a lady living with him," Luis added. "A lady wizard."

Caleb shrugged, as if this information was unimportant. "If I can be of further service, please come by. Otherwise, I'll contact you once I've made the talisman."

Eddie and Luis got to their feet and returned to the street.

"You buy that crap?" Luis snorted. "Enlightenment! He's no more enlightened than a pickpocket."

"I don't know, Luis," Eddie considered. "He knew you'd seen the three werewolves and there was the red one, the gray, and Howell."

"He was doing some kind of trick, gauging my reactions, the way a mentalist does."

"We've seen what he can do with those little disks. He even fooled the wizards for a while."

"I still don't buy that he's changed."

Eddie hoped Caleb could come through with the talisman, because they were running out of time as well as ideas.

TEN

Returning to Washington Square Park and the park office, Luis picked up one of the animal control nooses that Perry left for them.

"This might actually work out better," Eddie reflected as they patrolled the park. "Without the animal control guys around, I can use my magick. I don't have to hold back or try to hide it."

"That might be the thing to save our necks. I don' wanna get bit. Turning into a wolf every month would make things tough at home."

"You think?"

"Maria doesn't like dogs," Luis grinned.

Walking together with Luis holding the noose, Eddie enjoyed not having the talkative animal control agent with him. His camaraderie with Luis meant that any spot Eddie wasn't watching, Luis was. They knew each other, how to work together, and it was all second nature and easy.

They strolled their way around the pathways of the park as the sun set and twilight fell upon the city. The street lamps, designed to mimic old-style gas lamps with their tall black iron poles, sprung to life, each surrounded with an orange halo, creating pools of light up and down the walkways. Over the treetops, lighted windows on tall buildings appeared just beyond the park, which was only a few blocks long and wide, on land that measured less than ten acres.

Pacing up and down the walkways was hardly exciting work, and staying alert was difficult, but Eddie and Luis both knew the tricks to help them keep their focus.

"Man, it's like walking a beat again. I haven't done that in years."

"Being out there in daylight is a waste of time. We know the animal will only come out at night, if at all."

When they were in public, they decided to call the werewolf, 'the animal,' in case anyone overheard them.

"That Glade lady will be here later," Luis said. "She's got that whistle to bring it to us."

"Yes, but we can't let our guard down, even if it is daylight."

"No way, partner."

They paced the park, stopping at benches to sit more often than in the earlier part of the evening.

The park wasn't busy, but it was growing colder, and even with coats and suits, the wind added a chill.

Finally, Eddie stepped to a metal wire trashcan, checked to make sure no one was watching, and whispered, *"Flamma."* A fire appeared on top of the can. If anyone had been close enough, they would have seen that the contents of the can were not burning. The blaze merely sat on top, giving the illusion it burned, while the flames floated in the air. Luis huddled near the fire. Eddie wasn't chilled, as his wizard powers enabled him to maintain a steady body temperature at all times, but he enjoyed the warmth.

"Good to know you haven't forgotten how to do all this stuff," Luis said.

"I'm out of practice," Eddie said, staring into the flames. "Luis, can I ask you about this whole wizard thing?"

Luis shrugged his large shoulders. "If you can't ask me, who can you ask?"

"I'm thinking of giving it all up."

Luis gazed at Eddie. "I kinda thought you already did. I mean, you didn't do it anymore, and after a few months, I figured you got a refund or something. I didn't ask, because I figured you'd tell me when you were ready."

Eddie smiled. "Thanks for that."

"On the other hand, you handled yourself good last night."

"It's the part where I don't age that bothers me. I mean, Marlowe, Vasant, even Bankrock talk about how they have continued to live while the ones they love die and their memory fades."

"That's kinda sad."

"It was over centuries. I have a hard time accepting that they just sat back, ageless and perfect, and watched their spouses wither and die." Eddie swallowed. "It means I would stay the same while Cerise fades away—and you—and my kids. I don't think I could deal with it. I don't know if I want to."

Luis held his hands over the fire. "What if you did age, like normal?"

"What do you mean?"

Luis shrugged. "Ask Marlowe if you can do a spell so you *look* like you age like a normal person. Would that solve the problem?"

"It would solve one problem," Eddie groaned. "But then there's the whole defend New York from whatever supernatural situation comes up."

"Like a couple of rogue werewolves?" Luis asked his eyebrows raised.

"Exactly. How did I even get pulled into this?"

"You got a sense of duty, man. You figure if you got these powers, you wanna help the other wizards, and your buddy, Marlowe. Protect and serve, y'know."

It was well after eleven when Drusilicus and Vasant, both in wizard robes, walked into the park. Of course, being New York City and the Village, no one paid any heed of the two people walking about in flowing robes of blue and gold.

"What are you two doing here?" Eddie asked, surprised to see them.

"We are here to create a barrier that should dissuade any mortals from entering the park," Vasant explained.

"Yes, and to witness the talents of the great and powerful Matchitehew," Drusilicus added sardonically. "We want to see if Matchitehew does indeed have better luck than we did last night."

"Did you see either wolf this night?" Vasant asked.

Luis sighed and held up his empty animal control noose. "We saw nothin'."

Vasant nodded. "Not uncommon. Only the full moon makes the beasts come out."

"That red one showed up last night even before Glade conjured it," Eddie said. "I think there's more to this than we know. Are we any closer to a cure for Marlowe?"

Drusilicus sighed. "So far, the potions in Latin and Cuneiform, have proven to be variations of potions I have already tried."

"The Sanskrit writing I brought also contained a potion, but it proved ineffective," Vasant said. "When I attempted to mix it, it exploded."

Eddie frowned. "Anyone hurt?"

"Vasant was able to contain the explosion," Drusilicus explained. "Now, all we have left is the one potion that requires some of the fur of the werewolf that bit Marlowe,"

"Jeez," Luis complained. "How the Hell can we get that?"

"Obviously," Drusilicus said, "we ask the great and powerful Matchitehew to get some from the werewolf."

"If he'll do it," Eddie grumbled.

"We will depend upon your people skills to convince him," Drusilicus said, and with a nod, he and Vasant headed off in different directions.

"Great, more on me," Eddie muttered and turned to his partner. "Luis, you should go home."

"No way, man," Luis replied, folding his arms over his enormous chest.

A sound drew their attention to the nearby woods.

"What was that?" Eddie glanced up.

Luis paused and peered into the woods. "Looks like two people and a couple of dogs."

Eddie gazed around quickly. "I thought Vasant and Drusilicus were going to keep people away."

"Maybe they didn't get the spell going fast enough."

As the couple came out into the light, Eddie saw that it wasn't New Yorkers out on a stroll, but Glade and Matchitehew. Next to them trotted, not a couple of dogs as Luis had thought, but a pair of black wolves obediently following them.

Both of the animals had fur that was jet black and looked wet, more like the feathers of a raven than the fur of a canine. One was larger than the other, and both looked powerful and vicious.

"Well, this is cozy," Luis mumbled.

"Too cozy, if you ask me," Eddie murmured in reply, and with a gesture, he extinguished the flaming trash can.

Matchitehew drew closer and stopped, crossing his muscular arms in front of his body, as if to prepare for battle. "Do you come to confront us, wizard?"

Eddie kept his eyes on the pair of black wolves. "I am here to help in any way I can and to… um… ask a boon of thee."

"What boon do you seek?" Matchitehew asked.

"A few hairs from the gray werewolf's fur, nothing more," Eddie said.

Matchitehew shrugged. "Easy enough."

"We have the situation well in hand, Wizard Berman," Glade announced. "I be able to bring the errant wolf here, and Matchitehew will capture it."

Eddie inclined his head toward the black wolves. "Seems like you already captured a pair."

Matchitehew glanced down at the wolves. "These are my companions in their true form. Magnificent, are they not? In your world, we act as humans. But in our true form, we are hunters and creatures of the night. To take on the mantle of the wolf allows one to live the desire of all creatures."

"What's that?" Eddie asked.

"To be the true predator. To possess teeth that rip and tear, feel the dirt beneath your paws, and to run as fast as the wind." He curled his hand into a fist. "To strike down your prey."

"I'm… glad you enjoy it," Eddie said, his eyes still on the wolves. "Are you changing as well?"

"Only if I have no choice. I will try to win over our errant child with words. If it is necessary to fight, my associates can easily defeat a lone wolf without harming it."

Eddie shook his head. "I don't know. Both the red and gray wolves are tricky."

The corners of Matchitehew's mouth turned up in a sly grin. "For you, yes, but not for us. I would advise you and your fellow wizards to stay near the arch." He glanced over at Glade. "Except for you, good lady. Your skills will bring the runaway here to us."

Glade pointed at Eddie. "Wizard Berman, if ye be able, bring the lights down. It be too bright for the wolves."

Eddie gestured and the spotlights on the arch and the plaza faded dramatically.

"Come on, Luis, let's wait for Drew and Vasant," Eddie said, and he headed for the arch.

"Man, that Match guy has a high opinion of hisself," Luis grumbled.

"Just keep a grip on that animal control noose in case we need it."

They stood near the large monument, and in a few minutes, Drusilicus and Vasant joined them. They watched as Glade was very busy in the center round stone of the fountain for a second night.

"Vasant, did you bring your knives with you?" Eddie asked.

"My silver ones, Wizard Berman? Yes, I did," she answered, and in proof of her words, she produced a sparkling knife from her robes.

"Perhaps us being this far away is helpful," Drusilicus suggested. "We moved as a group the night Marlowe was bitten, and that was a mistake. If we had waited to see the wolves first, we could have struck them from a distance, safely."

"Yes, and I assure you," Vasant said as she held the glittery knife in her hand. "My aim is quite excellent."

Drusilicus' head snapped up. "I believe Wizard Glade is about to begin."

Eddie called forth his staff and covered his group with a dome of protective red light.

"Is this really necessary?" Drusilicus asked.

Eddie glanced at Luis. "Just in case. That red wolf likes to attack me."

Glade stood in the empty fountain, and with a gesture the tall thin tapers she placed in candleholders burst into flame. The lady wizard moved into the center of the circle and raised the small tubular whistle—the same one as the previous night—to her lips and blew. Eddie watched as Matchitehew and the pair of wolves all grimaced in reaction to the ultrasonic sound, and the smaller of the two wolves raised her head and emitted a brief howl.

Eddie looked around and the group waited.

And waited.

After about five minutes, Glade put the whistle to her lips a second time and blew an even longer note. Once again, the black wolves and Matchitehew reacted to the noise, while Eddie only heard a faraway hissing sound. The red protective dome kept out more than merely a physical attack.

"It don' seem to be working," Luis observed.

"Quite right, sergeant," Drusilicus agreed. "It would appear that our werewolf expert might not be up to the task."

"You needn't be so pleased about it," Vasant chided.

Glade looked at the burning candles and stepped out of the fountain area. She approached Matchitehew and said something to him, too quietly for Eddie to hear. She then went down one pathway into the woods, while Matchitehew spoke to his wolves.

"Where is she goin' this time?" Luis asked.

"Perhaps if the wolf does not come to her, she goes to the wolf?" Drusilicus suggested.

Something moved through the underbrush, just beyond the paved pathways through the park.

"What's that?" Luis said, pointing at the moving brush.

"We're about to find out," Vasant said.

The gray timber wolf came out of the bushes. The animal stopped, turned, and changed direction.

"Bring her in!" yelled Matchitehew as he pointed at the wolf. The pair of black wolves were off like a shot, moving incredibly fast. They moved in, going past the gray wolf and cutting off her escape route.

"What are they doing?" Luis asked.

"I don't know," Eddie admitted.

The gray wolf attempted to get out of the park, but one of the shiny black wolves got between her and the exit. Then, growling and running at her, it drove her back toward Matchitehew.

"See, wizards?" Matchitehew announced to the group still under the red dome. "I do not have to chase the child. I have others to bring her to me."

Drusilicus' jaw muscles twitched, looking at Matchitehew, but the wizards remained under the dome of red light. Vasant relaxed and returned her knife to its hidden pocket.

The black wolves manipulated the third, guiding her back toward the plaza where Matchitehew stood with his arms crossed, like a king observing his domain.

The gray wolf slowed down and allowed the black wolves to shepherd her without resisting.

All three wolves moved to the plaza, and Matchitehew stepped forward, clearing his throat. "Child, I am Matchitehew, father of the werewolves. I am here to guide you, and to help you."

The gray wolf shot him an annoyed doggie look and then sat down, panting.

Eddie dropped the red dome, and the four people drew closer.

Matchitehew still spoke to the gray wolf. "I will take you out of this city, so you can become a member of my pack, which has many of our breed. With us, you can hunt, live free, and avoid humans and hunters. We know that you have bitten people, and perhaps killed when the moon fever took away your wits. But that is in the past, and if you willingly go with me, then all shall be forgiven."

"Don't forget we need a few hairs of her fur," Eddie announced.

Matchitehew glared back at Eddie. "We have made an agreement with the wizards. They shall allow you to leave, provided you will give a few loose hairs so they may attempt to cure the wizard that was bitten."

The gray wolf sat listening to Matchitehew, as calmly and patiently as a household pet. It was panting less and had recovered quickly.

"Is everything under control now?" Luis asked.

Eddie murmured, "I don't know. It looks good."

Matchitehew spoke up again. "If you wish, your fellow wolves will escort you to a vehicle I have nearby and we shall drive you upstate to a place of unspoiled wilderness shared by your brothers."

The she-wolf lay down and lowered her head on her front legs, submissively, her eyes still focused on the big man.

Matchitehew turned to the wizards to smirk at them.

Vasant grumbled. "He is quite full of himself, is he not?"

"Yes, my dear," Drusilicus whispered. "But we are about to get what we want without a battle. Let us not lose sight of our goal."

Eddie sighed. They were right. Matchitehew had tamed the troublesome gray werewolf with no problems at all—but what about the red one who had been the genuine threat? Why hadn't that one shown up?

Eddie pulled an evidence bag he had secreted upon his person and moved away from the group toward the silver-gray wolf.

"Eddie," Luis warned.

"Miss... um... wolf," Eddie started, and the wolf tensed as he drew closer. Eddie glanced at Matchitehew, who nodded. He returned his attention to the canine. "If you will allow me, I wish to touch you, and… um… get a few of your hairs."

The wolf stared at Eddie with her white eyes, then lowered her head, offering to let Eddie touch her. Eddie slowly moved to his knees, and carefully reached out to stroke the wolf's head gently. Her fur was soft and luxurious, and he easily gathered a few hairs and put them in the clear plastic evidence bag.

"Thank you," Eddie said, and with his eyes focused on the eyes of the wolf, he rose and stepped back. He couldn't fight the feeling that he knew this wolf personally, but dismissed it as a crazy idea.

Eddie nodded at Matchitehew and joined his partner and fellow wizards, standing several yards away.

Matchitehew lifted his head back and he smiled. "Now, shall we go?"

The gray wolf quickly rose and took several steps, getting closer to Matchitehew, its eyes focused intently on him.

He pointed at one pathway, and the two black wolves moved to be on either side of the gray wolf. The three of them began to slowly saunter down the path away from the open square.

"Well, that's that," Luis said.

Like lightning, the gray wolf turned and in an unexpected move ran straight toward Matchitehew. She launched herself into the air, striking the big man in the middle of his chest with all her weight, knocking him to the ground with the impact of her body.

Matchitehew fell with a cry, and the two black wolves moved toward their fallen leader. The gray wolf took off in a totally different direction.

"Enough of this." Vasant pulled a knife and in one fluid motion threw it at the gray wolf, just as one of the black wolves was almost upon it.

In a flash of movement, the gray wolf flattened and slid as the silver knife passed inches above her, piercing the front shoulder of the black wolf.

The animal howled and fell back, its body shifting and changing as it writhed in pain on the ground. The fur disappeared, exposing the pale flesh of a woman.

The second black wolf, the bigger one, turned from pursuing the gray wolf, and charged at the wizards, teeth exposed, growling as it ran.

It only took the black wolf a few leaps, and it was almost upon the wizards, but Drusilicus lifted his staff and a blast of blue light struck out, toppling the creature out of the air and throwing it over a fire hydrant and into the greenery beyond.

"You dare!" Matchitehew said as he got up to his feet. He looked at the wolf hit by the knife. The wolf had finished the transformation, and was now the woman Eddie thought of as Biker Chick. She lay naked on the pathway, the hilt of the silver knife sticking out of her shoulder as she screamed in agony.

"I'll help the woman," Drusilicus said, moving towards her, but the larger black wolf, unharmed, leapt out of the bushes directly at Drusilicus.

This time, Eddie fired a blast of light, sending the creature sprawling. Vasant stood, another knife in hand, trying to get a clear throw at the attacking wolf.

"This shall not stand!" Matchitehew bellowed, reaching a hand under his shirt. Instantly, a large gray monster stood where the man had been a moment earlier.

It was like a wolf, but bigger than any of the others, and it stood upright like a man. The shoulders on the creature were massive, with a mane of fur around its neck and shoulders, giving it a leonine look. There were long claws at the ends of his paws which resembled fingers more than a canine forepaw. Even his feet resembled a human hand, with long sharp claws at the end.

This new creature gave a mighty roar and charged directly at Eddie, moving at the speed of a freight train.

"Eddie, look out," Luis yelled.

Eddie ducked to the ground and threw his dome of protection over himself, putting extra effort into the creation as this immense creature was more like a hybrid of wolf, human, and lion.

The monster landed upon Eddie and the protective shield crackled and flashed like it had an electric current running through it. Eddie felt the space within the dome compress, and his ears made a popping noise. With a cry, Eddie pushed back, focusing on the power of his staff.

There was a flash of light and the Hell-hound flew off Eddie, dozens of feet away. It landed on its feet and rose, looking to resume the attack.

Eddie yelled, *"Flamma!"*

A ring of fire blazed up around himself, Luis, and Vasant.

The Hell-hound paused, staring at the flames.

Vasant covered herself and Luis with a dome of golden light and held a silver knife aloft. "Cease your attack!"

Eddie gestured to Vasant. "Lower the knife."

"He attacked you!" Vasant declared.

"You hit one of his pack—we have to back down," Eddie shouted back. "Everyone, stand down."

"Wizard Berman is correct, let us all stand down," Drusilicus shouted. He was sitting on the ground next to the naked woman, both of them covered with a dome of blue light he had conjured. He extracted the knife from her shoulder, and a pink light surrounded the wound as blood dripped down her arm.

Drusilicus tossed the bloody knife to the ground and pulled at his own robe to rip strips of cloth to make a makeshift binding. He applied the cloth to her shoulder as she lay there.

The giant Hell-hound stood looking from wizard to wizard, its mouth opened and drool dripped from its jaws. The flames that encircled Eddie danced in the creature's red eyes.

After a minute, the monster sat back on its haunches, and one of his arms or forepaws moved to touch his waist. Instantly, the creature transformed back into Matchitehew, fully dressed, unaffected by the sudden shift.

The larger black wolf ran to him and Matchitehew hissed, "Get her clothes."

The wolf nodded and ran off.

Eddie dissipated the fire circle, taking a few steps closer to Drusilicus, but keeping his guard up.

Matchitehew approached slowly, and Drusilicus removed the dome of light.

"What has happened?" came a woman's voice.

Wizard Glade walked back into the open square, staring angrily at the wizards, and Matchitehew.

Glaring at the wizards, Matchitehew picked up the naked woman as if she weighed nothing, and she wrapped her undamaged arm around his shoulder. "The wizards attacked us! They came with silver!"

"What?" Glade said and focused on Eddie, Vasant, and Luis. "Are ye mad?"

"Wizard Vasant threw a knife at the gray wolf, because it attacked Matchitehew," Drusilicus stated plainly.

"She only startled me," Matchitehew scoffed.

"And if your lady wolf had kept back, it would be the gray wolf shunted back to human form instead," Drusilicus pointed out. "We regret we injured one of your pack, but it was an accident."

"You bring weapons of silver, and ye call it an accident?" Glade snarled.

"Once again, you wizards ask for our help and then lie about your intentions," Matchitehew scolded. "You did this to spy upon me and injure one of my pack. This will not stand. I shall return with many more of my pack and we'll see how you fare against their teeth and claws with your tricks!"

He turned his back to the wizards, and Biker Guy, in human form, stepped into the plaza holding clothing and boots. Matchitehew carrying the woman and his bodyguard headed off toward the east side of the park.

Glade shook her head. "I be done with the lot of ye."

She walked away, following Matchitehew, with one final glance back at Eddie.

"I'm sorry," Vasant said, approaching Eddie. "I thought if I could wound the gray wolf…"

"I know," Eddie said. "And when big boy became… whatever the Hell he was… we had to stop him." Eddie held up the small evidence bag. "But we have some fur from the gray wolf."

Drusilicus looked at the hairs in the clear plastic bag. "We can see if that potion works." He handed the plastic bag to Vasant.

"I have to report what happened—cleaned up a bit—to Detective Thomas. He'll make the call to see if we continue these patrols or what NYPD will do next."

"What would that entail?" Vasant asked.

"I don't want to think about it," Eddie confessed.

Luis spoke up. "Am I the only one who noticed that Glade went into the woods and then the gray wolf showed up?"

ELEVEN

"Sorry to hear things went badly last night, Lieutenant Berman," Captain Santaro told Eddie from behind his enormous desk. Eddie was in the city by 8:00 AM after a few brief hours of sleep, to speak to the commander of the Sixth precinct.

Santaro ran a tight ship—a skill which wasn't reflected by his office. Knick-knacks, little statues of comic book characters, and other paraphernalia filled every open space. Cute little toy statues stood in front of stacks of police files and thick books, but the man had a solid reputation as a no-nonsense cop and an excellent captain.

"We could have a better chance tonight," Eddie said.

"Look, from your reports, the animal control guys, and experts I've spoken to in the field—this was too big for you and Sergeant Vasquez to handle. These animals attacked you. I think I have no choice but to close the park down and bring in a SWAT team."

"I worry about bringing in a large force. It might escalate the conflict."

"Escalate the conflict?" Santaro repeated. "We're talking about a pair of wolves, not a terrorist cell."

"Sir, if we could sedate the animals and transport them to a location where they won't interact with people—"

"And where would that be? Alaska?" Santaro demanded, looking stern. "Look, these wolves might be killers. You told me yourself you had a death in Central Park. We've received numerous sightings and complaints in Washington Square. The mayor has stuck his nose in, talking to reporters, complaining about the job NYPD is doing. I need this taken care of fast. Detective Thomas suggested we bring in the SWAT team, and I am going to approve it. You can be there, but we are taking these animals out."

Eddie sighed. He could see he wouldn't win this. "Yes, sir. My partner and I will be out there tonight, providing backup for your team."

"Good. I have a plan in place to shut off the entrances and the sidewalks around the park before sundown. We'll keep the public out of the park and safe."

"Yes, sir."

Eddie left the office and got into his unmarked police car parked out front. All the NYPD precincts had parking arrangements, and with the Sixth precinct, they lined up spots on the street reserved for police cars.

Eddie turned the rear-view mirror so it showed his eyes and said clearly, "Drusilicus."

In only a few moments, the glass silvered over and Drusilicus' was staring at him from the oblong glass.

"I so dislike talking to you in a car mirror," Drusilicus complained. "All I see are your eyes."

"I needed to talk to you as soon as I could. They're going into the park with a SWAT team tonight."

"What is that?"

"It stands for Special Weapons and Tactics—highly trained police officers with lots of heavy equipment and big guns."

"Couldn't you stop them, lieutenant?"

"It wasn't my call," Eddie said. "Contact Bankrock, have him get in touch with Matchitehew, try to make peace and keep him out of the park tonight. If he acts on his threat to bring more werewolves—"

"I shall do so, though I doubt we shall have much luck," Drusilicus explained. "You must go to Marlowe's townhouse in a few hours. Vasant and the other wizards are attempting the potion made with the fur of the gray wolf."

Eddie sighed. "I'll be there. When will you try it?"

"This morning about eleven. But first, I need you to meet me at my townhouse. Can you do so?"

"What's it about?"

"All will become clear when you get here," Drusilicus explained.

"That's a big help," Eddie grumbled, and waved his hand over the mirror, which made Drusilicus' fade away and the mirror to reflect Eddie's surroundings.

Eddie parked near Drusilicus' townhouse and, upon knocking on the door, was let in by Howell.

"What's going on, Howell? Drusilicus asked me to come."

"Yes, sir," Howell said, closing the door as Eddie entered. "The master has had success."

Eddie brightened as Howell led him down the hall. "Really? He has a cure for Marlowe?"

"No, sir. However, he has fabricated the inhalant that you requested."

Eddie nodded as Howell led him into an office. Bookcases lined the walls, made of fine wood that gleamed with wax. Drusilicus sat at an old-style open roll-up desk. As Howell left the room, Drusilicus showed Eddie to a bookcase where three dark balls sat in front of the books. Each was a little larger than a golf ball and a dark shade of purple.

"That's it?" Eddie said as he picked one up.

Drusilicus cautioned, "Easy, lieutenant. I made these recently, and they will be delicate for a few more hours."

Eddie turned it over in his hand carefully. "How does it work?"

"You merely throw it into the air and strike it with a small blast from your staff. The casing will explode and release a mist that will cover a rather extensive area. If it comes in contact with a werewolf, it should instantly transform them back into human form."

Eddie stared at the purple ball. "Drew, that's brilliant."

"The combination of wolfsbane, silver, and a few other ingredients should make it quite effective. Since it is water-based, it will dry out, which is when the other ingredients I added will neutralize the wolfsbane, so there is little or no residue left behind."

"Sounds great. Where did you test it?"

"Test it?" Drusilicus scowled. "How would I test it?"

"Drew, you said that this combination can be deadly. We have to make sure it doesn't kill the people we're trying to stop."

"In theory, it should work," Drusilicus said defensively.

"It's too big a risk," Eddie cautioned. "Look, Drew, you have a werewolf living here. We could try it on Howell."

"What?" Drusilicus said, taken aback.

"If the reaction is terrible, you can use your magick to cure him."

Drusilicus' expression grew hard. "I would not ask Howell to do such a thing!"

"Look, Drew, we have to test it before we release it on these werewolves, and we might face quite a few, if Matchitehew acts on his threat."

"Sir, he is right," said a voice from the doorway.

Eddie and Drusilicus turned to see Howell.

"I forbid it!" Drusilicus fumed.

"Sir, if we set it off in the basement with the door closed, it won't get into the house, and we can attest to its potency. I helped you with the mixing of it, and my fear is that it may be too weak to stop a charging werewolf."

Eddie turned to Drusilicus. "Which is something else we need to know before our lives depend on it."

Drusilicus went back to scowling.

"We could test it in that underground passageway you have down there," Eddie suggested. "Now that the vampires are gone, it's just a big, empty tunnel and no one goes into it."

Drusilicus threw his hands up. "Fine, but I do so under protest."

"Gentleman," Howell said. "If you will excuse me, I must change my clothing into something more… flexible."

Howell left the room and Drusilicus carefully took one of the purple balls off the shelf and handed it to Eddie.

Eddie took the small sphere and turned it over and over in his hand, examining the smooth purple surface. Neither man spoke until Howell returned. The older man was wearing a long hooded robe that only went to his bare knees and slippers on his feet.

Howell wore a wry, embarrassed smile. "Excuse the informal attire, sir. I need clothing I can divest easily and not get tangled in."

"Completely understandable," Eddie said.

The three men headed out into the hall, Drusilicus in the lead. He brought them to the stairway, where he stopped and pressed on a hidden door built into the wood paneling. It sprung open, exposing a staircase that went down into darkness.

Lights came on as Drusilicus stepped through the doorway and began the descent. All three went down two landings before they reached the bottom of the stairs. Even with the overhead fluorescent lights, the basement was dark. The walls were made from cut stone in large blocks. There were shelves along the wall with many size boxes and an enormous, well-supplied wine rack.

All three walked past a large steel door that resembled a bank vault with an impressive digital lock. They moved into an adjacent chamber through an archway and stood before a large, empty bookcase.

Drusilicus' staff appeared in his hand, and as he gestured at the bookcase, it opened to reveal a large tunnel on the other side, hewn directly into the solid bedrock under lower Manhattan. "I think this will work. With the bookcase closed, the excess mist will travel into the tunnels and not the house."

His voice echoed down the subterranean passage.

"Should you and I protect ourselves in our magickal domes?" Eddie asked.

"The potion is a mist. Our protective dome might not keep it out completely."

"Then should we wear gas masks or something?"

Drusilicus considered this, one eyebrow raised. "It would be wise for me to wear one, just in case."

"Why not me?"

"Because, lieutenant, if Howell and I were to collapse, you would stand there, useless, with no idea what to do. While if the mist poisons you or Howell, I have the knowledge to cure the both of you."

Eddie winced. "I really don't like the way you put that. It would really bother me if it weren't true. I have to admit, I'm a bit nervous."

Howell stepped close to Eddie and murmured, "I am also nervous. No one has ever seen me change except for Master Greywacke. I hope you will not think less of me."

"Howell, the more I find out about you and the man you are, the more I am impressed by you. I'm only nervous that it might seriously injure you."

"I assisted in the mixture. The bigger problem might be that it does nothing at all."

"Thank you for your help."

Drusilicus walked into the tunnel, only he was now dressed in wizard robes and carrying his staff. He also had a gas mask suspended over his free arm. It was a cloth and rubber monstrosity with a hose and a canister hanging from it.

He gestured with the staff, and the bookcase behind him slammed shut. A blue light appeared on top of the staff, lighting the dark tunnel.

"Do you understand how to activate it?" Drusilicus asked.

"I throw it into the air and hit it with a blast from my staff?"

"Correct. Please take out your staff."

Eddie held out his right hand and the wood-grain credit card flew out of his pocket, transforming into the six-foot tall wooden implement. A small, bright pink light appeared on top, adding more light into the dark space.

Drusilicus nodded to Howell. "Would you prefer we turn away as you change?"

"No, sir," Howell said, and Drusilicus appeared surprised. "I believe it will help Wizard Berman to know what the change entails."

"If you are… comfortable with that…" Drusilicus stammered.

"There is nothing comfortable about it, sir. And I think Wizard Berman should know that," Howell replied.

He stepped out of the slippers, moved to a spot on the cavern floor and lowered himself to his haunches as he pulled the robe off over his head. His naked body was not hairy, but his chest hair was as white as the hair on his head.

He closed his eyes, his face pinched in pain, and he moaned. As Eddie watched, white hair sprang out all over his body. His skin seemed to bubble as bones and muscles shifted underneath.

Eddie took a step back in horror. There was a popping and crunching noise as the body shifted. Howell's sinews stretched and bones moved into different positions. These changes had to be extremely painful, yet Howell only moaned quietly.

The older man's hands extended into paws, as his feet grew longer, reshaping into the long canine back leg. There was a loud 'crack' as Howell's heels extended and a tail jutted out behind. Howell's mouth fell open as his teeth grew long and pointed, his face twisting as his nose pushed out into a canine muzzle.

The process had taken almost a minute, but now, in place of Howell was the large white wolf Eddie had seen the other night.

"That looked like it hurt," Eddie said, shaken by the hideous transformation.

"It does," Drusilicus said, readying the mask. "But Howell has stated that there is an odd pleasure in the transformation as well."

"I find that part hard to believe," Eddie said.

"I trust you are ready to do your part?"

Eddie held up the purple ball as Drusilicus slipped the mask over his head.

Eddie turned his attention to the white wolf. "Okay, Howell. Here goes." He gently tossed it underhand into the air, and with his staff, shot a blast of fiery light that struck the sphere. The ball exploded into a thick fog that descended onto the three of them and instantly filled the huge tunnel.

Eddie wasn't sure if he should hold his breath or not, so he tried to just inhale and exhale naturally. The mist had an earthy smell, reminding Eddie of wet dirt and grass.

The white wolf howled and fell to the ground. With grunts, groans, and the sound of cracking bones and sliding flesh, Howell quickly shriveled back into human form, twisting into the fetal position, all the time panting heavily.

Eddie moved to him, the fog not affecting him at all. He got down on one knee. "Howell, are you all right? Can you breathe?"

Howell nodded and coughed, but he still seemed in pain and unable to get up.

Drusilicus waved his staff, and a breeze passed through the room, blowing all the mist away and down the tunnel. He pulled off the gas mask and joined Eddie, kneeling next to Howell.

Drusilicus put his staff on the rock floor, lifted the old man's head, and rested it on his knees.

Howell was sucking in deep breaths of the clean air and shivering. Eddie took the robe and lay it on top of him.

Drusilicus looked at Eddie. "Any unusual reactions for you?"

"What?" Eddie said, still shocked by the strange events of the last few minutes.

"Tell me anything you are feeling," Drusilicus demanded, losing patience.

Eddie had to pause for a moment to think about it. "My tongue feels numb."

"How numb?"

"A little."

"Eddie, this is serious. Aconite poisoning can kill a man in an hour."

"Very little," Eddie said, stretching his jaw several times. "In fact, it's back to normal now."

"It was quite effective, sir," Howell croaked. Drusilicus and Eddie stared down at the man, who forced a weary smile. "It changed me back. I had no choice. And it has made me quite tired."

Drusilicus still looked stern. "Any other symptoms? Nausea or a need to vomit?"

"Not yet," Howell reported.

"Burning, tingling, or numbness in the mouth, face, or abdomen?"

"Not at all, sir, though as the lieutenant noted, my tongue felt like it was coated."

Drusilicus' mouth set in a hard line. "Most important—motor weakness or tingling and numbness of the skin?"

"No, though I do feel weak. Might you gentlemen help me stand and assist me with my robe."

Drusilicus helped Howell to his feet, and Eddie wrapped him in the robe. With a gesture of his staff, Eddie pushed open the bookcase as Howell put on his slippers. The two wizards, one on each side, helped Howell out of the tunnel and down onto the cement floor of the basement.

"It would appear, gentlemen," Howell said. "That we have created a most effective anti-werewolf weapon."

"A bit too effective," Drusilicus muttered.

"No," Howell disagreed. "If you need to stop an attack, it is merely enough."

Drusilicus and Eddie helped Howell up the stairs into a small room up on the third floor. In it, there was what looked like a hospital bed on wheels, complete with controls to raise the head or the feet. There were several machines about the room, a heart monitor and a stand that held a blood-pressure cuff and devices that Eddie did not recognize.

"What's all this?" Eddie asked as they helped Howell into the bed.

"As I told you, lieutenant," Drusilicus said, "I have attempted to help Howell in the past. We set up this room so I could keep watch of his vital signs after we tried a potion."

"Though it has been a while since our last attempt," Howell reported. "But that aerosol bomb really knocked me out. I do feel quite weak."

"We must be careful not to expose you to it a second time," Drusilicus reasoned. "It is a fine weapon in an emergency, but the wolfsbane could build up in your system, and that could be fatal."

"I don't know, Drew. You saw that thing that Matchitehew turned into last night. If he attacks police officers, that could be fatal to a lot of cops," Eddie asserted. "We need this invention of yours to stop him or any other werewolf."

Drusilicus wrapped the blood pressure cuff around Howell's upper arm, and the machine hummed and swelled the cuff. "Yes, then we could start a full-fledged war with the werewolves. Lieutenant, you may have vanquished all the vampires in New York City in one fell blow, but werewolves are heartier and possess fewer weaknesses."

"I don't want to start a war with any group, but Matchitehew threatened cops, and in case you forgot, I'm a cop!"

"As you have reminded me far too many times. If you focused on learning the skills of a wizard, instead of—"

"Gentlemen!" Howell said in a stern voice. "You are in my sick room, and the last thing I need right now is the pair of you sniping at each other."

Drusilicus and Eddie went silent and stared at Howell, surprised by this change in the usually polite and subservient man.

"Much better," Howell said, a small grin on his face. "I am going to take a little nap. Check on me in an hour if you like. You may continue your discussion downstairs, but please do so quietly."

With muttered apologies, Drusilicus and Eddie headed downstairs to the living room. Eddie immediately went to the enchanted tea trolley and ordered a coffee, which the magickal implements served him. Drusilicus got tea, and the two men sat across from each other stirring their beverages.

Eddie began, "It's good to have those inhalant weapons as a backup. I would prefer that we cure Marlowe and settle the whole thing peaceably."

"There are two of the wolfsbane spheres left," Drusilicus reported.

"Are you needed to mix the potion with the fur for Marlowe?"

"No. Ahbay or Vasant are both more than up to the task."

"Good. I'm going to head uptown. Can you make more of those spheres?"

"How many would you like, lieutenant?"

Eddie considered this. "Enough for each of us to have two."

Drusilicus gritted his teeth. "A tall order. I shall do what I can."

"If the gray werewolf arrives, we can change her to human form with that mist, and find out who she really is."

"Your partner, the good sergeant, believes that the gray wolf is Wizard Glade," Drusilicus said, sipping his tea.

"I know," Eddie said. "It is suspicious that she's been gone both when the red wolf and gray wolf show up. But I have my doubts."

"Why?"

"Because I just saw how difficult it is to transform. I don't think she had the time to go through that process so quickly and then scamper back to face us."

"You saw how quickly Matchitehew changed, and his transformation didn't seem to be unpleasant to him at all." Drusilicus frowned. "That was quite odd. As well as the creature he became, it was totally unlike a regular werewolf."

"Drew, there's more going on we don't know about."

"Let us hope we find out what we can before this night."

TWELVE

E ddie banged on the door of Marlowe's townhouse, where Wraith opened it a moment later.

"Hey Wraith, is everyone here to make the potion?"

"Marlowe and the guests are in the breakfast room—"

"Ahbay, Eugenia, and Vasant?"

Wraith nodded. "Yes, sir. But it appears we have a problem, if I may."

"Sure, Wraith. What do you need?"

"The messenger from the other night has… manifested in the basement."

Eddie turned to face the ghost. "Manifested? He's here?"

"Yes, sir, and he says he won't go away until you meet his demands. Really, he was quite rude."

Eddie let out a deep sigh. "All right, I'll go down and talk to him."

"Thank you, sir. I'll let the others know to expect you shortly."

He walked to the basement door and trudged down the stairs, unsure of what to do. If he was now bound to grant a demon a behest, would it be something terrible? And was he knowledgeable enough to grant it? He considered going to the other wizards and asking them to assist. He quickly dismissed this idea. He was the one to make the deal with the demon and he would have to handle it.

Mist filled the basement, and the cauldron was once again in the middle of the room on its raised platform. The demonic creature lay back in the cauldron like it was a hot tub, having a relaxing time, even though the liquid appeared to be boiling.

It raised its misshapen head at Eddie's arrival and peered at him with watchful, yellow eyes. "Wizard, art thou here to grant me my boon?"

Eddie stopped directly in front of the enormous cauldron. "What?"

The creature rolled its eyes, sat up, and leaned on the front of the cauldron. "You gonna give me what I want?"

"Why didn't you just say so?"

The demon gave an enormous shrug. "Most wizards expect the Oldspeak, with all the thee's and thou's. I find it pretty tedious, but hey, I make my living off tips."

Eddie nodded, trying to look sage. "What do you want?"

"You don't beat around the bush, do ya?"

"I got a lot to do today, and you're the least of it. You want it in the fancy talk? Okay…um… foul creature, what wouldst thou ask of this wizard?"

The demon smiled. "That's not bad. I like the 'foul creature,' nice touch."

"So?" Eddie demanded, his patience growing thin.

"I wanna be human," the demon said in a small voice.

"What? Like, forever?"

The creature sat up straight and waved its arms in the negative. "No, nothing like that. Just for a day."

Eddie frowned. "A day? Okay, what are you going to do?"

The creature leaned forward on the cauldron edge again. "The usual—lead people into temptation, corrupt their souls, convince them of the pointlessness of life. Y'know, demon stuff."

Eddie considered this carefully. "When was the last time you were human?"

The demon tapped his head. "I think nineteen-oh-one."

"You want this for only one day? And here, in New York City?"

"You got it. You make me human, and I may roam freely with no limitations."

"But you'll come back?"

"I would be duty bound. Hey, I got the paperwork right here. Look for yourself."

The demon reached into the boiling cauldron and extracted a scroll of parchment, which steamed as it came out. He blew on it several times to cool it, then offered it to Eddie.

Eddie took the damp scroll and stepped back to read it. It was only about a page and although the language was archaic, it made more sense than other legal papers Eddie had read in the past.

The agreement stated that the demon, whose name was Faap, was to be granted a day in human form by Wizard Berman. Upon the passing of twenty-four hours, the demon must return and resume his duties. The parchment also clarified that if the demon failed to return, the wizard would hunt down said demon and utterly destroy him.

"I kill you if you don't come back?" Eddie said, his back to Faap.

"I always come back. I like my job."

Eddie faced the demon. "What do I do? I'm not signing this in blood or anything, am I?"

"Just pull out your staff and say, 'so mote it be', and I'll take it from there."

"Do you need clothes or anything?"

"A few bucks would help. But I can't touch 'em until I'm human."

Eddie stepped back, held out his right hand, and his staff slapped into it. He allowed the energy to rise in him and all around him, and then focused on the parchment and declared loudly, "So mote it be!"

The parchment glowed, and a small tornado caught the demonic creature and spun him. Wind blew through the room and Eddie shielded his eyes from the flying dust particles.

The tornado rose above the cauldron and moved down to the floor, shrinking as it went. Then, all at once, it dissipated, and before Eddie stood an average height Caucasian man in an old-fashioned suit. Although human, his features possessed the large nose and pointed chin of the emaciated demon. At least he wasn't as rail thin as he had been in his demonic visage.

Eddie placed the rolled-up scroll contract on the platform for the cauldron, leaned his staff against his shoulder, pulled out his wallet, and gave the well-dressed man twenty dollars. "Here, will this do?"

"I guess," he said, his voice no longer demonic. In fact, he sounded like a used-car salesman. "In nineteen-oh-one, this was a lot of money, a month's pay."

"It might get you lunch, but not dinner."

"I won't have any problem. Humans are easy to trick into giving me things."

"I have other duties to perform. Allow me to walk you out."

"That's awful nice of ya."

They strode up the long staircase. Faap pulled at his fingers and stretched his legs as they went. Finally, Eddie led him to the front door and opened it for him to exit. He went with a huge smile on his face, just as Bankrock walked up the steps, passing right by the demon.

"Who was that?" Bankrock asked with a puzzled look at the retreating Faap.

Eddie watched the former demon head downtown, then turned to Bankrock. "A demon temporarily granted human form."

"Honestly, Wizard Berman," Bankrock snapped. "If you don't want to tell me, just don't."

Eddie and Bankrock headed into the large living room which was darker than usual as the curtains that covered the large windows were closed. Stepping into the breakfast room, he saw that this chamber also had the curtains closed, casting it into darkness.

Eddie was pleased that Marlowe was there along with Vasant, Eugenia, and Ahbay. The large table was leaning up against the wall, out of the way, and in its place was a small, round wooden table. On it was a bowl that contained several open cans of Sterno alcohol gel fuel and tongues of blue flame lapped at a small cauldron which hovered in the air above it.

Ahbay was standing next to the empty cauldron, looking at jars of ingredients as Vasant reviewed a parchment with Eugenia.

Marlowe sat in a chair, and Eddie worried that the old man was pale, and looked... fragile. Despite his mentor's advanced years, he had always been a dynamic man—now, he appeared smaller and old.

"Eddie," Marlowe said as he came in. "Where have you been? Wraith said you'd arrived, and I thought you would be in here."

"Clearing up a debt," Eddie said, and pointed at the hovering cauldron. "What's all this? Why are the windows covered?"

"Preparation to make the potion for Marlowe," Ahbay explained. "Vasant brought us the fur from the animal this morning."

"Some of the ingredients are affected by sunlight," Eugenia explained. "So we darkened this entire floor, to make sure they are not damaged."

Eddie nodded. "Did Vasant tell you that Matchitehew showed up in Washington Square last night? It didn't go well."

"Yes," Marlowe said sadly. "Do you believe that Matchitehew will no longer work with us?"

"I am afraid so," Bankrock confessed. "That's why I came here this morning. I have attempted to communicate with Matchitehew, and he will not respond. I also attempted to reach Wizard Glade, but she is not answering her mirror!"

"I think something is going on with those two," Eddie said. "They were far too cozy last night."

"Matchitehew has threatened to bring more of the pack to Washington Square and confront us," Vasant reported.

"What?" Bankrock croaked. "What are we going to do?"

"Right now, Banky," Eddie said. "We are going to concentrate on mixing the potion to cure Marlowe."

"I must concur with Wizard Berman," Vasant said as she moved a bottle filled with dried herbs to a spot on the table closer to Ahbay.

"Fine," Bankrock said, annoyed. "But I expect a full report after."

Eddie walked up to the Asian wizard. "Got everything you need?"

Ahbay nodded. "Yes, but I have concerns. Some ingredients are exceedingly rare and we only have enough fur for one attempt."

"But you can make it?" Eddie asked.

"I hardly think that you are in a position to question other people's potion making abilities," Bankrock grumbled.

Ahbay ignored Bankrock. "We have all the components. The colloidal silver and tincture of wolfsbane, made safe for human consumption. The final ingredient was a tincture made from Night Phlox, which Vasant also brought to us this morning."

"How are you feeling, Marlowe?" Eddie asked.

"Well enough," Marlowe waved a hand at Eddie in a dismissive gesture. "Do get on with it."

Ahbay leaned close to Eddie and whispered. "It will be a miracle if he is up to this."

"Aren't miracles what we wizards do?"

Ahbay looked sternly at Eddie. "Even wizards have limits, my friend." Eddie stepped back as Ahbay raised his hand and said, "Let us begin."

Ahbay picked up a blue bottle and poured it into the cauldron, where it steamed and hissed. Then he picked up other canisters and bottles from the table, first adding a small amount from a corked bottle, and then a liquid from a tiny vial.

An odd smell filled the air, the scent of sweet and bitter herbs, combined with the perfume of fresh-picked flowers.

Finally, Vasant handed Ahbay the animal fur held in a small plastic bag from an inside pocket of her robes and he carefully added the fur to the potion.

Now the air was filled with the odor of a wet dog.

Ahbay and Eugenia held their staffs aloft as they spoke words in an ancient tongue, reading it off the parchment Eugenia held in her hands. As they finished, they pointed their staffs at the cauldron and light flew to it, making it glow.

Ahbay stepped back from the levitating cauldron and waved at the others to move back as well. The cauldron emitted one more last flash of light before lowering to the stone floor.

Eddie, using his power over fire, gestured at the cans of Sterno and they all went out.

Vasant brought Ahbay a brass chalice, and he levitated the cauldron so that the hot liquid poured into it. Considering the amount of the ingredients, the finished potion barely filled the chalice half-way.

Ahbay returned the cauldron to the floor to cool, as Vasant brought the chalice to Marlowe, who looked down at the steaming contents.

"Whoa, Marlowe," Eddie said. "You'd better let that cool a bit before you try to drink it."

"Agreed," Marlowe said, holding the goblet by its stem.

Vasant nodded. "If we made the potion correctly, one sip should be enough."

The other wizards drew near, staring at the potion as the steam lessened and the mixture cooled. The animal smell was gone, and only the scent of the herbs filled the air.

"Well, down the hatch," Marlowe said nervously, blew on the mixture, and took a tentative sip.

Vasant put her hands over Marlowe's, and took the chalice from him, as the wizards all leaned in close.

"Could you all back away, please? You're making me claustrophobic," Marlowe said.

Mumbling apologies, they all backed a few feet away, still focused on Marlowe.

"Do you feel anything?" Eugenia asked, frowning. "Anything at all?"

Marlowe sighed. "Maybe I need another sip."

He took a step forward and all at once doubled over, making a sound like "Oof."

Eddie stepped closer. "Marlowe, are you all—"

Marlowe stood up straight. His eyes were red and his mouth opened to expose pointed canine teeth as he made a growling noise.

Eddie jumped back, his staff at the ready.

Marlowe raised his hands, and his fingernails extended into claws.

"Is that supposed to happen?" Eddie yelled to Ahbay.

"I don't think so," Ahbay replied, worried.

Marlowe extended his taloned fingers, and white energy struck out.

Eddie threw up a protective dome around himself and the others, but it was too little, too late. The dome collapsed and the force of Marlowe's powers threw them all against the wall as easily as leaves in a stiff wind.

Marlowe threw his head back and howled at the ceiling. The sound sent a shiver up Eddie's spine. The baying noise was so primal, so filled with frustration, anger, and aggression. Eddie forced himself to his feet and held out his staff as nothing more than a simple weapon, a club to stop an oncoming predator.

Marlowe's face twisted with rage, and he made an animalistic growl as he stepped toward Eddie slowly.

Vasant sent a burst of golden light at the transformed wizard, but a simple hand movement from the beast that had been Marlowe knocked the light off course and it struck the wall harmlessly. The beast gestured, and a flash of white light threw the other wizards against the wall a second time.

With a howl, Marlowe leapt at Eddie, who threw up his protective dome. Unlike the werewolves Eddie fought in the park, Marlowe passed through the dome, without even slowing down.

Eddie fell back, lifting his staff to protect his face, but the beast stopped a foot from him, clawing at the air and snapping his jaws.

"I've got him!" yelled Daniel Kraft.

The tall vampire was holding onto Marlowe's robes, using his superhuman strength to pull the transformed wizard back as he tried to claw and attack Eddie.

Marlowe turned and leapt for Daniel, but Daniel moved with lightning speed, and jumped out of the way, launching himself many feet back. Even so, Marlowe missed him by only inches.

"Somnus," Ahbay said, on his feet again, and a soft green light surrounded Marlowe. The old wizard clawed at the air, howled

again, but his eyelids grew heavy and he finally fell to the stone floor asleep.

Eddie carefully turned the old man over. His hands and features had returned to normal, but he was so pale that Eddie was afraid his mentor had suffered a heart attack.

Daniel drew closer. "Are you all right, Eddie?"

"Yes, thank goodness you were here."

Daniel knelt next to Marlowe and nodded. "I heard the howling upstairs and decided it was something bad—but this? How did he transform? It isn't the full moon."

"We made a potion to heal him from the werewolf curse," Ahbay explained.

"It didn't work very well," Daniel said.

"No, it didn't," Bankrock agreed.

Daniel stepped back to allow the wizards to get close to the unconscious Marlowe.

The others formed a circle around Eddie and Marlowe. Vasant touched Marlowe's face and pink energy of healing moved through her fingers.

"What happened to the potion?" Eddie asked, breathing hard.

"Spilled when he knocked us over," Vasant lamented, her attention focused on Marlowe.

Eddie glanced over at Ahbay. "What went wrong?"

"I do not know," Ahbay said. "We thought it would be a gentle process."

"The ingredients were meant to purge him of the beast," Eugenia explained. "Not call it out."

"The tincture of the night-blooming plant was, in part, to bring out the creature," Ahbay said.

"Yes, and the silver and wolfsbane were to force it from him," Eugenia added.

Vasant spoke up. "But Marlowe is a wizard, and the wolf seemed to manifest through his wizard powers." She took her hands away, and Marlowe's eyes fluttered open.

They were no longer red.

Eddie breathed a sigh of relief. "Good to have you back, Marlowe."

"How do you feel?" Vasant asked.

"It didn't work, did it?" Marlowe asked in a small voice.

"What do you recall?" Eddie said.

"I was going to take another sip," Marlowe said. "Now I am here on the floor."

Daniel Kraft bent and easily picked up Marlowe as if he weighed no more than a child. He carried him into the darkened living room, and placed him into one of the large padded chairs.

"What do you think happened?" Eddie asked as he followed Daniel into the living room.

Marlowe shook his head. "I sensed the beast fighting it, and it used my own magick to stave off the potion's effects."

"There was no mention of such a situation in the writings," Ahbay said, gesturing at another padded chair which floated over close to Marlowe.

"Is it possible that you are the first wizard ever infected with the werewolf curse?" Eugenia asked.

"I have lived for a long time," Marlowe said. "I know of no stories of wizards cursed in this way."

"You have to try again," Bankrock decided.

"We cannot," Vasant lamented. "We used up the fur on that attempt."

Marlowe weakly waved his hand at Bankrock. "We must make other plans, one based on the fact you may lose me to this curse."

The others faced him in stunned silence.

"What does that mean?" Eddie asked.

Bankrock met Eddie's eyes. "As you've seen, we cannot allow a werewolf to possess the unbridled power of a wizard."

Marlowe spoke up. "I must give up my position as coven master and surrender the Staff of Spirit to one who is worthy."

Eddie wondered if anyone was worthy enough to replace Marlowe.

THIRTEEN

E ddie took Bankrock aside and spoke with him for a moment.

"Are you going to tell me what happened last night?" Bankrock asked.

"Not now. You need to redouble your efforts to communicate with Matchitehew and convince him not to come to Washington Square Park tonight and definitely not to bring his pack. NYPD is launching a major offensive to take out those werewolves."

The short man grew paler. "What do you mean, offensive?"

"A SWAT team. We're talking heavily armed men with machine guns."

"Oh dear! Matchitehew will not like that."

"Do what you can," Eddie said. "We don't want anyone getting killed if we can avoid it."

Eddie went out to the street, leaving the stunned Bankrock behind. It was only noon, but he felt as if he had worked an entire day. He wanted to get his head around what to do, but it just kept spinning.

How could he avoid the SWAT team becoming engaged in a battle with werewolves? Even if there were only two, the NYPD team could be hard hit. And the werewolf curse would infect anyone who survived if they were bitten. How could Eddie, or any of the wizards, keep a lid on an event like that? The team of trained specialists would shoot the werewolves, and the animals would just get up and keep fighting. Could he switch their bullets for silver ones? And where does one get silver bullets? If he did that, then it would be the werewolves who ended up slaughtered.

On and on his thoughts rambled, not making much sense, and no logical plan coming together in his troubled brain.

The only saving grace was that this was not a world-ending event, and there was no family emergency that was part of it. The last two major wizard battles, Eddie's youngest, Douglas, had been a captive, and when he fought the vampires, Cerise was giving birth to Ellie.

So far, no werewolves had been stalking his home or his kids.

At least he didn't think so.

Eddie's phone rang, and he pulled it from his pocket. It was Cerise.

"Yeah, honey, what's up?"

"Sugar, where are you?"

Eddie took a deep breath to calm himself. "In New York, near the precinct."

"Have you forgotten? You promised to drive Douglas to his magic show. You have to leave in a half-hour to be on time."

Eddie tried to get his thoughts together. Was it Saturday already?

"I'll be there in ten minutes," Eddie said and crossed Central Park West to use the forest to return to New Jersey.

In mere moments, he was walking out of the park near his home, and saw Douglas standing outside next to his car, waiting impatiently for him.

The young man was wearing a red shirt with a fancy black vest and black pants, looking very much like a showman. He was standing with his arms crossed and an annoyed expression on his face.

Eddie fought to remain serious, as he knew his son was angry. But the expression on Douglas' face was so similar to his wife's when she was annoyed that it almost made him laugh.

"You forgot, didn't you?" Douglas said.

Eddie smiled. "No, son, I just had to take care of a few things before we go. Do you have your stuff?"

"I'll get it, now that I know you're here," Douglas said sullenly.

Eddie got into his car. He couldn't really blame his son, after all, he had promised. Another reason Eddie didn't like his wizardly duties—it made his life far more cluttered than he preferred.

While Doug collected his equipment, Eddie caught his breath and tried to slow his racing thoughts.

Douglas came out of the house with a red suitcase and another vinyl box with a handle on top. He put his equipment in the back seat, next to a speaker with a headset microphone.

"No top hat?" Eddie asked, trying to be nonchalant. "Don't you need a cape or something?"

"Dad, magicians don't do the hat or the cape, and a lot of them perform in jeans. But grandma made me this outfit and I think it looks cool."

Eddie smiled. "Indeed it does. Let's go."

The day was warmer than it had been and clear, which was good, because Douglas explained that the show was going to be outside. Douglas talked about what tricks he was going to do and Eddie nodded, but his mind was still on werewolves and wizards, and the night that lay before him.

They finally pulled up outside a white house with blue shutters on a quiet suburban street. Eddie got out of the car with Doug and helped carry the sound system, while Doug carried the cases with his tricks.

They met with the hostess and the host, a Caucasian couple. She was thin and blond and the man was big and barrel-chested. They also met the birthday girl, Susie, who just turned eight.

"You're gonna do good tricks, right?" Susie demanded.

Douglas smiled. "Nothing but the best for your party, Susie."

This pleased the young girl. Douglas chose a spot on the lawn a suitable distance from a rented bouncy house. The host put together enough extension cords to reach the small sound system through an open window.

Doug got to work as the other children arrived. The red briefcase carried a stand within it, which turned the suitcase into a table that he could open to retrieve tricks. Doug borrowed a snack table from the host and put several items on top of it: a rectangular plastic box, a round metal ball that he covered with a black cloth, a candleholder with a candle, and an empty paper cup.

Eddie hung back and watched his son. He seemed to know where everything went and which direction he should face, and it all looked very professional. He didn't know that Doug could be so well-organized considering that getting him to clean his room was a major chore.

The kids mostly focused on the bouncy house, except for one heavy red-haired kid who came over to watch Doug set up.

"I'm Sterling," the kid announced.

"Hi! I'm Doug the Magician."

"I know all your tricks," the young man said, munching on a candy bar from the table full of snacks.

Doug said. "Really?"

"Yeah, they show them all on YouTube. You're busted."

"We'll see," Doug said, staying pleasant.

Eddie felt a passing desire to transform the troublemaker into a small rodent, but decided he was overreacting.

The host clapped his hands and told everyone to sit for the show, and Douglas turned on the sound system, just as the host announced: "Here he is, Doug the Magician."

Doug had an MP3 player and hit a button, and dramatic music started. Doug lit the candle, threw fire into the air, and the candle turned into a white silk handkerchief.

Eddie watched, surprised. When did Doug learn all this stuff? He had been so busy with Ellie over the last year, his son had become quite good with his tricks. As the music finished, Doug made a coin vanish several times, and for a finale pulled it out from behind Susie's ear.

All the kids clapped except the red-headed kid, who sat there with his arms folded, looking unimpressed.

Doug did a trick where he poured two packets of sugar into his hand. The powder disappeared and then reappeared from a chosen hand, and Sterling yelled out, "It's a fake thumb. He's got a fake thumb. I know, I saw it on YouTube."

Doug seemed a bit flustered by this, but he carried on. His next trick involved a large square block with dots on it to make it look like it came from an enormous set of dice. He put it in the rectangular box with four doors on it, two on top and two in front. He leaned the box over, and you could hear the die slide, and then he opened one front door to proclaim it was gone. Soon, all the children yelled out that it had just slid, and Doug kept leaning the box and only showing the empty half until the kids were in a frenzy. Then he opened both sides completely, and the giant die was gone. He then opened his red suitcase-table and pulled the die from there.

This made Eddie smile.

For his finale, Doug put on another dramatic melody and covered the metal ball with the cloth. As the music swelled, the ball rose into the air under the cloth Douglas held.

Eddie had seen Doug do this one. The ball was very light and there was a metal wire that wrapped around his fingers and went to the ball, holding it up and putting distance between his hands and the ball. The cloth hid the wire from the audience. Eddie had seen Doug drop the ball during some rehearsals and kept his fingers crossed it would stay on now.

The kids started saying, "Let it go!" as Doug acted as if he was using the cloth to keep the ball from flying away. Then, there was a small noise, and suddenly the ball slid off the gimmick and fell to the ground, even though the dramatic music soared.

Sterling pointed at Douglas and laughed. "Busted."

Eddie looked at the fallen ball and whispered, *"Volaré."*

By itself, with no covering, the ball slowly lifted off the ground, and there was a series of startled "ohs" from the children watching. The ball rose into the air, hovered for a moment, then circled over the heads of the children, and as the music came to its climax, it flew up into the air until it disappeared from view.

At first Douglas stood there with his mouth open, but when it flew out of sight, he composed himself and took a bow, hiding the metal wire in the cloth.

An announcement of pizza being served pulled the kids away, but Sterling came up to Doug and said, "That ball was a drone."

"If you say so," Doug said, and smiled over at Eddie.

Doug packed his props, and Eddie came to help. "Dad, can you get my ball back? That cost me ten bucks."

"Sure, Douglas," Eddie said. He closed his eyes and whispered, "*Revenité.*"

Doug was looking up at the sky, and at first there was nothing, but soon the small ball appeared and returned to earth at a slow pace, hovering on its way down. The kids all stopped chewing their pizza and watched in amazement.

With a gesture from Eddie, it lowered into Doug's hand and he put it away with the other props.

The host came over and said, "That was pretty good, especially the ending with the floating ball." He slipped Douglas cash and smiled as he returned to the party.

On the drive back home, Doug was counting the money, a big smile on his face. He made fifty dollars and a five-dollar tip. Eddie was glad to see his son pleased with himself.

"You know, Dad, if you came to every show, we could do that ball trick every time."

"I think you need to get a ball that doesn't fall off the wire," Eddie suggested.

"What did you think of the show?"

"It was good," Eddie said, and his son's skills honestly impressed him. "I like the coin trick the best. How do you get the coins to appear like that?"

This made Doug smile. "It's all misdirection, Dad."

"Misdirection?"

"Yeah, I gotta make you look where I want you to, instead of where you should."

The young man had become skilled at his simple collection of tricks, and the opportunity had given him a chance to be on stage, even if that stage was a backyard.

Eddie saving Doug's trick was the first time he had used his magick and really enjoyed it. When he first got his powers, Eddie focused on being ready to go up against the Great Evil. Then he had months of studying with Marlowe and struggled to learn the words and the unique skills.

He doubted he would ever feel the joy his son had, and Douglas did nothing more than simple tricks.

"Misdirection," Eddie repeated out loud.

Eddie dropped Doug off at home and told Cerise he had to go back to work. She frowned as she knew he was supposed to be off, but she nodded and said, "Get home safe, sugar. Take care of my big, black man."

Eddie transported back into the city and walked out of Central Park to Marlowe's townhouse.

Wraith, who appeared more doleful than usual, opened the door.

"Hey Wraith, everything all right?" Eddie asked with concern.

"Wizard Berman, I heard the potion didn't cure Marlowe. It concerns me greatly," Wraith lamented.

Eddie nodded, his jaw tight. "We'll do our best to find a cure that will work."

"I hope so, sir," Wraith said as he closed the door and faded back into the wall.

"I hope so, too," Eddie murmured to himself. He headed out to the breakfast room to find Drusilicus, Vasant, Rusty, Ahbay, and Eugenia. They had returned the large table to its usual position and in the center were ten of the purple spheres.

"Drusilicus," Eddie said, standing in the doorway. "You made the spheres—and so quickly."

"I had the impression it was urgent," Drusilicus responded.

"They appear to be quite simple," Ahbay said. "And only a wizard can activate them?"

"I thought it a wise precaution," Drusilicus said. "The last thing we want or need is an accidental use of one of them, considering the effects."

Eugenia smiled. "Edward, we're so glad you came back."

"How's Marlowe?"

"He is resting after the attempt this morning," Eugenia admitted.

The others exchanged worried glances.

Vasant spoke up. "If we cannot find a cure soon, I am afraid it will be too late and we cannot prevent the change."

There was a loud knocking on the door, and Eddie returned to the door as it continued. He paused and glanced out the peephole just as Wraith materialized by his side.

"Should I open the door, sir?" Wraith asked politely.

Eddie turned to the ghost and smiled. "No, I've got this."

He pulled the door open, and a disheveled figure fell through the entranceway. Still dressed in a suit, though ripped in several places, was the human version of the demon, Faap. There was a contusion under one eye, and a minor cut on his forehead, and he looked the worse for wear.

"Faap!" Eddie exclaimed. "What are you doing here? It's only been a few hours. You still have a lot of time left on your one day as a human."

"Please, kind wizard," Faap begged. "You cannot leave me out there."

"What's wrong?" Eddie asked, fighting to suppress a grin. "I thought you were going to take advantage of the population, convince people to give you things, lead them into temptation."

"What has happened to the mortal world?" the demon cried, as Eddie helped the man to his feet. He had a rancid smell that combined fear-sweat and pepper-spray. "They used to be kind, caring. It was easy to persuade them to do almost anything—but now, they are so aggressive. I spoke to one woman, hoping to lead her astray, and she sprayed me with a foul substance that made my eyes burn and I could not breathe!"

"New Yorkers are high strung," Eddie soothed the battered demon.

"High strung? Two men pulled me into an alley and beat me, and took the twenty dollars you gave me. I have had nothing to eat! They mistreated me— I want my old body back!"

"But you've got hours left on your wish—"

"I decline my wish," Faap insisted, clinging to Eddie. "Please, kind wizard, take me to the basement and restore me to my demonic self. Hell is one thing, but there I am the torturer. Here in New York, it is I who is the tortured!"

Eddie glanced at his watch, which was more for show than to look at the time. "I don't know…"

"Please. If you do, I… I… shall assist you when you need help. Free of charge. Don't make me beg, good wizard."

"Very well," Eddie said, and helped the smelly demon toward the basement door. "But if you try to trick me again, like you did this time, I'll stick you in human form and leave you on a sidewalk somewhere."

"I shall be a good and honorable servant. I just want to be back in my comfortable demon form."

Eddie helped the limping Faap down the many steps into the empty basement. The bubbling cauldron stood in the middle of the room, the contract lay in front, as it had been when Faap had left.

"Thank all that is unholy. It is still there," Faap said and fell to his knees to clutch the rolled-up scroll to his breast.

"Now what?" Eddie asked.

"We agree to end the contract," Faap said.

"You first."

The demon stood unsteadily, looking up at the ceiling. "By mutual agreement, the two parties consent that this contract is null and void."

He offered the scroll to Eddie. "We mutually consent that this contract is null and void."

He held it out to Faap, who whispered. "You gotta say, 'so mote it be'."

"Right, right," Eddie said, and conjured his staff. He held the wood aloft and added, "So mote it be!"

Once again, the parchment glowed and a harsh wind blew through the room. The cauldron boiled and hissed. A tiny tornado lifted Faap up and surrounded him, carrying him into the air.

Eddie covered his eyes. As the wind ceased, Eddie lowered his hand and gazed at the cauldron. Faap lounged in the steaming, boiling liquid. The spell had restored him to his overlarge demon body, though looking even more scrawny and undernourished than he did before. He sighed contentedly and lay back in the bubbling ooze.

"Are we done?" Eddie asked.

"Thank you, good wizard," he sighed.

"And you are going to do something for me someday?"

Faap nodded and waved at Eddie. "I shall serve you well."

Eddie couldn't think of anything the undernourished devil could ever do for him, but he headed upstairs to rejoin the others.

As he closed the door to the basement, Eddie heard raised voices in the breakfast room. He ran in to find Bankrock was there, and the small man was quite upset.

"This has only made matters worse," he was shouting.

"Hey calm down, Bankrock," Rusty implored.

"There was nothing we could do," Vasant attempted.

"Wait," Eddie shouted, louder than Bankrock. "What is going on?"

"Going on?" Bankrock repeated. "I'll tell you what is going on! I finally spoke to Matchitehew, and he told me you attacked him with magick and silver last night!"

Eddie shook his head. "Look, Bankrock, that isn't the way it happened—"

"And I gave him your warning of heavily armed police in the park, and he blew up at me! He became incensed, gave an entire speech about hunting down his children, then ended our communication."

"That ain't good," Rusty observed.

Eugenia spoke up. "If Matchitehew fights, he could bring his entire pack against your police, Edward."

"It's called a SWAT team," Eddie explained. "Highly trained officers with some pretty impressive firepower."

"Unless they have silver bullets," Ahbay interjected, "their guns would be quite ineffective."

"It's hard to say," Eddie said. "A werewolf can instantly recover from a bullet or two, but what about hundreds of shots from automatic weapons? Not to mention the use of a grenade or grenade launcher. I doubt even a werewolf could shrug that off."

Vasant frowned and shook her head. "That would turn the park into a war zone."

"The last thing we need is open warfare between the police and the werewolves," Bankrock said, his eyes bulging.

"I must agree," Drusilicus said, and picked up one of the purple spheres. "Even this might not be enough."

Eddie couldn't agree more.

FOURTEEN

"Contact Glade," Eddie said. "She and Matchitehew got along. Maybe she can calm him down."

"She's not answering her mirror," Bankrock moaned.

"Bankrock," Eddie insisted. "You know where any member of the coven is at any time. You can enter their arch whether they like it or not. I suggest you use those talents and track her down!"

"What will you do in the meantime?" Bankrock grumbled.

"Something to help us," Eddie stated. "Rusty, can you drive me downtown?"

"Sure, my cab's out front," Rusty said with a smile.

"Great, I have to call my partner," Eddie said and pulled his phone as they headed for the front door.

"What's up?" Luis said, answering the phone on the first ring.

"I want to head downtown and talk to Caleb. Can you meet me at his apartment? I need his help and with you there, it will be harder for him to say no."

"Do you think all that crap he was saying about changing his ways is for real?" Luis grunted. "I don't think so."

"I need to see if he could make that talisman, or any talisman that might help. Rusty's giving me a ride. I'll meet you out front of Caleb's apartment."

Eddie ended the call, and he and Rusty walked to Rusty's classic Checker Cab, parked in front of Marlowe's townhouse on Central Park West. It was a thing of beauty with its enormous frame, built in the style of a 1940s sedan. It had a huge rear seat and plenty of leg room, and the exterior was as shiny, clean, and bright yellow as the day it came off the assembly line.

Eddie got into the back and Rusty started the car, flipping the flag on the old style meter to activate it.

Rusty pulled into traffic. "Downtown? You got an address?"

"Drop me off at the corner of Avenue C and Eighth Street, please."

"Sure. You think you got something to stop the battle tonight? Maybe cure Marlowe?"

"Maybe both if I'm lucky," Eddie said.

Within a few brief minutes, catching every light the right way and not running into any major traffic jams, the enchanted cab reached its destination in record time.

The meter read: $2.00.

Eddie gave Rusty a five-dollar bill. "Thanks as always, Rusty."

"I'll be in the park tonight. If you need me before then, just whistle."

Eddie stepped out, and Rusty drove away. Eddie paced waiting for Luis, finally going into a bodega and getting a cup of coffee. Luis pulled up and into a lucky open spot near the corner.

"Hey partner," Luis said. "I did a rundown on Caleb this morning."

"Really?" Eddie said. "I've been running around since seven."

"Good thing you need less sleep than me. From everything I could find, there are no complaints about Caleb's little fortune-telling booth. My friend in the Division of Consumer Protection says they've had zero write-ups, and that's unusual for card-readers and fortune-tellers."

"Did you check anywhere else?"

"I looked on Yelp, and there as well, excellent reviews. People saying he's really wise and stuff. One guy gave a one-star review, saying that Caleb tried to up-sell him."

"Up-sell?"

"Yeah, Caleb claimed the guy needed a trinket that was a lot more than he wanted to spend."

Eddie nodded. "It sounds like maybe he is doing things honestly."

"I don' know. He was a punk. In my experience, once a punk, always a punk."

They walked up Eighth Street to the five-story brownstone where they visited Caleb in the past. It surprised both detectives that the building had new locks on the door and a new intercom system. Eddie pushed the button marked "Heinz."

"Lieutenant, this is a surprise," Caleb's voice came from the speaker, without asking who it was. A buzzing sound unlocked the door, and Eddie pushed through as Luis looked around.

"Got to be a camera somewhere," Luis grumbled.

They walked up the five flights to Caleb's apartment. The hall and stairwells were cleaner than in the past and well-maintained. Someone had made improvements throughout the entire building.

Arriving at the fifth floor, Luis was breathing hard and had to take a moment to recover. Eddie, with his wizard stamina, moved to the door and went to knock on it, but it was opened by a smiling Caleb. Again, he wore a long Indian-style shirt, though a different one from their previous meeting.

"Come in, lieutenant, and you as well, sergeant," Caleb said and moved back from the door.

Eddie and Luis stepped into the apartment, and it too had undergone a surprising transformation from their last visit over a year previously. Before, it had been an unkempt bachelor apartment with a sink full of crusted dishes, dirty floors, and piles of unwashed laundry.

To say that the apartment was immaculate was an understatement. The floors gleamed with polish. Gone was the old, cracked paint on the walls, and instead it sported several coats of a warm semi-gloss. Although the main room was small, it was clean and organized, with furniture that boasted built-in storage.

"Wow," Luis said. "Did your landlord redo this place?"

"No, I did," Caleb said modestly. "I restored the floors, repainted everything. Turns out I have a knack for it."

"The entire building looks better," Eddie noted.

"I talked with the other tenants, and we worked to improve the common areas. I negotiated with the landlord, offered him my time for free. Now everyone in the building is enjoying it, and it didn't cost the landlord much, so the rents are still good."

Luis grew solemn. "Okay, what are you trying to pull?"

Caleb stared blankly. "Pull?"

"Yeah, all this 'good citizen' and 'honest business-owner' crap. You think you can fool me with any of this?"

Caleb grinned but didn't smirk. "I understand. It's a big change. But I realized that trying to be cool was not working for me." He looked at Eddie. "Actually, you made me realize it, lieutenant."

"Me? What did I do?" Eddie wondered.

"You made me see that getting a staff and using it wasn't about power. That was my problem. I wanted power, but I didn't want to change or take responsibility. After you two visited me and I figured out the vampires had tricked me into giving them my old staff, I decided I needed to do things differently. I had to open my mind and learn, so that I wouldn't get used again. Then I worked to improve my life, my surroundings, not using magick, but just the plain simple ways that anyone could. I discovered a whole new power: working with my hands, working with other people."

"Let's see if you mean it, Caleb," Eddie said. "Were you able to make that talisman that can cure Marlowe?"

Caleb simply nodded. "It's almost done. But I must warn you there is something funny about it."

"What?"

"That's just it, I'm not sure," Caleb explained. "The instructions for making the talisman were on that page, written in German. But the spell to activate it is not there."

Eddie had another concern. "Could the talisman hurt Marlowe?"

"I don't think so. There are several talismans that grant the bearer wolf-like abilities, but do not turn the user into a wolf. This binderune might have the power to cure Marlowe, or to complete his transformation. I would have to see the activating spell. The only talisman I know about that can turn a person into a wolf—"

"Is made of a wolf's pelt with special stones and medallions," Eddie said. "I'm aware of that. Someone murdered the man who made such belts on the last full moon."

Caleb frowned. "Wait. Someone killed Harold Stubbe?"

Luis turned to Caleb. "How do you know the vic's name?"

Caleb looked stunned for a second. "Um...he's a famous... uh... enchanter. You must have found some strange shit when you went into his place."

"We did. Tools and a wolf skin, but his cousin interrupted us."

Caleb frowned. "Really? Maybe this cousin has the spell for the binderune."

"I don't know," Eddie said.

"She let us look through his book, *Lupus Libre*," Luis stated. "That's where Eddie found that page he sent you."

"Do you have the rest of the book?" Caleb asked.

"We scanned it and it's on my phone," Luis said.

This made Caleb smile. "If you let me see it, maybe the spell is there. I can also explain anything you might not understand."

"Hey, when did we ask you to become part of our team?" Luis challenged.

Caleb looked at Luis wide-eyed. "I assume I became a team-member when you asked me to make you a talisman."

"No way, man," Luis said, shaking his head.

"Actually, it's not a bad idea," Eddie conceded.

"What?" Luis grunted.

"Luis, calm down," Eddie said. "He has a point. If there was anything about werewolves and spells, that book might have it. And how would you or I know what is what?"

"Drew-silly-ass might know," Luis suggested with a shrug.

This made Caleb laugh. "Drew-silly-ass? Oh, that's good."

"Let him see your phone," Eddie insisted.

"Okay, but I'm doing it under duress," Luis said, and unlocked his smart phone, went to the correct app, and handed it to Caleb.

Caleb sat back in his chair, looking at the pages, still smiling, and Eddie saw that this annoyed Luis even more.

It was quiet in the room while Caleb examined each page, nodding and frowning as he did. Luis stared at him, as if trying to remember something.

After about ten minutes, Eddie finally said, "Anything?"

Caleb looked up. "There are several spells, but they are used to activate the wolf belt, not for the binderune design you gave me to make."

"How is that possible?" Eddie asked.

"I think someone—maybe Harold Stubbe—added this rune to the book, drawn on a blank page."

"Why would anyone do that?" Luis asked.

"That," Caleb replied, "I don't know. Is there anyone we can ask?"

Eddie and Luis exchanged glances.

"I guess," Eddie suggested, "Sophia Stubbe."

"Is she the one in possession of the book?"

"I don't know how much she knows," Luis admitted.

"She knew that her cousin made the belts," Eddie pointed out.

"But when I was going through the vic's datebook—" Luis started, and then stopped and turned to Caleb. "Hey wait a minute. C.H.—Caleb Heinz!"

Caleb rose from his chair. "What?"

Eddie turned to Caleb with equal attention. "Stubbe met with a C.H. several times, according to his datebook."

"Really?" Caleb squeaked. "That's quite a coincidence."

"Coincidence, my flabby ass," Luis roared. "It was you. That's how you knew Stubbe's name! You were meeting with the guy."

With a gesture, Eddie's clothes transformed into his scarlet battle robes and his staff slapped into his hand. He held out his staff to ward off any magical attack Caleb might attempt.

Caleb, though, stepped back and raised his hands in surrender. "Okay, okay, I met Stubbe, but I had nothing to do with him getting killed."

"Christ, Caleb's been our wolf the whole time!" Luis shouted. "I tol' you he was playin' us."

"No, I'm not. I don't have a wolf belt. Stubbe was giving me pointers about being an enchanter and he was helping me with a project."

A fiery glow appeared on the top of Eddie's staff. "Caleb, if you know anything, now would be the time to tell us."

"I… can't… I swore I wouldn't," Caleb said, his hands in front of his face as if to ward off a blow.

"Well, I swore I'd give you a chance," Luis fumed. "But maybe if I beat your ass—"

Caleb dropped his arms and stared at the floor. "I wasn't trying to get Harold to teach me how to make a wolf belt. I went to him to find a cure for a werewolf."

Eddie's clothes shifted back into his suit, and his staff returned to his wallet. He put a restraining arm in front of Luis, and the two men took a step back.

"All right, let's talk about it. You know a werewolf?"

"Yes," Caleb muttered. "But she's no danger to anyone."

"So it's a she?" Eddie said.

"Isn't it always?" Luis grumbled. "So—who's leading you around by your dick?"

Caleb's head shot up. "It's not like that."

"Let's all just relax and calm down," Eddie said.

Luis went to a nearby chair and barely fit in it.

Eddie gestured, and a chair went to Caleb and another flew over to him. He sat. "Here we are, nice and calm."

"I tol' you he was no good," Luis muttered.

"It's okay," Eddie said. "Caleb wants to do the right thing. Don't you Caleb?"

"Yeah," the young man muttered.

"Who is this werewolf?" Eddie asked.

"I can't say, I swore I wouldn't tell," Caleb moaned, visibly upset.

"Okay, then tell us what you were after with Harold Stubbe."

Caleb nodded, and Eddie saw he was truly upset. "There was a rumor, more like the hint of a rumor—"

"Get to the point, please," Eddie encouraged gently.

"Okay—word was that Harold was about to get a hold of an artifact that could cure a werewolf."

Eddie and Luis exchanged a glance.

"Didn't you think that was important to tell us, right from the start?" Luis asked through gritted teeth.

"But that's just it. I didn't know what it was," Caleb explained. "Stubbe was a secretive guy, but he said that he'd recently received a book from an uncle who passed away, and that it had a werewolf cure in the back pages."

"*Lupus Libre,*" Luis said.

"But, I didn't see any cure in those pages on the sergeant's phone."

Eddie shook his head. "The last pages of the actual book were missing."

"Harold said that he had a potion from the book and had tracked down the talisman he needed to make it work."

"I take it that was before he died?" Eddie asked.

"I saw him about two weeks ago. He said he had to get the talisman soon, and that he'd let… my friend… be the first one to try it."

"Okay," Eddie said. "So when were you going to admit that your werewolf friend is Drusilicus' new apprentice?"

Caleb jumped up from his chair. "How did you—did you use a spell—how could you—"

Eddie raised his hand.. "I didn't need a spell. I'm a cop and I played a hunch."

Luis couldn't help but smirk. "From his reaction, I got to say that you were right on the money, lieutenant."

Caleb fell into his chair, forlorn.

"While you were talking, I kept thinking about the other initials in the datebook," Eddie said and glanced at Luis. "L.W., right?"

"That's right," Luis agreed.

"And the new apprentice's name is Lovetta Wynter. Why are you protecting her?"

Caleb looked up, his eyes full of sadness. "I love her."

Luis crossed his arms. "Now all these improvements make a lot more sense."

"How did you meet her?" Eddie asked.

"She came to my shop to have me tell her fortune, and I kept getting images of her as a wolf. She finally admitted she was a werewolf and had been seeking a cure for years. I was the one who encouraged her to contact Drusilicus and ask about becoming an apprentice."

"How would that help?" Luis grumbled.

"I knew Howell was a werewolf and that he and Drusilicus had been working on a potion for years. I figured if she apprenticed with Drusilicus and they discovered a cure, she could find out how it worked."

"I'm going to use your mirror and call Drusilicus, and then the three of us are going over to his townhouse to have a little chat."

Caleb nodded helplessly.

"Why didn't you want to tell us?" Luis demanded.

"Because—Lovetta is the gray timber wolf," Caleb replied, not lifting his head.

"The one who bit Marlowe?" Eddie said.

Caleb nodded.

"Well, that *does* change things," Luis growled, sounding very much like a pissed off werewolf himself.

FIFTEEN

A t the townhouse, Howell opened the door to the trio..
"Lieutenant, sergeant," Howell said, and then gazed in wonder at who was with them. "Master Caleb?"

Caleb smiled shyly. "Nice to see you, Howell."

"This is most unexpected," Howell said, but he seemed to be pleased to see the young man.

"Sorry to surprise you, Howell. Is that apprentice, Lovetta, here?"

Howell's eyes grew smaller as he observed Eddie. "She is still in classes. But I expect her shortly. Is there a problem?"

"Is Drew here? Or Vasant?"

"The master is in his library, doing research. The lady Vasant stayed uptown to assist the others in preparing for this night."

"Can you get Drusilicus?"

"Of course, sir. Please make yourselves comfortable in the sitting room."

Eddie, Luis, and Caleb all went into the large room and availed themselves of the coffee from the enchanted tea trolley.

Eddie's thoughts were racing. If Lovetta was the werewolf that bit Marlowe, was she the one who killed Stubbe? Drusilicus said that the Wizard Willowdell told them that the werewolf who killed Stubbe would be in Washington Square Park, and the timber wolf was one of them. He found it difficult to believe the gentle young woman he'd met could be their killer. If not, and it was the Eurasian red wolf, how could they track that one down?

"Lieutenant," Caleb said, "if you just let me talk to Lovetta…"

"You're going to sit there and be silent unless I ask you a question."

"But lieutenant—"

Luis leaned over into Caleb's face. "He means silent, like, starting right now."

Caleb leaned back and sipped his tea.

"Whatever is it now, lieutenant?" Drusilicus complained as he walked into the room. "I'm in the middle of—" He stopped in the doorway as his eyes fell upon Caleb. "What is he doing here?"

"Never mind about Caleb," Eddie said. "What do you know about your apprentice, Lovetta?"

Drusilicus frowned, surprised by this question. "She's a student at NYU, raised by Wiccans, and has been studying the occult for years. What of it?"

Eddie nodded, his jaw tight. "I need to talk to her, and I need you to be here. And let me be clear, this will be an interrogation."

Drusilicus lifted his head. "What on earth is this about, lieutenant?"

"You'll find out when I speak to her."

Drusilicus pressed his lips together. "Playing your cards close to the vest once again?"

"I have to, Drew."

Drusilicus turned his head and called out. "Howell, as soon as Lovetta arrives, have her come in here."

Howell put his head in the door. "Very good, sir. Shall I arrange refreshments?"

Drusilicus glared at Eddie. "Well?"

"Sure, refreshments," Luis burst out. "Why don't we have freakin' canapés and caviar?"

"Very good, sir," Howell said and left.

Drusilicus' eyes narrowed as he looked from Eddie to Luis and back. "You both appear upset. What is it? Is there something I am not aware of?"

"No," Eddie said, calming down. "I just need to—"

The front door opened and both of them stared at the sitting-room door.

Eddie heard Howell talking to Lovetta, and the young woman came in.

"You wanted to see me, teacher?" Her eyes met Caleb's and grew wide.

Caleb lowered his head, embarrassed.

"Yes, please come in, sit down," Drusilicus offered. "The lieutenant needs to speak to you."

Lovetta straightened her back, strode in, and sat on the velvet-sofa near a window covered by heavy drapes.

"The lieutenant is going to ask you some questions," Drusilicus said. "You will tell him the truth. To do anything else will not go well for you, is that clear?"

Eddie glanced over. Drusilicus' tone carried the weight of a threat. Nice to know he could let Drew play bad cop.

Lovetta sat up straighter but swallowed hard.

Eddie pulled out his cell phone and looked at the dates Luis gave him from the date book. "My partner and I have been investigating the death of that man in Central Park. In going over his date book, we found the initials C.H. and L.W."

The young woman bit her lip.

"After speaking with Caleb, he admitted he was the C.H." Eddie looked up from his phone. "Though he admitted nothing about who went with him, I surmised it was you, Lovetta Wynter."

"Why did I not know that you were in contact with a purveyor of magickal talismans?" Drusilicus barked. "An infamous dealer like Stubbe?"

"You're quite correct," Lovetta said. "I did go with Caleb to meet Stubbe, as Caleb thought he could help my condition."

This made Drusilicus frown. "And what condition is that?"

She looked at the men, stiffened her back even more and admitted, "I am the gray werewolf."

They all stared at one another. Lovetta kept her jaw tight, but Eddie saw her lower lip quiver.

"Drew," Eddie said, his eyes focused on Lovetta. "Maybe you should get one of the wolfsbane mist balls?"

"She's not a monster," Caleb attempted. "She won't hurt anyone."

"You don't need protection from me," Lovetta said, chin up. "I won't try to transform, and I won't attack you."

"Please let me go to her," Caleb begged.

Eddie met his eyes and nodded, and the young man moved to the sofa and took Lovetta's hand in his.

Drusilicus gestured at a box of tissues, which flew into Lovetta's lap.

"Thank you," she sniffled and took one.

"So, you're a werewolf?" Eddie coaxed. "Born that way?"

"No, a werewolf bit me when I was a teenager," Lovetta explained.

"How have you been able to hide this from us?" Drusilicus challenged, still obviously quite annoyed.

"In the nine months I've been here, I made up reasons to be gone during the full moon," Lovetta clarified.

"Your family emergency, your sister's wedding, all of that was a lie?" Drusilicus said, lifting one eyebrow.

"I helped her out," Caleb chimed in. "I created fake flyers for events at NYU. During the full moon I helped her get to Pelham Bay Park." He glanced over at Lovetta. "I… I love her."

Lovetta gazed at him with eyes that glistened with tears.

"How touching," Drusilicus sneered.

"You sought Stubbe because you thought he might cure her condition?" Eddie said. "Why was he willing to help you?"

"I told him a wizard apprenticed me and showed him a few of my more impressive talismans, and he respected my work. He thought I was funny," Caleb said. "I can't believe he's dead. He was such a cool guy, always upbeat, always nice."

Eddie shook his head. "I'm still not convinced he would just share something as important as a cure to lycanthropy because you impressed him with your trinkets or to play a game of brinkmanship with wizards."

He looked at Lovetta, who met his eyes. "I also told him my girlfriend was a werewolf, and I was looking for a cure to save her."

"Your adolescent love inspired him?" Drusilicus said, his voice dripping with sarcasm.

"It was more than that. He said he had recently received an ancient book, and it had a potion that could cure her permanently. He said he wanted to try it, but he had to track down a magickal talisman to make it work."

"Was the book *Lupus Libre*?"

"I never saw it," Caleb confessed. "He told me the potion was elaborate, and he needed a talisman to make it work."

Eddie said. "What talisman?"

"I didn't know that either," Caleb admitted. "I offered to make it for him, out of gold, or platinum, or whatever he wanted." He looked at Lovetta. "Anything to cure her."

"But he was unsuccessful?" Drusilicus demanded.

"I don't know," Caleb said. "The last time we saw him, weeks ago, he was really excited, claiming he'd located the talisman, and that it was here, right in New York."

"Really?" Eddie said.

"Yes," Lovetta added. "He told us he needed to get it, and that we might need to use some special talismans."

"Which talismans?" Drusilicus demanded.

"The one I made that opens any lock," Lovetta admitted. "That was why I created it, to help Stubbe with his plan."

"We didn't have a plan yet," Caleb said. "But he told me we'd need a talisman that grants invisibility."

"Sounds like it was going to be a robbery," Luis conceded.

"Okay, let's move on. Lovetta, why were you out in Washington Square Park as a werewolf?" Eddie asked.

"I told her to go," Caleb said. "I had a vision of a wolf attack in the park, and people dying."

"I wanted to use my powers to stop whoever was doing it," Lovetta said. "Caleb used his talismans and told me where to be in the park the night that Eurasian wolf attacked you wizards."

"I saw that something bad was going to happen involving a wolf, but I wasn't sure what," Caleb added.

"I saved the old wizard from that Eurasian werewolf. She's the one who's been trying to kill people."

"You bit a wizard," Eddie snapped at Lovetta. "You infected him."

Lovetta grew pale and whispered, "I know."

"That was an accident. It was during the full moon," Caleb attempted. "She doesn't have as much control as she does during the rest of the month. I mean, she fought that red wolf. It would've killed Marlowe if she hadn't stopped him."

"Wait," Drusilicus said. "You have some self-control during the full moon?" He looked up at the door. "Howell, why don't you join us, please?"

The door opened and Howell stepped in. "Yes, sir."

"Have you been listening at the door all this time?" Eddie inquired.

"Everyone spoke in raised voices. It was hard to miss, sir." Howell stated respectfully.

"Were you aware that Caleb has been romancing the young woman, Howell?" Drusilicus said.

Howell didn't speak but looked at the two for a moment. "I was... aware of some odd scents in the house, the smell of wolves. I assumed it was because of your work fighting the werewolves. I knew that Master Caleb suggested Miss Wynter as an apprentice, and I helped with the process. I also knew Miss Wynter was sneaking from the house on certain nights, but I assumed it was because she sought to be with her beau in a place where they could be… intimate."

"You knew that there was a romantic relationship," Drusilicus challenged. "And you didn't tell me?"

"May I speak freely, sir?"

"Yes, yes, get on with it."

"You have been very involved in your own romantic circumstances with the Lady Vasant, a situation I was most grateful to see," Howell insisted, and then his jaw grew tight. "As far as the young people's romance, sir—I felt it was none of your business."

"She is my apprentice," Drusilicus stated. "Everything she does is my business."

Howell lifted his chin, and his back straightened. "No, sir, some things are not."

"So, I learn of it in the middle of a disaster?" Drusilicus spat.

Eddie spoke up. "I am more interested in the fact that Lovetta is a werewolf who doesn't completely lose her humanity during the full moon."

"Yes," Howell said. "I am most interested in that as well."

The three men stared at Lovetta, who still held a crumpled tissue in her hand.

"My parents were Wiccans, and we lived on a farm in Florida, far away from anyone. All the plants my mother grew were exotic, as she was an herbalist. My father was adept at making mixtures and tinctures. During my childhood, I traveled with my parents to farmer's markets all over the country to sell their wares."

She walked over to the tea trolley to pour herself a cup. "One weekend in the summer I was fifteen, a guy came up to us at an outdoor market. I think it was in Kansas. He confessed he was a werewolf and was seeking a cure. My parents wanted to help. That night, the first full moon of the month, they... we... attempted a ritual in the woods far away from the market. They made an enchanted circle using colloidal silver in water."

"Would that work?" Eddie asked, frowning.

"It should," Drusilicus explained. "If done properly."

"Please go on, Miss Wynter," Howell encouraged.

"My parents and I were in the circle and the guy was outside of it, and he drank this tincture my father created. My parents did all the things I was used to, blessing the circle, raising the athame, and saluting the chalice."

"But despite all that, the man transformed?" Howell asked solemnly.

"Yes. It was the scariest thing I'd ever seen. He was screaming from the pain, and his body twisted and—" She closed her eyes.

"It's okay," Caleb told her.

"If I had just stayed within the circle, I would have been fine!" she stormed. "Instead, I panicked and ran, despite my parents yelling for me to stay. I didn't get far when the wolf tackled me to the ground and sank his teeth into my neck."

Her hand went to the back of her neck as if remembering the bite.

"How did you survive?" Eddie asked.

"I wore a heavy silver chain around my neck, a gift from my parents. When the wolf bit me, the silver burned his mouth, made him fall back. I crawled away and looked back to see the creature getting up with its angry yellow eyes. I screamed as it leapt for me, there was a gunshot and the creature fell."

"Your parents had a gun?" Eddie asked.

Lovetta nodded sadly. "A shotgun loaded with silver pellets. My father was a crack shot. Where the wolf had been was just a dead man. We got out of there and we never went back."

"But he'd infected you," Howell said quietly.

"I was sick for days, and while I recuperated, my parents got us home and made an enchanted circle in the backyard, and embedded silver in the surrounding dirt. Then we began monthly rituals, before every full moon, where they would feed me a potion, and we would stand in the middle of the circle and chant."

"Did any of the rituals work?" Drusilicus asked.

"No. Every full moon I would stand there, listening to them chanting, and the next thing I knew, it was morning. Sometimes, my father would find me at dawn and carry me back to my bed. Other times, I'd just wake up in the woods near our house, often covered with mud, blood… or worse."

"And the circle treated with silver kept you from attacking your parents?" Howell said.

"Yes, but I didn't know that until one night, when they offered me a special potion, made with Fire Cider, which is—"

"A classic recipe to boost the immune system," Drusilicus interrupted. "I am familiar with it."

"But my mom added something else to it. I never knew what. That night, I remembered everything. I remember changing, and God, it hurt. I could remember running through the forest, and chasing small animals, and all the smells."

"Do you have any idea what that secret ingredient could be?" Howell asked hopefully.

"I don't know," Lovetta said. "But ever since, I still change during the full moon whether or not I want to, and I feel wild, but I'm still myself."

"Howell, I take it that is not your experience?" Eddie asked.

"No, sir," Howell affirmed. "Quite the opposite. I become a raging beast."

"That's what's supposed to happen," Lovetta admitted. "After I was bitten, I read everything I could find out about werewolves." She seemed to pull herself together. "That red Eurasian wolf is not from around here. She smells of distant places."

"We still don't know who that wolf is in human form," Eddie said.

"I say it's Glade," Luis ventured. "She walked into the woods before the red wolf showed up."

"Stubbe died the first night of the full moon," Drusilicus said. "It was the last night of the full moon when Marlowe was bitten. Do we know where Glade was on those days?"

"Could the red wolf be someone who got hold of a belt?" Caleb suggested.

"He has a point," Eddie replied. "If someone ordered a belt from Stubbe months ago and arranged the pickup at the Group Of Bears Statue. He could have planned to kill Stubbe on the first night of the full moon to make us think it was a regular werewolf and not an enchanted one."

Drusilicus shook his head. "An interesting theory but all of this is merely speculation."

Luis spoke up. "What if the buyer hadn't planned to kill Stubbe?"

Howell nodded. "Yes, if it was someone who transformed for the first time, it could have been the power of the full moon that made the buyer lose control."

Drusilicus sighed. "We still don't know if there even was a buyer—and none of this helps us confront Matchitehew or his pack tonight."

"We have a weapon that can stop the werewolves," Eddie said.

Lovetta raised her head. "Really? What is it?"

"It is a potion that is released as a purple mist," Drusilicus said. "It will transform any werewolf back into human form."

"Maybe not all of them," Luis said.

Drusilicus and Eddie stared at Luis.

"What do you mean?" Eddie asked.

Luis shrugged. "I mean, what if they got one of those belts? I don' think any potion will change them back."

"He has a point," Eddie agreed. "And what about that thing that Matchitehew turned into? That wasn't a traditional werewolf."

"It could be because Matchitehew received his abilities from a demigod," Drusilicus offered.

"What if he has a belt?" Eddie surmised.

"He has been a werewolf for hundreds of years," Drusilicus sighed. "Why would he need a wolf belt?"

"Drusilicus, you saw that Hell-hound he became. It was bigger and stronger than any normal werewolf." Eddie turned to Caleb. "You spoke to Stubbe, met with him."

"Several times," Caleb admitted.

"What would happen if someone who was already a werewolf put on a wolf belt?"

Caleb glanced at Lovetta. "He never mentioned that."

Eddie turned to Howell. "Howell, what do you think?"

Howell blanched. "Why... I am sure that I would not know, sir."

"Why would anyone do that?" Drusilicus said.

"I can tell you why," Luis said. "Power."

"That's what happens when I become the wolf, I am flooded with power," Lovetta admitted. "But—I was on a mission to stop that red wolf from killing people."

"Yet, you are the one that bit Marlowe," Drusilicus said.

"I told you it was an accident," Caleb argued, rising from the sofa, as if to confront Drusilicus.

The taller wizard's eyes narrowed. "You dare speak to me like that?"

Eddie got himself between the two men. "Enough! Let's not fight amongst ourselves. I wish there was some way to get one of those belts."

"Is that what you want?" Luis said, and grinned as he stood up. "I can handle that for you."

"What?" Eddie said.

Luis stepped out of the room into the hall and a minute later, came in holding a very long belt. It was covered with a thick brown pelt and had sparkling gems and shiny medallions. "Will this do?"

"Is that...?" Drusilicus asked.

Eddie's mouth fell open in surprise. "That's a wolf belt, the one we found at Harold Stubbe's apartment," Eddie met his partner's eyes. "Did you steal it?"

"No, that Sophia lady gave it to me… as a loan."

"A belt like that is worth a small fortune," Drusilicus said. "Why on earth would she loan it to you?"

Luis shrugged. "I dunno. She started asking me if I felt bad not having any powers like Eddie, and I tol' her I wished I could help in a fight. So, she put the belt on me and said some words. Then she said, if I needed it, I could just touch it and think about turning into a wolf."

"Have you tried it?" Eddie asked.

"Not yet. I figured I'd use it if things get outta hand."

"I cannot imagine that she'd just give it to you," Drusilicus muttered.

"Well, since we have it," Eddie said. "We can test my theory that a werewolf with this belt transforms into that monster that Matchitehew became."

"How do you propose to do that?" Drusilicus intoned.

"How about Howell transforms, and then we add the belt's power to him as well?"

Drusilicus looked stricken. "That is very dangerous."

"Think about it, Drew!" Eddie insisted. "It should be safe since it is daytime and not during the full moon. We have the backup of the purple mist." He turned to the major-domo. "Howell, are you willing?"

"If it would help, sir," Howell replied after a moment of hesitation.

Drusilicus looked at Howell with concern. "No. Howell, you are still recovering from your exposure to the purple mist this morning. I will not allow this."

"No," Lovetta said, rising from the sofa. "Let me do it."

Caleb rose as well. "Lovetta?"

"You?" Drusilicus scoffed.

"Howell isn't young, and it might be a strain," Lovetta explained and stepped toward Howell. "You've always been so good to me. I don't want you to get hurt."

Howell smiled at the girl and then grew serious. "She has a point, sir."

"One problem," Luis said. "The belt has to be touched by the person it was enchanted for."

"We could put it on her and you could touch it," Eddie suggested.

"Sir," Howell spoke up. "I would recommend we use the cage in the basement for safety."

"A wise precaution," Drusilicus agreed.

"I could reach through the bars to set it off," Luis said.

"Very well," Drusilicus ordered. "Howell, bring the belt and help Ms. Wynter find something with which to cover herself, and I will get one of the wolfsbane spheres."

"What do I do?" Eddie said.

"What you always do, lieutenant. Think outside the box."

SIXTEEN

I t took almost three-quarters of an hour before Eddie, Drusilicus, Luis, and Caleb assembled in the basement to attempt the experiment. Both wizards held their staffs and were in their battle robes of scarlet and blue.

Eddie passed through the heavy metal vault door to the empty concrete space where a single cage stood in the middle of the room. The cage was not at all like an animal pen, but more like a prison cell, with heavy metal bars that were sunk deep into the cement floor. There were even bars on top to prevent escape over the enclosure.

Many scratch marks had been dug into the floor, especially around each of the bars. The lock was a heavy metal thing with electronics under a solid steel cover that had scratches as well.

Eddie looked back nervously at the outer vault door. "That can't close and accidentally lock us in, can it?"

Drusilicus glanced at the door. "It is a very special timed lock. Once started, it makes a beeping sound and you have two minutes until it seals the cage lock and the outer door until morning. It cost a fortune."

"I can imagine," Eddie said.

"I had it installed so that if I were out of town or otherwise occupied, Howell could put himself in and let himself out during the nights of his tribulation."

"Yes, but what about now?" Eddie urged. "Are we going to get sealed in?"

"The unit also has a remote control." Drusilicus held up the small, black remote. "I can close and seal just the cage or the vault door. If something goes wrong, we can evacuate the room, and I can seal it once we are out."

"But if we do, what will happen to Lovetta?" Caleb asked. "We don't know what will happen if she uses that belt. She could be stuck in here all alone."

"Calm yourself, Caleb," Drusilicus said.

"We're in unfamiliar territory here, Drew," Eddie pointed out. "I can see why Caleb is worried."

"This was your idea, lieutenant. If you wish to not go through with it, we can simply—"

"No," came a voice from the open doorway. Lovetta stepped into the room with Howell next to her, carrying the furry belt. She was wearing a pink long satin robe, made in a Kimono-style. Her feet were bare. "We must find out what happens if a werewolf uses the belt. We have to know what we might be facing."

"Very well," Drusilicus said. "But you must be in the cage."

"Is that necessary?" Caleb asked.

"I believe it is, Master Caleb," agreed Howell, handing Caleb the belt.

The three of them went into the cage, and Howell stepped out. Lovetta put her back to the others and opened her robe, and

Caleb put the belt on her waist. It was so much larger than the slim girl, he had to wrap it around twice, and even then, it slipped down to her hips.

He stepped out of the cage and Drusilicus hit a button on the remote, which made the cage door swing closed and latch securely.

"Howell, if I use the wolfsbane mist," Drusilicus said, "you are to leave the room before I do."

"I agree, sir. I shall turn on the exhaust fans in the room upon your signal."

"Why do you have exhaust fans in here?" Eddie asked.

"I have to clean the area once I am human again," Howell explained. "In wolf form, I am not...terribly careful about my bathroom habits."

"Ah, I see," Eddie said.

Lovetta got down on her hands and knees and released her arms one at a time from the robe, leaving the pink satin covering her back for modesty.

"I'm ready," she said.

"Any time," Drusilicus called back.

She grunted in pain, and under the satin cloth, her body moved and shifted. She cried out and Caleb gritted his teeth as if he shared each part of the change with her.

Lovetta moaned hoarsely, and Eddie saw the gray fur sprouting on the exposed parts of her legs. The girl let out a gasp as her legs stretched and bones cracked, shifting from human to wolf. She lifted her head and howled as her teeth elongated and her nose and mouth pushed out into a canine muzzle, the bones cracking and popping as they did.

The pink cloth slid off and the gray timber wolf was in full view, panting with the exertion of the change, the brown fur of the wolf belt in sharp contrast as it sat wrapped around her torso.

Drusilicus pulled the small purple ball out of his pocket.

"Lovetta, can you hear me? Can you understand?" Eddie yelled out. "Luis is going to touch the belt now."

The wolf nodded its head, watching them with her white eyes. She moved close to the bars.

"See if you can activate the belt," Eddie said to Luis.

With a nod, Luis reached through the bars, which were so close together, he almost couldn't get his hand through. He reached out and gently touched the belt, closing his eyes in concentration.

The creature let out a new howl of pain, as again her body twisted, grew, and changed.

Luis pulled his hand from the cage and took a step back, whispering, *"Madre De Dios!"*

Lovetta grew larger, and the muzzle shoved back into her face as the canine legs shifted into more human-like arms and legs. The feet twisted into limbs that resembled hands and claws extended into razor sharp points on both her hands and feet. Her shoulders expanded as bone and sinew shifted and crackled, continuing to grow until she resembled a person wearing shoulder pads. The hair all over her body grew longer and thicker, all gray except for two lines of brown fur along the waist.

The monster suddenly jumped to its feet and leapt at the door of the cage, reaching through the bars to grab for the men, growling and howling in its frustration.

Caleb stepped toward her, and Eddie barely had time to pull the young man out of reach of the monster's claws.

"She's just like Matchitehew was last night," Eddie said.

"Now we have an additional problem," Drusilicus said. "How do we change her back?"

Lovetta, in her Hell-hound form, smashed against the bars of her cage as the men stared in horror and fascination.

"Howell, I'm going to use the mist," Drusilicus said.

"Very good, sir," Howell said as he exited the room.

The creature that had been Lovetta was pulling at the bars and then throwing herself against the door of the cage. Drusilicus hit the remote control and the bank vault door swung closed.

"You throw and I'll hit it," Eddie said, his staff at the ready.

Drusilicus nodded and tossed the purple sphere underhand. Eddie struck the ball with a blast of red light from his staff, and instantly the room filled with a purple fog so thick that it was hard to see the cage or each other.

The creature howled and Caleb called out, "Lovetta!"

Eddie raised his staff, and the mist around the cage cleared. On the other side of the bars, the Hell-hound blinked, but remained unchanged. She started to once again beat at the door of the cage and the heavy metal bars were bending from the onslaught. She reached through the bars again, trying to claw the wizards.

"She is no longer in her right mind," Drusilicus shouted.

"I'm getting that," Eddie gulped and turned to his partner. "Luis, can you turn off that belt? Do you know how?"

Luis faced Eddie. "I have to touch it to make it work. See that band of brown fur around her waist? That's the belt."

Eddie turned to Drusilicus. "Can you do restraining bands of light? I saw Marlowe do that to the vampires."

"It's difficult with her thrashing around like that," Drusilicus said.

Eddie set his jaw. "I have an idea." He faced Luis. "If I can keep her in one place shoved against the bars, can you go around the back and touch the belt?"

"I guess so," Luis said, nervously.

Eddie lifted his hand towards the cage and yelled, *"Oppressio!"*

The wolf monster was thrown against the back of the cage and pressed against the bars. Eddie lifted his staff and the dome of light pressed up against the creature, giving her little room to move.

"Go now," he yelled to Luis, as he fought to hold the creature in place.

Luis ran to the far side of the cage, and slipped his hand in to touch the belt, but Lovetta freed an arm enough to slash the big man's hand.

Luis called out in pain, as blood dripped from three long gashes on his hand. He stepped back as the restraining light faded and the creature was free once more. She renewed her assault of the cage door, throwing herself against the bars with renewed vigor.

"You have to do something!" Caleb yelled.

"We have to remove the belt to break the spell," Eddie said.

"Brilliant deduction, lieutenant," Drusilicus said. "And just how do you propose to do that?"

Eddie shook his head, trying to think. If he could make the belt fall off the girl, the mist should make her human again. He had to undo the belt buckle even though he could no longer see it.

"Wait," Eddie said, as a thought struck him. "A belt buckle isn't all that different from a lock."

Drusilicus stared at him. "What?"

Eddie lifted his staff, focused on the brown line around the wolf's body and murmured, *"Patentibus."*

There was a slight noise, and suddenly the wolf belt fell, the heavy buckle hitting the cement with a clunk. The woman was suddenly in the middle of a metamorphosis, as she fell on all fours and sucked in a breath. An odd look went over the animalistic face and she collapsed, no longer a wolf or the Hellish beast, but an unconscious, very human, and completely naked girl.

Drusilicus moved quickly to Luis and waved his staff over his wounds, and they instantly scabbed over.

"At least I didn't get bit," Luis muttered.

Large fans whirled on loudly overhead and, in seconds, they cleansed the room of the purple mist. The fans shut down as the door to the vault opened and Howell came back in.

Drusilicus hit the button on his remote and the cage door creaked open on hinges bent by the onslaught. Caleb covered the girl with her robe, and then picked her up in his arms.

"I shall escort Master Caleb and the girl to her room, sir," Howell said, as Caleb carried her out.

Drusilicus eyed Caleb. "Very well. But Caleb, do not leave the townhouse. I wish to speak to you further about this… situation."

Luis moved to the cage where the belt lay on the ground. He picked it up with his undamaged hand and slung it over his shoulder.

"Is it wise for you to be in possession of such a dangerous talisman, sergeant?" Drusilicus asked with a raised eyebrow.

"Hey, if there's a fight tonight, I want to hold my own."

"Luis, you saw how she lost control once the belt was activated," Eddie said.

"It was hard to miss," Drusilicus said.

"That won't happen to me."

"I think there's something wrong with that belt," Eddie suggested. "Lovetta says she has control during the full moon, and yet she completely lost it when she used the belt."

Drusilicus considered this. "I would suggest that minor imperfections in his belt's design caused the situation."

"Or maybe Sophia Stubbe gave you a belt designed to make a wolf that was out of control," Eddie said.

"Why would she do that?" Luis asked. "She's on our side."

"Why did she even gift you the belt to begin with?" Drusilicus pointed out.

"You said you thought you saw her leaving Washington Square Park after we confronted the red werewolf," Eddie recalled. "What if *she* is the Eurasian wolf?"

"No, that red wolf was Glade," Luis said firmly. "And that doesn't explain why she would give me a tainted belt."

"I think it's best to leave the belt here," Eddie said.

"I shall guard it for you, sergeant," Drusilicus offered.

Luis looked at the furry belt with a longing glance, then handed it to Drusilicus.

"I just wanted to give you back up," Luis said. "But if it might make me go *muy loco,* it's best I don't have it."

"Agreed," Eddie said.

"Besides, like I said, Maria doesn't like dogs. She wouldn't want me comin' home smelling like one."

The three men headed out the vault door.

"Hey, you gonna go easy on the kids, right Drew?" Luis suggested.

Drusilicus lifted his eyebrows. "Would you feel the same if this was a police officer under your supervision who had been lying to you?"

"That's different," Luis said.

"No, it isn't," Drusilicus commented as they started up the basement steps. "One must entrust an apprentice to keep hard secrets and wield their knowledge responsibly."

"She was trying to stop that red werewolf from killing Marlowe," Eddie pointed out.

Drusilicus appeared unimpressed. "Keeping secrets from their teacher is a reason to end an apprenticeship, and it is wise to do it before they carry a staff."

"It's not her fault she's a werewolf," Luis said.

"Perhaps not, sergeant. She didn't tell us, and Marlowe became infected, and may have to give up his position as coven master. We will lose a powerful ally, as well as his wisdom and leadership, if this forces him to surrender his powers."

Eddie had no comeback for these facts as the three men reached the first floor.

In the sitting room, they found Vasant having tea. She rose as the men came into the room.

Drusilicus hugged her. "How is Marlowe?"

"Not well, I am afraid. Eugenia was watching him when I left."

"I guess we should head down to the park," Eddie said, looking at his watch as Luis nodded.

Drusilicus held up one finger, walked over to a bookcase and took three of the purple mist spheres and handed them to Eddie, who nodded and put them in a pocket.

"Lieutenant, sergeant, may I ask you both to stay a little longer?" Drusilicus said. "I think you may have insights that would be helpful."

"What is this about?" Vasant asked.

Drusilicus turned to her. "Lovetta is the gray timber wolf."

"The one that bit Marlowe?" Vasant said, her hand covering her mouth.

"She's a werewolf," Drusilicus nodded. "Bitten five years ago."

Vasant shook her head. "No, that is not possible. She has been here on full moon nights—"

"She has been lying to us," Drusilicus interrupted. "All of those family emergencies were not true, and Caleb has been helping to cover for her."

"Caleb, your former apprentice?" Vasant frowned, confused. "Why would he do that?"

"He's in love with her," Luis said.

"They've been seeing each other secretly," Eddie said. "He's the one who suggested she apply for the apprentice position."

Vasant shook her head. "I didn't know, but I had suspicions. She went to 'classes' when I know she didn't have any. And she had... a look on her face. It was obvious she was smitten."

"I didn't notice at all," Drusilicus huffed.

Vasant smiled. "Of course you didn't, you silly man. If it was a potion or a spell, you would notice everything about it. You see her as a student, someone to teach, nothing more. I see her as a young woman and know what that entails."

This made Eddie smile as he took up the tale. "We had Lovetta change into her werewolf, then we used a wolf belt on her."

"Why would you do that?" Vasant said, shocked. "And where on earth did you get a wolf belt?"

"It was mine," Luis said, raising his hand. "Sophia Stubbe loaned it to me."

Eddie nodded. "Her new form was very similar to Matchitehew last night."

Vasant sat heavily on the sofa. "Do you think Matchitehew has one of these belts?"

"It's a logical assumption," Eddie said. "He certainly wasn't a traditional werewolf when he attacked us."

"With Lovetta, the process took several minutes," Drusilicus said. "Yet, last night, Matchitehew did it in moments."

Eddie speculated. "He could have mastered the ability to shift to his own werewolf along with the power of the belt, so he instantly becomes the Hell-hound. The odd thing was that Lovetta completely lost control. She claimed she doesn't during the full moon. Is it possible the belt made the user lose control?"

"I suggested the wolf belt had imperfections that caused her to lose her rational mind," Drusilicus said. "But you could be right, lieutenant, the belt may be designed to make the wearer go mad."

Vasant frowned. "Why would Harold Stubbe make a belt that made the user wild?"

"I'd like to know that too," Luis pondered.

"What if he didn't make it?" Eddie said.

"But we found it hidden in his apartment," Luis said.

"Yes, in a size that happened to fit you," Eddie said. "And Sophia Stubbe just gives it to you? Luis, if you had used that belt, you might have attacked us instead."

"That would be bad," Luis remarked.

Vasant shook her head. "Why would the Stubbe woman do such a thing?"

"And what does this have to do with Matchitehew?" Drusilicus asked.

"Let's look at the facts on the table," Eddie suggested. "We cast the vampires out of the park last year."

"Thanks to you," noted Luis.

Eddie went on. "We have animal attacks that point to werewolves."

"All that did was make wizards concerned," Vasant said.

"Which got the wizards to fight the wolves," Eddie surmised, "and contact Matchitehew to ask him to come to New York to help."

Drusilicus frowned. "Very well. Why the brutal slaying of Stubbe?"

"I don't know," Eddie said. "But let's go on. Let's say Matchitehew killed Stubbe and got a belt that makes him the Hell-hound. Then we have the attack in Washington Square Park."

"That got the NYPD involved," Luis said.

"That's right," Eddie said. "Animal control teams, increased police presence... and now the SWAT teams move in."

"Even so," Drusilicus said. "Despite not stopping Matchitehew last night, we defeated the werewolves handily."

"Yes, we stopped a small group," Eddie said. "What if Matchitehew acts on his threat and uses their defeat as a rallying cry to bring more werewolves in to attack New York?"

The four people stood in silence.

"If they struck all over the city, all at once, the wizards would be hard-pressed to stop them," Drusilicus said.

"What would the advantage be?" Vasant said.

"I have one theory, but it's pretty dark," Eddie proposed. "What if they don't kill people, but just bite them?"

Drusilicus blanched. "That would be foolish. By the next full moon, there would be more werewolves."

"What if that's the plan?" Eddie said. "A city of eight million people, living in close proximity? Every full moon, they would infect more people. And some werewolves would hunt people down on regular nights."

"Then, what you're sayin'—" Luis gasped, "—is that Matchitehew wants to infect the entire city."

Eddie nodded. "Use the werewolves to take over New York. And by making a show of force in the park, causing NYPD to put their forces all in one place—the idea would be to infect the NYPD first."

"And as we have discovered," Drusilicus stated grimly. "We do not have a cure."

SEVENTEEN

Heavily armed officers patrolled Washington Square Park as Eddie and Luis made their way down Fifth Avenue toward the barricades. At the end of Fifth Avenue, blocking traffic completely around the square, were a group of protestors holding signs: FREE OUR PARK! ANIMALS HAVE RIGHTS, TOO! GET THE PIGS OUT! ANIMAL LIVES MATTER! The two detectives carefully made their way through the crowd to the barricade, where Eddie showed his shield to the officer manning it.

As the officer pulled the barricade aside and allowed Eddie and Luis through, the crowd chanted, "Pig…. Pig… Pig," but they just kept moving. The only people in the park were police in riot gear.

"This isn't good. The last thing we need is more people," Eddie said, shaking his head. "If Matchitehew wants to increase his numbers, he has a buffet here."

"*Qué va!*" Luis muttered. "If the werewolves bite all these people, eventually the entire city would be like that movie, *I Am Legend*, where everybody's a vampire except Will Smith."

"You got it. Except the entire city is werewolves."

Luis frowned. "Does he know you got those purple spheres that can stop them?"

"No, it's our one advantage," Eddie sighed. "But, from our experiment with Lovetta, the purple mist doesn't work on a werewolf wearing a wolf belt."

"Didn't Sophia Stubbe say that if you're a werewolf using the belt and you bite someone, you can't infect them?"

"What if you are already a werewolf wearing the belt, like Lovetta?"

Luis stared at his partner. "Then you still can infect people, right?"

"You got it."

The two men walked on, and Luis asked, "Was she awake by the time we left?"

"Still unconscious, but Caleb is staying with her."

"So Match-man is already a werewolf, and he's also using a belt?"

"It explains how he becomes that Hell-hound," Eddie said. "If they attack tonight, there won't be killing so much as biting."

"Turn the cops first, then they can spread the infection?"

"Either way, it will destroy the city."

Luis looked back at the crowd of protestors. "And those people are just sitting ducks. They'd be the first to go down. How are the other wizards coming here?"

"They're teleporting directly into the park, wearing the illusion of police in riot gear, but you and I should recognize their faces."

"Any idea how the bad guys will get here?"

"They're wolves. They'll run right in," Eddie mused. "If my theory is right, Matchitehew won't only bring more, he'll bring a lot more."

Eddie looked over the plaza, and noted that they had filled the fountain today. It did make a lovely reflecting pool, as it mirrored the sky overhead.

Luis brought him out of his thoughts. "Hey, don' they got to go someplace where they can leave their clothes and stuff?"

Eddie paused. "What?"

"The werewolves. It make sense, even werewolves got to leave their stuff someplace."

Eddie snapped his fingers and reached into his pocket to extract a small disk. It looked like a face powder compact, but inside was only a pair of small round mirrors. "I think I know the one guy who would know." He flipped open the disk and looked into the top mirror. "Rusty, I need to speak to you."

In moments, the mirror silvered over, and the face of Rusty Claremont appeared. "Hey, Eddie, what's up?"

Luis and Eddie both looked around to make sure no one was close enough to hear the conversation. "We think the werewolves are assembling somewhere downtown where they can leave their belongings."

Luis moved his head into the mirror. "Hey man! Do you know someplace real secret and close to Washington Square?"

Rusty stroked his chin in thought. "There are a lot of places in dat part of town. I mean, for all we know, they're rentin' a building."

"Someplace close, but definitely hidden," Eddie suggested. "We're dealing with Matchitehew, and he's hundreds of years old, so someplace only he might know about."

"Depends how far back ya go," Rusty affirmed. "Downtown was fashionable in the seventeen hundreds and the early eighteen hundreds. By like eighteen-fifty, it got turned into tenements."

"But are there any secret places?" Eddie asked. "Marlowe took me into an interdimensional labyrinth under Central Park."

Rusty scratched his head. "If you go underground, dere's a tunnel near da park, if you know to look for it."

"Maybe Match-guy knows about it?" Luis asked.

"Where did this tunnel come from?" Eddie asked.

"It's one of da old cattle tunnels."

"Why would they need a tunnel for cows?" Luis asked.

"Until the middle of da twentieth century," Rusty told them. "Manhattan was one a da biggest meat-packing cities in the world."

"The meat-packing district," Luis agreed. "But that's uptown at 14th Street."

"It wasn't always." Rusty went on, "In da eighteen hundreds, they brought the cows right up the streets from da downtown ferries, stopping traffic all de time. Lemme tell ya, as a cabbie driving a hackney carriage, they were always slowing things down. Later, the city laid steel tracks for da streetcars, so between the streetcars, carriages, and da cattle mucking up traffic, da rich folk complained. Slaughterhouses all got together and dug tunnels underground, took the cattle right to the butchers so you never even seen 'em. Of course, you sure could smell 'em."

"Are you saying those tunnels still exist?" Eddie asked.

"Yes, and no. When the subway system got built, they used several of the tunnels dat were already there and closed the rest," Rusty explained. "Over da years, things got built on top of them but there's still a cow tunnel between da Christopher Street and da West Fourth Street subway stations."

"The West Fourth Street station is only two blocks from Washington Square," Luis noted.

"If they came from there, they could approach the square as wolves quickly," Eddie pointed out.

"Yeah, but I ain't sure how you get in or out," Rusty admitted, and looked troubled. "For all I know, they coulda built over dem tunnels."

"Eddie, you got a spell to reveal stuff?" Luis asked.

"No, but Rusty, you can see any road, even when it's hidden," Eddie said. "Maybe you could find this tunnel and its exits."

"I dunno." Rusty said. "I could try."

"Can you meet me at Sixth Avenue and 4th Street?" Eddie asked.

"Gimme a few minutes," Rusty said, and the mirror silvered over.

Eddie looked at Luis. "You want to come?"

"Someone should be here to meet with your wizard posse," Luis remarked.

"I don't like leaving you alone with the werewolves on their way."

"It ain't dark yet," Luis said, looking up at the setting sun. "I'll meet Drew and the others and stick with them."

"Okay, partner. I'll let you know anything I find."

Eddie went through the police barricade at West 4th Street and headed toward Sixth Avenue. As he turned the corner, a large yellow Checker Cab pulled up to the curb and parked in a conveniently open parking space.

"You're lucky that space was there," Eddie said as Rusty got out, took off his yellow cap, and threw it into the car, hanging the large ring of keys on his belt.

"What's luck got to do wid it?" Rusty said. "I arranged for the spot on my way here."

This made Eddie smile. "Your wizard powers come in handy for a cab driver."

"Use what you got, I always say. So where are we lookin'?"

"Wouldn't the first thing be to go down in the subway?"

"You got tokens?" Rusty said.

Eddie chuckled. "Rusty, they stopped using tokens about thirty years ago. I've got my OMNY card on my phone."

"Your what?" Rusty scowled.

"It stands for One Metro New York, and I can use it for buses, subways… pretty much everything on public transportation."

Rusty shook his head in disgust. "I'll stick to drivin' my cab."

"Let's head to the entrance on 3rd Street—"

Eddie glanced across Sixth Avenue where there was a brownstone with a bank on the street level and three floors of apartments above it. A man walked up to the side of the building, which was painted with a street artist's graffiti. The man paused for a moment, then walked into and through the brick wall.

Eddie grabbed Rusty's arm. "Did you see that?"

Rusty looked across the street where Eddie was still staring. "No, what?"

"A guy just walked into that wall," Eddie said, and pointed at the side of the bank building.

Rusty looked over, narrowed his eyes, then relaxed and smiled. "I think we found what we're looking for."

They crossed the street. There were two stained glass windows built into the wall with intricate designs in heavy leaded colored glass of green, brown, and tan. The colors formed floral shapes with three lines and a circle at the bottom of each.

There was plywood behind the glass to discourage anyone from breaking in.

Rusty stared at the wall. "Yeah, I can see it, a staircase behind that wall. I shoulda known, this is the obvious place. Did the guy walk right between these two windows?"

"I think so," Eddie replied.

"Yeah, well back in the thirties and forties, this was one of da exits from da subway station. Dat's why the glass windows are there, trying to make the subway exit look snazzy."

Eddie put his hand against the wall. It was quite solid.

"I don't see how he could've got in. Do you suppose he had a talisman?"

"Maybe, or maybe someone enchanted the entrance to let you through only if you're a werewolf."

"How?"

"Look, werewolves are all infected with dat virus, right? Maybe somebody put an enchantment that allows you through if you got that virus."

"That would take a wizard, right?" Eddie thought about Glade. Could she have set this up for Matchitehew?

"An enchanter could do it, if they had the right spell, and the right talisman," Rusty said, running his hand up and down the brick wall of the building. "But it ain't gonna stop us."

Rusty touched the ring of keys on his belt. There was a rabbit's foot hanging from the ring, and Rusty put his hand on it as he closed his eyes and mumbled a few words. He then opened his eyes and said, "You go first."

"What did you do?"

Rusty winked. "I surrounded us with the illusion that we got werewolf DNA."

Eddie carefully reached out to touch the wall, and his hand disappeared into the brick. He pulled his hand back with a gasp. "Is it safe?"

"Yeah, but get all the way through and you'll be near da top of a set of stairs, so don't move forward too far."

Gathering his courage, Eddie took a deep breath, set his jaw, and walked into the wall—

—and right through it.

Immediately, there was nothing but darkness all around him. Without hesitation, Eddie called forth his staff and lit a small ball of light on top of it, stepping to the side in case Rusty came through in the same place.

This proved to be a wise choice as Rusty appeared directly next to him.

"Fade the light," Rusty murmured. His voice, though quiet, echoed down the enormous staircase before them.

Eddie made the light less bright, yet still enough to see the steps. They had about four feet of pavement and then old concrete stairs went down into an underground area. The steps were long neglected, the concrete worn and cracked, and the guardrails on each side were rusty with one fallen loose at the bottom of the steps.

"How should we proceed?" Eddie asked.

"We use da invisibility spell," answered Rusty, as the rabbit's foot on his key chain grew and became his staff of wood.

"It's werewolves—they can still smell us."

"I'll create the smell of dogs around us. They'll think we're just anudder werewolf."

Eddie frowned. "We can do that?"

"Sure. It's da same way wizards who pretend to be homeless create the body odor smell around them." He pulled Eddie forward toward the stairs. "Let's move before someone else arrives and sees us. If they are planning an attack, there could be quite a few people comin' down here."

Eddie and Rusty both waved their staffs, and mists appeared around them—which let Eddie know they were now invisible. They carefully went down the staircase, staying close to the walls to be out of the way of anyone else who used the stairs.

The staircase led to a lower tunnel with cobblestones on the floor like a street from a century earlier and unfinished wood planking on the walls. The roof of the tunnel was over eight feet tall and also made of planks of raw wood. There were upright timbers that acted as supports on the walls that braced the roof and held up the dirt overhead.

There was a musty smell, as if someone had not aired out the tunnel in a long time. An animal smell like an old barn made it worse, as well as the scent of dogs.

Voices came from down the tunnel and Eddie, staying close to Rusty, moved in that direction. They soon arrived in a large open space, where twenty or thirty people were milling around. There were large wooden storage units about the room, each one with multiple cubbyholes. People were placing some of their belongings, like handbags and phones, into individual compartments, while they spoke in low tones.

Several participants put their shoes in their storage spaces and were walking about barefoot on the cobblestones. There were several battery powered lights around the room, but it was still dim with shadows in much of the space.

Rusty and Eddie moved carefully to the far side of the room, so someone didn't accidentally walk into them in their invisible state.

Eddie felt the three purple spheres in his pocket. It would only take one of them to fill this room with the mist and stop this entire group if it came to that.

"Why are they human?" Eddie whispered.

"Waiting until nightfall, I guess," Rusty replied. "Do you see Matchitehew?"

"He'll be here or he'll send someone. These are his faithful, and he's got to get them worked up for the attack."

The two men, unseen by the others, watched as the group interacted with one another. Some of the more fit men and women were doing stretches as if they were a dance company preparing for a show.

"Listen up, everyone," came a voice from the tunnel.

Into the room walked the man Eddie thought of as Biker Guy. In leather pants, tall boots, and a leather vest open in the front exposing his washboard abs and muscular arms, he looked like he'd be at home on a Harley. His shaved head reflected in the dim light and his big black mustache moved as he spoke.

This was the man who had turned into the large black werewolf.

"Matchitehew has sent me to speak with you," Biker Guy said and with nimble reflexes, jumped onto a raised platform along the far wall. "I take it you all heard what happened to our brothers and sisters last night?"

An angry roar came from the crowd.

"The cursed wizards attacked them and used silver to wound one of our own and strip her of her Wolfen powers!" he yelled.

The crowd voiced another set of angry howls.

"Now, they send more police to shoot at us and lock us in cages," Biker Guy yelled. "Our leader will not let this go unchallenged. Tonight, we will attack the park, and we shall strike the wizards first."

Eddie and Rusty stood frozen as the crowd went wild.

"Stay here," Eddie said under his breath. "Unless I'm in trouble."

"How will I know if you're in trouble?" Rusty hissed back.

"You'll know," Eddie said, and stepped forward, simultaneously shifting to his battle robes and dropping the veil of invisibility. With a slight movement of his staff, a ring of fire appeared around him in a flash that drew the attention of the entire crowd.

Eddie lowered the flames to waist level and faced the group. The crowd wore shocked faces realizing a wizard was in their hidden lair.

Eddie spoke in a loud voice. "I am the Wizard Riftstone." Eddie's true wizard name always sounded more impressive than his own. "I speak for the wizards and we have no wish to engage in battle with you. Disband at once, leave this place, and we shall all go in peace. Do not attack the NYPD, they are merely trying to protect the innocent."

Eddie saw some people pulling off their clothes in preparation to change into wolves.

Biker Guy turned to Eddie, pulling off his leather vest. "I will taste your blood, wizard."

Eddie sent another burst of fire around himself which made the group freeze. "This is my final warning. Hear me or it shall not go well for you." Eddie pulled out one of the purple spheres and clasped it in his hand.

"The wizard cannot stop all of us," Biker Guy sneered. "Come my friends, who will join me in taking him down?"

Looking around the room, Eddie saw that several people were changing, their flesh shifting, bones cracking, and muzzles appearing where mouths should be.

"Very well, let this be on your head," Eddie announced, then gave the sphere a light underhand toss and used his staff to blast it.

The sphere exploded, making a 'whump' as purple mist instantly filled the large chamber. The gathered group stared in shock and Eddie heard coughing, while others made odd choking noises.

Eddie quickly pushed the mist away from around himself, as he couldn't see if someone was moving toward him to attack.

Bursting through the fog was not the black, shiny werewolf that Biker Guy had been the previous night, but an overlarge Hell-hound. It sprinted into the open space and faced the wizard. It was not as large as Matchitehew had been, but Eddie saw that black shiny fur covered it, except for a ring of brown fur around its waist.

"Oh, shit," Eddie muttered. "He's got a wolf belt."

Eddie barely had time to erect a dome of protection before the creature leapt through his protective ring of fire and tackled Eddie to the ground, biting at the bubble of red light viciously.

People were running all around, trying to escape the magickal vapor and the enclosed room as Eddie lay on the ground, stuck in his dome with the enormous Hell-hound atop him.

There was a blast of yellow light, and the wolf went flying. Rusty stepped forward in his bright yellow battle robes, his staff at the ready.

The Hell-hound rose to its feet and with a roar, it leapt for the wizards again. Rusty merely gestured, and threw the canine across the room a second time.

Rusty approached with his staff aloft and held the fallen werewolf in a bubble of yellow light, pinning it to the floor.

"Change back," Eddie demanded. "We need to talk."

The wolf just growled.

"What can we do?" Rusty asked.

"I learned a little trick today," Eddie said. "Let's see if it works on him." Eddie held out his staff and whispered, *"Patentibus."*

Suddenly, there was a 'click' as a buckle opened and the wolf belt fell open. The monster's body began to shift and change, moving into wolf form. Since the purple mist was still in the room, in moments it was just a man lying on the cobblestone floor.

He still wore his pants and boots, and Eddie realized that the magic belt allowed a person to change even fully clothed.

Eddie dropped his dome of light. "Rusty, see if you can help the unconscious."

People were still coughing, and Rusty merely whispered, *"Ventus."*

A wind blew through the tunnel and room, sending the purple smoke out and away.

There were at least a dozen people still there, some on their knees coughing, several laying on the cobblestone floor, unconscious.

"You got a name?"

"I don't have to tell you shit," the man spat as he lay on the floor.

"Talk to me and we will leave you unharmed and go. Or I can show you some tricks I know with fire," Eddie said, his jaw tight, and he saw fear in the man's eyes. "What do you mean, telling these people that the wizards are hunting them down?"

"Because you are. That's why there were wizards in the park during the last full moon. You were after us." Then he smirked. "That's how one of your own was bitten."

"There was an animal attack in Central Park—the man killed is the one who made your wolf belt."

"Says who?" he replied, smirking again.

"Okay, where did you get it?"

"I got the right to remain silent. Besides, you're preparing to exterminate us."

"What?"

"As your attack today proves," Biker Guy replied and set his jaw. "Maybe we had someone lose control, but it was that gray bitch that bit the wizard."

"Why attack us at all?" Eddie persisted, he stepped back.

Biker Guy got to his feet. "You wizards are planning to chase us out of New York, from all the parks, get rid of us."

"Why do you think that?" Eddie said with a frown.

"You killed off all the vampires. Now you want to get rid of us," he said, as he picked up his leather vest and put it on. "That's what Matchitehew says."

"We didn't want to kill the vampires. They gave us no choice. Besides, the wolves and the vamps never got along."

"So now you're after us."

"I think Matchitehew is out for himself, and he's using you. What do you get out of this plan of his?"

"You think you know his plan?" Biker Guy sneered.

"Yes, to turn New Yorkers into werewolves. To spread the infection throughout the population, starting with the NYPD."

Biker Guy's mouth fell open in surprise, which Eddie found very gratifying.

He quickly recovered. "It's a goal I agree with. We turn Manhattan into the island of the wolves."

"It's a stupid plan."

"Because regular people will get killed?" Biker Guy snickered.

"No, because it will get the werewolves killed."

Biker Guy's tone became mocking. "I thought you didn't want to kill us."

Eddie shook his head. "You just don't get it, do you? What will happen if you bite people and they change? I give you a month, maybe two, before the authorities bring the army in here and annihilate all of you."

Biker Guy frowned. "That wouldn't happen…"

"Or let's say you infect the entire city. Do you believe they won't nuke NYC to end the infection and prevent it from spreading?"

Biker Guy gave Eddie a dirty look, but in his eyes, Eddie saw the dawning realization.

Eddie went on, "Werewolves have survived because they have lived in secrecy and hidden their curse—"

"It's not a curse!" Biker Guy snapped.

"All right, blessing, powers, whatever you want to call it. Exposing yourself and attacking people will not end well, because if the wizards don't stop you, other people will."

Biker Guy glared at Eddie. "You done? Can I go now?" He bent to pick up the fallen wolf belt, and Eddie put his staff on it, pinning the furry strap to the floor.

"Tell me who made your wolf belt and you can go," Eddie demanded.

"Like I would tell you," he said.

"Okay then, I'm keeping the belt." Eddie asserted.

Biker Guy spat on the ground and headed toward the way out without a look back.

Eddie picked up the belt, threw it over his shoulder, and walked over to Rusty, who was helping a half-dressed woman to her feet.

"You just going to let him go?" Rusty said nodding toward the retreating Biker Guy.

Eddie held up the belt. "He's no threat without this. He'll tell Matchitehew what I said, that we know his plan, and that we have the mist to stop him. Maybe that will dissuade them from attacking tonight."

The woman, a scrawny blonde with dirty fingernails who stood unsteadily, looked at Eddie through half-closed eyes. "No man—we're gonna strike a blow, get the respect we deserve."

Rusty murmured to Eddie, "A true believer." He then faced the woman and asked, "You gonna be okay?"

"I feel weird. I can't feel my wolf."

"It's temporary," Eddie assured. "You might not be able to change for a day or two."

She moved to the raised platform Biker Guy used, picking up a pair of jeans as she sat and slipped them on.

The two wizards looked around the room. Everyone who had been unconscious was waking up and being helped by their friends. All of them glared at the two wizards angrily.

"Well, at least tonight's attack is a bust," Rusty admitted.

"I don't know. Matchitehew wasn't here and neither was Biker Chick."

"Biker Chick?" Rusty repeated.

"One of Matchitehew's lieutenants. There could be another group," Eddie said. "We should head back to the park, just in case."

As Rusty led the way back to the stairs and the hidden entrance, Eddie shifted his clothing back to his suit as he extracted the small round mirror from his pocket. He called out for Drusilicus, and soon the other wizard appeared in the glass.

"Yes, lieutenant?" Drusilicus said.

"Drew, Rusty and I stopped a group getting ready to attack the park. Matchitehew's bodyguard had a wolf belt." Eddie patted the wolf belt that sat on his shoulder for emphasis.

Rusty stopped at the foot of the stairs and looked into the small mirror. "He's right. Da guy became da Hell-thing and attacked us right through da mist."

Drusilicus scowled. "What? How?"

"He didn't say. Perhaps he's the one who bought it and killed Stubbe," Eddie explained. "We stopped him, but we now know for certain that in combat, the purple sphere does not affect anyone with a wolf belt."

Drusilicus looked stunned. "Where are they getting all of these belts? Does Matchitehew have a wizard assisting him?"

"I don't know," Eddie finally replied. "But he and Glade were pretty chummy last night. Rusty and I are on our way to meet you in Washington Square."

"Make haste, lieutenant," Drusilicus said as the mirror became reflective again, and he faded from view.

EIGHTEEN

A s Eddie and Rusty passed through the magical wall and onto the sidewalk, the sun was setting, and they immediately headed for the park.

"Will your cab be all right?" Eddie asked as they passed Sixth Avenue.

"Yeah, after seven, there ain't no parking fee."

The wooden barricades with uniformed NYPD officers were keeping people out of the park, and in the plaza, near the fountain, were two large step vans.

Arriving at the barricades, Eddie flashed his shield and an officer moved the barrier out of his way so he could get in.

As they approached the plaza, Eddie noted that besides the step vans, there were now several light towers high overhead—wheeled units that ran off diesel generators, and the roar of the gas-powered engines filled the park. There were four of them, each pointed in a different direction, and the blinding lights cut through the gloom of the wooded pathways, eliminating every shadow.

Milling around the vans were men and women in dark blue uniforms, each wearing kevlar vests that read POLICE in reflective white letters. They each had a radio microphone near the shoulder on the vest. Each member of the team wore a helmet, a black balaclava, and gloves. Along with their side arms and supply belts, several carried M-4 carbine semi-automatic rifles.

It looked like an army had invaded the park.

One step van was open and had built-in benches where officers were sitting. The second van had a large dish and several antennas on the roof. Inside that van would be men and women stationed at computer screens and relaying information to the force.

He heard a buzzing sound over the diesel generators and looked up to see drones aloft above the park, getting a bird's view of the park and its surroundings.

Detective Brad Thomas was standing next to a big man with sandy hair and a full mustache, wearing the SWAT gear as if he'd been born in it.

"Here's the LT from the Central Park Precinct," Thomas said, and pointed to Eddie, who gestured to Rusty to stay back as he approached. "He's been on patrol the last couple of nights, and his report was why we brought your team in. LT, this is Captain Harris."

"Captain," Eddie said and offered his hand.

"Lieutenant," Harris replied, and took Eddie's hand in a firm shake.

"I need to call my captain," Brad Thomas said. "I'll let you two talk."

As Thomas walked away, Harris said, "You gonna tell me what's going on, or give me more bullshit, like the detective?"

"I would love to tell you what is going on, but I am still trying to figure it out myself," Eddie said.

This elicited a tiny smile from Harris. "At least you're honest about it."

"Look, captain, I will be honest with you. I was against the SWAT team from the beginning. What we had in my patrols was a pair of wolves in the park. I saw them."

Harris glanced at Eddie. "Well, now that the mayor's office is involved, we have to end this and fast. Do you want to be onsite?"

"Yes, sir, captain, if you don't mind."

"Stay close to the vans and get a vest," Harris ordered and glared at Rusty, who stood several feet away. "Who's this guy?"

"Doctor Claremont," Eddie said, thinking fast, and signaled Rusty to walk over. "He's an animal behavior expert. I thought he might offer some insights."

Rusty took the hint and nodded sagely.

"All right," Harris said. "Get yourself and the doctor a vest and stay close to the vans. Doc, can you identify these creatures if they show up?"

"I'll do my best," Rusty promised.

"You'll excuse me. I have to get those protestors moved out, and make sure we're ready if those animals show up."

"Any of the protestors being a problem?" Eddie asked.

"Not so far, but things can change," Harris said, and put a finger to his earpiece, then touched the button for his microphone. "On my way." He looked at Eddie and Rusty. "Duty calls."

He strode off toward the northern side of the park, where uniformed officers were working to remove protestors.

Rusty turned to Eddie. "Doctor Claremont?"

"He accepted you, didn't he?"

Rusty shrugged, and the pair headed for the larger van, where Eddie showed his shield and requested a pair of police vests.

Putting them on over their clothes, they walked to the arch, where they saw Luis waiting with two SWAT officers. The officers were actually Drusilicus and Vasant, surrounded by the illusion they wore tactical uniforms.

He handed Drusilicus the wolf belt, which made his eyebrow raise in surprise. "My, we are getting quite a collection of these."

"It is better if we have them, and not the wolves," Vasant said.

Luis drew close to Eddie. "I heard you tracked down the bad guy's lair."

"We sure did," Eddie said, "and hit them with a dose of the purple mist."

"Outta twenty or so," Rusty added, "none of them can become a wolf, tonight."

"But you think Matchitehew is bringing more werewolves here?" Vasant observed.

"I don't know," Eddie said. "That's our problem. We know what Matchitehew is planning, but none of the details. So far, we've faced two people who have wolf belts, which, combined with their own werewolf powers, turns them into those Hell-hounds." Eddie looked around the square. "If even one of those Hell-hounds was loose down here, the loss of life would be tremendous."

Drusilicus set his jaw and nodded, looking around at the police and the protestors.

A large rental truck, one that could move the contents of a small house, caught Eddie's eye as it turned off Sullivan Street on the south side of the square and turned right onto Washington Square South.

Luis was by Eddie's side in a flash. "What is it?"

"That moving van," Eddie said, pointing at the large vehicle.

Two uniformed officers attempted to wave the truck on, but it drove right at them, and the two men had to jump out of the way as the truck crashed into the wooden barricade.

The driver opened the door. It was Matchitehew's female bodyguard, the woman Eddie had nicknamed Biker Chick.

"This is it," yelled Eddie, and ran across the plaza, Luis lumbering by his side. Rusty, Drusilicus, and Vasant ran after them. As they drew close, several other officers moved on the truck, raising their semi-automatic rifles as they did.

Biker Chick went to the back and threw open the roll-up door.

With a cacophony of growls and howls, wolves sprang out of the back of the truck, jaws open, teeth bared, and hackles raised. The unnatural sound made even the strongest men freeze in place, and Eddie felt his knees go weak.

At that moment, there was a flash of gray light over the entire park. Eddie watched as the leaping wolves slowed. They stopped all forward momentum and hung in midair, frozen in place. Eddie glanced about to see that Luis also slowed in mid-stride and was stuck in one position like a mannequin.

Eddie, however, found he could move, and he turned to look back at Vasant.

She stood with her legs straight, her arms up in the air in her wizard robes, all illusions gone. Her raised staff shone light as bright as an aurora borealis, and she had her jaw set and her body tense.

"What is she doing?" Eddie shouted.

"She's freezing time," Rusty barked.

Eddie turned to the cabbie, who was also now in his robes with his staff as well. "We can do that?"

"Yeah, but not for long," Drusilicus said, concern showing on his face.

Rusty shouted. "We gotta get da wolves back in dat truck."

Without another word, Rusty stepped toward the truck slowly like he was walking underwater, but with a flick of his staff, one of the frozen wolves flipped end over end and tumbled back into the box truck.

Eddie walked as well, but felt the air resist his forward movement, and he had to force his way through it. He focused his attention on a wolf that was inches away from biting one of the uniformed policemen, its jaws open and a drop of drool hanging from its mouth. With a gesture, he made it levitate back into the truck.

"Please hurry," Drusilicus shouted. "She cannot hold it."

Eddie glanced back to see that Vasant had fallen to her knees from the strain. Drusilicus was behind her, energy flowing from his own staff to reinforce her power.

Eddie flung the unmoving canines back into the truck as quickly as he could, ducking under the wooden barricade as he did.

Rusty aimed a blast of his staff at Biker Chick and shoved her into the back as well. Eddie drew close, tossing the last of the wolves into the truck. He climbed up the three metal impact bars that formed the truck's rear bumper, stood on the platform, reached up to grab the handle and yank the roll-up door down.

It wouldn't move.

Eddie shouted, "It won't come down."

"It's da time freeze," Rusty yelled. "Da door won't move until it's over."

They both turned to see Vasant collapse, which instantly made the sky clear.

The wolves and the woman were falling all over themselves inside the box truck, as they ceased being frozen.

Rusty raised his hand and yelled, *"Oppressio!"* which threw the animals and woman farther back into the truck.

Before the wolves and Biker Chick could get up, Eddie grabbed the handle of the roll-up door, slammed it down with all his might, and threw the latch to secure it.

Immediately, there was the sound of banging and howls from inside.

Rusty, now wearing the illusion of a SWAT team officer, sprinted away from the truck and back to Vasant, who lay unconscious.

Captain Harris, also in an unfrozen state, ran to the barricade and yelled to Eddie, "What the Hell just happened?"

Thinking fast, Eddie shouted back, "The driver ran away! I think it's a truck bomb. I have to get it out of here."

He glanced over and saw Rusty and Drusilicus pick up Vasant, and the three of them simply disappeared. Eddie assumed they used the invisibility spell to hide their retreat from the park.

Without another word to Harris, Eddie ran to the front of the truck, and was relieved to see that the keys were still in the ignition.

He hopped in the driver's seat and started the vehicle, as the banging on the walls of the box truck continued.

Luis yanked open the passenger door. "I'm coming with you."

"Luis, I need you to stay here. Make up a story to explain what happened."

"I don' like you going with them alone," he growled, with a glance at the back of the truck where howling and thumping was still taking place.

"I know where to take them," Eddie said, "and I have a better chance of being unhurt alone. I'm sorry, Luis, but I need you here."

Not happy with his mission, Luis stepped back and shut the door. Eddie slammed the vehicle into drive and pulled out and away from the barricade, carefully maneuvering his way down West 4th Street, avoiding the cars parked so close on both sides.

Stopping at the traffic light for Cooper Square, he headed north, got on Third Avenue, and soon pulled onto the FDR North. As he drove, the howling and banging against the walls continued. At this time of night, the traffic was light, and he soon travelled over the Robert F. Kennedy Bridge and was on the Bruckner Expressway, getting off at the Pelham Bridge exit, where he pulled the truck into the expanse of Pelham Bay Park.

The streets of the park were in total darkness, except for the truck's headlights as Eddie drove deeper and deeper into the vast expanse. The trees faded in the blackness and their silhouettes stood out like an attacking army as Eddie pulled the vehicle into the empty parking lot for the Split Rail Golf Course.

Something jolted the truck, and Eddie saw the passenger seat pushed forward. There was now a hole in the metal and wood wall, and a muzzle poked into the cab, growling and snapping at the empty air.

Eddie grabbed the van keys, opened his door, and pulled himself up to the roof of the cab. The truck pitched to the left and right from the powerful creatures moving about inside, throwing themselves against the sides and back seeking release.

He wanted to stand up on top of the cargo hold, but it was being jostled so much he crawled. At the back of the truck, he hastily called forth his staff and with a simple gesture, he made the lock release and rolled the door open.

An explosion of animals leapt from the confines of the truck, growling and baying, worked into a frenzy.

One wolf saw Eddie, and with amazing strength, vaulted from the ground to the top of the truck, where Eddie smacked the creature in the head with his staff and it fell to the ground, whining.

"Hear me!" Eddie yelled, and the animals faced him, haunches raised and teeth showing. Eddie held his staff aloft and send a blast of fire into the night sky. This got the attention of the animals and they grew silent. Biker Chick was amongst the group as well, and she had remained in human form, but her hair was a stringy mess.

Eddie reached into his pocket and felt the mist sphere that was there. He could use that to transform these wolves back into people, but in this open space he might miss one, and even one werewolf could kill him.

Eddie shouted down to the crowd. "I could have burned that wolf just now. I could burn you all if it were my wish, and then your threat would be gone. However, the wizards do not seek to injure you. We do not seek battle with you. We are here to protect the mortals. You are free to go, but if you attack, the other wizards and I will be there. We shall not be so merciful next time."

Eddie threw another blast of fire into the sky to make his point. He hoped that since it wasn't the full moon, the wolves maintained enough of their intellect to understand his point without having to make good on his threat.

Many of the wolves got down on their haunches and growled. Then, one at a time, they slowly headed into the nearby woods.

The woman remained standing and stared at Eddie, hate in her eyes. "We shall kill you all," she promised.

"I met up with your friend," Eddie yelled back. "He had a wolf belt—even so, we stopped him." He lifted his staff. "Tell Matchitehew there is no benefit from going to war and his plan to infect the city will fail."

"We shall see, wizard," she said, and then a smile curled on her lips. "And you'd best spend the night up there if you value your life."

With that, she turned and walked into the woods herself.

She had a point. With the wolves hidden by the darkness, he couldn't get back into the truck, as they might attack him the moment he was on the ground. This also meant he couldn't walk into the woods and teleport to Washington Square or even Central Park. His dome of light could protect him from one or two werewolves, but what would happen if there were six or seven? And what if Biker Chick also had a wolf belt and became the Hell-hound?

Eddie stared over the edge of the truck at the ground below him—only to find himself on a grassy hilltop.

The change was so sudden that Eddie stumbled. He was on a hill with stars shining overhead and the smell of wood smoke in the air. There was a circle of stones and a fire just down the slope on a small plateau.

Eddie knew where he was—Stone Face brought him to the Watchung reservation.

Eddie took a deep breath of the fresh air and headed to the fire, relieved that the Sasquatch had gotten him out of that difficult situation. As he drew near, he saw the hulking shape of the mighty Sasquatch sitting on the large rock on the far side of the fire.

Eddie stepped past the ring of stones and bowed his head to his host. "Stone Face, thank you for your help."

The immense creature gestured to one of the large stones, and Eddie sat down upon it.

Stone Face held the pipe to his lips and blew out a plume of smoke before he answered. "I have been able to find the one you seek."

"You found Wisakachek?" Eddie marveled.

"He will join us around this fire shortly," Stone Face said, and offered the pipe to Eddie. With his long arms, Stone Face easily reached him.

Eddie took a tiny puff on the pipe, then stood and returned it to his host. He didn't want to be rude, but it was very strong tobacco.

"So we just… wait?" Eddie asked.

Stone Face puffed away. "You bored? Would you prefer I left you on top of that truck?"

"No, no, that's quite all right," Eddie said and leaned back, keeping his staff upraised. He wanted to project the right look for a wizard, as he was encountering a demigod.

There was movement beyond the circle of stones, and Eddie glanced about, not sure where the noise came from.

A man stepped into the firelight, tall and well-muscled, his skin ruddy. He wore his dark hair long and tied back in a ponytail, and a three-piece suit fitted him perfectly, complete with expensive shoes and a costly tie. Stepping into the light, he nodded to both Stone Face and Eddie, pulled a handkerchief from his pocket, and placed it on top of a rock before he sat down.

"This is a very inconvenient time," the man said.

Eddie's mouth fell open. "You? You're Wisakachek?"

"What did you expect?" the man said, eyebrows raised. "Did you think I'd be running around in a loincloth, carrying a bow and arrow?"

"No, I thought you'd be... I don't know... more god-like somehow," Eddie stammered.

"I'll have you know, I am the foremost creator of Native-American casinos in the United States," Wisakachek replied haughtily.

"Casinos?" Eddie repeated.

"Of course! The days of being a nomadic people living in simple shelters are long past. The founders of the country pushed my people onto reservations. Now we turn that land into multi-billion-dollar industries. That required someone with vision and finesse to create, as well as a bevy of lawyers. Do you think that just happened?"

"Um… I guess I did."

Wisakachek gave Stone Face a look that seemed to say, "Where did you find this rube?"

"This is the wizard, Eddie Berman," Stone Face told the well-dressed man.

"A wizard?" Wisakachek replied. "Except for the robes, you look like a cop."

"I'm also a detective with the NYPD."

"He needs your help," Stone Face added. "I would consider it a personal favor."

Wisakachek sighed. "What is this about?"

"Matchitehew," Eddie said simply.

Wisakachek frowned. "That's a name I have not heard in many years. What has that fool done now?"

"He is attempting to start a war between the werewolves and the NYPD," Eddie explained. "He has control over the other werewolves."

"That he does," Wisakachek grumbled. "I thought with an extended life he might develop some wisdom, but it is wasted on someone as witless as him. He merely used his wolf powers to create a pack and surround himself with followers."

"Is it true that he is the one who created werewolves here in America?"

"Some," Wisakachek said and shook his head. "Lycanthropy can be genetic, and every werewolf, while in wolf form, can infect others through its bite." Wisakachek considered this for a moment. "I didn't expect him to create an army when I transformed him."

"We asked him to help us deal with some werewolves in New York. One of them bit a wizard."

This got Wisakachek's attention. "Bit a wizard? Can't this wizard simply cleanse himself of the infection?"

"We've had no luck. Instead of helping, Matchitehew became angry and launched a werewolf attack in a park in lower Manhattan."

"I assume there was massive bloodshed?" Wisakachek questioned, watching Eddie's face.

"We stopped some werewolves with a potion. The rest were in a truck that I dropped off at Pelham Bay Park."

Wisakachek leaned forward, resting his elbows on his knees, his eyes watching the fire. "What do you wish of me, wizard?"

"You were the one that gave Matchitehew the ability to change and his long life. If you could undo it…"

"Impossible," Wisakachek said, shaking his head.

"But you have the power—"

"It's not as simple as that," Wisakachek maintained. "I used to shape-shift all the time, and I granted such abilities to others. To undo it after all these years would be impossible. These days, I help my people through financial means, the true power in this society."

"And enriched yourself as well," Stone Face pointed out.

"Why not?" Wisakachek demanded. "Unlike you, old friend, I can fit into modern life, and I have evolved."

"The problem is, as long as Matchitehew remains a werewolf, even if we capture him, he is still a danger any place we put him."

Wisakachek rubbed his chin. "I cannot make him human again."

Eddie sighed.

Wisakachek lifted his head and said, "But I could transform him permanently into a wolf."

Eddie frowned. "What could we do with him, then?"

Stone Face looked over at Eddie. "I could send him to a vast wilderness I know. He could live as a wolf and be no harm to others."

"Let me know," Wisakachek rose and looked at the expensive gold watch on his wrist. "I have to go. I have an important meeting in the morning."

Eddie rose as well. "How can I get in touch with you if we capture him?"

Wisakachek sighed impatiently, reached into his pocket to extract a business card, and offered it to Eddie. It read:

Wick Silverheels

Investment Advisor

Eddie frowned. "Silverheels?"

Wisakachek shrugged. "It's a name I've used before, when I worked in Hollywood. If you call, leave a message and say you're the man from New York. I will know what that means."

Stone Face rose from his own rock, and kept rising to his full height, which was almost eight feet tall. "It was good of you to come."

"You should spend a weekend at one of my casinos, my treat," Wisakachek offered. "Bring that mask you have that transforms you into a human. Believe me, you would have a blast."

"I shall consider it," Stone Face said. "It is kind of you to offer."

"Immortal beings have to hang together," Wisakachek remarked, and then looked at Eddie. "I guess I'll be seeing you over the next couple of hundred years. I have to go."

The man vanished. No gesturing, no walking off into the woods.

He simply disappeared.

Eddie stared at the ground. Is that what I want? To go through existence as an immortal being, only befriending those who have unending lives as well?

"Still troubled?" Stone Face asked, and Eddie gave a start.

"Yeah, I still don't have any way to stop Matchitehew," Eddie said.

"What we spoke of the other night troubles you as well," the giant said as he returned to sitting on his rock. "The idea of living a wizard's life still does not bode well for you."

"It's just the idea... I mean, you guys live so long, but look at you. You're all alone."

"I am comfortable in my solitude."

"I get that. But that was what happened to the wizard who passed his staff to me. He lived a solitary life, in the guise of a homeless man. Marlowe thinks that since he was a prophet, he sacrificed himself so I would get the staff and do what he could not."

"You have proven yourself a great Magus, Edward Berman."

"But at what cost? Does each year as a wizard, each loss and each victory, does it make me less human? I mean, I destroyed the

New York vampires, and the Drakula himself. Who am I that I get to be judge, jury, and executioner?"

Stone Face watched Eddie as he spoke but offered nothing.

"I gotta get back. Could you send me to Drusilicus' house? I really don't want to end up back on top of that truck."

"Picture the place in your mind," Stone Face said. "You have much to consider."

"Don't I know it," Eddie said.

And suddenly, where Stone Face had been standing was now the front door of Drusilicus' townhouse.

The door flew open with Howell behind it.

"Howell?" Eddie said, relieved to see the older man. "Did Drusilicus get Vasant home?"

Howell nodded. "Yes, sir, she is here. Unconscious, I am afraid."

"Will she be all right?"

"I-I don't know, sir," Howell said, and Eddie saw he was anxious. "The master is upstairs with her. Could you wait in the sitting room? It may be a few minutes."

"Of course," Eddie said and went into the room as Howell headed off to help Drusilicus. Eddie commanded the enchanted tea set to give him coffee, which it merrily provided. He sat in a chair, the long day washing over him in waves of exhaustion.

As he sat, Drusilicus came into the room.

Eddie jumped to his feet. "How is she?"

"She attempted a spell few wizards have ever been able to manage, and she may have injured herself."

"Drew, I'm sorry."

The other wizard's back grew straighter. "It wasn't your fault. Were you able to remove the wolves to someplace where they could harm no one?"

"Yes, I let them go in Pelham Park," Eddie said.

Drusilicus looked puzzled. "How did you get back here?"

"I have my ways," Eddie said, not wanting to talk about Wisakachek or Stone Face.

Drusilicus shrugged. "I suppose they can do little damage there at this time of night."

"Do you know where my partner is?"

"He's still in the park, Rusty is with him," Drusilicus said, sitting down with his cup of tea.

Eddie said, "Then, I have to get back to Washington Square. Matchitehew is still out there, and I didn't see the red wolf either. The police are still in danger."

"Take a moment and prepare yourself, lieutenant. Rusty is there to help the sergeant, and you have had a very long day."

Eddie took a large swallow of the coffee and put the cup down. "That's my partner down there, and I have to be there for him. Can you come with me?"

Drusilicus frowned. "I cannot. I must remain here for Vasant."

"I can come," said a voice from the doorway.

Drusilicus and Eddie turned to see Caleb standing in the doorway.

"Lovetta's asleep," Caleb said, "and I want to help."

"Don't waste our time," Drusilicus muttered. "What help could you be?"

Caleb reached into his shirt and pulled out the many medallions on their chains around his neck. He wore a determined look on his face. "I might not be as powerful as a wizard, but I can hold my own."

Drusilicus raised an eyebrow.

Eddie spoke up. "I'll take whatever help I can get. Let's go."

NINETEEN

E ddie and Caleb walked down Fifth Avenue in the dark.

"Can you become invisible?"

Caleb held up one of the medallions. "I got that one right here."

"Good. Now can you think of some way I could listen in on the police, hear what's happening?"

Caleb looked through the medallions, and carefully pulled one off over his head and held out the talisman to Eddie.

"This is the Fourth Pentacle of Mercury, and it empowers the wearer to gain knowledge in all things, and to penetrate the hidden thoughts of others."

"I would have preferred a listening device," Eddie said as he took it. "How does it work?"

"Put the chain over your head, place one hand on the pentacle, and the other on the wall of the place you want to listen in on. Say the word *Audité,* and you will hear everything. You break the spell when you remove your hand from the wall."

"That's pretty useful," Eddie mused, putting the chain over his head. "Why don't you become invisible and let's get in there."

Caleb nodded, put his hand over one pentacle and, with a whispered word, disappeared.

Eddie continued downtown, glad to see that the protestors were gone. He showed his shield to the officers at the barricade and kept the opening long enough for Caleb to go through before he went in.

He saw Luis and headed toward him.

"Eddie!" Luis said, happy to see his partner. "You got rid of the moving van?"

"The van and all the wolves are in Pelham Bay Park."

"There were wolves in the van?" Luis asked, his eyes wide.

Eddie frowned. "Yeah, didn't you see them all come out?"

Luis frowned. "Well, that truck arrived, and that *puta* opened the back. Then you were slamming down the door and running to the driver's side, yelling about a bomb."

"Vasant froze time," Eddie said simply.

Luis shook his head. "She did? All I saw was her falling to the ground, and then I din' see her or Rusty."

Apparently, Vasant's time freeze had stopped the gathered police force from seeing the wolves in the back of the vehicle. Since Luis didn't possess wizard powers, it affected him as well as all the other witnesses.

"That's good. I dropped them all off and got back here. Anything happen while I was gone?"

"After the truck thing, they cleared out the protestors really fast, and everyone's been on high alert."

"I've got Caleb with me."

Luis looked around. "I don't see him."

"I'm right here, sergeant," a disembodied voice said, and Luis jumped.

Luis glared at the empty air. "Don't do that, man. You almost gave me a heart attack. So, you're invisible?"

"You stay here with Caleb," Eddie said, his eyes on one of the step vans. "I want to go listen in on what is happening."

Luis frowned. "How you gonna do that?"

"I have ways." Eddie headed toward the van with the large dish and antennas on the roof.

Eddie placed one hand casually on the metal wall, and one hand on the medallion he wore, and whispered, *"Audité."*

"We're here all night?" a voice said.

An icy chill ran down Eddie's spine. He turned, but no one was near him. That voice sounded so very close.

"That's the orders," came a woman's voice, again sounding as if she was standing right next to Eddie.

"No wild animal is coming out of hiding with all these people here," the first voice said. "And all these lights."

Eddie relaxed. The voices he was hearing came from *inside* the step van.

"You think that van had a bomb or what?" the woman asked.

"There has been no explosion, so maybe everyone overreacted. Anyway, it's gone now."

"That was the only interesting thing that happened all night."

It surprised Eddie that the voices were so clear. It was as if he was standing in the room. He even sensed where the voices were coming from, as if he could see inside the vehicle. He had to give it to Caleb, when it came to making magickal talismans, he was the best.

"Team one, check in," the woman said.

"Team one," came the answer over a radio.

"Team two, check in," she then said.

"Team two," came the reply.

Eddie smiled. This talisman was so good, he could hear the radios on the teams as well. He glanced around to make sure no one was near and then pulled out the small makeup compact from his pocket. He opened the circular container with the hand not pressed against the van and whispered, "Rusty."

Rusty's face replaced the reflection. "Hey, Eddie, where are you?"

"I'm back. How about you?"

"I'm walking the west side of the park."

"Good. There are two police teams."

"Dey doin' anything?"

"Not yet. But at some point, they'll start a sweep."

"Okay. I'll call you if I notice dem movin'."

Eddie closed the compact and returned it to his pocket. With one more look around, he leaned against the step-van and waited, his hand still on the wall.

Eddie knew that they would soon do an organized sweep since it was well into the night.

As he stood, he heard check-ins and updates and the complaints of the operators within the communications van, which he soon realized were three people: two men and one woman.

He felt tense, on edge. Maybe Matchitehew had decided against attacking an army of police now that Eddie had neutralized his two teams of werewolves. Without his pack, he might just back down.

"We have movement on the west side of the park," the woman announced over her communications equipment. "Coming in fast."

"Team one moving to intercept."

The drones possessed thermal imaging, because there was no way they could see wolves by simple visual contact. That was a smart choice. If he had been in charge of an operation like this, he would have done the same thing. Animals, especially predators, are experts at hiding in their environment, but you can't hide from a thermal imager.

Unless you're a vampire.

Eddie pulled the mirror and spoke quickly, "Rusty, we have incoming."

The cab driver's face appeared in the glass. "I got—what?"

"Incoming… um… wolves, and the police are moving. West side of the park."

"On it," he said, and the glass silvered over.

Inside the step-van, Eddie heard communications back and forth.

"We do not have visual. How many?"

"Seems to be two, maybe three, low, moving fast. Definitely an animal."

Eddie waited. In moments, the NYPD would have an encounter with a werewolf, but which one? Eddie forced himself to breathe slowly and deeply.

"Hold fire, hold fire," the voice came over the radio. "It's a dog, repeat, it's a dog, a golden retriever, not a wolf."

Eddie still had the compact in his hand, and Rusty's face was now in the mirror.

"Eddie," he said. "It's only a dog."

"I know," Eddie said. "Can you make it go away before some nervous cop shoots it?"

"Sure thing."

Eddie heard the radio report inside the van again. "The dog is heading away from the park. Let it go, guys."

"Wait, Team One, I still have an animal."

"We don't see—Jesus Christ!" the man bellowed over the radio. Sounds of an animal growling and screams echoed through the park and through the radio in the van.

"Officer down, officer down," the woman shouted frantically on the radio to her team.

Eddie took his hand away, breaking his link to the communications van. He pulled from his pocket one of his two remaining purple spheres as he took off in a dead run toward the west side of the park. Retreating officers passed as they moved back to regroup in the plaza. He heard gunfire as he threw the sphere into the air, using all of his concentration to summon his staff and fire a red light at the small ball.

With a *poof*,' it exploded, just as a wolf ran down the path and leapt toward Eddie. Eddie saw the red fur and the white belly, and knew it was the beast they had been searching for.

Eddie projected his dome of light and the wolf fell on top of it, knocking Eddie to the ground as purple mist filled the west side of the plaza. Eddie looked up, expecting to see the she-wolf changed back into her human form.

Instead the wolf fell away coughing and whining.

Eddie rose to his feet, his staff glowing and ready. He would soon face the person behind all of this.

A very human moan from a nearby bush pulled his attention. Eddie moved to the shrubbery to find a SWAT team member on the ground, his helmet gone and several scratches on his face.

"Were you bitten?" Eddie shouted. "Did that animal bite you?"

"No, no," the man said, his voice tight with pain. "Landed on my chest, scratched me, knocked me down. I think it broke a rib. Jeez, it hurts."

"Lie still, I'll get you medical attention," Eddie said, and waved a hand over the man, reciting the few words of healing that he knew.

A ferocious growl came from behind him.

Goosebumps ran up and down his arms as he slowly turned to face a Hell-hound standing on two legs down the path from him.

The creature was huge, with its reddish fur now long and shaggy, the white belly bright in the artificial light. It had a mane of longer hair on the shoulders and head, and eyes that glowed with an inner fire. The monster curled its gums to reveal yellow stained teeth and then let out a low rumbling growl. A brown stripe of mis-matched fur ran around the creature's waist.

The red wolf had a wolf belt and had activated it.

The purple mist still hung in the air but it had no effect on the creature.

It came in huge, leaping strides toward Eddie, claws extended, mouth open, and eyes burning.

Eddie fired a mighty blast from his staff, unable to clearly see the Hell-hound through the mist, dodging as he fired. The huge shape pushed past Eddie, missing him by mere inches. The creature was moving so fast that even though it missed him, it spun Eddie off his feet and he fell to the ground.

He used his staff to get up to his knees. The Hell-hound turned to face him, the red eyes looking even more angry than before, as the purple fog moved in waves around them.

Before Eddie could do anything, the Hell-hound leapt a second time, its speed incredible. Right before it struck him with claws and fangs, hands pushed Eddie out of the way as the monster ran into something that wasn't there.

There was a sound like a clap of thunder, and the Hell-hound staggered back a step falling to one knee, as something human-shaped flew through the air and slid in the dirt to be stopped by a tree. Eddie's invisible benefactor could only be Caleb. Was the young man injured?

Eddie conjured a bubble of protective red light, making it as strong as he could as the creature pounced at him again. It knocked Eddie down to the ground, and he and the dome slid through the dirt. Eddie's head smashed against the inside of his dome and he saw stars as the world spun around him.

The Hell-hound was on him, scratching and clawing at the protective barrier, snapping its jaws and trying to break the magickal protection with its teeth. The dome was a creation of will and intent, and as soon as the hound ripped away at it, it instantly reformed.

Eddie was trying to focus, to send a blast of pure force against the thing gouging away at his shield, but the world still revolved around him.

"Get off him, motherfucker," a strained voice cried out.

It was the wounded SWAT team member with the scratched face. He rose into a kneeling position with his M-4 rifle pointed right at the creature, which turned to face the new threat. Eddie rolled into the bushes to get out of the way.

The officer set off a burst of bullets. He shifted the weapon to fully automatic as a barrage of explosions filled the night.

The weapon was powerful enough to knock the Hell-hound back against the tree, which was also damaged by the hail of bullets. The monster made a low keening sound of pain and outrage as it twitched and jerked spasmodically from the bullet strikes.

At last, the officer ceased firing, the extended magazine spent.

The Hell-hound lay against the tree on his back, in a position more human than wolf. Dozens of bleeding wounds covered the creature.

"You all right, man?" the officer yelled to Eddie.

"Yeah, just winded," Eddie shouted back, worried about how much the officer saw and about Caleb, wanting to know if he had been injured.

"How did you keep that thing off of you like that?"

Before Eddie came up with a convincing lie, there was a slight popping sound, and a bullet fell to the ground—expelled out of one of the Hell-hound's wounds.

The monster trembled.

A series of the little 'pops' continued and bullets dropped quickly out of the wounds, the holes closing up and sealing without even a scar as they knitted closed.

Eddie pushed himself up to a kneeling position. "Run!"

The man stared in disbelief—in that moment, Eddie knew the man was dead.

Leaping up with a speed that defied physics, the Hell-hound was on its feet, its jaws wide as it clamped its mouth directly onto the SWAT officer's throat. The young man barely had time for a gurgled scream.

With a gush of dark blood, the monster ripped the man's head from his body. Eddie cringed at the sound, like the tearing of wet fabric followed by a crunching grind as the Hell-hound smacked its massive jaws in satisfaction.

Eddie aimed his staff and shot forth a blast of pure fire. There was the stench of burning hair and the monster screamed an unholy howl, turned and ran, its coat ablaze as it sped blindly away. It ran through the lit plaza. The officers met it with cries, screams, and gunfire as it ran to the center fountain and plunged in.

With a hiss of extinguished flames and more shocked yells from officers, the creature put out the flames in the fountain's waters. The beast ran off into the darkness, its fur still smoldering as it went.

Eddie sat numbly next to the beheaded corpse.

TWENTY

R usty appeared, still wearing the police vest Eddie gave him earlier.

"We gotta go, Eddie," Rusty said. "I got to tell Ahbay, Eugenia and... everyone... what happened."

Eddie knew that by 'everyone,' Rusty meant Marlowe. More bad news about the werewolves, and still no idea of a working cure. "You go, I'll stay."

Rusty left as Luis walked up. "Eddie, you okay, man?"

"I've been better," Eddie said bitterly, his eyes on the dead man. "Caleb hit... um... the creature, he stopped it. I don't know how."

"I see him, hold on," Luis said, and headed out of Eddie's line of vision.

Beams from gun-mounted flashlights shone around the wooded area as the SWAT team approached. Eddie raised his hands, as armed and armored men filled the area, aiming their lights on anything and everything.

One man saw their beheaded comrade and cursed.

"You, two hands up!" one officer yelled, his light revealing Luis, who was helping a bedraggled Caleb to his feet.

"They're okay, that's Sergeant Vasquez and a civilian," Eddie yelled, his hands still in the air as he sat on the ground.

Eddie saw Captain Harris' tall frame as he approached.

Harris yelled out, "Is someone going to tell me what that goddamn thing was?"

Eddie stumbled to his feet. Harris helped him stand.

"Sir, I believe that was our wolf," Eddie said.

"Animal control, my bunion-covered toes," the older man said. "I've been a hunter my entire life, and I'll tell you, whatever that thing was, it was not a wolf. My men shot that thing more times than I can count when it ran into the plaza, and it didn't seem to feel it. If it weren't for whoever had that flame-thrower, we'd be still fighting it."

Eddie was relieved. The captain thought it was an officer with a flamethrower, which got him off the hook.

"If the media gets any video, how the Hell am I going to spin that so it makes any sense?" Harris said, his teeth clenched. He looked down at the decapitated officer. "And I lost a man. Damn it, we had enough fire-power to take down a small country, and that thing just runs away a little scorched."

Eddie met the captain's eyes. "What are your plans, sir?"

"Shut the park down, day and night. I'll contact the governor and ask for the National Guard to come to Manhattan."

"Is that necessary?"

"Look, lieutenant, if I have to bring tanks down Fifth Avenue, I will eliminate this threat and kill that creature. Am I clear?"

"Very clear, Captain."

"Good. Now, you'll excuse me, but I have to make sure my men are keeping this area secure," Harris said, and walked off.

Luis and Caleb stepped close to Eddie, and the three of them walked away as the SWAT team members took care of their fallen comrade.

"Caleb, are you all right?" Eddie asked. "That Hell-hound smashed right into you."

"It didn't touch me," Caleb said. "My talisman repelled it."

"What are you talking about?" Luis said.

Caleb held out one medallion from around his neck. "This talisman, the one that protects me from wolves? It literally repels them. When that Hell-hound ran into me, it repelled both of us from each other. Of course, it weighed more than me, so I went flying."

"Are you hurt?" Eddie asked.

"A few bumps and bruises," Caleb said. "But it could've been worse."

"Let's get you to Drusilicus," Eddie said and looked over his shoulder, adding, "I don't see how this could've been worse."

In the safety of the townhouse, Eddie sat with his eyes closed as Drusilicus waved his hands around Eddie's head, doing a healing spell. Rusty was working on Caleb's injuries and Luis just sat in a chair, exhausted.

"There you are, lieutenant," Drusilicus said, and Eddie opened his eyes. "Better?"

Eddie felt more invigorated and his head clearer. "Thanks, Drew." He turned to the others. "Has anybody checked the media for news coverage about tonight? We need to see how they're covering this."

"They're New Yorkers," Rusty said. "Dey won't think nuthin' of it."

Eddie shook his head. "I doubt it. We've been able to keep this in the background, reporting the previous occurrences as a troublesome animal. I think after tonight, that might be impossible."

Luis pulled his smart phone from his pocket and checked several news sites. "*Madre De Dios,* they got footage of the flaming werewolf."

"How is that possible?" Drusilicus wondered.

"Everyone has a smart phone these days," Eddie said.

Luis nodded. "From the angle, it looks like someone shot it from overhead. It makes sense, people live in those brownstones around the park."

"Are any of our team revealed in the footage?" worried Drusilicus.

"I doubt it," Eddie said, pulling out his own smart phone to look for the video. "I set off the purple mist from a wolfsbane sphere and it filled the plaza with fog."

Luis nodded. "Yeah, but the flaming werewolf running into the fountain stands out."

Luis turned his phone to show the creature leaping into the fountain. The news organization showed it in the original size and then the video repeated in slow-motion, closer and grainier, with the caption, "What is this thing?"

"We have no time to worry about this now," Drusilicus said. "Vasant is still recovering, as is Lovetta. We did not have enough wizards there this night. Have we any idea where Wizard Glade is?"

Eddie faced Drusilicus. "Bankrock was supposed to find her."

Drusilicus shook his head. "I doubt he'll have any luck. I take it the purple spheres did nothing to the Hell-hound, like with Lovetta downstairs?"

Eddie nodded. "Not at all. The werewolf that attacked was the red one we'd seen before, but she used a wolf belt before the mist could make her human."

"The fire worked pretty good against it," Luis said.

Drusilicus frowned. "Is it possible that a werewolf with a wolf belt may be too powerful to be stopped by magick?"

"My talisman repelled him," Caleb said. "I've almost finished the talisman you found in the book."

"Ah, yes," Drusilicus nodded. "The binderune."

"I just don't know how to activate it."

"I doubt it will cure Marlowe," Drusilicus said. "And let us not forget that is our priority."

"I faced two Hell-hounds tonight," Eddie said. "Where is Matchitehew getting these wolf belts?"

Luis nodded. "Yeah, considering the guy who knew how to make them is dead."

Drusilicus paced the floor. "A logical assumption is that Matchitehew got them from him when he was alive. You said you found Stubbe's tools and talismans in his apartment."

"I went through his datebook," Luis countered. "There was no meeting listed for anyone starting with an 'M'."

"I'm going home," Eddie said. "We stopped them this night, and that's the best we can do."

"Going into the park to teleport?" Drusilicus said.

"No, I want to ride up to Central Park with Luis and teleport from there," Eddie stated, getting tiredly on to his feet.

"Wizard Greywacke?" Caleb said respectfully.

Drusilicus, Eddie, and Luis all turned to look at him.

"If you would allow me, I'd like to stay here," Caleb said, turning red. "To be near Lovetta when she wakes, y'know?"

"I shall put you in the room next to hers, and you can stay," Drusilicus conceded.

"Thank you, sir."

Drusilicus pointed his finger at Caleb. "But, you and I will talk about your relationship with the young lady in the morning."

Drusilicus headed up the stairs and Caleb turned to Eddie and Luis with a shrug and followed the tall wizard.

It was after two AM when Eddie stepped out of the park near his home in Teaneck. The drive uptown with Luis had been quiet, with both men going over the day's events in their minds.

Eddie didn't think he could take another day like this, and he needed to formulate a plan to take out the werewolf threat. But how? The animals were all so powerful and fast, and many men could lose their lives if the battle escalated.

And where was Matchitehew tonight? Eddie had seen no sign of him.

The street lamps made scattered pools of light as he trudged toward his home. He paused and looked around, unable to fight the feeling that he was being watched. Fortunately, he knew how to handle that.

He faced the way he'd come and whispered, *"Ostendo."*

A circle of red light slid away from his body in all directions, making little sparks of white as it revealed leaves of trees, overhanging wires on poles, and a sleeping bird in a nest.

The circle of red light extended away from him, and then finally became a single circle in the darkness at the end of the block.

Eddie watched this as another red circle appeared.

Suddenly those red circles bounced up and down and came at him at a tremendous speed.

They weren't circles—they were eyes.

Werewolf eyes!

Eddie threw up the red protective dome as his staff slammed into his hand with such force it hurt. The creature was running straight at him.

In that moment, Eddie saw the overlarge creature with dark gray fur, almost black in places. It had a thick pelt around its neck and shoulders, suggesting a mane, and Eddie knew with certainty that this was Matchitehew in his pure werewolf form.

His foe had been lying in wait at his home to attack him.

The monster leapt into the air, and Eddie braced himself for the impact of a creature that had to weigh several hundred pounds.

But to his surprise, the werewolf pulled up short and fell to the pavement a good three feet in front of him.

Eddie's protections were now in place and he flashed a light onto the fallen werewolf, only to see that behind the animal was a man with a firm grip on the creature's tail.

"Nice doggie," the man said in an all too familiar voice.

The wolf shied away from the light and with amazing speed and all its viciousness set upon the unarmed man. It leapt upon him, knocking him to the ground, biting and clawing at him. Eddie raised his staff to blast the creature, but the man was laughing.

Eddie paused. From the flashing fangs and teeth, the wolf should have been ripping the man's face apart, but he appeared undamaged and kept laughing at the creature.

The huge animal appeared frustrated, paused, and with a glance back at Eddie, it jumped off the hapless man and ran off into the night as fast as it could.

Eddie found he was breathing hard and tried to push past his shock to go to the fallen man. But the stranger was sitting up and undamaged and Eddie helped him to his feet.

Eddie stared at him, looking for scratches and bites, when something in the stranger's face looked familiar. "Faap?"

"It's me," the man said jovially.

Eddie stood and pushed the man to arms length to look him up and down. "But you gave up the human form."

"Oh, this is just an illusion," Faap replied, and he snapped his fingers. Though he remained human size, his body now shifted into the demonic form Eddie recognized from Marlowe's cauldron. Fortunately, this guise was not nearly as ugly, and the demon was not naked, but wearing a pair of pants.

"How are you not hurt?" Eddie said, stunned.

"Werewolves can't hurt me," The demon said merrily. "Or anything else, for that matter. I was only vulnerable when I was human."

"Wha-what are you doing here?" Eddie stammered, looking up and down the street to make sure no one was looking out a window at them.

"Keepin' my pledge. I said I owed you, and I've been watching over your house at night."

"I'm… uh… grateful," Eddie said. "Wait, how did you know where I live?"

Faap snapped his fingers, and the human illusion returned. He started off toward Eddie's house. "You were pretty easy to find, what with the Half-Fae girl running about and all."

Eddie stopped, grabbed Faap's arm, and turned the demon to face him. "Half-Fae? What are you talking about?"

"Your daughter," he said, a surprised look on the human face.

"What does that even mean?" Eddie said, feeling as if the pavement had disappeared under his feet.

"She's touched by magick," Faap explained. "You're a wizard, and word on the street was the mom got bit by a vampire." He shrugged. "Probably those two events gave her a certain amount of inherited magick. It happens more often than you think."

Eddie's legs suddenly gave out on him, and Faap grabbed him and kept him upright. "Hey, you okay? I heard you had a big fight in the park. Were you injured?"

Eddie straightened his back, planted himself solidly, and took a deep breath. "No, I'll be okay. Thank you Faap, you can consider your debt paid."

Eddie took two steps away, and Faap asked, "Hey, is it okay if I peek in on the kid now and then? She's really cute."

Eddie faced the demon. "What?"

"I mean, she can see me and everything, and I make her laugh," Faap said, as Eddie stared at him. "She's got a cute laugh."

Eddie couldn't get his mind around this. "She's seen you?"

"Yeah, I was guarding the house, and she teleported right outside next to me."

"She teleported?" Eddie whispered.

"Yeah, she's gonna do that a lot. We'll talk about it when you've gotten some sleep."

The demon turned away and vanished as Eddie stood staring after him.

Eddie went into his house, pulled himself up the stairs, and stopped at the baby's room to stare down at his sleeping daughter.

His child was magickal? Why hadn't he thought of that?

He stared at her peacefully sleeping face, aghast at the ramifications of the demon's revelation.

And what was worse, Matchitehew knew where he lived, had waited for him. If he only defeated the werewolf, he might come back seeking revenge against his family.

He was exhausted, but felt he might never be able to sleep again.

TWENTY-ONE

T he next morning was Sunday, and Eddie opened his eyes to see Ellie holding onto the bed with one hand and pulling at his hair with the other. Her chubby face broke into a grin showing tiny teeth, and she giggled as drool dribbled from her mouth.

"Hey there, Ellie," Eddie croaked. "How's my little girl doing?"

She burst into an excited babble that had a few actual words in it, like "Ma," "Gra," and even "Doo," which meant her brother Doug. Otherwise, it was incomprehensible.

Eddie took the child in his arms as she squealed with delight. As he lifted her, he felt all the sore muscles from his battles with the werewolves. Being a wizard meant he needed less sleep and healed faster, but werewolves had pounded him more than once in the last few days.

He sat her on his hip and looked at the clock, which read 10:00. Still in his pajamas, Eddie carried the girl out into the hall. The baby gates at the top of both sets of stairs were closed and latched.

Eddie sighed. "I have a child that can teleport."

This inspired Ellie into another chain of babbling, as if she wanted to explain her sudden appearance.

He went downstairs and into the kitchen, where Eleanor was mixing dough, flour sprinkling the front of her apron.

"Look who came to visit me," Eddie said.

Eleanor frowned. "Visit you? What do you mean?"

"She was in my bedroom, pulling on my hair."

Eleanor put down the bowl of dough and grabbed a towel to wipe her hands as she hurried out to the dining room. She returned a moment later, a look of wonder on her face.

"That's the strangest thing. I put her in her playpen in the dining room while I was makin' biscuits. I heard her out there."

Eddie carried Ellie over to the playpen and put her into it. She immediately picked up the toys and happily played with them.

"How did she get out?" Eleanor said. "I know she can crawl up stairs, and I always worry because she wants to come down them."

Eddie and Eleanor stared down at the little girl, who was very busy talking to a long-eared stuffed rabbit.

Eleanor stared at her son. "I got the feeling you know something about this, but you ain't tellin' me."

Eddie smiled at her. "I need coffee."

She nodded and headed back to the kitchen. "I got to finish the biscuits. I guess you'll tell me when you're ready."

"Thanks, Momma," Eddie said, still looking at the girl, trying to get his head around what he had learned.

He thought back to Cerise's pregnancy, which was a miracle in itself. Both he and Cerise were over forty when they conceived the girl on a second honeymoon in Aruba. It was a surprise as Eddie had a low-sperm count and Cerise's gynecologist told them she probably wouldn't get pregnant again.

That was before Eddie gained his staff, and Marlowe explained that the process that extended his life also meant he no longer fired blanks. The pregnancy thrilled Eddie and Cerise because they always wanted a third child.

During the last trimester, a vampire broke into their house and bit Cerise, giving her anemia. Between his wizard powers—which restored his ability to procreate—and the vampire's bite, Ellie must have gained some kind of magickal talent that Faap recognized. What had he called her? Half-Fae?

He would have to monitor the girl, alert Cerise, and talk to Marlowe or Drusilicus about what it all meant.

Eddie poured himself a cup of coffee.

"How much longer you gonna be gone all the time like this?"

Eddie sighed. "Not much longer, I hope."

Eleanor frowned. "Edward, you're missing out on watching your sons grow up, and Ellie looks around for you all day."

"Momma, please, the last thing I need right now is a guilt trip," Eddie said brusquely.

"Well, pardon me," Eleanor replied haughtily, and went back to making biscuits.

"Momma, I'm sorry," Eddie apologized. "It's just—I'm working with those wizards again and I'm annoyed that I even got involved."

Eleanor looked up at him through her thick glasses. "Must be somethin' important."

"It is."

She patted his arm. "Do your best, son, and get back here to your family. We need you more than those wizards do."

"I will, Momma."

Marlowe rubbed his eyes. He looked even more fatigued as Eddie and the others reported the events of Washington Square Park the previous evening. As the story went on, he just kept looking more and more weary.

They all sat around the large breakfast room table. Besides Marlowe, Bankrock, and Eddie, there were Ahbay and Eugenia who insisted on hearing the tale as Eddie explained the events.

Bankrock shook his head. "I knew Matchitehew could be difficult, but I'd hoped that since it meant saving werewolves, he might be reasonable."

"The SWAT team leader, Captain Harris, has sealed the park completely, no one but police in or out," Eddie reported.

"Who was the wolf you set afire? Was it Matchitehew?" Ahbay wondered.

"No," Eddie speculated. "It was the red wolf. I don't know her human identity, but I know that it's a werewolf using a wolf belt. That's how they become the Hell-hound."

"The incident with the truck I find the most appalling," Eugenia said. "There could be no other purpose other than to kill members of your police force."

"I still think it was to bite them," Eddie said. "I questioned Matchitehew's right hand man last night in that underground tunnel. When I told him I knew the plan was to infect the city, I could tell by his reaction that I guessed right."

"Personally I was shocked that a werewolf attacked you outside your home!" Bankrock commented. "How did he find you? How did he know where you live?"

"One of them must have tracked me down," Eddie said.

"Are you sure it was Matchitehew?" Marlowe asked.

"I'm only sure it was a werewolf, but my instincts tell me it was him," Eddie said.

"It is good you were able to fight him off, as tired as you were," Eugenia said.

Eddie had not mentioned the demon Faap, or the revelation about his daughter.

Ahbay's mouth set in a hard line. "We must remember that werewolves are only unthinking monsters during the full moon. After that, they can make plans."

"To be honest," Bankrock admitted, "I didn't think Matchitehew was this clever."

"Could someone be advising him?" Eddie said. "He has multiple wolf belts. His right-hand man and the red wolf both became Hell-hounds. Where are the belts coming from? Only Harold Stubbe knew how to make them."

"So why would they kill him?" Bankrock wondered as there was a knock at the door.

Drusilicus and Rusty walked in.

"How is Vasant?" Eddie asked.

Drusilicus looked as if he hadn't slept. "I gave her a potion. She has a severe case of psychic shock. After all, she stopped time."

"How did she learn to do that?" Eddie asked.

"I am aware of the spell, but I have only heard of one other wizard who ever successfully used it." He turned to look at Eugenia.

Eugenia raised a hand to her mouth. "Ah yes, it was me, and I ended up in bed for a week after I did it. You should know she didn't stop all of time. Her spell merely affected it in that very specific location, around the park."

"That is still quite impressive," Marlowe marveled.

Drusilicus looked at Marlowe and Eddie could see the old man's appearance shocked him, though he tried to hide it. "Yes. She didn't see another solution to the attack."

"You kiddin'?" Rusty beamed. "You shoulda seen her. She just lifted her arms and everyone in the whole freakin' park just slowed down and stopped—"

"No need to bore Marlowe with the details," Drusilicus muttered.

"What we should be concerned about," Bankrock said. "Is what is Matchitehew planning for tonight?"

"An important question," Ahbay said.

"You burned the red wolf, Eddie?" Marlowe asked. "Werewolves do not heal so quickly from fire. Perhaps she is incapacitated?"

Eddie shook his head. "No, she put out the fire pretty quickly. I am afraid we will face her again.

Bankrock spoke up. "So, you think everything that's happened has been a plan by Matchitehew?"

Drusilicus shook his head. "And that his scheme was to manipulate us and justify an attack on humans to take over all of New York?"

"That's how I see it," Eddie said.

"If you are correct, it is a very intricate and cunning ploy," Marlowe offered. "As Bankrock mentioned, he does not appear clever enough to have thought this up on his own."

Eddie frowned. "Matchitehew has a big ego, but he seems very self-involved."

"Yet, he has manipulated us," Drusilicus emphasized.

"I think a warlock is helping Matchitehew," Rusty said. "I mean, nobody's seen or heard from Wizard Glade in days."

"I have attempted to speak to her on my mirror," Bankrock remarked. "But she does not respond."

"By Zoroaster," Marlowe cursed, "it's difficult enough to stop a werewolf, never mind a warlock. We don't even know what their next attack will be, or how many Matchitehew will have serving him."

"Plus, we are short-handed," Drusilicus acknowledged. "Marlowe, you cannot fight in your condition, and Vasant must rest tonight."

"What about your apprentice, Lovetta?" Eddie asked.

"You mean, my soon-to-be ex-apprentice," Drusilicus spat.

"We told Marlowe that the young woman is the werewolf that infected him," Eugenia said.

"In my day," Ahbay said, "an apprentice would never keep such things from their master."

"I agree. She screwed up," Eddie said. "She had no right to keep it a secret and to be out where there were people during the full moon—but let's not ignore what she did. The girl stopped the Eurasian werewolf from killing Marlowe, and she saved me as well. If we're gonna fight werewolves, it would make sense to have her on our side."

"The lieutenant has a point," Drusilicus agreed. "If nothing else, the girl can move faster than we can, and as a wolf, she is aware of sights and smells that we are not."

Eddie nodded. "Also, Caleb helped me fight the Hell-hound last night. His talismans make him a powerful ally."

"I dislike the idea of mere apprentices in this battle," Ahbay worried.

"Both of them have already been in the fight," Eddie said. "We just want them to be part of our group, not fighting on their own. Last night, we stopped what could have been a slaughter with minimal casualties on both sides. I doubt we can do that for another night."

"When will it end?" Bankrock said.

"We cannot spend night after night fighting them off," Drusilicus agreed.

"We need a decisive victory," Ahbay proposed.

"Yeah," Rusty chimed in. "Something that will make dem give up and go home."

The group became silent, contemplating the situation.

"I can't fight that feeling that we're missing something," Eddie complained, then his face when blank. "Misdirection."

"What are you babbling about?" Bankrock grumbled.

"I must admit, I am not following you, lieutenant," Drusilicus said.

"It means looking in the wrong place," Eddie said.

"Are you saying that someone is distracting us, so we don't see something else?" Bankrock said.

"If so, what are they after?" Eugenia pondered.

"Well, y'know," Rusty said, "the best way to figure out somethin' is to see what doesn't fit."

Eddie pointed at Drusilicus. "You tracked the red Eurasian werewolf down to Washington Square Park because that's where the prophetess Willowdell said it would be."

"Correct," Drusilicus stated. "Is there a point to this?"

"Yet they killed Stubbe in Central Park. That's what alerted you and Marlowe to become involved. Every other attack was downtown. Why?"

"I thought we had agreed that Mister Stubbe was selling a belt," Ahbay proposed.

Eugenia nodded. "Yes, and that the buyer lost control of himself."

"Since Matchitehew has a wolf belt," Drusilicus added, "it would be logical to assume he bought the belt and killed Stubbe."

The wizards all nodded, except for Eddie.

"That's been what we were thinking, but Matchitehew has several belts," Eddie replied, and snapped his fingers. "It's misdirection."

"There is that annoying word again," Bankrock complained.

"You guys found out about a person killed by a werewolf in Central Park. You checked with Willowdell. She advised you to seek the werewolf in Washington Square and confront it?"

"Are you suggesting that Willowdell sent us incorrect information?" Ahbay asked.

Rusty shook his head. "Hey, I know the lady and she ain't no warlock—"

"No, I think the werewolf went to Washington Square and made its presence known to pull you down there," Eddie said, and then paused as a new idea flooded his brain. "To pull *me* down there. Which is where I've been since I got involved in the case."

"Edward, this sounds very convoluted," Eugenia maintained.

"Who would want to keep us downtown?" Drusilicus questioned.

"The person pulling the strings," Eddie said. "To keep us—especially me—out of Central Park."

Bankrock tightened his tie. "It is a place of power."

"And any talisman kept within the park increases in power," Eugenia said.

"We all know that from our battle with the Great Evil," Ahbay said.

Drusilicus looked around the room. "What could be in Central Park they don't want us to know about?"

Eddie smiled. "Stubbe died near the Metropolitan Museum of Art. He had a note in his datebook that said: Group Of Bears-G.A."

"As useless as the first time you told us, lieutenant," Drusilicus snapped.

"But G.A.?" Eddie said. "What if that stood for Glade Arch?"

Bankrock sat up straighter. "Glade Arch is only two or three blocks from the statue where you said Mr. Stubbe was killed."

"There ye go!" Rusty blurted. "She's our warlock!"

Marlowe appeared troubled. "This does not sound correct to me."

"She has a secret room in the arch, right?" Eddie insisted.

"Yes, all the arches have one, but only that wizard can access it," Bankrock acknowledged.

"Except for you, Bankrock. You have the power to enter any wizard's arch, am I right?" Eddie said.

"Myself, or the coven master," Bankrock said, with a glance to Marlowe. "But I prefer not to enter uninvited."

"Could she be hiding in her own arch?"

Bankrock's jaw grew tight. "One's arch is the only place where I cannot perceive them."

Eddie rose. "Then let's go look right now."

"What do you think you will find, Edward?" Eugenia asked.

"I don't know, but if there is someone pulling the strings, they've been very busy trying to keep us away from Stubbe's murder scene."

"Very well," Drusilicus agreed. "Since it is on the other side of the park, Rusty, would you be kind enough to drive us over there?"

"Sure," Rusty said.

"I fear you might be on a wild goose chase, Eddie," Marlowe said.

"I know, but I need to get out of here and take another look at that crime scene and the arch," Eddie explained. "Maybe something will click."

"Come, lieutenant, let us get this fool's errand over with," Drusilicus grumbled as he, Bankrock, and Rusty headed for the door.

TWENTY-TWO

They were soon in Rusty's cab and crossing the transverse road on 86th Street to get to the East Side. No one spoke as the car reached Fifth Avenue and headed downtown.

Rusty was soon in front of the four-block facade of the majestic Metropolitan Museum of Art. He drove past the main entrance and pulled the car into a parking space that magically opened up at 80th Street.

There was an enormous banner on the building that read "Artifacts of Arcadia", giving a date that was ending soon.

The four men walked up the path into the park next to the museum, which led them to a circular plaza where the bronze statue of three bears frolicked. It was only a few hundred feet from the southern wall of the museum.

"This is where we found the body," Eddie said, pointing at the stepped pedestal that formed the base of the statue.

"I suspect they thought it was an animal from the Central Park Zoo?" Drusilicus asked.

"First thing they checked," Eddie said. "Luis and I saw the mangled body before the forensic team got here. Throat ripped out, chest opened. It was a real mess."

"Was da heart eaten?" Rusty asked.

Eddie stared at Rusty with surprise. "It was missing. Why?"

Rusty shrugged. "Sign of betrayal. In ancient days, they'd cut out a traitor's heart."

"Whoever killed Stubbe might've thought he betrayed them," Bankrock added.

"Shall we continue our quest?" Drusilicus demanded. "Or shall we stare at the metal bears all day?"

"I'm trying to get ideas, Drew," Eddie responded, annoyed. "It's a process."

"If you could process more quickly, things might go faster."

The four men took a path that led deeper into the park, then headed downtown. In a few minutes, they were standing in front of Glade Arch. The arch was made from cut stones and was one of the park's widest, with a diamond design façade and hand-hewn stone balustrades on the roadway above.

"You know how to get into the room, right?" Eddie asked Bankrock.

"Certainly," Bankrock answered. "It's been a while since I went into another wizard's arch, but I know what is involved. Please check for any pedestrians."

Rusty and Eddie peered at each end of the tunnel.

"All clear," Eddie said. "Rusty, you stay out here."

"Am I the watch out?" the cabbie said as he positioned himself at the arch's entrance.

"That's 'look-out,' and yes, you are," Eddie assured him.

Bankrock stepped into the tunnel with Eddie and Drusilicus right behind him, then took a right turn to face the solid wall.

With a touch, all three wizards passed into a room that actually wasn't a room at all. They were in a forest that appeared to go on for miles. It was twilight in the woods, and a slight mist moved around the bushes and trees, giving the entire glade an ethereal character.

Eddie turned back to see the brick wall they'd passed through before he surveyed the expanse of forest with trees stretching into the distance.

With a flash, a blue light appeared over Drusilicus' staff, and Eddie saw that Drusilicus and Bankrock were in their blue and gray battle robes.

"Fourth dimensional physics," Bankrock huffed as Eddie continued to gape at the expanse. "But I believe she exceeded the recommended use of space."

Eddie shook his head. "She said she preferred living at one with nature."

"Lieutenant," Drusilicus said in a low voice. "Since we may face a warlock and a murderer, I think your battle robes would be wise."

Eddie's suit melted into his scarlet robes, as his staff slapped into his hand and a red light appeared atop it. The three men stepped stealthily forward, going around the large trees that rose up out of sight.

A hammock that appeared to be woven out of vines and leaves was hanging between two trees.

"Unusual accommodations," Eddie noted.

"Gentlemen," Drusilicus murmured as he shifted and turned to look around them as they advanced. "She could be anywhere, and she knows the lay of the land, while we do not. Please focus your attention on the task at hand."

"Banky, is she here?" Eddie hissed. "Do you sense her?"

Bankrock stopped and lifted his head. "I'm not getting anything."

Drusilicus faced Eddie. "I told you this was a waste of time."

There was a rustle in the underbrush about fifty yards from them.

"What was that?" Bankrock squeaked.

Drusilicus sneered at the little man. "Do calm down. We are in a forest. There are bound to be some animals here."

"Not like that," Bankrock exclaimed and pointed.

A large animal was charging right at them, moving with incredible speed.

"Werewolf," Eddie shouted as he conjured the red protective dome over himself and his companions. The creature was approaching rapidly, and Eddie closed his eyes and held his staff aloft, braced for the impact of a leaping werewolf.

The impact—didn't come.

Eddie opened his eyes and lowered his arm to find the wolf was sitting on the grass in front of them, tongue lolling and panting like a household pet. It was indeed a wolf, but it differed from the others he had seen. This wolf was a tawny brown and had a long muzzle and short ears, but the red in its eyes gave him pause.

"What is it doing?" Drusilicus frowned.

"It's not attacking," Bankrock hissed.

"Hello?" Eddie said, unsure what the animal was doing.

He stared into the creature's eyes and realized that they weren't really red at all. The red he'd seen was a reflection of his own protective dome. This wolf's eyes were violet.

Just like Wizard Glade's.

His confusion increased when the sitting wolf reached back with a forepaw and touched a line of dark brown fur that wrapped around its middle, and instantly Glade, in her green-blue wizard robes, was there, crouched on her haunches.

Eddie stepped back in shock. "Glade?"

The petite woman stood, twisted to adjust her back, and said, "Aye, 'tis me. I thought you might be here to attack me."

"You're a werewolf?" Drusilicus said, surprised.

"That's forbidden," Bankrock said, rising to his full height, which really wasn't any taller than Glade. "Any wizard struck by the werewolf curse must surrender their staff."

"Oh, now—do they lose their staff if they use a talisman?" she challenged.

Bankrock stood stone still. "No, I guess not."

She unbuckled the fur belt around her waist. "Well, that's what I have, a wolf belt. Made it meself, with the help of Harold Stubbe, that is."

She rolled up the belt and slipped it into her robes.

"But how…why?" Eddie stammered.

"How else could I get close to Matchitehew and find out his plans, except as one of his own?" She looked from man to man. "I couldn't truly become a werewolf, as the coven would take away me staff."

"We've been trying to get in touch—" Eddie began.

"I know, but I've been workin' undercover, as you police say. Bankrock's been calling me day and night," Glade explained, then looked at Bankrock and grinned. "Ye're a persistent bugger, I'll give ye that."

Bankrock tried to regain his dignity. "I… was… concerned."

"Undercover?" Eddie repeated. "What have you been doing? What have you found out?"

"Matchitehew is putting together an army, he is."

"Tell us something we don't know," Drusilicus retorted.

Eddie nodded. "We fought off two groups last night, and we believe he is bringing reinforcements this night."

"But that's not the only problem," Glade said. "He has a warlock working with him."

"We thought it might be you," Eddie said. "You seemed very chummy with him."

"I was trying to find out who was helpin' him," Glade said. "If you talk to Matchitehew for five minutes, it's obvious the man doesn't have enough brains to put together a scheme like this."

"Do you know his plan?"

"To infect all of New York with the werewolf curse," Glade said.

"Starting with the NYPD," Eddie added.

"I dinna think of that," Glade exclaimed. "But, aye, that makes sense."

"What about this warlock?" Drusilicus demanded.

"Well, it be Harold who told me that someone—and he dinna know who—was making wolf belts, and wantin' to steal the book his uncle left him in his will."

"Lupus Libre?" Eddie said. "We found that book, on a bookshelf in his bedroom."

"He were afraid a warlock or enchanter was going to steal it."

"Why didn't you tell us this before?" Eddie asked.

"I wasn't sure if any of the wizards in your group be the warlock he feared," Glade said. "He made me promise to keep his secrets, and he gave me something I was told only to give to a wizard I truly trusted."

"I hope you trust us," Eddie said.

"No, to be honest—I only trust ye, Wizard Berman. The reason I do is that I saw the werewolf go for ye, and only ye. Methinks it wanted to kill ye and that means ye are the one Matchitehew and his warlock fear."

Drusilicus glared at Eddie. "Once again, you receive undue praise."

Glade stepped away and ran into the trees, only to return a moment later with an envelope in her hands.

She wore a serious face. "I met with Harold on the night he died, and he entrusted me with this. He tol' me to hold it for him, or if anything should happen, give it to a wizard I could trust. I don't know what this is, but I think ye need to see it."

Eddie opened the large envelope and pulled out several folded pages. They were heavy and made of parchment, and when he unfolded them, he could see that they had been cut out of a book.

There was a title page written in elaborate hand printed letters in gold-leaf and a brilliant red ink.

Lupus Remedium

Eddie frowned and showed it to Drusilicus. "What does that mean?"

Drusilicus looked over Eddie's shoulder and said, "It translates to—curing the wolf."

Bankrock pulled at the pages to glance at them. "Is there a potion or an incantation?"

"Both," Drusilicus snapped.

"But what does it—" Eddie started.

Drusilicus held up a hand. "Please, I am trying to concentrate."

Eddie handed the pages to Drusilicus and took a step back to stand next to Bankrock, who rolled his eyes. Apparently, Eddie wasn't the only one who found Drusilicus tedious.

"This differs a great deal from the potion Vasant made for Marlowe, but there are some similarities," Drusilicus reported, going through the pages again and again. "I'm pleased to say I can make it from simple ingredients, all of which I have in my stores."

"Do you think it will work?" Eddie asked. "I mean, cure a werewolf?"

Drusilicus pursed his lips in thought. "I believe it could not only cure a recent infection, but even a person living with the curse for years."

"Great!" Bankrock effused. "We can cure Marlowe."

Eddie turned to Glade. "Did you know that this was what was in the envelope?"

Glade shook her head. "No. If I knew it was a cure, I would've brought it that first day."

"It looks possible," Drusilicus said and continued reading. "But there is a problem—"

"Now what?" Bankrock groaned.

"It speaks of a talisman necessary to activate the potion," Drusilicus finally told them. "This claims that the best talisman would be the *Mentagió tou Zeus Lycaeus* —I believe I pronounced that correctly—with a specific spell to cleanse the curse."

He turned the page toward Eddie and Rusty, and on the parchment was a circle with a drawing. The drawing was of a muscular man holding lightning bolts in one hand and a staff in the other. His head was that of a wolf.

"Oh, do ye have it?" Glade asked.

"Afraid not," Eddie said.

Bankrock sighed. "Where are we going to get that?"

Eddie thought for a moment. "What's the name of that talisman again?"

Drusilicus exhaled with frustration. "It's Greek. It translates as the *Medallion of Zeus Lycaeus* if that's any help."

"Isn't that the Greek wolf guy you told me about?"

Drusilicus set his jaw, as if answering Eddie was an obvious strain on his patience. "Lycaon was the King of Arcadia that Zeus turned into a wolf. It all began—"

"Wait!" Eddie interrupted, pulling out his cell phone. "King of where?"

"Arcadia," Drusilicus replied dryly. "Lieutenant, do you wish to hear the story again or not?"

Eddie pulled up google on his phone. "I think I know why he was killed near the MOMA. He was going to the museum."

Drusilicus looked annoyed. "You were the one who told us he had the Group Of Bears listed in his datebook."

"That's where Harold said he was going after he met me," Glade said.

"Did he mention if he was meeting anyone?" Bankrock asked.

Glade shook her head.

Eddie was focused on his phone. "My theory is that he was on his way to see a specific exhibition... and here it is."

Eddie held out his phone. On the display was a Metropolitan Museum of Art webpage for *Artifacts of Arcadia.*"This is where Harold Stubbe was going,"

"Arcadia?" Glade said, looking at the phone.

Bankrock frowned. "Where Lycaon was the king?"

"Yes," Drusilicus said, also studying the page . "He built a temple to Zeus on a mountain he named after himself, Mount Lykaion. They destroyed that temple in the second century." He backed away from the phone and glared at it. "This display is of artifacts found there in a recent archeological dig." His eyes narrowed. "You don't suppose—"

"They may have found the medallion!" Eddie said. "Remember what Harold wanted from Lovetta and Caleb? A talisman to open any lock and one to become invisible—"

Drusilicus' eyebrows shot up. "As if he were planning a robbery."

"That's why Stubbe was interested in the exhibit," Eddie said. "He was casing the place, planning to steal something."

"Only one thing doesn't fit, Wizard Berman," Bankrock stated. "The man made werewolf belts. Why would he be interested in a cure?"

"I don't know, but it matches what Caleb told us," Eddie answered. "He said Stubbe was excited about being able to cure

Lovetta, and that he figured out how to do it. He found out someone was making wolf belts, a warlock or enchanter, and he must have felt threatened."

"So he cut out the pages in the back of the book that contained the cure," Drusilicus theorized.

"And gave them to me?" Glade said.

"It makes sense," Eddie admitted.

Bankrock looked at Eddie. "It still does not tell us who the mastermind is behind all of this."

"We need to go to the museum!" Eddie declared. "To see if the medallion really is there."

"And if it is, what do we do then?" Drusilicus huffed. "Steal it?"

Eddie's jaw tightened. "If it'll save Marlowe? Damn straight." Eddie walked to the wall where they had entered and stopped. "How do we get out of here?"

"Carefully," Glade said and stepped up to the wall, placing her hand upon it.

"What are you doing?" Eddie asked.

"Sh!" Glade hissed.

Bankrock leaned close to Eddie's ear. "She's checking if anyone is out there before we go."

Glade gestured at the wall, and the four people stepped through it.

The Metropolitan Museum Of Art first opened in 1880. A famed architect, Richard Morris Hunt, designed the current facade, completed in 1902 and featuring ornate Beaux arts designs: three grand arches surrounded by four sets of two-story high pairs of Corinthian columns atop a grand staircase.

"I believe that all of us going in together might attract more attention than we wish," Drusilicus advised as the five of them stood at the bottom of the wide staircase outside the ornate entrance.

"I still have me wolf belt," Glade said. "I shall go downtown and meet up with the werewolves. There be more arrivin' each day."

"You're still undercover?" Eddie asked.

"If they think I'm one with the cause, I might find out things," Glade said.

"Be careful," Eddie warned. "NYPD has shut down Washington Square Park."

"I'll have a care, don't worry about me, Wizard Berman," Glade said with a smile, and headed back toward the park.

Bankrock cleared his throat. "I have no skill for thievery, and I need to let the others know what we found out. I am going back to Marlowe's townhouse."

Bankrock headed off, and Eddie noticed he caught up to Glade and was speaking to her as the pair walked away.

"I guess dat leaves us," Rusty said and started up the stairs.

"Apparently so," Drusilicus said, exchanged a glance with Eddie, and the pair of them followed Rusty.

At the front desk, Eddie grabbed a flyer that featured information about the *Artifacts of Arcadia* display, probably a copy of the same flyer forensics had found on the dead Harold Stubbe.

They entered the Great Hall, constructed from limestone, with a unique ceiling built with three domes far overhead, braced by eight supporting arches springing from enormous bases. These interior domes corresponded to the three arches on the front of the building.

After a quick perusal of the brochure, Eddie led the other two directly into the Greek Art exhibit, then down a long hallway with a curved ceiling and skylights that allowed natural light into the room. They passed colossal standing statues that were decapitated or missing limbs.

The three men entered an exhibition hall which had more banners, and a large display that showed photos from the archaeological dig that led to the discoveries.

"If we require any shenanigans, I think I would be the most qualified to carry them out," Drusilicus murmured.

"Shenanigans?" Eddie repeated sardonically. "Yeah, I'll keep you in mind if I want any malarky or tomfoolery as well."

"Really, lieutenant," Drusilicus huffed. "Must you mock me constantly?"

"Not constantly, but you invite it," Eddie said as he examined the display cases filled with treasures from jewelry to stone reliefs. There was a small statuette of a bronze horse from the eighth century BCE, a sculpture in marble carved to look like a seashell, a gold bowl used for libations, and a small plaque with ancient Greek lettering.

Rusty stopped in front of a display case. As Eddie drew near, he saw within it a shining gold medallion that featured a man with a wolf's head holding lightning bolts and a staff.

"By Zoroaster," Drusilicus whispered. "It is here."

"This is what Stubbe was on his way to see," Eddie said. "And he wanted someone to come with him."

"Why?" Rusty asked.

Eddie shrugged. "Maybe to help steal it? Whoever he met at the Statue of the Three Bears killed him."

"But if this artifact can cure a werewolf, why would anyone want to stop him?" Drusilicus asked.

"Yeah," Rusty said, "think of all the people he coulda helped."

Eddie glanced around the room. "Could we grab it and teleport out of here?"

"Nah," Rusty said. "It's a talisman of power."

"He's right," Drusilicus agreed. "We don't know what might happen if someone teleported with it. And as you know, teleporting in Manhattan is—"

"Yeah, I know, difficult and dangerous," Eddie said, annoyed..

"Let's walk." Rusty headed for the doorway that led to the main hallway again. Drusilicus and Eddie followed, and once they reached the hall, Rusty quietly said, "Head outside and across da street to da cab and wait for me there."

Eddie and Drusilicus exchanged a glance and headed out of the main entrance. They walked across the street to the checkered cab without speaking.

Drusilicus whispered *"Patentibus"* and the doors of the vehicle unlocked.

They both got into the back and stared at the museum.

"What do you think he's going to do?" Eddie asked.

"If it were me, I would use an invisibility spell, then try to remove the item surreptitiously when the cameras could not see me," Drusilicus said.

"I don't see how he could get it out of that case," Eddie said. "Isn't it alarmed?"

"Once again, you point out your limited knowledge of your powers."

"I'm pretty good in a fight," Eddie grumbled.

"Yes, but to a hammer, everything is a nail. You can wield great power effectively, but you lack the knowledge to use the finesse which many situations require."

The front door of the cab opened and closed quickly, but there was nothing there.

"Rusty?" Eddie said to what appeared to be empty air.

"Yeah, be quiet until I get us outta here," a disembodied voice said.

Rusty's use of the invisibility spell impressed Eddie. Usually, the wizards could see each other until they stepped several feet away, but Rusty created an aura of invisibility so effective that even inches away, Eddie could see nothing.

The cab pulled into traffic, heading south on Fifth Avenue.

Onlookers should be surprised to see a cab moving with no driver, but of course, being New Yorkers, no one noticed.

After five blocks, Rusty materialized at the steering wheel as he guided the cab toward the transverse road at 66th Street.

"Did you get it?" Eddie asked.

Rusty said nothing, merely reached into his jacket and extracted the medallion, and handed it back to Drusilicus.

Drusilicus caressed the medallion and said, "I sense great power within."

"How did you get it?" Eddie asked as Rusty pulled off Fifth Avenue.

"Went to the men's room and used the invisibility spell. Then I merely walked up to the case, made sure I shut the alarm off—"

"We can do that?" Eddie wondered.

"Yeah, sure, then I made one of the glass side panels disappear, reached in, and grabbed the medallion. I made the side panel reappear, and I was outta there."

"Finesse, lieutenant," Drusilicus gloated. "Rusty, if you could take me to Marlowe's, I can prepare this new potion."

"No," Eddie exclaimed.

Drusilicus stared at Eddie. "Are you insane? We have a way to cure Marlowe."

"And we have Matchitehew and I don't know how many werewolves getting ready to go head to head with NYPD in a few hours. That has to be our primary mission."

Drusilicus looked at Eddie as if he were daft, but then his expression softened. "What do you propose, lieutenant?"

"I have an idea for a plan, but it'll take all of us to make it work," Eddie said.

"It better be a good one," Rusty added.

TWENTY-THREE

A s twilight fell, Eddie made his way down Fifth Avenue toward Washington Square, alarmed by what he saw. The police still had barricades around the park with the SWAT team vans on the plaza. The bad part was that there were many more protestors filling the streets on all sides of the square, blocking his way into the park.

Eddie wondered if he should try to get into the square another way, perhaps going to nearby Minetta Green, a tiny park on Sixth Avenue and teleporting using the trees. He dismissed that because the green was just too small. The other choice was to return to Drusilicus' townhouse and attempt teleportation from his room of mirrors, but since he'd just left the dour wizard, he dismissed that idea as well.

Finally, he decided to just work his way through the crowd. With a sigh, he wove in and out of the protestors. They carried signs that read: FREE OUR PARK, and PARKS ARE FOR PEOPLE AND ANIMALS, NOT COPS.

The odd thing he noticed was that there seemed to be some kind of dress code. Most of them were wearing large ankle-length squarish robes, what might be called a caftan or a muumuu. The garments ranged from brightly colored to plain tan and brown, and both men and women wore them. It made Eddie think of photos he'd seen of hippies in the 1960s at some of their anti-war protests.

He eventually slipped his way through to the wooden barricade manned by three uniformed officers. He flashed his shield despite the catcalls and jeers from the assembled mob. He made his way to the arch, where Luis was waiting.

"Quite a mess out there," Luis complained, with a nod to the crowds.

"Yeah," Eddie said. If his plan with the other wizards didn't work, the number of people bitten or killed would be staggering. He pulled out the hand mirror from his pocket and whispered, "Drusilicus."

The hawk-faced wizard replaced his reflection. "Now what, lieutenant?"

"How is it going?"

"It would go better if I didn't have interruptions," Drusilicus said gruffly.

"Sorry, Drew. There are protestors all around the park—you should teleport in."

"Protestors?" Drew said. "Are they mad?"

"They don't know it's dangerous, Drew. That's why I'm counting on you to come through."

"As always, lieutenant, you ask the impossible," Drusilicus fumed, and the mirror silvered over.

Eddie shook his head and moved Luis near the arch, where they were out of sight of the protestors. "Your handgun is a Glock 19, right?"

"For the last five years. What's the problem?"

"No problem. Pull the magazine and give it to me."

Luis scowled but took his weapon out of his shoulder holster and ejected the small rectangular box from the handle, which he handed to Eddie. Eddie pulled the bullet cartridges out of the top and put them in his right coat pocket.

"What're you doin'?" Luis asked.

"Upgrading your weapon," Eddie said, and pulled out a cartridge which he handed to Luis. The projectile peeking out of the top of the nine millimeter casing was bright and shiny.

"Silver bullets?" Luis marveled.

"Drusilicus gave us some nine millimeter rounds," Eddie said as he slipped shiny cartridges into the magazine from his left pocket. "I don't want to kill the werewolves, but I don't want you unable to defend yourself, either."

"What choice do we got if they try something like that truck last night?"

"Agreed." Eddie handed the magazine to Luis. "I have a plan."

Luis reinserted the magazine into his Glock. "Is it a good one?"

A muscle in Eddie's jaw twitched. "I don't know. In fact, it might not work at all. And I know it won't work on all the werewolves."

Luis grimaced. "Sounds like a shitty plan."

"It's all I've got."

Luis looked over at the busy men in their SWAT uniforms and the crowd of protestors. "How are you gonna do it without all these guys knowing about the wizard thing?"

"I don't know that either."

Luis frowned. "Are you sure you made a plan?"

Eddie shrugged. "We'll find out, won't we? Let me check in with Captain Harris."

"What do I do, watch the perimeter or somethin'?"

"Ahbay, Eugenia, Bankrock, and Rusty should arrive soon. They are cloaked in an illusion of SWAT gear, but they'll actually be in their wizard's robes."

"Okay, so I wait near the arch," Luis sighed.

Eddie headed for the pair of vans. It was rapidly growing dark, and the enormous lights on poles were firing up. The diesel generators roared to life and the elevated bank of lights brightened the surrounding area.

"Lieutenant," Harris said as Eddie drew near. He was talking to a group of three men and broke away from them as Eddie approached. "Pretty fast thinking with that truck last night. Anything come of it?"

"There were just some noisemakers in the truck, no bomb. Probably just a prank," Eddie lied. "Are there signs of any animals?"

"No, I think we may have scared them off," Harris said. "I just want to get this done and get out of here. These protestors are the last thing we need."

"Agreed, sir," Eddie said. "Any fallout from that creature that was on fire?"

"The one the press calls 'the flaming werewolf'?" Harris said and shook his head. "Werewolves! We get a couple of wild animals, and the press goes with werewolves."

"Any chance we could just capture them?"

"Not after it killed one of my men. We have to face the facts, lieutenant. Whatever that thing was, it's dangerous and probably rabid. If we get more infected animals, I don't have to tell you what a disaster that would be."

"I'll be standing near the arch if you need me, sir."

"We'll get it done," Harris said. "Just be somewhere safe when the shooting starts."

The night was growing darker and the bright lights in the park made the buildings outside of the square look like ghosts.

Eugenia, Ahbay, and Rusty, all in their SWAT team illusions, stood near Luis. Next to them was Bankrock, who appeared ludicrous in the gear, as he was too short and too skinny to be very threatening.

Near the arch, a big SWAT team member stood, a balaclava covering his face. He was facing the crowd of protestors. He was almost as big as Luis, and the black uniform and vest seemed to be one size too small for him. An AR-15 hung from a strap, and he wore a handgun on his hip.

"Glad to see all of you," Eddie said as he drew near, lowering his voice because of the proximity of the SWAT officer. He focused on Eugenia. "Are you sure you're up to this?"

"I have Ahbay and Claremont to help me," she said, also glancing at the large SWAT agent. "I am unsure how long I can maintain the spell when the time comes."

"Do your best, Eugenia."

Luis leaned close to Eddie and whispered, "You gonna tell me this plan, or do I wing it?"

Eddie put his hand on Luis' shoulder. "Just try not to get hurt, partner."

Luis shrugged and stepped away, looking out at the protestors. Eddie stepped back with the three wizards, putting some space between them and the arch.

"Any word from the Wizard Greywacke?" Ahbay asked, keeping his voice low.

"He's working on it," Eddie murmured. "I'm sure he'll be able to do it. It all depends on whether—"

"Hey Eddie," Luis interrupted, still at the arch, peering at the protestors.

Eddie glanced at Luis as the big man stepped closer. "Yes, Luis?"

"Did you notice what the protestors are wearing?" Luis asked, pointing at them with a thumb over his shoulder.

Eddie glanced over at them. "I figured they're bringing back the 'hippy' look. What about it?"

The other wizards looked over the crowd.

"They're all in those baggy outfits and sandals on their feet," Luis said.

"So what?" Eddie replied impatiently.

"Like robes," Luis said. "Robes that are easy to get out of..."

"Oh, my!" Eugenia gulped.

"Dat can't be good," Rusty added.

"Oh dear," Bankrock fussed.

"Ah, I see what you mean, sergeant," Ahbay agreed.

"What are you all looking at?" Eddie said, as he gazed at the crowd, really focusing on the mass of people. The garments flowed loosely with no hint of clothing underneath.

Eddie gaped.

Luis said quietly, "Most of those protestors aren't wearing anything under the robes. And sandals are very easy to slip out of."

"I believe we may have found the werewolves that will lead the attack this night," Eugenia said.

Eddie looked over the crowd. "There must be hundreds of them."

"Glade said that Matchitehew has been busy pulling together an army," Bankrock said.

Rusty nodded. "He must've got Wolfen from all over da country, telling 'em to come."

Eddie said, "He's been conscripting werewolves to come here."

"Some regular people are mixed in with the caftan-wearers," Luis pointed out.

"They'll be the first to get bitten," Eddie said, his jaw tight. He glanced at the SWAT agent to make sure he was out of range and yanked the mirror out of his pocket. "Drusilicus!"

Drusilicus' face appeared in the small circle of glass. "Lieutenant, I am doing the best I can—"

"Drew, listen to me. This is important. The protestors around the park are werewolves in human form."

Drusilicus frowned. "Are you sure?"

"I'm not, but there are many people wearing caftans and sandals, which seems a little chilly for early spring."

"I see," Drusilicus replied, understanding at once.

"Did you get it to work?"

"I think so. But, lieutenant, we are talking of an untried potion and an unproven spell. We have no way of knowing what will happen—"

"Just get down here, Drew. I don't know how much time we have until this thing gets ugly."

"On my way as soon as I can," Drusilicus said.

Eddie tucked the mirror back into his pocket.

"Eugenia, Ahbay, Bankrock, and Rusty, get to your positions in the middle of the plaza near the smaller step van." Eddie pointed at the one with the satellite dish and antennas on its roof. The four wizards nodded and headed for the vehicle.

Luis was still examining the crowd. "What do you think they're waiting for?"

Eddie gazed at the milling pedestrians. "A signal or an order or something."

A SWAT team member trotted over to Eddie and raised his hand to get his attention. "Lieutenant Berman?"

"Yes, I'm Berman."

"I just got a radio message from a patrolman on the barricade. Some guy says you asked him to come here? His name is Caleb. Says he has something you need."

Eddie nodded. "Ask the officer to send him through and have him report to me here, please."

"Got it," the man said, and strode away, talking on the radio.

"What does Caleb want?" Luis asked.

"I guess he finished that talisman we asked for," Eddie said and tried to keep his eye on anything unusual happening in the crowd or in the park. The large SWAT guy was still close by, and he made Eddie nervous. "I don't know if we can make it work, but I'll take all the help I can get."

"How come?"

"We located the missing pages from the weird book we found at Stubbe's and it recommended a different talisman," Eddie explained.

Luis frowned. "Where did the design that Caleb is making come from?"

"I don't know, but we'll see if he can tell us anything."

Eddie glimpsed the young man, only to see him stopped and questioned by a SWAT team member. A woman was walking with him, and she was wearing a head scarf, dark glasses, and gloves, so it took Eddie a moment to recognize her.

Sophia Stubbe.

"Ms. Stubbe, what are you doing here?" Eddie asked as the two of them drew close.

"Ms. Stubbe contacted me," Caleb answered.

"How did she know your number?" Eddie asked.

"She showed up at my shop, told me I had to close up and come help you," Caleb said and then frowned. "Didn't you ask her to come get me?"

"Vhat does that matter, lieutenant?" Sophia smiled. A few strands of her red hair peeked out from under her head scarf, and Eddie found it odd that she was wearing sunglasses and gloves, as it was night and not that cold. "I am here to help."

Caleb turned to Eddie. "There's something weird with the talisman."

"Did you find the spell to activate it?" Eddie asked.

"I have the spell," Sophia said. "But, I felt ve shouldn't try until ve vere in the park."

"You have the spell?" Eddie said. "You're an enchanter?"

"Ja, as all of my family," she said and smiled again.

Eddie frowned at this, and stared at Sophia, concerned.

"We have a problem," Luis said, keeping his voice low. "We think the protestors are actually werewolves."

Both Caleb and Sophia glanced at the crowd.

Sophia lowered her voice as well. "You may be correct."

"Can this binderune stop them?" Eddie asked and glanced around. No one was very close, except Luis, though the big SWAT officer was still milling nearby. "Let me see it."

Caleb pulled a medallion about the size of a silver dollar out of his pocket. It was on a delicate chain, and both the talisman and the chain had the rich dark yellow of fine gold, glowing from the radiance of the overhead lights. Caleb had etched deep symbols into the metal.

Sophia smiled. "Your young friend vouldn't let me see it until you did."

Eddie took the medallion in his hand, examining it. "Nicely done."

"May I?" Sophia asked, and Eddie showed her the talisman, without letting go of it. Her smile grew. "Yes, quite vell done."

"By the way, we found the missing pages from your cousin's book," Eddie told her.

"Really?" she said, her eyebrows raised in surprise.

"Yes. It turns out those pages were a cure for werewolves. He cut them out and left them with a friend for safekeeping."

"Harold vas obsessed vith finding a cure for lycanthropy," she said, her eyes hidden behind the dark lenses. She sighed, "It is vhy I had to kill him."

Eddie's jaw set. "What?"

"Ja. I had to go to his apartment the next day, and alter the volf belt, so it would make whoever vore it lose control. I knew a vizard vould search his place at some point. I also had to find the old book and add the drawing and instructions for this delightful rune your friend crafted so vell." She shrugged. "I vas afraid I vould have to make it myself."

Luis took a step closer. "What are you sayin', lady?"

"It's obvious, isn't it? If you possessed a cure for a verevolf bite, that would have ruined everything."

An unnerving howl filled the air.

Eddie, Luis, and Caleb all looked up, trying to discern where the cry had originated, while Sophia stepped back out of the way.

"I'll take that off your hands," a familiar voice said. The big SWAT agent yanked the medallion from Eddie as he knocked him to the ground. With his free hand, he struck Caleb who crumpled like paper. As Eddie lay on the ground, the big man threw the golden medal to Sophia Stubbe, who caught it easily.

It was Matchitehew.

"You two are working together," Eddie grunted, trying to get up and conjure his staff, but Matchitehew lifted the AR-15, pointing the barrel right at Eddie's chest.

His finger moved to the trigger.

Before he could fire, Luis slammed against him and grabbed the gun's stock to point it harmlessly toward the sky. Matchitehew pulled the trigger and released a burst of shots. Luis threw his full weight against the man. Matchitehew was big, but even he could not stand up to the full strength of Luis.

Eddie sprang to his feet, his staff appearing in his hand and a dome of red protective light around him.

Matchitehew threw Luis off with inhuman strength, leaving him open.

Eddie struck him with a blast from his staff, knocking Matchitehew not only off his feet, but crashing the big man into the base of the Washington Square Arch twenty feet away.

Eddie ran to his partner and helped him up. "You okay?"

"I been worse," Luis croaked.

"You've lost, vizard!" Sophia screeched, and Eddie turned to see Sophia holding the binderune medallion high. A bright white light surrounded the talisman. In the brief battle with Matchitehew, Sophia must have recited an activating spell, and now the binderune was releasing its magic. It was so dazzling, Eddie had to shield his eyes. A wild wind whipped up all around the park.

Sophia laughed maniacally, and pulled off her head scarf. Eddie saw patches of missing hair and burns on her scalp, though they seemed to be healing.

"You're the red werewolf!" Eddie shouted.

"Of course, and now you will see my full power!" Sophia hollered back and held up the glowing medallion.

Eddie looked out to the plaza where SWAT officers were coming in their direction, reacting to the gunfire. Suddenly, all the officers stopped, grabbed their stomachs, and collapsed one by one.

"What are you doing?" Eddie shouted.

"Attacking Manhattan with verevolves," Sophia cackled, and pulled off her gloves, which revealed small burns on her hands that were almost healed. "This was my plan all along."

"Why?" Eddie demanded.

Her features were dark and hideous. "Because I'm a genetic verevolf. Harold knew how to make wolf belts, had been doing it for years. But when he received the old family book, he decided he vanted to cure me."

"Why did you kill him?" Eddie demanded.

"He was close to locating the medallion and planned to force the cure on me." She hung the glowing binderune around her neck. "I killed him because it was my due as a predator."

"I'll stop you," Eddie said.

"You'll be too busy," she sneered.

Her hand went to her waist, her fingers reaching inside her clothing.

"She has a wolf-belt," Eddie yelled, leaping in front of Luis as Sophia instantly transformed into the Hell-hound, huge and unstoppable. Like the previous night, the monster was covered in red hair with a white stomach, but Eddie saw the burn marks, though they were small.

The Sophia monster raised her head and howled, receiving answering howls from the crowd. The people beyond the barricade had pulled off their robes and were transforming and still others had already become wolves.

Screams of fear accompanied the howls of the wolves, and the protestors not dressed in caftans, like the SWAT officers, crumpled over and collapsed.

Secrecy was no longer important. Eddie ran toward the barricade, his clothes melted into his wizard robes, as he fired a blast of light from his staff. He needed to force the fierce animals back.

A fist struck at him, bouncing off his protective dome, but still knocking Eddie off his feet. He looked up to see Matchitehew pull off the balaclava, revealing his human face.

"You have more to fight, wizard," Matchitehew shouted. "Look at your SWAT team!"

Matchitehew reached into his waistband, and instantly the man was gone. In his place, a massive Hell-hound stood. Without a second glance, the creature turned and ran into the nearby bushes, making a chuffing noise that Eddie realized was the sound of a wolf laughing.

Ahbay, Rusty, Bankrock, and Eugenia ran back to the arch. His battle with Sophia and Matchitehew, which seemed long, had merely been a few moments. They dropped the illusion of being SWAT team members and were in their battle robes and each carried their staff.

"What is happening?" yelled Ahbay over the howls and the wind.

"I don't know," Eddie yelled back and looked at Luis, who was helping Caleb to his feet. Although the SWAT team members were falling to the ground, his partner and Caleb seemed unaffected. "Are you two all right?"

"Yeah," Caleb yelled, and held up one of his medallions. "I have protective charms."

"And the spell ain't affecting me," Luis said, helping Caleb along to join the others.

Suddenly, Luis stopped and got a strange look on his face as he fell to his knees with a loud, "Oof." His body shifted under his clothes and he screamed.

"Luis," Eddie yelled, getting on one knee next to his partner.

"G-Get back," Luis shouted. "Protect yourself."

Luis fell back to the ground. He screamed as his knees reversed direction and the bones relocated all over his body. Two powerful leg kicks shoved his pants off and on to the ground next to his empty shoes. His nose punched out as the long wolf's muzzle extended. The screams he made turned into a long howl as gray fur sprouted from his body, and his clothing tore away from his body as his muscles changed in size.

He became a large gray wolf staring at Eddie with yellow eyes.

Eddie fell back to the others and threw up a protective dome as the wolf turned to them, growling.

"Is that the sergeant?" Ahbay asked.

"He's been enchanted," Eddie said, backing away, making sure the dome of red light completely covered himself, Ahbay, Caleb, Eugenia, Bankrock, and Rusty.

"Enchanted to attack us?" Bankrock whispered.

"It appears so," Eddie said, as the Luis wolf leapt at the protective dome and bounced off.

"Dat ain't all," Rusty called out, pointing at the plaza. "Look!"

Eddie turned to see the collapsed SWAT agents moving about, their clothing shifting.

The wolf that was Luis launched itself at the protective dome again, biting at it and bouncing back off to the ground, where it continued to snarl at the wizards.

"They're crawling out of their clothes," Eugenia said.

"No!" Ahbay yelled. "They are wolves."

"How is this possible?" Bankrock said.

"It must be that binderune talisman I made," Caleb said.

"Sophia Stubbe tricked us all," Eddie barked. "That talisman doesn't cure a werewolf, it transforms regular people into wolves."

The Luis wolf leapt again and Eddie yelled, *"Oppressio!"*

This sent the wolf flying back ten feet, where it rolled and was back on its feet in seconds.

"We're surrounded," Ahbay said.

"With no way to escape," Eugenia said. "We can't even get to the woods to teleport away."

Eddie looked out at all the wolves as they poured into the plaza under the barricades, their fierce eyes glaring at the wizards with a hungry look.

TWENTY-FOUR

"We have to get into the arch," Eddie said. "Move there as a group under the dome."

"We must give up the plan." Eugenia's eyes were huge.

"No, we stick to the plan," Eddie insisted. "But we're outnumbered and we have to move to higher ground. If we can get up to the top of the arch, we can attack the wolves, but they can't get to us."

"We could levitate to the top," Ahbay said, as the group crept toward the arch within the large projected dome.

"Best to go inside," Eddie said. "That way, if they find a way to strike us on the top, we can still hide in the building."

Dozens of wolves were moving at them, and around them, trying to stop them with sudden lunges. Some were fighting among themselves, and Eddie knew that any bitten non-werewolves would become infected with the curse unless his plan worked.

The wolves kept rushing at Eddie and the wizards, throwing themselves against his dome, or leaping on top of it with abandon. Eddie kept the group moving, which was hard as they had to ignore snapping jaws and claws as they struck his dome.

Each time the animals hit, red light flashed as the wolves damaged the protective shield and it re-formed.

Eddie backed to the doorway and extended his dome so it linked with the outer wall of the vast arch. Ahbay gestured and the door came open. One at a time, the members of the group ducked low and went inside the monument. Eddie was last, and he slammed the door before a wolf could get its muzzle in.

"Will it hold?" Caleb asked.

Rusty gestured with his own staff, and a rectangle of yellow light covered the door. "That will keep them out for a while, at least."

"Quickly, all of you get to the top and out onto the roof," Eddie said.

As the others went up the spiral staircase, Eddie retrieved the small mirror and called, "Drusilicus."

"Yes, lieutenant," Drusilicus said, appearing in the glass. "I am on my way—"

"The situation has changed," Eddie snapped. "Not only were the protestors werewolves—that talisman Caleb made? Sophia Stubbe activated it and it turned everyone but the wizards and Caleb into wolves."

"What? How far does the effect extend?"

"I don't know," Eddie replied helplessly.

Drusilicus considered it. "Probably not beyond the square."

"We're inside the arch, heading for the top."

"Lieutenant, our plan will not work if there is a talisman making them into wolves."

"What can we do?" Eddie asked. "Is there a counter spell?"

"Destroying the talisman will be the most effective way to break the spell."

"Sophia Stubbe has become a Hell-hound and is wearing it around her neck."

"That complicates things—but there may be a solution. I am on my way to join you."

"The streets are full of werewolves."

Drusilicus smiled. "Who needs streets? See you shortly, lieutenant."

Eddie slid the mirror into his pocket and climbed the stairs to the roof. The pair of doors at the top of the stairs were open, and the other wizards were out looking down at the carnage below.

The lights on top of the arch were projecting up into the sky, making it hard to see. With a gesture of his staff, Eddie made the floodlights on top shut off. It was darker, but the illuminated light-poles the police set up still brightened the entire park.

Eddie peeked over the edge to see growling and howling canines surrounding the entire arch. They were circling the two supports, some of them even trying to leap and climb up the marble, and falling back to the ground. The feral howls made Eddie's skin crawl.

"What can we do?" Ahbay asked.

"We need to destroy the binderune talisman," Eddie said. "It's what's causing the non-werewolves to change."

"I don't see either Matchitehew or dat lady," Rusty said.

"They have to be here," Eddie murmured. "This is what they've been working for. They have to stop and savor their triumph."

"Is Drusilicus on his way here?" asked Eugenia.

"He said he was," Eddie answered. "But I don't see how he can get past the wolves."

"Actually, here he comes now," Bankrock interjected.

Eddie raised his head to see Drusilicus in his blue battle robes flying toward them, a stick between his legs.

"Is he sitting on his staff?" Eddie asked.

Eugenia smiled. "I am quite sure he is using a broom."

Eddie recalled the old-fashioned broom he'd seen near the front door of Drusilicus' townhouse. "You have got to be shitting me."

Drusilicus flew past the arch and Eddie saw the bristles of the old broom as Drusilicus banked and landed on the roof and placed the broom down.

"Do you have it?" Eddie insisted.

Drusilicus pulled a sphere the size and color of a baseball from his robes. "Right here, lieutenant. Completely untested and we only have one shot at it." Drusilicus looked over at Caleb. "Do you have any way to track the binderune?"

"None," Caleb responded. "But if we could get a hold of it, I know how to break its effect." Caleb pulled a small metal hammer out of his pocket and quickly unscrewed the bottom of the grip, which came off to reveal a thin chisel that nested inside.

"What good would that do?" Eddie asked.

"One need not destroy a talisman," Drusilicus stated and smiled. "One need only alter it."

"I change the design," Caleb said, "and the spell is broken."

"So far, we haven't been able to locate Stubbe or Matchitehew," Bankrock explained.

"Over dere!" Rusty said, pointing. "I see 'em."

All the wizards looked to the eastern side of the park. Standing with their forepaws on the ground and sitting back on their haunches looking more simian than canine was the pair of Hell-hounds, watching the wolves as they surrounded the twin bases of the arch. The hound that was Sophia still had the medallion around her neck, though it wasn't glowing nearly so bright, now that it had worked its evil magick.

"What can we do?" Eddie asked. "Can we levitate the necklace off her?"

"The woman is wearing the talisman in her wolf form?" Drusilicus asked.

"Yes, why?"

"Because I have some people on it," Drusilicus affirmed.

Only because they were so high were they able to see a pair of animals rushing in through the northeast side of the park. One was a gray timber wolf, and the other was pure white.

"Is that Lovetta and Howell?" Eddie pointed.

"They wanted to help, so I gave them a specific mission."

"Those Hell-hounds will tear 'em apart," Rusty muttered.

"They shall have to catch them first," Drusilicus said grimly.

"How will they know where to go?" Caleb asked.

"Simple," Drusilicus noted. "They can smell Matchitehew."

Without hesitation, the pair of wolves veered and made a beeline for Matchitehew and Sophia, who had their backs to them, watching the wolves around the arch. As they drew near, the white wolf lunged forward and leapt over the sitting pair, surprising them.

With a roar, the larger Matchitehew Hell-hound jumped forward to pursue the white wolf. At that exact moment, the gray wolf leapt on the other Hell-hound, grabbing the medallion in its mouth, and yanking hard to break the chain.

The Lovetta wolf continued forward even as Sophia got purchase to run after her.

"She got it," Ahbay cheered.

"How do we get her up here?" Eddie worried.

"Under control, lieutenant," Drusilicus said, and with a gesture, the broom on top of the arch lifted and went flying off.

"How can that help?" Eddie hollered.

"Oh, ye of little faith," Drusilicus boasted, his eyes focused on the broom as it swept down and turned, hitting the Sophia Hell-hound with its sturdy bristles, knocking her aside.

Lovetta's wolf was drawing closer to the arch, and the dozens of werewolves turned to face her, ready to attack. The broom, under Drusilicus' guidance, flew under the timber wolf and lifted her into the air, taking her up off the ground.

Wolves jumped, leapt, and snapped at the flying werewolf, but they missed, and the broom carried her up and landed her right next to the wizards on the roof.

"Howell! Matchitehew is gonna get Howell," Rusty yelled.

Eddie looked over to see the Hell-hound tackle the white wolf, who fell and rolled over and over, obviously injured.

Rusty lifted his staff and a yellow dome of protection covered the fallen wolf as the Hell-hound attacked and tried to break through.

"How are you doing that from all the way over here?" Eddie said.

"It ain't easy," Rusty replied through gritted teeth.

All at once, another wolf broke from the crowd and leapt upon the Hell-hound's back, sinking its teeth in the mane around Matchitehew's head. Eddie looked down at the tawny wolf as the Hell-hound howled in pain.

The attacking wolf had a ring of brown fur around its waist.

"That's Glade!" Eddie yelled.

Rusty waved his staff, and as the Hell-hound tried in vain to reach the wolf on its back, the white wolf flew up into the air inside a yellow ball of light and toward the arch. The Hell-hound thrashed but could not break loose. The yellow sphere landed on top of the arch with the others.

Rusty fell to one knee, and Eddie caught him. "Are you all right?"

Rusty smiled. "That was harder than driving a cab all dese years."

With the White wolf safe, the tawny wolf let go and fell off the back of the Matchitehew Hell-hound, moments before the Sophia beast leapt at her.

Without hesitation, Glade turned and ran, the pair of Hell-hounds in pursuit.

Bankrock grabbed the fallen broom and turned to Drusilicus to say, "May I borrow this?" Not waiting for an answer, Bankrock launched it into the air.

Lovetta dropped the medallion from her mouth in front of Caleb and then went over to the unconscious white wolf, whining the entire time.

Eugenia went to the fallen Howell. "I can heal him."

Eddie moved to her. "Eugenia, you need all your strength if our plan is going to succeed."

"I'll do it," Rusty said. "But I'm supposed to be back up for Eugenia, and I'm already pretty wiped."

"I'll back up Eugenia," Eddie offered. "Help Howell."

Eddie moved to Bankrock, who held his staff aloft. Down on the square, the pair of Hell-hounds were still chasing Glade, but Bankrock controlled the broom and sent it flying toward the female wizard.

"Can you do this?" Eddie said, amazed that Bankrock could control the flying implement with such dexterity.

Bankrock was concentrating fiercely. "It's difficult. Please be quiet."

The broom got under the running wolf and lifted her up and into the air. Both Hell-hounds came to a stop and stared up, unbelieving. The wolf touched a forepaw to its waist, and instantly it was Glade riding the broom. She gave a battle cry and rose up, flying over the heads of the wolves toward the top of the arch.

She landed, dropped the broom, and laughing, ran to pull Bankrock into a hug. "I told ye—ye're a persistent bugger."

The smile on Bankrock's face lit his eyes.

Caleb picked up the medallion and put it up on the stone floor. He put the chisel on top of the disk, but a flash of light knocked the tool off.

"What is wrong?" asked Ahbay.

"I don't know," said Caleb. "Runic inscriptions hold magical powers. I guess the talisman is projecting its magic, which stops me from breaking the charm."

Drusilicus looked over Caleb's shoulder. "I sense power coming from it. If we only knew the spell."

"Maybe there is something on the page from the book." Eddie pulled out his phone. He found the page with the rune and the written words and held it out to Drusilicus. "Any ideas?"

"Let me see it," Eugenia said, and Eddie turned the phone to her. "Ah yes, this is reminiscent of a double or triple stacked Tyr binderune found in the *aanz-b-mutt* sequence."

"Can you break the enchantment?" Eddie pleaded.

"No, but I know what I can do." She held out her hand to Caleb. "Young man, may I borrow your chisel?"

Caleb glanced at the implement and put it into Eugenia's open palm. She lay her other hand on top and then chanted in strange words with a Norwegian sound to them. She then handed the chisel back to Caleb. "Give that a try."

Caleb nodded, just as there was a crash far below them and the sounds of claws rushing up the ceramic steps.

"They've broken in the door downstairs," Rusty yelled, and Caleb pulled the medallion off the floor as Drusilicus and Eddie quickly slammed the two glass doors closed. Eddie put a binding spell over the door and red light flashed inside and out. Through the glass doors, he saw the fierce muzzles of the wolves as they slammed themselves against it, trying to reach them.

"It won't hold," Eddie said. "We have to put the plan in motion now!"

"We have not destroyed the charm," Ahbay said, looking at Caleb.

"I must be on the ground in order to stop time," Eugenia said.

Ahbay smiled. "Down is easier than up."

"What?" Eddie shouted, but it was too late.

Ahbay gestured with his staff, and he, Eugenia, and Eddie launched into the air, levitating down to the plaza.

"Remember," Eugenia shouted as they floated quickly down. "Your powers are being used to support me."

Eddie was too busy staring at the ground that was rising to meet them. Just before they hit, they slowed and landed on their feet next to the large fountain.

The wolves around the bottom of the arch turned and ran toward them. In his peripheral vision, Eddie saw that the Matchitehew Hell-hound was up and rushing toward him from his left, as the Sophia Hell-hound attacked from the right—all of them less than ten feet away.

Eugenia raised her staff, and with a crash of thunder, the sky overhead darkened. The wolves racing toward them slowed, as did the overlarge Hell-hounds, moving slower and slower until they stopped, frozen in mid-stride.

Ahbay fired a green light from his staff going to Eugenia, and Eddie focused on giving her his strength as red light flew from his staff to empower her.

The next part was up to Drusilicus, standing on top of the arch with his hands extended. He took the baseball-sized sphere and threw it into the air, hitting it with a blast of his blue wizard light. The sphere exploded and a white mist hung frozen in the air over the entire park as Drusilicus chanted strange words and held the stolen *Medallion of Zeus-Lycaon* aloft.

"Ahbay," Eddie yelled. "When we let go of the time freeze, there are Hell-hounds attacking from the left and right."

Ahbay nodded. "I know that."

Drusilicus finished, and the circle in his hand crackled with power that flashed over the entire park.

Eddie shouted. "Okay, Eugenia."

Eugenia lowered her arms and instantly surrounded herself with a dome of violet light as Eddie and Ahbay pulled back their power and also surrounded themselves with protective domes.

Things began to move again.

Something that felt like a city bus smashed into Eddie and bowled him over, knocking him completely off his feet. The Sophia monster was on top of him, clawing and biting at him, ripping apart the magickal dome.

Up on top of the arch there was a flash of light and she howled wildly.

Caleb had broken the binderune.

Eddie yelled *"Oppressio!"* and threw the surprised Sophia not only off him but twenty feet away.

White mist filled the entire area.

Eddie got up and saw that Ahbay and Eugenia were standing too, though he couldn't see much else in the artificial fog Drusilicus created. With his dome still in place, he moved toward the other wizards.

"Are we still under attack?" Ahbay looked around.

"Back to back," Eddie advised. "Caleb broke the medallion, but I don't know if this potion worked on anyone else. And we still have people wearing wolf-belts."

An enormous gray wolf slammed into Eddie, propelling him to the ground again.

"Luis, stop it!" Eddie yelled, but the creature looked at Eddie and chuffed.

As the mist descended from the sky, the wolf looked up, took a deep breath, sneezed, and suddenly Luis was crouched on his hands and knees, naked.

"What the Hell just happened?" Luis groaned. "Where are my pants?"

Eddie quickly extended his dome around Luis just as the pair of Hell-hounds fell upon them.

"Madre De Dios," Luis yelled in shock.

Eddie turned to Ahbay. "Use the lock spell to open the wolf-belts."

In unison, the three wizards pointed their staffs at the two Hell-hounds and ordered, *"Patentibus."*

Two belts fell off their wearers and Matchitehew was suddenly in human form wearing the stolen SWAT outfit, as well as Sophia in her dark pantsuit.

"How did you do that?" Sophia blurted.

Eugenia rose to her feet, swung her staff and clocked the woman, knocking her to the ground, unconscious.

"What did you do to me?" Matchitehew bellowed on his knees. "You've corrupted me!"

Ahbay set his jaw. "Would you be so kind as to shut the Hell up."

The Asian wizard hit the big man with a blast of green light and he collapsed to the ground.

Eddie helped Luis to his feet. He waved his staff and pieces of Luis' clothing flew to them. His big partner slipped them on, but they were more like rags than clothes. With a gesture from Eddie, the jacket and pants repaired themselves, and Luis looked as good as new.

"Did we win?" Luis asked.

"We're about to find out," Eddie said, looking out into the mist. "Be ready, everyone."

The mist was fading fast, and a naked woman came out of the fog, looking dazed. She was a brunette with long brown hair that curled down her back. She was trying to cover her breasts as she looked at the wizards in disbelief.

She finally spoke. "My wolf is—gone."

Eddie lowered his staff. "Yes, you've been cured."

The distraught woman said, "I don't want it to be gone."

Luis pulled off his coat, put it on her shoulders and said, "Let's see if we can get you your clothes."

The dazed woman nodded bleakly, but allowed herself to be led away.

As the mist faded, Eddie saw people all over the plaza, some sitting, some laying down, and some standing—but they were all human.

Many of them had the same dazed look on their face, and Eddie couldn't tell if those were people transformed by the binderune or had been wolves for years and were just cured by the white mist.

At the arch, the access door was wide open and there were people stumbling out of the small space.

"I wish I could get up to the top without having to get past all those people," Eddie said.

"As you wish, lieutenant," Drusilicus shouted from above, and suddenly the broom lowered down next to Eddie where it hovered two feet off the ground.

"Is that a flying broom?" Luis asked.

"Yeah," Eddie said, staring at it.

"You gonna get on it?"

Eddie considered it a moment, then finally said, "Hell no. I'm taking the stairs."

Luis shrugged. "I'll wait out here. See if I can help."

Eddie nodded tiredly, and ducked to go inside, sliding past people walking out of the confined space. He was soon on the roof, as Drusilicus opened the doors.

He went directly to Howell, who was now in human form, and Rusty had conjured a blanket to cover him. "How is he?"

"I've done some healing," Rusty said. "If it weren't for Glade, Matchitehew would've ripped him apart."

Eddie glanced over at Glade, who was off to the side talking with Bankrock. From their body language, both seemed incredibly shy, like a pair of introverts on a first date. Eddie smiled, it looked like the start of a beautiful friendship.

Sitting on the open frame of the glass doors, Lovetta and Caleb were holding each other. Caleb was bare-chested, as he had taken off his long shirt and put it over the girl to cover her.

Eddie leaned in and focused on Lovetta. "You did pretty well out there. How do you feel?"

She considered this. "I can't feel the wolf anymore."

"The mist was a potion to cure the curse," Drusilicus said, walking over.

"All of those people—they will never be werewolves again?" Lovetta asked.

"I believe it only cures those who received the curse from a bite," Drusilicus cautioned. "It might temporarily affect a genetic werewolf like Howell, but it cannot cure him permanently."

"I can't tell you how long I've waited for this," she said and smiled. "I've dreamed of being cured for years."

"Once we finish up here, we can go cure Marlowe as well," Eddie said.

"What'll you tell da captain of your SWAT team?" Rusty asked.

Eddie shrugged. "I'll think of something."

Drusilicus smirked. "That should be amusing."

TWENTY-FIVE

"What did you tell your Captain Harris?" Marlowe asked.

The group sat around in chairs in the large breakfast room of Marlowe's house. Once again the vast table was up against the wall and Drusilicus was mixing the potion to cure Marlowe of the werewolf curse.

Everyone else was there from the battle: Ahbay, Eugenia, Rusty, Luis, Caleb, Howell, Lovetta, Bankrock, and Glade. Even Vasant felt well enough to join them.

Drusilicus was mixing a special brew of the potion in the levitating cauldron that hung over the burning cans of alcohol fuel. He held the parchment papers in his hand to review it as he added different liquids and herbs.

"I suggested there was a release of hallucinogenic gas," Eddie said. "It made people see things, probably from a rave."

"A rave?" Eugenia repeated, confused.

"Yeah, that's an illegal party. I told him it was a group trying to get high in one of the brownstones near the park, and they miscalculated. That's why everyone saw so many weird things."

"And he accepted such a ridiculous idea," Marlowe replied with raised eyebrows.

"At the time, the captain was in a state of undress," Drusilicus pointed out, "I am sure he would've accepted anything that sounded plausible."

Eddie smiled. "It helped that we had Matchitehew and Sophia Stubbe sitting on a bench in handcuffs, claiming that they were responsible. The pair of them will spend the night in jail."

"Is that safe, Wizard Berman?" Howell fretted, his arm in a sling from his battle with Matchitehew. "Ms. Stubbe is a genetic werewolf and Matchitehew gained his abilities from a demigod. Surely, the cure did not purge them of their wolves."

"I doubt they will have the ability to change for several days," Eddie assured him.

"I don't believe I shall be able to transform again until the full moon," Howell added.

Eddie looked at Howell. "Just like you couldn't transform after we hit you with the purple mist."

"What are you going to do with them?" Ahbay asked.

"Tomorrow, I am going to magically create a release order, giving their custody to me, saying they have outstanding warrants upstate. Then, Luis and I will drive them out to the Watchung Reservation where Wisakachek will meet us."

Drusilicus snapped his gaze over to Eddie. "What?"

Bankrock also stared at Eddie. "How do you have a direct line to Wisakachek?"

Eddie shrugged. "I know people."

"What is the solution, then?" Ahbay asked.

"Can he make Matchitehew human again?" Eugenia wondered.

Eddie shook his head. "He can't. But he can transform him into a wolf permanently and take him to a wilderness. I am going to ask that he do the same with Sophia. With her werewolf power and knowledge of making wolf-belts, Sophia is a danger in human form. This way, they both can live out their lives in the wild."

"That seems harsh," Ahbay said.

"Edward is correct," Eugenia said. "They are far too dangerous for prison."

"Yes," Bankrock said. "And too much of a threat to leave free."

"We have weapons that can stop them," Rusty reminded them.

"They've lost their humanity," Glade said. "So takin' their human form from them seems fair. Besides, living in the forest is the best." She looked at Bankrock. "How do you feel about camping?"

Bankrock smiled, but it looked forced. "I'm… uh… willing to try it."

"What about the werewolves at the park?" Marlowe asked. "Were they arrested as well?"

"Some were," Luis said. "Without their powers, they ain't no problem. The police mostly charged them with public nudity."

"A difficult charge to pursue, when most of the SWAT team and police officers on site were also undressed," Eddie chuckled. "They'll be released or given community service."

Luis nodded. "They brought ambulances in and got the few people who got injured to hospitals."

"Many of them just put back on their caftans and left," Eddie said. "I guess they went to where they stashed their clothes and got out of town."

"Probably their stuff was in dat hidden tunnel we found," Rusty insisted, then paused. "Hey, now dat de spell cured them they might not get into that tunnel again."

Eddie nodded. "You're right! They need to be werewolves to pass through the wall."

"That's gonna piss dem off," Rusty snickered.

"The point is, word will get out," Eddie concluded. "Werewolves are going to avoid New York City."

"A glorious victory," Ahbay said.

Marlowe turned to look at Lovetta. She had dressed and was wearing a simple top and jeans.

"How do you feel, my dear?" Marlowe inquired.

"Different," Lovetta said and sighed. "Safer. When you have the wolf inside of you, there is always a part of you that feels that predator instinct all the time."

"You're free of it now," Caleb said and took her hand, which got a smile from Lovetta.

Marlowe nodded, still watching the girl. "I also think it is time for the truth to be told."

Lovetta blanched and looked down at the floor.

"What is it, child?" Vasant asked.

"I am ashamed," she said, still focused on the floor.

"Tell them, my dear," Marlowe said, kindly. "We all need to hear the truth."

Lovetta glanced up, and at the wizards all around her. "The bite… when I bit you… it wasn't an accident."

"What?" Ahbay declared.

"How could you?" Eugenia asked.

"Dat ain't good," Rusty said.

Eddie held up a hand. "Hold on. Why did you do it, Lovetta?"

"I thought… I thought…" Lovetta stammered, gripping Caleb's hand tightly. "If one of you had the curse… you'd find a cure… and fix me."

"You didn't need to be fixed," Caleb argued. "You've always been perfect."

"No, I wasn't. I couldn't have a relationship, I couldn't ever have children, and I knew I could never carry a staff," Lovetta protested. "I was a monster."

The other wizards talked and argued, as Eddie remained silent.

"Everyone calm down," Marlowe soothed, quieting the group. "Everything has worked out for the best."

"Yes," Drusilicus said, adding one last ingredient to his potion. It was obvious he was not pleased. "Because Harold Stubbe had enough sense to remove those pages before his cousin could destroy them. We were also lucky that the correct talisman was here in New York."

Eddie spoke up. "Luis and I will return the talisman to the museum tomorrow, before we pick up Matchitehew and Sophia Stubbe."

"I would like to believe that the Divine has watched over us and allowed us this victory," Marlowe declared.

"Still, if one thing had gone wrong, all of this could have been a tragedy." Drusilicus shot an annoyed look at Lovetta.

"Ease off the poor girl, Drusilicus," Marlowe said. "It gave me the chance to reevaluate."

Drusilicus levitated the cauldron, so it poured its contents into a floating bronze goblet. "We did not cure you yet, Marlowe. But the potion is prepared."

He stood above the steaming mixture and took out the large Greek medallion. The room fell silent as he chanted the words of the spell and the cup glowed with a golden light.

The cup floated to Marlowe, who took it by the stem, waiting for it to cool.

"Would you care for a sip, my dear?" Marlowe said to Lovetta. "Just to make sure that you are indeed completely cured?"

"If you would allow me," Lovetta said in a small voice.

"Of course," Marlowe said with a broad smile. "You did nothing wrong. You were merely a part of the unfolding of the Divine's plan."

Lovetta walked over to Marlowe. He gave her the cup and she took two small sips and returned it to the wizard, who then took several sips himself.

"So mote it be," Marlowe said as he finished drinking.

Everyone throughout the room repeated the words, even Luis.

"Now things can go back to normal," Drusilicus stated.

"No, they can't," Eddie said, rising from his chair and speaking loudly. "I've made my decision. I cannot in good conscience remain one of the Five."

This drew gasps from the other wizards.

"However, for reasons I do not wish to discuss, I believe I need a staff to protect my family. I wish to exchange the Staff of Fire with another wizard, one whom I deem worthy."

"We cannot give an apprentice the Staff of Fire," Drusilicus objected, his eyes darting to Lovetta and Caleb.

"Nothing of the kind," Eddie said. "The person who I would like to exchange the Staff of Fire with is—Rusty."

Rusty got up slowly from his chair. "Me? You want me to be one of the Five?"

"Of course," Eddie said with a smile. "You're an experienced wizard, knowledgeable and most important, you can think outside the box. You are the perfect selection."

"And you would get my staff?" Rusty asked.

"Yes," Eddie said and glanced at Bankrock. "If that is acceptable according to the wizard rules."

The little man straightened his bowtie. "Well, it is unusual… but I see no conflict."

Marlowe rose from his chair as well. "I am glad you have told us of this choice, Eddie Berman. It makes what I have to say easier."

All eyes focused on the old wizard, whose color had already improved from the potion.

"Even though I am cured, and no longer a danger, the time has come when I must lay aside my staff and rest from our many battles."

The others in the room stood, crying out, "No," and "We need you," but Marlowe merely held up a hand until everyone was silent and returned to their seats.

"As I said to the young lady, this incident has given me a chance to reevaluate. The Five are important, and only an experienced wizard should step in to lead the Five and the coven." He looked over at Vasant. "Vasantbainkon, will you take the Staff of Spirit and lead this coven?"

All eyes went to the Indian woman, who lifted her chin. "I shall, Marlowe."

Marlowe smiled and sat. "Then I shall rest easy."

"Now I have to award my staff to another," Vasant said.

"There is also my old staff," Drusilicus said. "From when I received the Staff of Water." He looked over at Lovetta and Caleb. "Do you two believe you are ready to become full wizards?"

"Me?" Caleb said with genuine surprise. "I didn't do well with the staff when I last received it."

"No, you didn't," Bankrock agreed.

"Aye, let him talk," Glade encouraged, patting Bankrock's arm.

Eddie spoke instead. "I think you've grown, Caleb. I believe you can handle it now." He looked to Drusilicus and Vasant. "And you'll have people to help guide you."

"Then—I accept," Caleb said with a smile.

"If you will allow us," Lovetta said.

"That is the correct answer, child," Vasant said.

Drusilicus scowled. "But be aware, your training will begin in earnest, and I have not yet forgiven the fact that you bit Marlowe."

Vasant glanced at Drusilicus fondly. "Let them have their moment, dear."

Drusilicus agreed, and a small grin slipped out before he became stern again.

"Since we have settled all," Marlowe said. "Let us put the table back in place and feast. My appetite has returned."

As they levitated the table back to where it belonged, Luis came over to Eddie. "Are you sure about this, man?"

"I am, Luis," Eddie said. "I want to be a second-stringer, only called in during an emergency. I want to get back to being a cop, and just a cop."

"But having a little magick when you need it, won't hurt either," Luis said and clapped him on the back.

As the table and chairs flew into their correct locations, a smiling Wraith entered the room pushing a large trolley ladened with food.

Eddie sidled up to Marlowe. "I wanted to ask you about something."

"Anything at all, Eddie," Marlowe said as he levitated food from the trolley onto the table.

"My daughter has been appearing upstairs when she can't have gotten up there, getting out of her crib. I mean, I had a... being... tell me she is Half-Fae."

"Ah!" Marlowe said, poking out his lips in thought. "I wouldn't worry."

"Why not?"

"Her powers are probably just a phase she is passing through. I am sure with time, they will fade."

Eddie sighed. "That's a relief."

Marlowe paused. "Unless, of course, she is a natural Magus. Only time will tell."

Eddie glared at his mentor with annoyance. "You mean she might end up being a wizard?"

"Don't get too far ahead of yourself, Eddie," Marlowe reassured him. "Besides, who better to raise a child with such gifts than you?"

Eddie sat at the table, staring at the food. He hoped he was free of some of the weirdness.

But maybe not...

EPILOGUE

T he full moon was high over a desolate field beyond a large grove of trees, as Eddie stepped out of the forest with Luis and Cerise. Eddie and Luis both wore a suit and tie, and Cerise was formal in a long dress.

Vasant walked out of the forest with Lovetta and Caleb, carrying a battered metal broom stick. She wore her Indian style robes, and the apprentices were in plain white tunics and sandals. Last of all, Rusty stepped out in his cab-yellow robes.

"Where are we?" Cerise asked, gazing over the landscape.

"It is a place hidden from all but the wizards," Vasant said.

"This is where I was initiated," Eddie explained.

Luis looked around and nodded. "Not bad." He turned to Eddie. "You sure it's all right that we're here?"

Eddie smiled at his partner. "I got a special dispensation from the coven master himself. This one time."

Lovetta looked up at the moon. "This is the first time in five years I have looked upon the full moon with no fear."

"And you never need fear it again, my dear," Vasant said.

Rusty pointed at the large circle of stones in the field downhill from them. "Hey, they're waiting for us."

The stones were huge and white and over ten feet tall. Around them, silhouetted figures moved.

"Wait a second," Caleb said, stepping forward. "Before we go down there. Sergeant...um... Luis, I wanted to give you this."

Caleb handed him a disk on a chain with symbols etched into it.

"A talisman?" Luis asked. "What does it do?"

"It protects from all earthly harm," Caleb said. "I know Eddie will still have a staff, but as a cop, you might need it."

Eddie and Luis exchanged a smile.

"Don't put it on until after we leave. The magick here might mess with it," Caleb cautioned.

"That's really nice, man," Luis said.

"You guys are part of the reason I straightened out. I wanted to give you something that would help you."

"I know Maria will appreciate it," Cerise said.

"Shall we go?" Vasant said.

"Dey can't get started until we're dere," Rusty pointed out.

The group began the walk through the grass, which was only a few inches high. Even from this distance, they saw Marlowe standing on a flat stone in the middle of the circle, his staff in hand. Drusilicus stepped from the crowd and joined Marlowe on the flat rock.

As they walked past the first large stone marking the circle, Marlowe planted his staff into a small hole in the center of the stone, and the top of his staff burst forth with a glittering white light.

From shadows between the standing stones, small globes of light hovered above the staves of the members of the coven. The balls of light at the top of each staff of the robed and hooded figures glowed in the different hues of the rainbow.

The wizards who came into the circle were all shapes and sizes, all ethnicities with robes of different colors and styles. They moved slowly, with purpose.

As if by a secret signal, they stopped walking, raised their staffs, and the different colored radiance shone forth, uniting with the energy above Marlowe's own to create an overhead canopy of pure light.

They began a low, soft chant. It was the same tune as Eddie's own ceremony, with an odd familiarity which spoke to a primal force in his soul. Marlowe held up his hand, and the group stopped approaching.

Drusilicus gestured to Caleb, and Vasant handed him the broomstick she'd carried. Caleb advanced to Drusilicus and the metal broomstick became a wizard staff.

Marlowe spoke, and Caleb pledged his faithfulness, and as they bequeathed the staff to him, an ivory light surrounded him.

"Huzzah!" the crowd yelled as the transfer was complete.

Lovetta was next. Vasant joined Marlowe on the flat stone and repeated the same words. Vasant produced her staff and gave it to Lovetta, who also gave her oath to follow the path of the wise.

"So mote it be!" reverberated through the crowd.

As Vasant and Lovetta stood down, Rusty took their place, and Eddie approached him. Marlowe spoke different words, the two men exchanged their staves. As the chant rose to its climax, Rusty's robes shifted to scarlet as Eddie's transformed into the bright cab yellow, and red and yellow light surrounded them both.

Eddie smiled. He knew Rusty would respect the power of the Staff of Fire and keep the other wizards on their toes.

Finally, Vasant went up again, and this time the ceremony was different.

The silence was as thick as a fog, but Marlowe broke it. "Since the dawn of time, there have been those who walk the way of the wise, but there have been few coven masters who carry the Staff of Spirit. This night we present the new coven master to you all."

Marlowe gently placed Vasant's hand on his staff and stepped back.

White light flowed over her and through her, and she appeared to glow as every part of her body shimmered with it. She appeared to gain height and stood ramrod straight, looking at the crowd.

"So mote it be!" the wizards shouted again.

Marlowe looked around at all the gathered wizards and smiled. "It is said that the reason there are not more prophets is that great prophets will always see their own ending—and even a great soul can shy away from such a revelation. The idea that the world will continue without oneself can drive a weaker mind quite mad."

"What is he doing?" Eddie hissed to Drusilicus, who stood with the apprentices.

"I have no idea," Drusilicus said, obviously concerned.

"There comes a time when one has seen so much, done so much, and has lost so much. A person wishes nothing more than to be at peace. When one has fought great evil, as I have done—I know that there are beings who wish nothing more than to strike me down."

The group was in a state of hushed reverence.

Marlowe smiled at Eddie and the others. "I leave the protection of the world in safe hands, and with good people. I thank you all for allowing me to serve you and this world. The time has come for me to go."

"No," Eddie whispered.

Marlowe lifted his arms, and his body glowed. Eddie stepped forward, afraid for his mentor, but on Marlowe's face was a look of pure bliss. His body sparkled and became thousands of tiny lights that formed his shape. The lights swirled, undulated and moved, until they all came apart and flew into the air, spreading themselves out and filling the open field with their tiny luminescence.

The tiny lights circled and danced through the crowd, then rose into the night sky, vanishing into the darkness.

Cerise came to Eddie, as did Luis.

"He's gone," Eddie lamented, as tears stung his eyes.

The beams of light that formed the canopy above them all returned to the individual wizards and Vasant stood in the center of the flat rock, the white light shining above her. She pulled the staff loose, and that light faded as well until the entire site was only lit by the soft silver radiance of the moon.

Vasant's robe was still the Indian design, but now it was pure white. She reached into her robes and pulled out an envelope, which she handed to Eddie.

"He left this for you," Vasant said. "Come, let us return you to your home."

Eddie nodded. He would never see Marlowe again.

Taking a few vacation days, Eddie stayed home to reconnect with his family. He did not open the envelope, because the idea of reading the letter just overwhelmed him. He could not bear to read the last words the old man left him.

He was sitting in the living room, holding the envelope, when Cerise came into the room, carrying a fussy Ellie.

Eddie said. "Give her to me, you relax."

Cerise smiled gratefully and handed the whining child to Eddie. She looked at him and said, "Da!"

"I'll put her to bed," Eddie said.

Ellie reached out a free hand, and her stuffed rabbit sitting in the playpen rose into the air and flew to her, and she giggled when she took it.

"Eddie!" Cerise said, shocked. "You shouldn't do your magick with the child."

Eddie looked at his wife sheepishly. "Actually, I didn't do that."

"I just saw you," Cerise said, then her eyes went to her daughter, who hugged the bunny with one hand and giggled again.

Cerise's jaw fell open. "You don't mean…"

"Don't worry, it's just a phase… I think," Eddie said. "Let me get her to bed and we'll talk."

Cerise fell into a chair still staring at her daughter.

Eddie brought Ellie to her nursery, changed her diaper as the little girl pointed at a wall and gurgled excitedly, "Faap… Faap!"

Eddie turned to see nothing where she was looking, but sternly whispered. "Faap, show yourself."

The demon appeared, but he was no longer the towering figure he had been in the cauldron, or even in a human-sized form. He was now about the size of a stuffed teddy bear, and despite his big ears and nose, he looked rather cute, more like a stuffed toy than a living being. Eddie was also thankful that he was again wearing pants.

"I… I was just checking on her," Faap said warily, looking at Eddie tentatively.

"Faap!" Ellie stated loudly, as Eddie picked her up from the changing table.

He smiled and waved at her.

Eddie stared down at the little demon. "You won't lead her astray or anything, will you?"

The small demon moved his hands to his hips. "Hey, I'm a demon, not a monster. She's a total innocent!"

"Give me your word, Faap. I'll only allow you to visit her, if you swear to be a help to her. If not, I'll put a barrier around the house so powerful you will not pass through it."

"You have my word, good wizard," Faap said. "I'll just look in from time to time to see how the little thing is doing."

Eddie lay Ellie down in her crib, and she fussed and pointed at Faap.

"Let me tell her a story," Faap said. "She likes that."

"What kind of story?" Eddie asked with suspicion.

"A good one. You can stay if you want."

Eddie sat in a chair and Faap went into a rather charming tale about a princess who was saved from a monster by a friendly demon. Eddie found his own eyes grew heavy and Ellie was fast asleep by the end.

When the story was done, Eddie turned to Faap and said, "You're not a bad baby sitter."

"My rates are reasonable," Faap said. "But gold coins only!"

With that, the demon disappeared.

Eddie went back to his wife and explained the concept of Ellie being Half-Fae. Cerise was not pleased, but she accepted it was another one of the strange parts of their lives.

"After that, I need a glass of wine," Cerise confessed. "How about you?"

"I'm good. There's something I need to do."

Cerise kissed him and headed off to the kitchen.

Eddie picked up the letter and pulled out the folded paper within.

My Dear Eddie,

I am sure my choice to not remain on this plane of existence saddens you, but this is what I wish. I have seen my end for many centuries and used to fear it.

I no longer do, thanks to you.

You've made me realize a person can stay around too long, and with my life lasting more than a millennium, I am ready and willing to move on.

You helped me because of your simple humanity. I had grown too proud and too powerful, and you reminded me what it was like to just be human, a person doing the best they can.

I see great things for you. Maybe you will no longer save the planet from demons, vampires, and werewolves. Instead, you

will save New York City from criminals as you raise your
children and act as a boon to your community.

And to be honest, isn't that enough?

Blessed Be

Your Friend, Marlowe.

Eddie wiped away a tear, but he knew it to be true. He would do his job, honor his friends, love his wife and kids, and be the best man he could be.

For himself and for Marlowe.

THE END

ABOUT THE AUTHOR

Known as the "Wizard Of Odd", Arjay Lewis is an actor, magician, and multi-award-winning author.

I write tales of the strange and the horrifying.

I have spent my life as an entertainer, amusing people as a street-performer in the 1970s; a Broadway and casino artist in the 1980s; a party performer in the 1990s and 2000s; a cruise ship performer in the 2010s.

Stories have always been in my mind, and I have been writing since the 1990s. My reason to write is simple: to entertain. I write the type of books that I like to read: murder mysteries, strange tales of unnatural gifts, odd happenings and horror.

Please visit my web site and sign up for my mailing list to be "in the know" for upcoming books. Visit me on Facebook, Twitter, or my Amazon Author page.

And thank you for reading. You are the reason I write.

www.arjaylewis.com
www.facebook.com/arjaylewis
www.twitter.com/arjaylewiswrite
www.amazon.com/Arjay-Lewis

ALSO BY ARJAY LEWIS

Doctor Wise Series
Fire In The Mind
Seduction In The Mind
Reunion In The Mind
Haunted In The Mind
Devotion In The Mind
Asylum In The Mind
Specter In The Mind
Vengeance In The Mind
Echoes In The Mind
Infection In The Mind
Justice In The Mind
Ritual In The Mind
Vanished In The Mind

Horror
The Muse
Kept In The Dark
The Vanishing
Digger

Romantic Suspense
(with Debra Snow)
A Study In Murder

NYPD Wizard Detective
The Wizards Of Central Park West
The Vampires Of Greenwich Village
The Werewolves of Washington Square

FREE NOVELLA

VOWS

AND OTHER TALES OF THE MACABRE

For those who enjoy a good scare, here is a collection of stories designed to give you nightmares. These stories that have been published in *Weird Tales, H.P.. Lovecraft Magazine Of Horror, The Ultimate Halloween,* and *Sherlock Holmes Mystery Magazine.* If you tried to get them from their original source they would cost over $20.00. But you get them for FREE by signing up for Arjay's Newsletter

VOWS: A story of devotion that extends beyond death itself.
SIREN: A Sci-Fi fantasy of a condemned prisoner lost in space.
THE DARK: A guard sees creatures in the night...are they really there?
DREAMCATCHER: A walk in the woods...but you are not alone.
THE TRAVELER: What do you do if your flight is delayed...forever?
INTO THE ABYSS: A makeup artist gets the dream job...at a price.

www.arjaylewis.com/free-stuff.html

www.ingramcontent.com/pod-product-compliance
Lightning Source LLC
Chambersburg PA
CBHW050902250626
47155CB00001B/71